THE

LIGHT

OF

EPERTASE

Epertase Publishing
Second American Paperback Edition

Editing by Becca Brown

Cover art by Steve Murphy. Contact Steve
Smurphyart@gmail.com

Visit Douglas R. Brown at Epertase@blogspot.com
Email Douglas R. Brown at epertase@gmail.com.

Printed in the United States of America
10 9 8 7 6 5 4 3 2 1
The paper used in this publication meets the minimum requirements of the American National standards of Information Services - Permanence of Paper for Printed Library Materials, ASNI Z39.48-1992.

DEDICATION

To my son, Aiden: You are my life.
You make me proud at every turn and I am
the happiest father in the world because you are here.

I love you, little guy.

ACKNOWLEDGEMENTS

The act of writing a book is an intensely personal experience between the author and his or her story. That is not to say that writing a book is a one-person job. Many people must come together for a book to be presented to the masses, and I would like to thank a few of those people here.

I could not have accomplished this dream without the support of my beautiful wife. To Angela: For your encouragement and patience while I peck away at my computer, I thank you. Even if I were to become the most elegant, majestic, and successful author in the history of man, I would be unable to find enough words to express my love for you in a way that would do it justice.

To all my proofreaders: I do not envy your task, as reading my drivel in various stages of completion must be excruciatingly painful. But I understand as it is painful for me and I'm the sap who wrote it.

I would like to thank Rhett, Emmaline, Kara, and the entire Rhemalda staff for taking a chance on me.

When I began writing several years ago, I was an amateur in every sense of the word. To my aunt, Bobbe Ecleberry: I cannot thank you enough for your undying support and for helping me learn my craft then and now.

To Breanne Braddy: You were like a lantern in this publishing cave of darkness. You are unselfish in your knowledge and gifted in your talent. I feel fortunate to consider you a friend and have no doubt J.S. Chancellor will be a household name. And I'm sorry, but she'll never be Ripley again.

Also, thank you to the following people for their help and support: My mother, Lillian Dove, for your unwavering support and being a wonderful mother. The Amazing Mattman McNemar, whose creativity and talent I aspire to approach. The Columbus, Ohio Division of Fire for giving me a continuing wonderful career. Everyone at Smokin' Station 22 except for John. Brett Shearer, for being the muscles on the cover. My fantastic cover artist Steve Murphy, who is as talented as anyone I have ever met and who gets it in every sense of the word. Mick Cecil, Jeff Stanforth, Mike and Betty Donahoe, Cory and Aimee Knight, Bryan and Kara Young, Alex Sundberg, Greg Ecleberry, Sean and Helena Wooten, my grandmother, Lona Davis, and all my family and friends. For those who have inspired my character names, I thank you as well.

And last but certainly not least, I'd like to thank everyone who buys this book. I hope you enjoy reading it as much as I have enjoyed writing it. Wait until you see what I have planned for Rasi and Epertase in book two.

VOLCANIC REGION

INFINITE SEA

Bluefields of Sorrow

Danduke River

The Lands of Muéi

LITHIA

Wastelands

Tek Camp

Farmlands

Pataska

Havens Ravine

EPERTASE

LEGENDS REBORN
THE LIGHT OF EPERTASE
BOOK ONE
DOUGLAS R. BROWN
1

CHAPTER 1

FALL OF A WARRIOR

After years of conflict, the end of the Heathen War sparked celebrations all over Epertase. The festivities became a royal affair in the capitol, with Prince Elijah putting on an extravagant gala for the men in his command. Rasi, one of Elijah's top commanders, stood in the courtyard with his wife, Edonea, and the soldiers from his regiment and their families. The gala had been going for hours, and Edonea was getting restless. She pulled on Rasi's hand as a troupe of jesters climbed onto the stage.

"Can't we watch for a few minutes?" he asked.

She cocked her head to the side. "Are you serious? How can you watch that childish garbage?"

Rasi looked past her as one of the jesters tripped over the other and they both conveniently smashed pies into each other's faces. He muffled a giggle.

Edonea's hands went to her hips. "Really? That's funny?"

He shrugged. "A little?"

She cupped his cheek and turned his head away from the show. "You're so silly sometimes. I love that about you."

Rasi grinned and leaned down to kiss her, but she playfully pulled away. He followed until he got his kiss.

As Rasi let Edonea lead through the crowd toward the exit, soldier after soldier stopped him to pat his shoulder and introduce him to their wives and kids. After he pried himself away from a sergeant's wife whose name he had already forgotten, Edonea whispered, "You're like a celebrity around here."

"Nonsense." Rasi hated praise. He'd rather enjoy the army's victory in relative obscurity with his wife and a few close friends.

"Everyone wants to see you."

"They're probably just getting bored."

"Maybe they don't like that you're growing a beard and are trying to find a way to tell you."

"Maybe they don't like it." He gave her a sly grin. "But you do."

She rubbed his chin and bit her lower lip. "Yes, I do."

She hugged his thick biceps as they walked, sighing dramatically as a soldier no more than nineteen years old ran up to him.

"Commander Rasi, I want you to meet my girlfriend, Patty."

Rasi nodded graciously and kissed her extended hand. "It is a pleasure to meet you, Patty."

As Rasi straightened, he noticed Tevin the Third behind Patty, standing alone near the ale table with a fresh tankard. When their eyes met, Tevin curled his upper lip and turned away. They had butted heads several times during the war. Tevin's methods were too brutal in Rasi's opinion. But since Tevin was Elijah's closest friend, Rasi would be wise to cool the embers between them at some point.

Edonea resumed leading Rasi through the crowd, and it took him a moment to realize she was pulling him toward his good friend Atticus and his wife, Celia. Atticus saw them coming and his eyes brightened. He held out his hand, and when Rasi grabbed it, he pulled him in for a hug. Atticus was tall and strong and overly self-conscious about the scarring on his upper lip from a heathen's bite. "Any idea when the jesters go on?" he asked.

Rasi turned toward the stage, but he couldn't see the show from that angle. "They're on now," he said.

Atticus's eyes widened with panic. "What? I've been waiting all evening to see them. Come on."

Rasi hesitated.

Atticus turned back. "Well? Are you coming?"

Rasi looked over his shoulder to where Edonea and Celia were talking. Edonea looked up with a smile. He loved her smile and the slight gap between her front teeth. She noticed Atticus shuffling his feet and grudgingly flicked her hand at Rasi.

"Are you sure?" Rasi asked.

She rolled her eyes and nodded.

"I love you," he mouthed.

"Whatever," she answered.

While Atticus hurried toward the stage, Rasi was stopped two more times before he got caught up in time to see the jesters taking their bows.

The herald crossed the stage as the jesters bumbled off. He shouted, "Ladies and gentlemen."

The chatter died down, and all eyes turned toward him.

The herald cleared his throat. "The great Prince Elijah has an important announcement to make." He bowed and stepped aside. Prince Elijah crossed the stage. The crowd politely applauded until he stood ready to speak.

"Thank you for coming out. It is a pleasure to be able to host such fine men and women on this historic evening. Tonight marks the formal end of the years-long Heathen War. From this day forward we will know this, the year 1012 of the great King Matthew, as the year we finally rid Epertase of the heathen scourge, thanks in part to all of you."

The crowd applauded again. Elijah waited until they finished before continuing. "We have been fighting those savages for many years, but thanks to my flawless leadership, we have assured a peaceful future for your children and grandchildren." He swigged a half-full tankard of ale, the seventh that Rasi had seen him consume that evening. Elijah loved his ale a bit too much. He spilled some down his embroidered silk jacket.

"Before I let you get back to my celebration, I have one major announcement." He scanned the crowd until his drunken eyes fell on Rasi. He smiled. "Rasi, could you come up here for a moment?"

Rasi's forehead creased and he looked around for Edonea.

Elijah clapped his hands together. "Come on, everyone. Let's get Rasi up here."

The crowd began applauding again and parted to open a path to the stage. Rasi hesitantly started forward as people hooted and hollered his name. They whistled and patted his back as he walked by. He couldn't imagine what the prince wanted, unless he was announcing that Rasi had resigned his commission to be a farmer again. Maybe Elijah just wanted to send him on his way with a thank-you.

He joined Elijah at the center of the stage and bowed. The ovation continued. Rasi heard his name shouted a dozen more times in between the whistles. As he studied the crowd, he finally saw Edonea and Celia near the back. Edonea gave him a questioning look, which he returned with a slight shrug. The crowd's ovation continued uninterrupted. Eventually, Elijah leaned over and said in Rasi's ear, "Are they ever going to shut up?"

It was no secret Elijah didn't like being overshadowed. Rasi stepped forward, bowed to the crowd, and then signaled for them to be quiet.

Once the last cheer died, Elijah shouted, "Thank you, thank you. We all know *everyone* loves Rasi." The crowd cheered again, but Rasi felt the annoyance in the prince's words. "Rasi, do you remember what we talked about during the last days of the final battle?"

It hit him like a horse kick what Elijah was doing. While keeping a smile on his face, he whispered through his teeth, "Don't do this, Your Highness. I told you I didn't want a promotion. I'm not fighting anymore."

With a politician's smile, Elijah ignored him and stepped forward. "You will all be happy to hear that I am promoting Rasi to my old position as High Commander of the mighty Epertasian army. He has earned it."

The crowd erupted. Rasi searched for Edonea again. With a bewildered expression, she lifted her hands as if to say, "What's going on?"

Rasi shook his head. He had promised her he was done, and there wasn't anything that could make him break his promise, not even a royal decree. He turned to Elijah. "Your Highness, I am forever humbled and grateful for this honor, but—"

Elijah cut him off. "I feel it's time for me to take a more public role as Prince of Epertase. I've been wanting to step away for some time, and now that I have defeated the heathens there's no better time."

"Your Highness, I regret that I cannot accept."

Elijah's eyes darkened.

Rasi knelt and bowed his head. "Your Highness, Edonea is with child. It's time to put down my sword and raise a family."

Elijah gave a forced chuckle and told Rasi to rise. He unfastened the High Commander's chain of office he wore around his neck and extended it toward Rasi.

Rasi subtly shook his head. As Elijah leaned in and fastened it around Rasi's neck, he whispered, "Accept this honor now and we'll discuss it later. *Do not* make me look the fool at my own celebration."

Rasi bowed again and then turned to the crowd. Fists lifted in the air in sync with chants of "Rah—sai. Rah—sai."

Rasi turned back to Elijah. "Am I dismissed?"

Elijah nodded. He thanked the crowd for coming and joined Tevin the Third at the side of the stage.

Rasi could think of nothing but getting to his wife and explaining everything. He fought through the crowd as his friends and fellow soldiers shook his hand, patted his back, and shouted their congratulations. As he reached the back where the crowd thinned, he saw Edonea standing with Celia and Atticus.

Before he could cross the courtyard to them, Tevin stepped into his path. "Good evening, Rasi."

"Tevin, I don't have time to deal with you right now." He started to step around him, but Tevin moved into his path again. "What is it, Tevin?"

Tevin looked toward the stage. "I think Elijah wants to have a few words with you in private." He firmly grabbed Rasi's shoulder and steered him away from Edonea.

Rasi looked over his shoulder and mouthed, "I'll explain later." Her hands were on her hips again.

Tevin escorted him to the side of the stage where Elijah was waiting with a fresh tankard of ale. He turned back toward the crowd as if standing guard while Elijah motioned for Rasi to join him.

Out of earshot of the guests, Elijah asked, "What is going on with you, Rasi?"

Rasi didn't want to anger the legendarily short-tempered prince. He needed to choose his words carefully. "Though there are few honors greater in life for the son of a farmer than to lead your glorious army, I could never command as well as you, Your Highness. I'm sorry. I was only made to look good because of your excellent leadership."

Elijah brushed his compliment off with a wave. "Nonsense."

"As much as I'd love the honor, I cannot accept."

Elijah flashed one of his politician's smiles at someone behind Rasi as he said, "You know I can't take no for an answer." It wasn't his words that turned the brisk evening air even colder as much as the way he said them.

The band started playing on the stage. The prince chugged his ale and then tossed his tankard into the grass. He grabbed a succulent tornment fruit from the table beside him and chomped on it. Dirty-yellow juice leaked from the corner of his mouth. He wiped it away with his sleeve before it could harden and become sticky. Some people ate tornment fruit for its nutrients while others, like Elijah, ate them for the buzz. He offered Rasi a bite.

"No, thank you, Your Highness."

"You know you can call me Elijah when we're out of earshot of the peasants. How long have we known each other? Ten years?" Elijah set the half-eaten fruit back on the table and licked the sticky juice from his fingers.

"That sounds about right. I joined your service when I was seventeen."

"Time sure flies, doesn't it?"

"Yes, sir." Rasi figured it best to rip off the bandage. "I'm sorry, Elijah, but as much as I'd like to help you, I promised my wife I was done. I'm going to be a farmer. There's no amount of convincing that'll change my mind."

Elijah put his arm around Rasi's shoulders, still smiling to the crowd. "A farmer, huh? Now why would you want to do that?"

"My father's a farmer."

Ever the politician, Elijah nodded and politely waved as he spoke through his teeth. "You're a soldier to your bones, Rasi. Some people train for years to become good soldiers and others are just born that way. You're the latter."

"That's not what I want anymore. I want to be home. Edonea's with child."

"Yeah, I heard you the first time." His arm slid from Rasi's shoulders. "A farmer, huh?"

"Mm-hm."

"Well, you might farm, but you'll never be a farmer."

"I grew up farming."

Elijah shook his head. Though he was only a decade or so older than Rasi, his manner was that of a disappointed father. "Why would you want that hard-scrabble peasant life when you could have gold and fame commanding my army?"

"I didn't want to be a soldier in the first place. I only joined to help stop the heathens." He noticed Atticus and Celia making their departure near the back. "What about Atticus? He's a brilliant strategist."

Elijah turned back to him. His false smile faded. "I didn't give Atticus the position; I gave it to you. Besides, my father likes you.

It's an easy sell." He tapped his chin. "Yeah, I think he'll accept my resignation with you taking my place. I'm tired of being around soldiers all day. I've gone to war. I've done what's required of me. I'm ready to live like the royalty I am. Yes, I think my decision is made. Congratulations."

"Your Highness, as generous as your offer is, I'm officially declining it. My word to Edonea means more to me than anything in the world."

Elijah licked his teeth, making a godawful sucking sound. "I hate to hear that. You know you can't refuse."

"What? Are you going to lock me up if I do?"

"Oh, I don't need to lock you up. You're going to do just what I ask. That I promise."

Rasi felt his breaths quicken. "It doesn't have to be like this, Elijah. I've served you and your father well. Maybe we should talk to King Cecil."

Elijah calmly shook his head. "We don't need my father involved. I am quite capable of making decisions for the kingdom. As I said, I have a real tough time taking no for an answer."

In any other life, Rasi would have loved to take on the challenge, but it just wasn't to be this time. What Rasi said next might have been the hardest thing he'd ever said. He lowered his head. "Well, that's my answer. I have loved serving you and your father. The promotion is more than I deserve, and it would be the greatest honor I could receive. But I have made promises I cannot break."

"You know what, Rasi? I think your answer's actually yes. I think you're just a little confused. Maybe you've had too much ale tonight."

"I haven't been drinking."

Through clenched teeth, Elijah said, "Damn it, Rasi. You're starting to piss me off."

"May I be dismissed, Your Highness?" Rasi turned to rejoin his wife.

Elijah grabbed his arm and sank his nails into Rasi's flesh. "No, you are not dismissed. I'm not done with you."

Rasi turned back. Some of the crowd quieted as though they felt the tension, but their mood lightened when the court musicians struck up a cheerful tune. The music had no effect on Elijah, who was getting red. Rasi needed to de-escalate fast. "Let me get you another drink, Your Highness." He grabbed one from the table and offered it.

Elijah swatted the full tankard from his hand. "Listen to me, you shit." He leaned close. "You're going to do exactly what I said. Do you know why?"

Stone-faced, Rasi shook his head.

"Because if you don't, I'm going to have Tevin pay a visit to your lovely wife." The music nearly drowned out his words, and Rasi hoped he'd heard him wrong.

"Elijah, what are you saying?"

"I'm sure you've heard stories of what Tevin did to the heathen women in the fortresses we captured. They're all true. Hell, sometimes I even watched. He's quite messy. Maybe I'll watch him give it to your whore wife."

Rasi nearly choked on the rage and disgust rising in his throat, but he forced it down. He had to stay calm. "Come on, Elijah. Stop it. You're drunk. You don't mean what you say."

"Don't tell me what I mean." He hiccupped, and it smelled like shit. "Come to think of it, Rasi, maybe Tevin's already paid your wife a visit. She probably gives it to everyone in the city."

Rasi took a calming breath, though it was getting tougher to hold his tongue. "Elijah, stop it."

Elijah grinned. "Let me ask you. Are you even sure that's your kid she's carrying around?"

Rasi had sunk his fist into Elijah's gut before he realized what he was doing. The music halted. The crowd gasped. He yanked his fist back to his chest. The crowd stared in stunned disbelief.

Elijah doubled over and splattered the stone walkway with unsettled ale. He straightened. His face was pale and concerned. He wiped his chin with his sleeve.

"Elijah, I'm so sorry. I didn't mean it."

Elijah tilted his head. "What did you just do, Rasi?"

Rasi heard armored guards rushing up behind him. He spun around to plead his case, but one of the guards slammed the hilt of a sword against his forehead. Everything went blurry. He tried desperately to focus from his new seat on the ground. His head throbbed with each beat of his heart and he rubbed the newly formed knot. It felt like an apple had been jammed under his skin. Two soldiers from the Elite Guard, Elijah's hand-picked unit, grabbed his arms and yanked him to his feet.

Elijah led them back into the courtyard in front of the stage. The crowd parted. Rasi scanned the spectators for Edonea and found her standing with her hand over her mouth. Had she seen his terrible lapse?

Elijah shouted, "You all saw what Rasi just did. Striking any member of the royal family is strictly forbidden."

Rasi's eyes lingered on Edonea's terrified face.

"What is going on?" an old, weathered voice called from behind him. It was King Cecil. The soldier turned Rasi so he faced the king.

Rasi opened his mouth to speak, but Elijah ordered the guards to keep him quiet. One wrapped a cloth around Rasi's neck and tightened it just enough to silence him.

Elijah stepped toward the stage. "He struck me, Father."

Cecil rubbed his chubby, bare chin. "I can't believe that. Why would Rasi strike you?"

"I don't know. We had a minor argument and he hit me out of the blue. I think he's lost his mind."

Cecil's kind eyes met Rasi's. He tilted his head slightly. "Is this true, Rasi? Did you strike my son?"

Elijah nodded to the guard holding the choking cloth. He let up just enough for Rasi to answer. "I did, Your Majesty. But I—" The cloth tightened again, cutting off his voice to no more than a wheezing whisper.

Elijah glared at Rasi and then looked back to his father. "Everyone saw him do it, Father. There's no other choice. The punishment is death."

Rasi heard Edonea's muffled shriek behind him. King Cecil's shoulders slouched and his head drooped. Someone in the crowd shouted, "King Cecil, please don't kill Rasi. He doesn't deserve to die, despite what he did tonight."

Others agreed. Their pleas grew contagious until most of the crowd pleaded for mercy. If only Cecil knew what had triggered Rasi's anger, he would surely understand.

Cecil rubbed his forehead. "Rasi, I have no wish to execute you."

Elijah shouted, "Father, you must. Our sacred laws demand it."

"Shut up, Son."

Elijah wilted under his father's glare.

"As I was saying, I have no desire to execute you, but striking royalty cannot be tolerated. It pains me greatly to do this, but you've left me no choice. You are hereby banished from my kingdom forever."

Edonea openly sobbed.

Rasi felt the king's sadness as Cecil turned away, but it didn't change the fact that he wasn't getting a fair deal.

Embarrassed and angry, Elijah turned and snapped at the crowd, "Everybody leave. The party's over." The crowd mostly stood stunned. Elijah's face reddened and spittle sprayed as he shouted, "NOW. Everybody leave." The crowd filed toward the exits. When Elijah noticed the servants starting to clean up, he screamed, "Leave it till morning. Just go. The lot of you."

Edonea stood motionless as the crowd shuffled past. Rasi bobbed his head for her to leave with them, afraid of what she might see next. She shook her head.

Once the courtyard was cleared of everyone but Elijah, four members of his Elite Guard, Rasi, Tevin, and Edonea, Elijah stepped before Rasi. Two guards held him on his knees. Elijah studied his face. "Why, Rasi? Why did you have to do that?"

Rasi looked up. The cloth loosened around his neck slightly. "You know I didn't mean it, Your Highness."

"Well, it's too late now. You've ruined everything."

Edonea approached and knelt before Elijah. "Your Highness—"

Rasi caught her eye. He shook his head. "No, Edonea. Don't. Just leave. Go home."

Elijah turned to her. "Your husband's right. You should go home. In fact, Tevin, see that she gets home safely." As Tevin passed, Elijah spoke into his ear and their eyes lifted to Edonea. Tevin nodded with a sick smile.

Rasi's stomach dropped. "Wait, Elijah. Don't do this."

Elijah grabbed Rasi's face and leaned in with his rank breath. "I told you what would happen if you refused me. You caused all of this, Rasi."

As Tevin reached for Edonea's hand with a false comforting smile, Rasi shouted, "Run, Edonea." He yanked one arm free, sprang to his feet, and knocked the front teeth from the guard still holding him.

One of the guards struck the back of Rasi's head with something hard and blunt. Rasi tasted dirt.

Elijah crowded in and kicked Rasi in the ribs. "You wanna fight, tough guy?" He nodded to the three other guards. "Teach him some manners."

Rasi slowly pushed to his feet, dizzy and nauseated. A look to the exit found Tevin leading Edonea away with a tight grip on her upper arm. Rage seared through Rasi's veins. He had one choice left: Violence. Though he wasn't completely lucid yet, he charged the biggest guard. He chose that one for no other reason than getting rid of the largest threat first seemed like a solid plan.

Rasi tackled him, knocking the air from the big man's lungs. *Don't let him recover.* He rolled onto his stunned foe's chest and drove fist after fist into his face while Elijah watched, laughing.

A second guard plowed into him, knocking him to the ground and landing on top. Rasi's lip exploded in pain and blood. The next punch, while connecting with Rasi's cheek, left the guard's wrist exposed. Rasi caught it and twisted with everything he had. The wrist turned unnaturally and snapped. The guard reared back, clutching his forearm. His wail was invigorating. Rasi shoved him aside and rolled to his hands and knees. Before he could push himself up, the sole of a military boot met his chin, sending whiteness flashing behind his eyes. His face hit the ground.

Someone jumped onto his back. Two thick hands grasped his ears. The soft underside of his neck pulled taut and then his face hurled back toward the unforgiving dirt.

He wanted to beg the hammer to stop hitting his head from the inside. He wondered how long he'd been out. The ground was cold, and he shivered.

Elijah stepped next to him. "Give it another go?"

Rasi rubbed his forehead. Of course, he'd give it another go—he had no other choice. He had to save Edonea. He rolled to his stomach. A death grip on the ground did little to stop it from swaying.

People were speaking. Although the voices sounded like they came from the end of a long tunnel, he knew they were right beside him. "He's getting up again, Your Highness," one of them said. "Should we take him from the city and start him on his way?"

Rasi turned his bleary eyes on Elijah.

"Take him from the city?" Elijah's forehead creased.

"Yes. So he can leave Epertase. Like your father commanded."

"After what he's done? Spoiling my plans and humiliating me in public? No, no, no. I know what my father said. But that's not what you're going to do. You know where I want you to take him."

"But, sir, your father s—"

Elijah grabbed the guard's chestplate at the rim around his neck and yanked him close. "Are you disobeying my order?"

"No, sir."

"This will be our little secret. Is that understood?"

"Yes, sir."

Rasi envisioned himself leaping from the ground and bringing justice to them in the bloodiest way possible, but his body moved like he was stuck in mud. He pushed to his knees while the two men finished their discussion. With his feet under him, he studied the exits for the best path to potential escape. If he could just make it, he could get Edonea to safety and seek another audience with King

Cecil. It would be better to say his piece when tempers weren't so high. He staggered. Every second they gave him helped to right his spinning mind.

Elijah glanced over. Seemingly bored, he said, "All right. Finish this."

Rasi stumbled toward the exit where Tevin and Edonea had gone. A set of hands grabbed his shoulders from behind. He spun, pinned the guard's arms to his side with a bear hug, and slammed his own head against the man's forehead, dropping him.

Elijah trailed him. "Where do you think you're going, Rasi?" From behind, he took out Rasi's feet with a sweeping kick. Rasi slammed onto the stone walk and immediately rolled to his back. Elijah held his own stomach as a wet-sounding belch puffed his cheeks. His face paled and his eyes swam.

Rasi scrambled to his feet as the guard he had head-butted shook away the fuzz and staggered toward him. The other guard with the broken arm followed. Rasi started to back away, but Elijah reached out and grabbed his shirt. "You're not going anywhere."

Rasi's fist caught him on the cheek. He tried to flee again, but he was too slow. The guards pinned his arms to his side as Elijah approached, his cheek already swollen and discolored. He put a hand on Rasi's shoulder and then sank his fist into Rasi's gut, doubling him over. "Doesn't feel so good, does it?" He lifted his fist in front of his face and worked it, massaging his palm. Rasi hoped it was broken. The soldiers released his arms and let him fall to his face. He rolled over and looked to the dark sky.

Elijah looked down at him. He reached down and ripped the chain of office from Rasi's neck. "You won't be needing this anymore."

His wind returned enough to whisper, "If Tevin hurts my wife, I'll kill you."

Elijah winced. "Threatening a prince as well. You're just digging deeper." He looked to his guards. "That's enough. Put him to sleep." He started to walk away and then turned back. "Oh, and make sure he doesn't talk anymore."

A guard stood, straddling Rasi's head between his boots. He hovered the butt of his sword over Rasi's face as though searching for the perfect shot. "Goodnight," he said, and then drove it down.

CHAPTER 2

STRAPS

*W*here am I? Rasi fought to open his eyes against the vice that squeezed his brain. His mouth ached deep in his jaw like his teeth had suddenly rotted. He tried to focus. A torch lay at his feet, highlighting the dank stone walls of his prison. He could see no ceiling, only the moon in a ragged circle of sky.

A wad of goop trickled down his throat, gagging him. He spat it out and wiped his chin. The torchlight revealed what he'd feared: Blood.

Something's very wrong. He poked his finger into his throbbing mouth, which caused ten thousand raw nerves to scream for him to stop. He winced away from his own touch as a realization smashed him like an axe in the face. He prayed he was wrong. He tried to call for help, but he couldn't form the words.

By the gods. Those bastards cut out my tongue ...

Something poked his lower back and he pulled it away. It was a man's femur. He fumbled for the torch by his bare feet. They'd even taken his shoes. The floor was littered with skulls and ribcages and femurs, some with rotten chunks of meat and maggots still attached.

The stench of blood and feces and wet dog burned his nostrils. His breath hovered in the chill air like he'd taken a toke from a weed stick.

A sick feeling washed over him. He knew there was a rashta pit near the mountainous region, and worse, he knew that it was among Elijah's favorite means of execution.

He struggled to his feet. A constant *rat-a-tat-tat* pounded in his head and he realized it was his teeth chattering. He gagged again and coughed up another glob of syrupy blood, which dangled from his bottom lip in a string before splatting into the dirt.

A guttural growl rose from the darkest recess where the pit opened into a cave. Rasi turned his head toward the sound. Slowly, he squatted, picked up the man's femur, and then slammed it against the wall, snapping it in two pieces with splintered points. He slid the longest one into his waistband and dropped the other.

A shadow moved in the dark. Rasi wiped his forearm across his chin, trailing gore over his cheek. *Show yourself, creature. Let's get this over with.*

A blood-red tentacle slithered out of the blackness, moving along the floor. A second one emerged soon after, floating slightly above the first. They were thick like a cow's tongue, and veiny. *What kind of rashta is this?*

Rasi held his torch out, trying to get a glimpse of the creature. One of the tentacles hovered inches from his face, as if studying him.

The silent shadows behind the tentacles erupted into angry screeches as the rashta leaped into the light of the torch. The creature moved like a bear with front legs shorter than the rear. The body was shaped like a donkey, and it was covered with scales and blotches of fur. It was an ugly bastard. Snot and spit sprayed from its bloodstained, wolf-like snout. When it reared up on its hind legs, Rasi stood to the beast's chest. He stared up in awe as seven long tentacles danced from the creature's back. They snapped like whips and hissed in the air, alive and thirsty.

The creature lifted its massive front paws with a deafening roar.

I do not fear you, creature, Rasi thought, even as he retreated until his back met the cave wall. The creature crouched but hesitated.

Maybe, just maybe, it fears me ...

The rashta lunged. Rasi dove to the side and barely out of reach. The creature's teeth snapped past his head and he felt the wind on his ear. One of the tentacles grabbed his ankle and slung him across the cave floor.

His back collided with the merciless rock wall; the torch fell from his hand. He rolled to his knees, taking in gasps of moldy air. A meaty tentacle smashed his cheek, bending him backward onto his own leg. His knee screamed and he squirmed to straighten it. Another tentacle hurled toward him. He dropped to his back as it whiffed past his nose. He rolled to his hands and knees. Another attack shot at his head, but he dove out of its path.

The creature sniffed the air and licked its lips. Its tentacles floated above it, preparing to strike again. Rasi tried to catch his breath as he followed the wall deeper into the cave.

A slab of meat crashed into his chest. His body smacked against the stone wall and he crumpled to his knees.

He yanked the bone shank from his waistband as he fell to his back beneath the charging beast. The rashta drove its mammoth paw down, its dagger-like claws glistening in the dull lighting. Rasi thrust his shank upward. The creature yelped. The weapon pierced the pad of its paw and burst through the top. Rasi twisted the shank with both hands and yanked it free. The rashta, shrieking with pain, scurried back to the farthest wall, giving Rasi a chance to gather his wits.

The small respite was cut short as one of the tentacles crashed into his side. His weapon bounced from his hand into the shadows. The torch rested just out of reach. Rasi scrambled for it.

The wounded creature released an echoing howl. Rasi howled back at it. The rashta stumbled back in surprise.

He sprinted toward the beast, still howling like a wild animal, dodging tentacle after tentacle as he barreled forward. The assaults were relentless. One of the tentacles cracked the side of his head, driving his face into the ground and splitting his cheek open. He didn't stop, but instead crawled toward the retreating beast, torch still in hand.

The rashta reared up on its hind legs again. Rasi plunged the torch into its gut. The creature's pale, scaly skin crackled and blackened at the flame's touch. It sent another piercing squeal throughout the cave and lunged for him.

Rasi ducked, but not quickly enough. Pain exploded in his left shoulder as the creature sank its razor teeth so deep into Rasi's flesh they scraped along his collarbone and shoulder blade. He tried not to scream, but one left his lungs just the same. The torch hit the ground. With his other hand, he pried at the creature's locked jaw, but its muscles were too strong, its teeth too deep.

The creature jerked Rasi from his feet and shook him like a dog would a toy. Crimson gore splattered the walls. His left hand went numb.

For a moment he felt weightless as the creature flung him through the air. Then his spine and wounded shoulder bashed against the stone wall. He hit the ground with a bone-jarring thud and crumpled onto his face.

It's over. I've lost.

His shoulder burned with pain that radiated into the side of his neck. He pressed his hand against the wound, but blood squirted from between his fingers. A tentacle coiled around his ankle. He had no strength to fight it while it dragged him toward his death.

Out of the corner of his eye, he saw his torch lying on a pile of bones just within reach. As the tentacle dragged him past it, he clutched it with his good arm.

The creature hoisted him feet-first into the air. The blood from his shoulder flowed like a waterfall, splashing onto the cave floor. One of the tentacles looped around his neck like a noose and tightened. Rasi gasped, unable to feed his thirsty lungs. With every bit of strength he had left, he shoved the flaming torch against the tentacle that was wrapped around his neck. The beast flinched. Rasi thudded to the ground as the tentacle retreated. He thrust the torch at the monster's chest, pushing it backward.

Rasi tried to lift his injured arm, but it weighed a ton. It hung limp, streaming blood as he tried to crawl away from the beast. Two more tentacles curled around his waist. He wanted to scream, "Just give me a second," but they squeezed the air from his lungs. The tentacles dragged him along the floor like a piece of dead meat.

The orange blur of his torch flickered just out of reach. He wanted to give up. Edonea's face flashed through his mind and he couldn't wait to see her on the other side.

And that's when he saw his salvation, something better than any treasure he could imagine, better than the torch. It was his last hope. His bone shank. He extended his weary arm and touched the makeshift weapon's rough surface with his fingertip. He wanted to smile, but hadn't the strength to spare.

The creature lifted him into the air over its snapping razor teeth. Rasi grimaced and squeezed his weapon. The rashta opened its mouth for the killing bite.

Rasi thrust his precious shank into the soft underside of the beast's lower jaw. The shank continued through and into the roof of the creature's mouth. The tentacles let go, and Rasi fell, landing hard on his injured shoulder. The rashta wailed, a harrowing sound that shook dust from the ceiling, and Rasi imagined the ghosts of every life taken in that pit smiling from the heavens.

Lying on his stomach, Rasi forced his head up enough to see the wailing beast trying to shake the shank free. One of the tentacles twisted around the exposed part of the weapon and yanked it out, spraying blood like a fountain from the gaping wound. The creature staggered and crumpled to the ground. The tentacles flailed above as the rashta seized in a growing pool of red.

Rasi, lacking the strength to press his hand against his wounded shoulder, watched his own blood pool around him and ooze into the cracks in the cave floor. *You may have gotten me,* he thought, *but I took you as well, you bastard.*

The world faded to a view through frosted glass.

The creature's tentacles gyrated frantically around the rashta's carcass. One by one, they tore away from the scaly flesh and slithered along the cave floor toward Rasi. He was too weak to fight, too weak to move, too weak to care. They swarmed his body until he was buried beneath their hot flesh. One of them curled around his injured shoulder and cinched tight enough that he winced. The bleeding stopped. Another one dug into the muscle on his back, which he was sure would be the last pain he'd ever feel. He welcomed death. Each tentacle burrowed into the meat and muscle of his back while he lay helpless.

Every rip and tear of his flesh reminded him that the gods were too cruel to take him before the torture had ended. He shivered despite the tentacles' fevered heat.

So cold.

Tired.

Out of fight.

He gave in to the long sleep.

Rasi opened his swollen eyes. The two suns brought morning light and heat to the pit. The torch lay just out of reach, only a dull ember proving there was ever a flame.

He strained to see the rashta's body in the deeper recesses of the cave. His fallen foe seemed to move. A closer look revealed bristling maggots infesting the corpse.

Rasi's back tickled with the sensation of a thousand insects crawling beneath his skin. He wondered if the maggots had found him as well. His shoulder itched to the bone. He was too tired to move and dozed for most of the morning and into the afternoon.

When he woke again, his stomach rumbled so loudly that he feared another creature might hear. He rolled to his side and sat up. His every muscle ached like he'd been gnawed by a dragon with dull teeth.

Something darted past the corner of his eye and he spun his head around, the movement sending agony through his shoulder. One of the creature's tentacles hovered in front of his face. He recoiled only to find three more of the red, strap-like tentacles floating above him. Too weak to fight back, he watched and waited for their attack. But they didn't attack. When he leaned to the side, they leaned with him. Each time they moved the skin on his back tugged like a freshly sewn wound. He reached behind him with his good hand to investigate.

By the gods.

The tentacles had melded with his skin. He fell to his side and passed out again.

The suns were almost gone by the time he next woke up. Without their heat, he braced for the maddening shivers to return. One of the straps brushed his foot and he was surprised at how warm it felt. When he tried to move his arm, another tentacle pressed it tight against his side. The others coiled around him as if wrapping him in a cocoon. With only his face exposed, he felt strangely peaceful. He slept through the night.

He woke in the morning to the tentacles dragging him along the cave floor toward the rashta's carcass. Once near the rashta, Rasi's new appendages perched above the dead creature. Did they miss their previous host? Were they grieving?

One of them grabbed the rashta's front leg while another coiled around its shoulder. They tightened and ripped the leg away from its body. While some of the maggots fell from the flesh, the others continued their feast. With a dull thud, the straps dropped the leg at Rasi's feet like a gift.

Rasi stared at it. One of the straps nudged it closer to him. He had no fire, so he was forced to risk sickness from the raw flesh if he had any hopes of gaining enough strength to find a way out. He picked it up and stripped some of the scales away. Then he sank his teeth into the cold flesh, maggots and all. His mutilated tongue throbbed, but the protein would be well worth the pain, and it didn't taste as bad as he'd feared. In fact, it didn't have much flavor at all. Once he had the meat in his mouth, however, he encountered an unexpected problem. With half of his tongue gone, he couldn't move the meat to his teeth, so it sat like a rock in the bottom of his mouth. He retrieved a large sliver of bone from the cave floor and used it to push the meat between his back teeth. It wasn't perfect, but it worked. His straps danced in the air, invigorated.

By afternoon, Rasi had noticed a tree root protruding near the top of his would-be tomb. Reaching that became his goal. Healthy, Rasi would have welcomed a new rock-climbing challenge, but in his current condition he hadn't a chance to save himself. Still, he had to try.

His fingers found a small crevice just above his head. With a grunt, he wedged his cold, numb toes into gaps in the stone. He pulled with his good arm. He couldn't raise his other arm above his damaged shoulder. With an all-or-nothing lunge, he pushed with his feet, released with his good hand, and grabbed for a protruding stone. He missed.

He was kidding himself to think it was possible. He pressed his forehead against the wall and silently cursed his luck. While he felt sorry for himself, the skin on his back tugged. His feet lifted from the ground. A glance up revealed one of the meaty straps with its tip crammed into the wall high above.

He shoved his fingers into the crevice again and pulled. The strap held his weight as he reached higher. Then the other straps joined the effort. Though his biceps burned and his injured shoulder ached, he continued slowly up the wall with the help of his new appendages.

Near the top, he dug his nails in for one final thrust toward freedom. He found a toehold and prepared to lunge when he heard crumbling rock and the strap broke free. Another strap clawed at the wall to no avail. Rasi lost his grip. He had time for one thought.

I've lost.

The skin on his back jerked, twisting him around with a halt, facedown above the floor. He looked over his shoulder. A single strap clung to the root near the top. Another strap scrambled to find a new crevice. Once it did, Rasi glided back to the wall. He dug his fingers into a crack and pulled himself higher. Another strap reached over the edge of the hole and grasped something solid. With a heave, it pulled Rasi to freedom.

He flopped onto his back on the surface and inhaled delicious breaths of the fresh, frigid air. His pupils constricted in the brightness. A single snowflake landed on his nose.

CHAPTER 3

A NEW HOME

The snow fell in blankets at the base of the mountain known as Shadows Peak. Rasi stood exhausted but proud, having just survived his own execution. He looked to the Forest of Concore that stood between him and the capital city of Thasula. His mind twisted with flashes of his conversation with Elijah. He couldn't believe it had escalated so quickly. In his confused haze, he saw images of Tevin escorting Edonea away. His fists tightened at his sides. That bastard better not have hurt her.

Before he could do anything for Edonea, he needed somewhere to hole up until the snowstorm ended and his thoughts were clearer. As a soldier, Rasi had studied every map known to Epertase, including the maps of the mountainous region. From his studies he knew that on the southern face of Shadows Peak sat the entrance to a cave that could only be reached by a treacherous path. He and Atticus had talked more than once about taking a holiday and exploring that very cave, but family and soldiering always took the time away. Now he had a chance to explore it himself, though he wished the circumstances were less dire.

The snow drove sideways at times during his journey up the mountain, but he pushed forward. Soon he couldn't see his bare feet beneath the deepening snow. He wondered why they hadn't turned numb and dead in the cold, and why his face still felt feverish.

As night fell, so did the temperature, biting him for the first time. Thunder cracked as loud as if he were in the very clouds, announcing a coming mountain storm. Travel would soon be even more precarious. The snow fell heavier, blinding him and covering his tracks as quickly as he made them. He stumbled several times on the narrow ledge, yet he somehow kept his footing. His stomach rumbled again, but food was not his most pressing priority.

Fresh and strong, this trip would have been manageable, but in his weakened state it felt increasingly futile. He could no longer feel his toes. The black bite of frost that he was so fortunate to have avoided so far would not stay away much longer.

Finally, he fell to his knees. His legs quivered as he tried to push himself to his feet again. He had nothing left. With no more strength to push forward, despair tempted him.

Maybe I could lie down and rest for a moment.

But Rasi wasn't a quitter. He lifted his head, searching for landmarks. And then the driving snow parted enough for him to see his goal. He didn't know whether it was real or a mirage, but either way it was hope. Salvation was near. All he had to do was push past his pain and weakness. With the brutal wind beating his exposed skin, he willed himself back to his feet.

Using his straps to steady himself, he pushed through the snow to the mouth of the cave. He dug away at the snow drift covering the entrance until he could see the cave floor inside and wriggle through. His arms shook as he crawled deeper into the cave before collapsing onto his face. He needed sleep, even if he never woke up. It wasn't despair this time; it was acceptance.

As he lay motionless on his side, a frost beetle scurried past his cheek. One of his straps snatched the bug and shoved it into his mouth. The bitter insect squirmed across the stinging tender stump of his tongue. After several failed attempts, he caught the squirming beetle between his teeth and choked as the carapace scraped down his throat. One by one, his new straps lay down over him, warm like a blanket fresh off a wood stove.

The moonlight slowly faded as whiteness covered the cave's entrance. Fears of a predator also choosing the cave as its refuge were hard to shake, but there was no sense in worrying. If that was his fate, he would be food by morning.

Rasi awakened long enough to wonder if he was alive or dead. Either way suited him fine. He was dimly aware of something digging at the snow at the top of the cave's entrance.

Rasi opened his eyes again, stunned he was able. A dark blur stood before him. Was it Death? Rasi smiled. *I've been waiting for you.*

Like a dream, the bitter eyes of Death faded to be replaced by a blurry human face. If the cold and starvation hadn't taken him, he was sure the stranger would.

Gloved hands grabbed him beneath his armpits and pulled his limp body deeper into the cave.

The heat of a small fire warming his face forced his crusty eyelids open. His mouth was dry like he'd been chewing on cotton.

He moaned as he tried to lift his arm.

"Easy, old friend," a familiar voice said. "It's me. Atticus."

Atticus?

He touched Rasi's shoulder and regarded the cave. "Rest, Rasi I can't believe I found you. I guess you found a way to explore this cave after all."

Just as the gods had brought such a horrible mountain storm upon him, to redeem themselves they brought him a savior.

"Could you tell those things on your back to take it easy, though? They've nearly killed me three times."

Rasi would if he could.

"Hold strong, Rasi. This is going to hurt." He shoved a salt rag against Rasi's shoulder before wrapping fresh bandages tight around the salt. The straps sprang into the air, but they didn't attack. "Open your mouth," Atticus ordered. Melted snow dripped onto Rasi's stinging, cracked lips, as refreshing as a stream at the end of a desert.

"Chew this." Atticus stuffed something into his mouth. "It's japsy weed."

While Atticus tended the small fire, Rasi sat up with his back against the wall, using a kindling stick to help him chew the japsy weed. Atticus tossed a piece of jerky to him and sat down just out of reach of the straps. "Wondering how I found you?"

Rasi nodded. He tried to speak, but without his tongue the words came out as garbled noises.

"It's all right, Rasi. Don't try to talk. One of Elijah's Elite Guard used to be in my command. He told me what happened, and that Elijah sent you to the rashta pit. He's a sick bastard. When I went to the pit and found the dead rashta, I knew you were still alive. Something, maybe just a hunch, guided me here." He poked at the fire with a stick, unable to look Rasi in the eyes. "I'm sorry I wasn't there for you. Why would you ever strike Elijah?"

Rasi looked away, the mention of Elijah making him angry again.

Atticus paused, removing the stick from the fire. The end burned with a tiny flame. He blew it out. "There's something else I need to tell you, Rasi, and I don't know how." His tone carried a terrible weight.

Rasi's heart seemed to constrict in his chest.

Atticus absently drew doodles in the dirt with his stick. "Edonea never made it home after the party."

An almost inhuman noise bubbled up Rasi's throat.

"I'm so sorry."

A tear streaked Rasi's cheek. While he'd known in his heart that Edonea was dead as soon as Tevin grabbed hold of her, he'd been clinging to a tiny morsel of hope that Atticus had just taken away. *Remember this pain,* he told himself. He'd use it to steel his resolve in the coming months and prepare him for what he needed to do.

"The city guard found her in an alley near your home. It appears she jumped from the inn roof. They found a note. It said … it said she couldn't live with the shame …"

Rasi considered telling his best friend how Edonea had really died, but he knew how Atticus would react and what the consequences of that would be. He couldn't make Celia a widow. It was a burden he alone needed to carry. He turned away to hide his tears. Something about the ache in his chest told him it would never go away.

Atticus tossed his stick into the fire and straightened. "I found your horse in the castle stables and took him to my home. I'll bring him to you when the weather breaks."

Rasi nodded.

"For what it's worth, King Cecil has struggled with what he had to do. He truly liked you."

If he liked me so much, why am I out here?

"No one's looking for you. As far as they know, you've left Epertase. Some people think you headed for Lithia while others believe you'll simply wander the Wastelands. I think you should go to Lithia and lay low. You can start a new life there."

With these straps? I don't think so. Rasi flashed back to Edonea's final smile before their world collapsed. *She deserves justice. No, I will stay here until I'm ready to be seen again. These mountains are my home for now.* He nodded.

Atticus walked over and patted him on the shoulder. "Good."

Rasi couldn't look him in the eye.

"I'll be back next week with some supplies."

Rasi stared at the floor as Atticus gathered his bag, wrapped a fur around his shoulders, and left.

True to his word, Atticus returned when the weather broke with Rasi's horse, Salient, his sword, some rations, and a bag of clothes. The rations were the most welcomed, since Rasi had eaten enough fish from the river near the mountain's base to grow gills. When Atticus left, it was for the last time. "I will look you up in Lithia one day, my friend."

Hatred for the prince consumed Rasi, keeping him warm through the rest of the bitter, lonely winter. He decided spring would be the perfect time to make his violent return to Thasula. He must do it right. He must plan carefully. Elijah would not be easy to get, but it could be done.

CHAPTER 4

SCORNE

S pring brought Elijah's thirty-eighth birthday. To celebrate, Tevin treated him to a rare evening of drinking and gambling outside of the castle. By evening's end, Elijah was up twelve coins and ready for more. They made their way deep into the city, seeking out more games of chance and suckers to swindle. It was late. Most of the citizens were safely tucked away in their homes, which made finding an active game more difficult.

They happened across a sleazy, rundown tavern bearing a hand-painted sign that read "Arthur's Dive" with the "D" written backward. While Tevin clearly understood the dive status of the bar, Elijah had consumed too much ale to care. He pulled Tevin toward the entrance while two members of the Elite Guard took up posts outside.

Elijah plowed through the door as though everyone awaited his grand entrance. He counted five patrons inside. It was definitely a shithole, proven by the putrid stink of an outhouse that pervaded the common room.

"My gods," Elijah said, covering his nose. "What is that smell?"

A man shouted from behind the bar, "You'll get used to it."

Elijah didn't want to get used to it. He scanned the bar and found no tender, only the massive back of a hulk-sized patron.

"Pretty soon you won't notice it at all," the man continued, and that's when Elijah saw the top of a balding head behind the bar.

"Have a seat anywhere, hon," a waitress hollered. "Be right with ya."

She leaned over and shook the shoulders of an unconscious man who lay on his back atop a table. The drunkard's gut protruded like a whale stuck on the beach. He didn't budge, so she put her ear to his mouth to confirm he still drew breath. He mumbled something she must not have appreciated, most likely concerning her thick breasts pressing against his chest.

She stepped back. "Don't talk to me like that, dung hole," she snapped. She yanked up the end of the table, dumping the drunkard, along with several mostly empty tankards, to the floor. He rolled to his side, unaffected, and began to snore. "Shut up," she said, kicking him in his bloated gut. His cheeks puffed out with a half-gagging, half-choking sound before he swallowed, rolled to his opposite side, and continued to sleep.

She made her way to Elijah and leaned on the wobbly table he had chosen. Her belly, in all its stretch-marked glory, hung below her shirt. Her hair was curly, dirty, and short. "What can I get for ya?" she asked.

Tevin nudged Elijah and whispered into his ear, "Looks like an old blister, does she not?" Elijah chuckled, diverting his gaze to the knotted table.

"I recognize you, Your Highness," she said.

He smiled at her like a politician.

"But you and your friend can leave just the same if you're gonna be rude."

"Just serve me something strong," Elijah said.

Tevin indicated that he'd have the same.

"Hey, Frank," she shouted. "Two whiskeys over here."

"All right, Marge," the bald head hollered back.

After a moment, she returned with two dirty tankards full of piss-colored liquid and splashed them onto the unbalanced table. A tiny, dead bug floated, trapped in the bubbles of Tevin's drink.

"Excuse me?" he said, pointing to the bug.

"Oh, sorry 'bout dat." She fished her dirty finger into his drink, removing the insect and flicking it to the floor. She went to the big guy at the bar and whispered something to him. He glanced over his shoulder and then turned back. They laughed.

The night dragged on as Elijah imbibed whiskey after whiskey in a manner more befitting the town drunk than a future ruler. He periodically shouted, "What stinks in here?" with increasing volume, though no one answered.

Marge walked by, announcing last call, and Elijah took the opportunity to smack her rear. She swatted his hand away. "Your Highness, that's not appropriate behavior for our future king."

"Shhh," he whispered. "Are you trying to embarrass me in front of my sheep?"

He grabbed her wrist; she yanked it free. He liked her sass. She lowered her voice while keeping her intensity. "With all due respect, sir, I'm not interested." He snatched her hand again, and again she yanked it free.

Tevin tugged on Elijah's shoulder and chuckled. "You've had enough. Leave her be or we won't have anyone to bring us our alcohol. And I do need more alcohol."

She cocked her head to the side and said, "Maybe you didn't hear me. Last call."

Over her shoulder, Elijah watched a scrawny, toothless patron in need of a scrub-down and clean clothes stagger to the corner. He stumbled over a knee-high can, spilling its contents onto himself and the warped wooden floor.

"Marge," the tender yelled. "Someone knocked over the piss pot again."

"I saw him," she yelled back, annoyed. She grabbed some rags and headed to the mess.

Elijah leaned toward Tevin's ear. "That explains the smell. Here I thought we got rid of all the heathens. You ready to head home? I'm awfully tired."

Elijah nodded and the two stood up. Tevin placed his hand on the back of Elijah's neck and escorted him toward the door. But before they could leave, Elijah pulled away from Tevin's grasp like he had forgotten something of vital importance. "I will not be sad if this place burns to the ground," he yelled across the room.

He staggered and slammed into the back of the big, slouching patron sitting at the bar. The hulk straightened, revealing his full size. He wrenched his head to the side, releasing a symphony of cracks.

Elijah took a drunken step backward, almost tripping over his own feet. "Turn around, big man. If you are going to clench your fists, then turn around."

Tevin stepped between the man and his prince. The big man took a deep breath, but didn't turn. Tevin pushed Elijah through the doorway and onto the street.

Elijah's stomach twisted and gurgled. Putting distance between him and the stench of the bar helped his nausea, though not much. If he could stop the town from spinning, he would be delighted. Finally, the nastiness came. He tried to choke it back, but failed. He dropped to his knees and spewed warm whiskey onto the dirt road.

Tevin patted him on the back. He was laughing.

"What's so funny?" Elijah asked.

"Do you know who you tried to start a fight with back there?"

Elijah rolled to his rear end and wiped his mouth with his sleeve. He shook his head.

"Does the mercenary Simcane ring any bells?"

"Yeah, I know Simcane." He raised his voice, "Bring him out here. I fear no man."

Tevin laughed again as he helped Elijah to his feet. "Let's go, tough guy. No fighting legends tonight."

"He is not a legend, he's a coward."

Tevin continued laughing as he looked around. "Where are your guards, by the way?"

Elijah contorted his mouth as he tried to think. He rubbed his face. "I don't know," he answered. Then he swung his arm in a horizontal arch and shouted, "Fire them all." He put both of his hands on

Tevin's shoulders, leaned closer, and whispered, "Tevin, old friend, you needn't walk me home like one of your floozies."

"Your breath, Elijah." Tevin pushed him away. "You're sure?"

"Of course, I'm sure. I am the prince. I am untouchable."

"So, you say. Very well. I will see you soon."

The castle towering above the town gave him the direction home. Though the trip took three times as long as it should, he reached the castle's perimeter before morning.

Short of the guard towers, a stranger startled him, speaking from a shadow alongside the wall. "Rough night, P-P-Prince?"

Elijah spun with his hand on the hilt of his sword. He saw no one. "Show yourself, stranger."

A man stepped into the poor light of the street lamp, looking more dead than alive. His thin gray hair hid part of his gaunt face. He wore no shirt and his skin was covered with festering, seeping scabs. In Elijah's drunken state, some of the scabs appeared to move.

"What do you want from me, leper?"

"I only request a moment to s-s-s-speak."

"Make it quick." Elijah slid his sword partway out of its sheath.

"I can help you," the stranger said.

"You?" Elijah chuckled. "Help a prince? How could that be?"

"I've heard whispers throughout Thasula of your d-d-displeasure over your military obligations. I've h-h-heard King C-C-Cecil refused your resignation. Are you angry about it? After all, you're b-b-better than a lowly s-s-s-soldier. You shouldn't have to b-b-be at their l-l-l-level. You should be k-king."

"And?"

"I have a talent, one that can help you end your p-p-pathetic military servitude."

"You don't say? And how would you rid me of my burden?"

The stranger's grin cracked his raw cheek and pus trickled down the side of his face. "Leave that to m-m-me."

"What do you ask in return, creature?"

"Just some f-f-f-f-freedom to explore certain, how should I say, activities in your kingdom?"

"What kind of activities?" Even as he asked, he had an inkling of the stranger's murderous intentions.

"Just some occasional f-f-f-fun within the kingdom for me and my f-f-friends without your soldiers interfering. You know, T-T-Tevin's t-t-type of f-f-f-fun."

"No, I don't know."

"Surely you haven't f-f-found some new scruples. Maybe I don't know you as well as I th-th-thought."

"You don't know me at all, heathen. I don't care what you do in the shadows. I just don't know how a dirtball like you can help with my problem."

"I have ideas."

Elijah studied his face. What could it hurt to let the maniac try? "All right. I'll tell you what. You get me out of my military obligations and I'll make sure my men look the other way once in a while. As long as you don't get out of control and attract too much attention."

With a sick grin, the stranger nodded and retreated to the shadows from which he came. Elijah rubbed the back of his neck. He wondered what he had just agreed to.

CHAPTER 5
TASTE OF VENGEANCE

Rasi's heart beat like a hummingbird's as he stood near the door. He had been pleasantly surprised at how easy it was to get past the guards and scale the wall to Elijah's bedroom. Knowing how much Elijah liked his ale, especially on his birthday, made this the perfect night. The prince would be drunk, tired, and easy pickings. Rasi was almost giddy at the thought of Elijah's throat in his grasp.

A smile broke through his hardened scowl. His straps floated aimlessly around him. Though he had never enjoyed killing, on that night he would savor it. He could afford no pity, no quarter, because he knew that what lay ahead would be hard and messy and satisfying. Though he had no illusions of escaping after the blood started spilling, he didn't care. His entire life had become that moment.

Clumsy footsteps from the hallway made his heart skip. By the time the door latch rustled, his hands were shaking. *Steady,* he told himself. Before the door opened, he pictured Elijah's cold eyes for that final push. He filled his lungs, then pursed his lips together and slowly blew out his breath with a sigh. Now he was ready.

The light from the hall spilled through the opening door. Rasi waited behind it. Silent. Excited. A thin piece of wood separated him from sweet vengeance and he almost blew it with a quivering breath.

From behind the door, Elijah's "goodnight" to his guards sent shivers up Rasi's spine. That voice, and the anger it sparked, had kept him warm many nights. His revenge was within reach.

Elijah's foot appeared in the doorway. Rasi prepared for blood. But before Elijah stepped completely into the room and Rasi's clutches, he froze.

What is he waiting for? He couldn't have heard me.

Elijah's foot retreated and he screamed, "Caimen, get help."

Rasi ripped the door open. Elijah tried to run, but Rasi's straps enveloped him and yanked him into the room. Rasi kicked the door shut while his straps pinned Elijah's arms to his side. The prince's eyes bulged with beautiful terror as he was pulled face to face with his death dealer.

This is what I've been waiting for, Rasi thought. It was as perfect as he had dreamed. A growl emanated from deep within his gut. Each of his angry breaths sprayed spittle onto Elijah's stunned face.

"Wait, wait, wait," Elijah begged, until a strap squeezed his windpipe shut.

Elijah gasped and clawed at the straps in magnificent impotence. They could have ripped his head clean off, but Rasi had promised to make him die slowly. Rasi clenched his jaw so hard he feared his teeth would break.

The guards racing down the hall forced Rasi to change his plans. *Snap his neck,* Rasi demanded. *Do it now.*

But then, just as vengeance was so near, the straps released their prey. *No. What are you doing?*

Elijah coughed and scurried backward across the floor.

Rasi's straps recoiled for their next fight. *No, no, kill him first. You're blowing it. Let me die. Just kill him.* But it was no use. His straps lashed out at the first soldier through the door, knocking him against the wall.

That Elijah was still breathing infuriated him. Nothing else mattered, not his life, not the guards, nothing but revenge and justice for his wife and unborn baby.

More and more guards spilled into the room, backing Rasi toward the very window through which he had entered. "Get behind us, sir," one of them ordered.

Rasi scanned the dark room for a way to get to Elijah again, but too many guards had filled the space between them. The guards closed in, hesitant, wide eyes on Rasi's straps. When one guard stepped within range, a strap tossed him to the side.

"Kill him," Elijah screamed, his voice hoarse.

Another guard advanced and a strap tossed him through the window like he was weightless. Two down, but Rasi could hear more reinforcements on the way.

Next time, Elijah.

A guard charged, avoided the straps, and tackled Rasi through the window. One of the straps caught the sill, jolting him to a stop while the guard screamed the three stories to his neck-breaking end.

Rasi looked up at the sill in time to see a soldier stabbing at his strap, causing it to let loose in a spray of blood. The other straps clawed at the wall on the way down, but barely slowed him. At the last instant, the straps reached for the ground to cushion his fall. His lower back screamed in pain. There was no time to nurse his wounds. He scrambled to his feet. His lower back tightened and he groaned as he hobbled through the Royal Garden toward the perimeter wall.

"There he is," someone shouted from the window. "Fire."

An arrow plowed into the dirt beside him. Another one whizzed past his head.

He glanced over his shoulder as soldiers poured from the castle. With the wall and freedom within reach, he leaped. His straps reached for the top and pulled him up.

An arrow shattered against the stone beside his waist, but he ignored it, focused on his goal. With two of his straps holding on to the top of the wall, Rasi jumped. White-hot pain seared his thigh. He let loose a grunt loud enough to let those bastards know they got their target.

The straps let loose. Hitting the ground sent another wave of searing pain down his leg. He somersaulted with his hand firmly around the arrow protruding from his thigh.

"Rah," he grunted. Salient raced along the wall, ready to retrieve his master. Rasi grabbed his mane as he passed and pulled himself onto his back. With a grimace, he snapped the arrow's barb from the front of his thigh. Every bounce, every movement, every surge of blood through his femoral artery, sent pain shooting through his pelvis and into his abdomen. He wanted to vomit with each grind of the arrow against his femur. His teeth found his lower lip as he clenched his fingers tight in Salient's mane.

He crossed the Great Plains into the Forest of Concore as soldiers on horseback spilled from the gates. He knew he could lose them once he reached the mountains, but it would be close. Salient had to give his all, weaving around trees and leaping over downed branches. He knew the woods better than anyone, even in the dark, and it wasn't long before the sounds of pursuit faded. He and Salient were safe in his mountain cave by morning.

For the next two days, Rasi treated his thigh wound with salt and rags. While each treatment stung less than the one before, the pain of his failure did not fade. He replayed the night over and over in his head while cursing his defiant straps.

Even catching fish only reminded him of how easily Elijah had slipped through his fingers. His constant self-admonishment made him sloppy, and while he filleted his catch for dinner, he was caught off guard when his straps slowly lifted into the air.

Rasi froze. Had they found him?

Without his instruction, the straps hoisted Rasi to the ceiling. Someone or something was outside. Rasi hoped it was a bear. If it was soldiers, he was done.

He glanced at his sword leaning against the wall and wished he'd had more warning before he took his elevated perch. A man with a wrap hiding his face entered the cave, oblivious to the danger above. The crackle of the fresh fire surely told the intruder that Rasi was near. A fight was assured.

He studied the thick, bundled trespasser, wondering how long he had before reinforcements arrived. He doubted Elijah would be foolish enough to send a single assassin, even a highly skilled one.

Rasi waited. Slowly, the trespasser crept within range. *A little farther* ... Rasi extended his arms, ready to pounce.

Then the stranger saved his own life by calling out, "Rasi?"

Atticus?

Rasi dropped behind his friend without a sound. He tapped Atticus's padded shoulder, causing his friend to jump. Atticus fumbled for his sword and spun to face him. When Atticus recognized Rasi, he lowered his sword with a relieved sigh.

"Rasi, why are you still here?" He took a deep breath, clutching his chest as if his heart was about to stop. "You promised you'd go to Lithia."

Rasi shrugged, grabbed the tree branch he was using as a walking stick, and limped to the fire.

Atticus sat down across from him. "You really did it this time. What were you doing in the castle?"

Rasi pictured Elijah's terrified face and smiled. With the charred point of a stick from the fire, he wrote, "Revenge."

"Revenge? On King Cecil? Why?"

Rasi raised his brow and cocked his head. *Not Cecil. Elijah.*

"Tell me Rasi, did you kill the king and queen? I'll believe you if you say you didn't."

What? He shook his head. *No, no.*

"They say you killed them both. Then you attacked Elijah. Witnesses saw you fleeing. They saw your tentacles. They say the princess found their mutilated bodies."

Rasi kept shaking his head. He couldn't believe Atticus's words.

Atticus's posture softened. "You really didn't do it, did you?"

Rasi shook his head again.

"I believe you, Rasi. I do. But what were you doing there, then?"

Rasi didn't think explaining his plot to kill Elijah would buy him much sympathy. Besides, there was nothing he could tell his friend that wouldn't drag Atticus into the whole mess. He turned away.

Atticus seemed to accept the silence. "Well, it's safe to say you've lit a fire under the kingdom. You'll never be safe coming back now. I wouldn't even go back to your parents in Puimia if I were you."

Rasi didn't want to go back. If he had indeed drawn the guards away while someone else killed the king and queen, it was just as much his fault as if he had done it himself. His own blind hatred had led to this. With the sudden guilt crowding out some of the anger Rasi had lived with for so many months, he realized his attempt to get vengeance had completely crushed any chance he had of fleeing to Lithia and starting a new life. His actions had slammed that door shut forever. What had he done?

Atticus stood up. "You're my friend, Rasi, and I'd help you till the end of time, but I can't come back here anymore. It won't be safe for either of us."

Rasi agreed. The last thing he wanted was for Atticus to face the same fate as he.

Rasi rose to his feet, his tense straps agitated and restless.

Atticus backed away, his eyes trailing them. "I should head back, my friend. I hope something changes one day and I am able to see you again."

Rasi hoped so as well, but didn't expect much to change. As Atticus disappeared through the mouth of the cave, Rasi bowed his head. *I'm so sorry, Cecil. I will never forgive myself.*

CHAPTER 6

A CHANCE
ENCOUNTER

Rasi's self-pity and depression didn't dull over the next three years. The weather in the mountains was brutal, though not nearly as brutal as the loneliness that accompanied it. Rasi had become a prisoner to Shadows Peak and the forest near its base.

Rarely did he think about Epertase anymore, as most of his focus centered on survival. His only comfort came each night before he drifted to sleep as he remembered his beautiful wife and used her smile to lead the way to his dream world.

The suns were hot and the air was muggy. Rasi cursed his long hair as he tied it into a tail. He'd like to hack off his locks altogether, but he knew better. As miserable as his mane made him in the summers, he was thankful for every strand during the harsh winters.

He moaned and stretched his kinks away. The straps reached for the ceiling, doing the same. He breakfasted on crushed berries in a hollowed-out river stone. Though he couldn't taste the sweetness, he remembered enjoying berries and hoped for something. Other than the texture, he didn't get much. At least they were nutritious. He took stock of his situation.

His hunting the day before had been lazy, and the only game he'd come across had been scared away with clumsiness. He was sick of the smell of fish, so he'd gone to bed without eating anything, and his straps weren't happy about it. Their restlessness had kept him awake most of the night. Even the berry juice didn't make them happy. *How about we find something substantial today?* His straps danced in approval. Maybe a bear. Or an ochrid. Ochrids were trickier prey, but if you could avoid the paralyzing leaches in its hollow tail, the meat was nutritious and the long whiskers had many uses. After another drink of berry juice, he gathered his sword, sandals, and water pouch. Then he slung a cloak over his shoulders and the straps wrapped loosely around his body beneath it.

Rasi led Salient down the treacherous path from his cave to a stream near the base of Shadows Peak and left him grazing in the grass. Rasi followed the stream on foot as it led into the woods. The base of the waterfall at the end of the stream was the perfect place for grizzlies since the fish were so active that time of year. The walk was long but peaceful. His straps squirmed beneath his cloak. One of them drew his sword and playfully waved it in front of him.

Knock it off, he demanded. The strap sheathed the sword, but defiantly remained outside of the cloak. Rasi didn't bother fussing with it. In fact, he looped his cloak around his neck so it hung over one shoulder and draped his front, releasing his straps to explore. As they grabbed at branches, stuffed themselves into gopher holes, and explored every knothole in every tree, he regretted his leniency. They drove him nuts sometimes.

He reached the edge of a waterfall that overlooked his destination. The clear blue water dumped into a reservoir lined with olive-green trees bathed in light from the gorgeous suns in the cloudless sky. The most legendary Epertasian artists had toiled their entire lives trying to create such beauty, mostly without success.

A bald eagle swooped down, snatched a fish from the water, and then flew to a nearby tree. Rasi followed the stream with his gaze until he saw what he was looking for: a bear wading through the water in the distance. Rasi smiled. Now all he had to do was piss it off so it would charge instead of flee.

His straps effortlessly scaled the jutting rock wall alongside the waterfall as Rasi kept his focus on his game. At the bottom, he stepped into the cool, rushing water, cupped his hands, and drank. His straps played in the water, plunging deep and then exploding into the air like it was a game. One of them returned from its dive with a trout the size of Rasi's forearm.

Not this time, Rasi told them. *We're out for bigger game today.*

Once he'd had enough to drink, he splashed his face. It was cool and soothing, the calm before the coming storm. Rasi waded to the embankment and then focused on his playful straps. They shot above his head, instantly poised for the coming battle.

Rasi approached the shore close to the bear, intentionally snapping twigs to announce his arrival. The bear sniffed the air and then rose to its hind legs. When the bear roared, the straps flared out in an intimidating array.

The bear dropped to all fours and charged. Rasi stood his ground on the shore, knowing the first charge was likely a bluff. The bear stopped short and roared again. Drool hung from his snout as he bared his teeth.

Rasi snarled, baring his teeth as well.

The bear rose to his hind legs again. Rasi drew his sword. The bear slammed his front paws into the water, splashing Rasi's face, and charged again.

Rasi dove out of its way, but the creature's massive paw clipped his hip, spinning him across the rocks. He glanced at his straps. *Where the hell were you?* Rasi bounced to his feet. *Maybe a little more effort this time, guys?*

One of the straps snapped like a whip.

That's more like it.

The creature circled back, lunging with snapping teeth. A strap wrapped around the bear's snout and tightened while two more grabbed its front paw. Rasi's back slammed against the rocks, the bear straddling him and jamming his muzzled mouth against Rasi's chest in a desperate attempt to take a bite. Rasi stabbed his sword toward the side of the beast's neck, but the bear swatted it away with his free paw. One of the straps caught the weapon in the air.

The bear pushed Rasi into the water, letting up just enough for Rasi's face to break the surface. He gasped a breath before the beast's weight forced him back under. The bear repeatedly ground his snout into Rasi's chest, trying to dislodge the strap-muzzle. The creature wasn't going to kill him by eating him; he was going to drown him. The straps weren't strong enough to push the bear away, and Rasi wasn't strong enough to free himself for another breath.

Pull me tight, he ordered.

All the straps except for the one around the bear's snout released their holds and wrapped around its chest. Rasi was drawn flush against it. He was still beneath the surface, but the bear was confused and charged the shore, trying anything to shake free the large leech with the strange tentacles. Each stride slammed Rasi's back against the rocks until he was too broken and tired to hold on any longer. He ordered his straps to let loose, but they ignored him. They knew letting loose now might mean the loss of a good meal.

The bear ran on, battering Rasi's body raw and bloody. And then his straps, perhaps recognizing a losing fight, released. The bear's rear paws crushed Rasi's thigh and cracked the side of his face as it barreled over him.

The straps slipped and weaved to avoid the stampede. Once free of the bear's legs, Rasi found himself in a thorn bush. The bear continued retreating deep into the forest until it was gone. With a throbbing jaw, battered back, and thorns jammed into nearly every orifice and piece of exposed skin, Rasi looked up toward the trees. His seven straps floated into his line of sight and pointed down at him as if judging him.

What kind of a fight was that?

They didn't react.

Rasi tried to move, but the thorns raked his flesh.

How 'bout a little help?

Two of the straps wrapped around a thick hickory branch above. They lifted Rasi from the thorns and placed him on his feet. *Thanks.* He worked his thigh to make sure nothing was broken, hoping it was just a deep bruise. Actually, his whole body felt like a deep bruise. *Add being trampled by a bear to the list of firsts.*

He was absorbed in removing the dozens of painful thorns when one of his straps presented his sword.

Now you give it to me? He snatched his blade and sheathed it. *You couldn't maybe stick it in the bear?* Rasi swooshed back his wet hair with his hand. *Looks like it's gonna be fish again today after all.*

Rasi picked at the thorns and cursed at his straps as he limped back to the stream and the waterfall. While his straps carried him up the rocks to the top, he wondered what the bear must have thought, and it made him chuckle.

A last look over the falls reminded him how beautiful life could be. He closed his eyes and filled his lungs with the fresh air. It was oceans better than the mildew of his cave. *I should come here more often.* He stretched his arms above his head, be damned the pain, and his straps mimicked him. As he started his journey back to his cave, a sound he hadn't heard in years stopped him cold.

"Over here, Blair," a woman shouted. "It's beautiful."

Rasi crouched and surveyed the streambank for the source. In the distance, a young woman spun with her hands above her head, dancing. She hadn't seen him yet. Using his straps, Rasi lowered himself back over the edge of the waterfall until only his eyes were above it. He watched.

A young man ran from the tree line carrying a basket. He wore a sword at his hip, though he didn't look like a fighter. Just his movements and lack of awareness of the danger he was in told Rasi as much. There were more dangerous creatures than bears so far into the forest. The man set the basket beside the woman and lifted her into his embrace. Together they spun and giggled and then ran hand in hand to the water's edge.

They were far enough away and sufficiently preoccupied that Rasi decided he could move closer if he used the trees as cover. It had been a long time since he'd had company, and though he would never actually talk to them, just hearing human conversation for a change would do him good. He snuck to the trees and moved closer until he was close enough to hear them better. His straps lifted him into a tree.

Judging by his clothes, the man was royalty. His face appeared soft and feminine, more suited for paintings than for war. Though

Rasi didn't recognize the man, there was something familiar about the woman. She wore a plain blouse and riding pants, but he didn't think she was a commoner. If she could just turn toward him once so he could see her face.

When they spread out a blanket for their picnic, she lifted her gaze toward the trees as if she had suddenly caught wind of Rasi. In that brief second Rasi knew exactly who she was. She was beautiful, no longer the teenager Rasi had met several years ago, but a grown woman of at least twenty-one. He was stunned that Elijah would allow his daughter to travel so deep into the dangerous Forest of Concore with only a single protector. Or maybe he didn't know.

Looking to the sky, Rasi calculated the amount of daylight left and the time it would take for the couple to get back to Thasula. Even if they had horses tucked away somewhere, they had dangerously misjudged their time. He should tell them. If they rode fast, they could make it, but it would be close. He had no choice. Alina had always been kind and sweet, and though Rasi hated her father, he saw her as the ruler Epertase would need once Elijah was gone. He dropped down from the tree.

His straps sprang to attention, but Rasi ignored them. He needed to be careful to not startle the couple. When he opened his cloak for his straps to hide, they didn't obey. He jerked at his cloak, ordering them down, yet instead of obeying they turned toward his rear.

Too late, he realized his mistake. He spun in time to see the scorpion-shaped tail of an ochrid strike his chest and slam him against the tree. His breath left his body with a grunt. He dropped to one knee, trying desperately to catch his breath.

The ochrid stared momentarily, its long white whiskers extending from its round, flat face and brushing the ground. Then its pointed ears perked at the sound of Alina's laughter and it charged the unsuspecting couple, its eight legs moving too fast for Rasi to grab.

He heard a scream. The ochrid was upon them. The man called Blair valiantly shoved Alina out of the way and screamed for her to run as the ochrid pounced. He pulled out his sword, but it was no use. The ochrid barreled into him and knocked the sword to the stone as Alina ran along the water's edge.

The ochrid flicked its tail toward her. A glistening leach flew through the air, smacked her arm, and slithered under her blouse. She screeched.

Rasi pushed to his feet and staggered toward them. Alina wobbled like a drunkard before collapsing face-first. Blair made the most godawful sounds beneath the creature as it tore into him. There was nothing Rasi could do for him now.

The ochrid turned its attention to Alina. Blair lay motionless within a puddle of blood, his bare rib cage protruding outward. The ochrid charged Alina. Rasi raced to meet it, but it was too fast. With one of its legs, it rolled her to her back. Her eyes were wide with fear, yet she didn't move.

Rasi leaped onto the creature's back and wrapped his straps around its neck. The ochrid screeched and flailed back and forth. Its neck was too thick for Rasi to choke it, but he could hold on. The creature speared its barbed tail toward Rasi's exposed back, but a strap intervened, stopping it short of its target. Rasi fumbled for the sword at his waist.

The strap around the beast's tail stiffened and then fell limp. Rasi's fingers started to tingle.

A couple more straps curled around the beast's gut. The tail lunged again toward Rasi. This time, instead of defending Rasi dove from its back. His straps, however, held strong.

The ochrid galloped into the thick brush. *Not again.* He was going to have to get the straps on the same page. Rasi bounced along the hard ground with his worthless limp strap dragging behind. Branches whipped his arms and face, opening small, stinging cuts wherever they struck. He was sick of being dragged.

Release. "Unh." *Come on, you idiots, release ...* "Unh." He knew his pleas were in vain. His straps weren't letting another meal get away. *Let go,* he begged.

Another strap entangled the creature's front legs and tightened. The ochrid's growls and hisses were replaced by frantic cries as its front two legs snapped and it crashed to the ground. The creature caterwauled while struggling to its feet.

The strap around its waist quivered as it squeezed tighter. Another strap coiled around the ochrid's open jaw while a third wrapped around its head. Rasi stood up. The straps flexed. The ochrid's jaw popped. Then, with one brutal, final flinch, the straps ripped its jaw away from its skull.

The creature collapsed into a growing pool of blood.

Rasi's strap hoisted the creature's messy, severed jaw into the air like a trophy. He hadn't time to celebrate, though.

Alina.

He turned to go back, but one of his straps held on to the ochrid's waist. *Let go,* he insisted. The strap held firm. Rasi rolled his eyes. He understood—he was hungry too—but Alina needed him. *We'll eat fish tonight and I'll find something else tomorrow.* Still, the strap held firm. Rasi groaned. *Okay, okay. Bring a piece.*

He turned back toward Alina. His straps ripped one of the thick legs away and carried it as Rasi raced to her.

He felt strange, as though he'd had too much to drink, but he pushed through it. His limp strap still dragged on the ground. He was surprised by how much it weighed when it wasn't supporting itself.

Alina's panicked eyes followed him as he closed in. The ochrid's venom was a paralytic even stronger than the leeches. He dropped to his knees alongside her. Her lips were as blue as the ocean. He rolled her to her side and lifted her blouse to expose her back. *There.* He tore away the ochrid's leech and threw it against a tree.

Come on, breathe. He pressed his lips over hers like he'd learned in military training. Her chest lifted with each puff of air from his lungs to hers.

Breathe, damn it.

Again and again, he blew into her mouth until she gasped like a newborn taking its first breath. She inhaled another lungful before coughing and choking. Rasi sat back on his haunches with a relieved sigh. Alina rolled to her side with her knees to her chest, trying desperately to catch her breath. She was going to be all right. Rasi sat with her until she gathered herself.

With Alina out of imminent danger, he turned his attention to his paralyzed strap. As he searched it for leeches, he wondered why the other straps hadn't helped their brother.

As though another threat had arisen, the other straps shot into the air. One of them slithered around his neck and tightened slightly. Another one curled around his wrist. He froze. *Eaaasy,* he told them, withdrawing his hand from the injured strap. The straps around his neck and wrist loosened slightly. Once his hand was far enough away for their comfort, they released.

Alina sat up and scooted away, her eyes fixed on his straps.

He wanted to tell her everything was all right, but was afraid his jumbled speech would frighten her even more. He decided silence was a better route.

"Stay away from me," she said.

Rasi bobbed his hands in front of his chest in calm, nonthreatening movements.

"Tell me who you are."

Rasi shrugged and opened his mouth to point to his stub of a tongue.

"Oh," she said. Her voice was soft and kind. She asked without speaking, *Who are you?*

You don't recognize me, Princess? I am—He cocked his head. *I heard your thoughts, not your voice. How is this possible?*

She ignored his question and turned her attention in Blair's direction. *We have to help Blair,* she said, again in his head.

Rasi shook his head. *I'm sorry.*

"No," she cried. "He's dead?"

Rasi nodded.

"He can't be dead."

Rasi wanted to comfort her, but he didn't think it would be appropriate. *We can't stay here.*

"Are you sure he's …?"

Rasi nodded again.

"I wanna see."

No, you don't. Rasi had forgotten how stunning her emerald eyes were. One could lose themselves in them.

"I need to get home. Will you escort me?"

I cannot. The forest is too dangerous at night. There are more of those creatures. They rarely stray far from their packs.

Alina gasped and covered her mouth as if a terrifying thought had washed over her. "Allusia's out there."

Who?

"My horse."

Does she know her way home?

"I think."

Then she will be all right. I have a place we can go for the night. We should be able to make it before dark if we go now.

Other than that he'd saved her from the ochrid, there was no reason for her to trust him, but she stood up and nodded.

I will come back tomorrow and properly bury your friend. Though he knew there wouldn't be much left to bury by morning, he thought it might ease her worry.

She shook her head. "No. We need to take him back to Thasula."

That I cannot do. I will bury him. If you choose to send men to retrieve his body later, that'll be up to you.

She wiped her eyes before nodding again.

Darkness had settled by the time they reached Salient. Dragging the paralyzed strap so far had caused Rasi's legs to ache, his sides to cramp, and his head to spin worse than before. He helped an equally exhausted Alina onto Salient's back and started the trip up the mountain.

Once in the cave with a makeshift door made of branches and leaves across the opening, Alina was full of questions. Rasi rubbed two leaves of japsy weed together until a trickle of smoke lifted. He continued until a flame took hold and ignited the wood in his fire pit. Alina sat next to it.

Hungry? he asked.

"No, thank you."

Do you mind if I eat? These things—he nodded toward his straps—*can be real nuisances when they're hungry.*

"It's fine. What is your name?"

He hesitated to tell her in case she'd heard stories about him. *Rasi,* he finally answered.

She tilted her head and studied his face. "I remember you. You fought under my father in the Heathen War."

That I did.

She pulled her knees closer. He saw the concern grow in her face. "They say you're evil—that you've killed many people." She covered her mouth and gasped. "They say you killed my grandparents." Her eyes shot toward the entrance, the only route to escape.

He sighed. *You're safe, Princess. I would never hurt you. Not everything you are told is always truth. I have killed, that's undeniable, but I was a soldier. It was my job. And I would never hurt your grandparents.* Despite what he told her, the guilt over drawing the guards away that night still clawed at him.

She stared at him with wondering eyes.

He kneeled on one knee, careful to keep a comforting space between them. He swayed, drunk on the leech's poison, and braced himself with his hand against the floor. All but one of his straps floated behind him, cautiously following Alina's every movement.

Staring at his floating straps, she changed the subject. "And those? How is it that you now wear those on your back?"

Again, young princess, life is difficult here. But that's a story for another time. A strap handed him his roasting skewer as if reminding him what he needed to be doing. Rasi retrieved the ochrid leg and began cooking it. *How is it that you hear my thoughts?*

She seemed more concerned with her surroundings than his questions. "What? Oh. I don't know. I've always been able to communicate this way. I was born with the ability, I suppose."

Can you hear all my thoughts?

She stared at his hypnotic straps.

Princess. Can you hear all my thoughts?

"No. Only those you project outward. Like talking."

Could you hear me from a great distance?

She shook her head. "I can only hear as far as a voice carries."

One of Rasi's straps floated past her face. She poked it as if no longer afraid. She was indeed brave, or at least curious to a fault. The startled strap retreated behind Rasi and cocked back for a strike.

Rasi snatched her wrist. *Stay back. Sometimes I can't control them.*

But she swatted his hand away and reached for it again. Her movements were gentle and inviting. The other straps flared out, watching for the slightest wrong move. But she didn't cower, and they didn't attack. Rasi's heart pounded.

Don't hurt her. Don't hurt her. Don't hurt her.

She touched the one nearest to her. The strap balked at first, flexed, and then relaxed into her hand. "It's heavy. Are they heavy on your back?"

Not really. I think they balance themselves somehow. Or maybe I'm just used to them.

Another strap drifted toward her face and brushed her cheek.

Incredible, Rasi said. *They do not trust even me.*

"Maybe they just need a woman's touch."

Rasi grinned for the first time in years. His grin faded as he wobbled and again slammed his hand to the ground.

"What is wrong with that one?" she asked, pointing to the paralyzed strap.

It was injured. The ochrid left a leech on it, like the one that was on your back.

She crawled toward it, determined and fearless. She touched the wounded strap, which sent the others into the air again.

Rasi reached over his shoulder for her hand, but she pulled out of reach. *They will hurt you.*

Again, she ignored him. She slid her fingers along the strap until she came to the leech. Fearlessly, she ripped it away. The injured strap sprang into the air and retreated behind the others like a scared child. She threw the leech onto the cave floor. Rasi stepped on it and squished side to side. The dizziness and nausea were fading already.

The two talked through the night. Rasi repeatedly steered any conversation back to her, as nothing he had to say about himself would be anything she'd want to hear. When she talked about her father, he was forced to bite his tongue, figuratively speaking. When the suns broke the horizon, he knew it was time to go. *They'll be looking for you. We'd better get you back.*

He escorted her from the cave, helped her onto Salient's back, and led her down the rocky path into the forest.

It took hours to get to the edge of the Great Plains. Rasi stopped and looked at the distant wall of Thasula for the first time in years. It took his breath away. He had forgotten how much he missed civilization. *This is as far as I go, young princess.*

She climbed down from Salient's back. "Come with me. You deserve praise for rescuing me." She touched his hand.

He shook his head. *You shouldn't be seen with me.*

"We can tell my father that you're innocent. We can explain everything. I'm sure he'll believe you."

No. It's much more complicated than that.

"I'd like to hear the whole story."

You know I'm wanted for regicide. You might believe me, but there are many who would see me hang. I suspect your father would be chief among them. I'm sorry, Princess. It was wonderful seeing you again, and I thank you for the conversation, but we shall never meet again. If you truly believe what I've told you, then you must promise to never speak of me.

"Well, that's ridicu—"

I mean it, Alina. If you tell anyone about me, they will never stop hunting me until my head is on a pike. Now please go. I have work to do.

He turned his back and rode into the woods. By the time he buried what was left of Blair and reached his mountain home, it was midnight. He fell asleep picturing Alina's warm smile instead of Edonea's.

CHAPTER 7

EMERALD MEMORIES

The rain fell with stinging regularity as Rasi ended another day of successful hunting. The cotee he had just killed, though feisty, had barely stood a chance. He salivated from the memory of the extra-salty meat of the rare creature, and it pissed him off to know he'd never enjoy that taste again. Now all he could look forward to was the cotee's soft coat. It would make a fine pelt, he was sure. Maybe he would give it to Alina … if he ever saw her again.

He slung the creature's carcass onto a flat rock by the stream. He drew a sharpened stone from his waistband and squatted over his catch. With a handful of fur clenched in one hand, he guided his makeshift knife through the creature's gut.

While dressing his meal, his mind continuously replayed his encounter with Alina, as it had for the three moons since they'd met. His straps stood guard while he worked. The cotee's guts washed cleanly into the water.

Rasi was almost finished when his straps rose up. He slung the carcass over his shoulder and turned toward the tree line. One of his straps whipped the rocky bank in a display of dominance.

Stop drawing attention, he screamed in his head. The straps lowered. If Rasi didn't know better, he might think they had actually listened.

A horse neighed in the distance and Salient shuffled nervously. Could it be Elijah's men? Had they found him after all this time? He knew he shouldn't have brought Alina to his home.

A horse emerged from the trees. Rasi forgot how to breathe. *She came back? Is it a trap?*

When Alina saw him, she smiled. Rasi focused behind her in search of the soldiers who surely followed.

"Rasi," she called out.

Alina? What are you doing here?

The rain had slicked her dark hair to her cheeks. A blanket covered her shoulders. "I needed to see you again." She climbed from her horse.

Why'd you come in the rain?

"It wasn't raining when I left."

You know it's too dangerous for you to travel the forest alone.

"Allusia's the fastest mare around."

It's still too dangerous.

She brushed off his concern.

You need to go back.

"The moon will be up soon. Now it's too dangerous." She grinned.

Rasi grimaced and shook his head. *You're playing a dangerous game, Alina.* He wanted to scold her, but something about her innocent eyes stopped him. He groaned. *Well, we should get out of this rain and get you by the fire.*

Salient led the way up the mountain to the cave. The embers in the fire pit were still warm, allowing Rasi to stir flames up easily. Alina leaned over his shoulder as he worked.

This couldn't be real. He felt her breath on his ear, and it sent a chill up his neck. Against his every instinct, for a reason he still couldn't explain, he trusted her completely. Maybe because she smelled like an angel.

You shouldn't have come, he whispered in his mind.

"I had to see you again. You saved my life. I'll never forget that. I wasn't followed, I assure you. My father believes I've gone to town for a few days."

Rasi sat on a rock across from her. *Did you ask about me?*

"You said not to."

He cocked his head to the side and lifted his eyebrows.

"A little," she confessed.

Rasi glanced at his lazy straps as they lay on the floor. *Why don't you fear me, Alina?*

"Maybe it's because you call me Alina and not Princess or Your Highness."

I don't have use for such formalities around here.

"I like that about you. Besides, I'm a good judge of character, and from what I've seen you have character in spades."

You are a princess. You cannot be here with a criminal.

She brushed him off with a wave of her hand. "Nonsense. I brought supplies." She hurried to Allusia and removed a saddlebag. Full of enthusiasm, she presented it to him like a Matthew's Day gift.

I don't understand.

"I just thought … maybe … you could use some things." She dug into the bag with tremendous zeal and pulled out a frilly white handkerchief wrapped around something silver. With the huge grin never leaving her lips, she unrolled a set of eating utensils.

Rasi forced a smile, but his labored attempt gave him away. Her shoulders slouched as the realization struck her. "Oh. How silly of me. You don't need things like this out here."

Rasi strained to come up with something to comfort her. *Perhaps not, but I do appreciate it. Do you know how long it's been since I was able to enjoy a meal like a regular man?*

She gazed at him, seemingly searching for a hint that he was lying. "Are you sure?" she asked.

Everything that can make me remember life away from here is something I cherish. Thank you.

She smiled, pleased with herself. "Wait, that's not all." She dug through the pack and pulled out a folded piece of fabric. "I made a blanket for you." She unfolded the multicolored patchwork blanket for his inspection, and it was the ugliest yet most beautiful thing he could imagine.

I love it, he told her with sincerity. It was soft against his cheek. She shivered, so he draped it over her shoulders.

"But I brought it for you."

He retook his seat. *I know. But you could use it more right now. Alina, I wanted to ask you something that might be hard for you to answer.*

"Anything."

Are you doing all right? After losing your friend, I mean.

Her green eyes saddened. He regretted asking. She turned back to her bag and pulled out a dark knitted hat, a pair of leather shoes with laces, and a bag of gold and silver coins. "Here."

What's this?

"I want you to think about what I say and really consider my offer before answering."

He squirmed, unsure of what to expect.

"I want you to come back to Thasula."

He was already shaking his head.

"Listen. I want you to wear this hat. Cover your straps with your furs. And shave that dreadful beard. I will help hide you until I can convince my fath—"

That can never happen. Rasi leaned back. *I cannot go back. I won't hide in a kingdom where the people in charge call me a king-slayer. I can only imagine what the people say about me now. No, I will return on my own one day when I'm welcome. Or I'll be carried back when I'm dead.* He could tell his words made her sad, but it was best to be blunt.

She searched for comfort. "Well, I'm leaving this here in case you change your mind. I can only hope that the gold and silver will aid you someday."

Rasi nodded. *Are you hungry?* he asked.

"No. But you are, aren't you?"

His stomach rumbled even as he shook his head in denial.

"Please, don't let me stand in your way."

Rasi cooked the cotee. He used the utensils to eat, but he turned away so he could poke the food between his teeth without her seeing. He wouldn't eat in front of her at all if he wasn't starving. *Are you sure you're not hungry?*

"Maybe just a bite."

Rasi cooked her a piece, and watched her eat. It was too hard to hide his sloppiness as he ate, so he decided to hold off on the rest until she wasn't watching, despite his angry stomach. She caught on quickly and went to the cave entrance to watch the storm while he finished his meal.

As the night passed, Rasi told her about his wife and the life they'd wanted to build together. She listened with the same warmth he remembered from Edonea. She told him about the pressures of royalty and about how much she loved her father, even when he was a bit harsh.

While they talked, his straps lay sleeping on the floor. They were as exhausted as he was, though he would forego sleep for days if it meant hearing Alina's stories. He gorged on her every elegant word, only replying when necessary to keep the conversation going. But mostly he just listened.

Before the suns broke above the southern mountains, she whispered that she wanted to stay longer. Though it crushed him, he refused.

She sighed. Her last words to him that morning were, "I'll come back again. I promise."

He wanted to tell her that she mustn't—to protect her, to protect him—but he couldn't bear the thought of her not returning. She brushed her hand across his arm, and he closed his eyes. Her touch, however brief, was almost more than his senses could handle. He helped her onto her horse and stood next to her. The urge to take her hand and ask her to never leave was strong, but he knew it was selfish. She reached down and caressed his cheek.

Rasi grabbed his sword, climbed onto Salient, and trailed her down the path. Once she was safe in the Great Plains, he headed back home. *Today,* he thought with a smile. *Today is a good day.*

Her visits grew more and more frequent over the next four summers, and they were all that got him through.

CHAPTER 8

FORBIDDEN

R asi rarely slept soundly when Alina was with him. Like she had on so many recent nights, she tossed and turned beneath his blanketing straps. He would do anything to take her night terrors from her.

She cried for her grandmother and grandfather. "No," she screamed. "Please … don't leave me."

Rasi brought her out of her dream with a loving nudge, as he had many times before. She mumbled incoherently, stretched, and then drifted off again. Her breathing calmed, and she slept through the rest of the night while he watched.

When first light reached the cave, his straps wriggled and stretched into the air. He tried to will them back over Alina, but they were more concerned with breakfast than keeping Alina warm. Her hands searched for a blanket that wasn't there. Rasi brushed her hair from her face. There was no better part of life than seeing her green eyes when she first opened them.

Good morning, Alina, my love.

She stretched her arms above her head, still not quite awake. Rasi stroked his finger along the outline of her ribs. She shuddered. *Good morning, my love,* she replied, and opened her eyes. Her dimples showed as she smiled shyly.

You are as beautiful as any sight I have ever seen. Even the suns and stars in the sky envy your beauty.

She ran her hand along his chest and over the scars on his shoulder. When she touched his old wounds, her eyes wore a look of pity that always made him uncomfortable. He pulled away and stood up, the morning light projecting his muscular silhouette onto the cave wall.

"I see why people fear you," she said. "If only they knew how gentle you are."

Rasi smirked. *You've never seen the bad in me.*

"I don't believe there is any."

His pulled his long hair off his shoulders. A single braided lock that he had tied years ago to remember his wife brushed his hand. He twisted it around his finger and fiddled with it, suddenly overwhelmed with guilt. He turned away.

"What's wrong?" she asked in her angelic voice.

He shook his head.

"You miss her, don't you?"

I miss the world, he snapped, and stormed from the cave.

He stared through the light fog to the faded outline of Widows Run, the next tallest mountain in the region. The air wasn't as cold to him as it would have been before the feverish straps, even wearing no more than his animal skin kilt.

While his mind was distracted, a rodent scurried past the cave's entrance. One of his straps snatched the squank, snapped its bones with a quick squeeze, and dropped the carcass at Rasi's feet. *All right. I get it.* He picked up the limp squank and carried it back into the cave.

Alina whispered, "I'm sorry for upsetting you."

I love you, Alina.

She nodded with a smile.

Are you hungry?

"Yes."

He tossed three pieces of wood onto the smoldering fire and fanned the flames. While the fire grew, he dressed his prey with his back to Alina so she wouldn't have to watch.

You're getting better at hunting with your straps, she said.

I didn't do that. They're just hungry.

He tore away a cooked squank leg and handed it to her. She sank her teeth into the meat and ripped a chunk away as though she had never eaten before. Squanks were small creatures without much meat, so Rasi nibbled a small piece while giving the rest to her. His straps followed each piece angrily as he passed them to her, but they didn't try to snatch them away. He promised them more food soon.

A large creature swooped past the entrance, grabbing Alina's attention. "Did you see that?"

What? The eagle? He comes by often.

"That is the biggest eagle I've ever seen. I thought it was a dragon at first." She lifted her eyes and flashed him a crooked grin. "I've heard one lives in these mountains."

Rasi peered up from stoking the fire.

"Have you seen one?" she asked, and her green eyes grew wide.

Rasi grunted and shook his head. *No. Why?*

"Oh, no reason really." Her shoulders drooped a little. "I've heard tales and was curious, is all."

Though Rasi had no idea why she was so fascinated by dragons, he decided to humor her. *I have seen one once.*

She snapped her head up. "You have?"

When I was a child, several of my friends and I snuck into the woods near my family's farm. We had heard rumors of a nest in the forest, and though we were forbidden to go there, one night we did.

"What happened?" she asked, looking like she would burst if he ended his tale too quickly.

It smelled us coming, growled at us, and we ran.

"That's it?"

That's it.

"But you saw it?"

Yeah.

"What did it look like?"

It was big, almost as big as your castle. And colorful. I think it was a female.

"It didn't attack or give chase?"

No. Dragons are more passive than anything nowadays. Since the Epertasian-Dragon Wars, the few dragons left tend to avoid humans. So, to answer your first question, no, there are no dragons in these mountains that I'm aware. And to answer your last, if you ever come across one, stay out of its nest. He threw another hunk of wood onto the fire, sending sparks floating to the ceiling. He peeked at her as she stared at the flames.

She smiled, then draped a cotee pelt over her shoulders and carried the rest of her breakfast out onto the rocky cliff.

Don't get too close, he cautioned. She glanced back with a grin, then sat and dangled her legs over the edge. *You should back up. I don't want you to fall.*

She continued to grin. "Nothing can hurt me when you are around." He touched her shoulders. She shivered.

It's cold out here. You should come back inside. His straps wrapped around her.

She brushed them away. "The cold lets me know I'm alive. I want to stay with you. I never want to leave."

Your father will worry. He'll send trackers.

"Let's run. We can flee these lands. We'll go to Lithia or the Islands of Torick. You will protect me."

He would be lying if he denied that it was his dream as well, but life on the run was hard. *Your father is king of Epertase. His reach stretches the entire known world. We could never be free.*

"I know," she said, resignation in her voice. "But every moment we're apart, my heart dies a little."

He wanted to tell her how his heart ached as well, but it would only make their goodbye more painful. *You'd better head back. You will be missed soon.*

She glided her hand along his cheek. "I like it better with your chin bare."

I know you do. That's why I shaved it.

She disappeared into the cave.

Rasi brought Salient and Allusia from deeper within the cave. Salient's black coat wasn't as vibrant as it used to be, and his mane hung over his eyes. Rasi brushed it back. The inky shades of black were now woven with streaks of gray. Rasi stood facing his long-time companion and stroked his muzzle.

Alina returned wearing a teal dress with white laces and golden filigree adorning her collar. The voluminous sleeves hung low enough that she could catch fish in them. She twisted her hair up into a bun and then carried her travel bag to Allusia.

Now that's more befitting a princess.

She curtsied.

Rasi wrapped his arms around her from behind. She turned in his embrace and squeezed him. He scanned the mountainous landscape again, always on alert for any threats. The only threat that day was the cold. *Take this.* He draped his cotee fur over her shoulders.

Despite her objections, he accompanied her back to the Great Plains. Since the threat of another brutal winter drew near, he knew he'd probably not see her again for a while. He felt it was going to be harder to endure the loneliness than in years past. While he watched her cross the Great Plains, for the first time he considered accepting her repeated pleas to hide within the city. It was a fleeting thought. He was too stubborn and too proud. Maybe next year, he told himself, which is what he told himself each year. He was now convinced that his destiny was to grow old and die on Shadows Peak.

Rasi's breath left his mouth and hovered in the air. He started the long trip home. *I grow tired of this life.*

Instead of going straight to his cave, he rode Salient along the stream near the waterfall. His first and perhaps most important task before the winter was locating enough japsy weed to get him through. Not only would the fire it produced keep him warm, but in a pinch the herb could serve as nourishment. Since the fire-starting plant ironically grew near water, he kept his head down, searching the streambank.

It wasn't long before he came upon a patch of the clover-shaped weeds. *This will do nicely.* He patted Salient's neck and dismounted, leaving Salient to graze while he filled his pouch with the weeds. Satisfied with his take, he tied his bag around Salient's midsection.

Then he turned to the frigid flowing water and waded in. The current almost tumbled him over. His straps hovered just above the surface, waiting. A coppafish as large as his thigh leaped from the water. Without thought, a strap snatched it from the air and slammed it against a rock before tossing it to the shore. After catching three more healthy-sized fish, Rasi made his way back to Salient, removed several winding ochrid whiskers from another bag, and poked the ends through the fishes' mouths. Then he tied them together and slung them over his shoulder.

At nightfall, Rasi relaxed outside of his cave, his straps draped over the edge of the cliff, ready for a well-earned rest. He hoped Alina would come this night, but then, he hoped such most nights. She didn't come. The snow began to fall.

CHAPTER 9

TEKS

Long before the other Tek commanders had awakened, Supreme Leader Zaffka sat up on the hard cot he had called a bed for most of his adult life. Nearing the twilight of his life, he had known nothing but war and crusades, as was the fate of most Tek males. He stretched his arthritic arms to the music of cracking joints. He gritted his teeth, fighting the urge to cry out as his back twinged. It would eventually loosen up after he moved around a bit, but the first few minutes were torture. Years of battles and birthdays had not been kind.

He wore not a stitch of clothing as he crawled out of bed. He made his way across the cabin to a pail of piss-warm water. With cupped hands, he splashed the water into his face. A piece of smudged steel, buffed to give reflection, hung on the wall above his pail.

His cabin swayed with the waves of the ocean, but he had long grown used to the motion. He remembered the stomach rot of his first mission as a teenager and how long it had taken him to get his so-called sea legs. With more gray stubble than dark on his leathery chin, he hardly recognized his reflection anymore. Every scar on his face was a sign of his dedication as a soldier, and he remembered receiving every one of them. If he was ever fortunate enough to retire, he wondered what his many wives would say about the missing chunk of his upper lip, bitten off during his last battle. Or his missing front teeth, the result of a war hammer to his face. Many years had passed since he'd last seen his wives, and he wondered if they even still lived.

He sucked in his gut and puffed out his chest, remembering a time when his muscles had been solid and tight, a time when the markings inked into his skin hadn't faded, their edges more defined. With a disgusted sigh, he let his stomach sag back into its customary bulge.

This next part had become his most dreaded ritual of the morning. Unable to muffle a pained groan, he tried to relieve himself into the piss pipe protruding from the wall. His forehead met the metal as he winced with the effort. His urine dribbled out in weak, agonizing spurts, drawing beads of sweat from his forehead with each strain. Every time he thought he was finished, another wave of sharp pain preceded a few more drops of thick, cloudy gunk. He feared he'd never pass water peacefully again, despite the doctor's repeated assurance that his condition would pass. After two weeks of medications, he had his doubts.

Since the rest of his command staff would be awake soon, he needed to complete his morning routine before joining them. First, he stretched, touching his knees and then pushing his fingertips to his toes. Then he walked laps around the large cabin to loosen his muscles. It wouldn't bode well for him to let his staff see how stiff and slow his body had become. Teks by nature were ruthless bastards always looking to who could best lead them in the future. Though there was no doubt his time was nearing an end, there was no sense in giving them more reason to push him out to sea. This next invasion would probably be the last of his storied career.

Once finished with his exercises, he slipped a set of war fatigues over his sagging skin before wrapping a heavy cloth coat around his shoulders. With a deep breath, he stood up straight and pulled the cabin door open.

A cacophony of screeching machines and grinding metal filled the outside. He followed the passageway to a balcony overlooking the deck and hundreds of working Tek soldiers. Thick, black smoke billowed from tall cylindrical stacks at the ship's center, blocking out the suns and turning morning into night. Though the smoke announced the Tek fleet's arrival, a warning would do his future enemies little good.

Young General Rayles, his second-in-command and greatest threat to his power, joined him on the balcony.

"Zaffka. Teok el Masika," he shouted over the screeching machinery.

"Sholon par seefa," Zaffka answered.

"We arrive at the so-called Wastelands soon," General Rayles said, continuing to speak in their native language.

"Very good. Any resistance?"

"None, sir."

He surveyed the fleet of massive ships that stretched as far as he could see. Nearly a hundred thousand battle-hardened warriors were at his command, most of whom hadn't seen their families since they'd been drafted as children.

Supreme Leader Zaffka grinned at the barrenness of the desert terrain beyond the shore. "This shall be an easy landing."

"Most of them are, your excellence," General Rayles replied.

"Have you sent a force to the south as ordered?"

"A thousand men are already on their way. The ship will stay hidden until the appointed time, and then they will make landfall and move into position."

"And they know to wait until they hear our thunder?"

"They do, sir."

"Very well. Leave me be until we've secured our landing."

"Of course, sir."

"Kill all who move," Zaffka ordered.

"We always do."

General Zaffka returned to his chambers to make final adjustments to his war plan. He studied a hand-drawn map of the continent they approached. His scouts had done well. More than half of the land was covered with a single country labeled "EPERTASE" in large Tek letters.

Two years of planning had made his strategy sound, but since he was a meticulous man, he ran through them one last time. First, make landfall in the Wastelands and set up camp. The barren desert would allow him, for the first time in his long career, to build a stronghold and launch his initial attack from land instead of by sea. He would take his time draining the west of the ground's black blood before moving east toward civilization. He was excited at the prospect of sending home boatloads of the vital substance before initiating a single battle. His masters would be pleased. Maybe they'd even let him retire before General Rayles challenged him. Or maybe General Rayles would have an accident during the coming battles.

He pointed on the map to the smaller country to Epertase's northwest and smiled. "You will be first, Lithia," he whispered.

Though he fully understood the cruelty he was about to visit upon the land's inhabitants, once the violence began he would have no remorse. This was his duty, his people's way of life, his destiny. Tonight they would make landfall and the invasion would begin.

For the rest of the day he studied his maps, losing track of time until a knock at his door announced his dinner. His servant brought in a platter of overcooked hog and set it on the table. Zaffka devoured the food with the same restraint he planned to show his newest foes—none. In hindsight, that turned out to be a mistake as terrible indigestion took hold and tormented him for most of the evening.

The massive warship belched and eased to a stop as close as it could get to the shore. The time was near.

He moved to the glistening black suit of form-fitting armor hanging in a display case on the wall. He opened the case and dragged his finger along the sleeve, which bore steel cylinders extending from elbow to wrist. The armor's solid black was only broken by two parallel red stripes along the side of the neckpiece, indicating his rank. "Soon," he whispered.

A knock on his door announced it was time. Three of his top bodyguards awaited in full Tek armor outside his door. Air hissed from vents along their necks with each of their movements. Of all the Tek weaponry, the mechanical suits of armor were Zaffka's favorite.

"Ready, sir?" one of the soldiers asked.

He nodded. They followed him down a ladder into his command vessel at the side of the ship, while two other soldiers lowered his armor case into the boat. The small motor whined as they bounced along the turbulent waves toward the shore. Zaffka didn't speak during the trip and his guards knew better than to open their mouths.

The shore was alive with commotion. Heavy digging machines as large as small castles worked at a frantic pace. Massive ground movers carried sand from fresh holes to newly formed mounds. His Teks were efficient and hard-working and he was pleased.

Within five moons, the first pits would be finished, and the pumpers would be siphoning their treasure. Early tests of the soil by his scout teams had indicated plenty of black blood to fuel the rest of their invasion. He surveyed the horizon. Thousands of bonfires littered the landscape as far as he could see.

Now was a good time to be a Tek. Now was a bad time to be anyone else.

General Rayles met Zaffka on the shore. "Our spies were accurate. This land is indeed desolate. The Machine God has smiled upon us."

"Do not let this emptiness mislead you. Epertase is reported to be a powerful country and we mustn't take them lightly. Well," he paused, "as powerful as any primitive country could be, I suppose."

Rayles's top lieutenant approached. "Sir, we came across an outpost a few miles inland. There were several enemy soldiers living there."

"Did any of them escape?"

"We don't believe so."

"Very good." Zaffka turned away.

"What would you have us do with the prisoners?"

Zaffka glanced back. "Hang them, of course." He started walking with Rayles. "How are the defensive perimeters coming along?"

"On schedule, sir."

Zaffka nodded his approval. "And what of the water supply? Is the river called Danduke plentiful enough for our needs?"

"It is, sir. Though we will leave it dry when we are finished."

"Perfect."

Day and night, the rumble of machines echoed relentlessly, making sleep next to impossible without earplugs. Seemingly bottomless wells of thick, black fluid filled the desert landscape.

A foreigner would be amazed at the speed in which entire Tek cities developed. As for Zaffka, he thought it barely adequate.

On the fourteenth day, a Tek scout returned from his explorations. "Sir, the country called Lithia has begun to strengthen its western borders. It appears its scouts have seen us and they prepare for war."

"Let them prepare. It will do them no good. We will advance when we are ready."

"Perfect, Supreme Leader."

CHAPTER 10

THE DAY OF MATTHEW

T he winter brought record snowfall and more days of complete isolation for Rasi than all the winters he'd been on Shadows Peak combined. By the time the spring thaw came, he'd lost all the weight he had gained in the fall and some of the muscle. Prey had been scarce, and he'd gone through nearly all the japsy weed. But hunger was not what almost drove him mad. It was the loneliness. If not for Alina's arrival as soon as the mountain trails became passable, he might have opted for a blindfolded walk along the path.

That morning, for the first time, she was awake before he stirred. She was building the fire when he opened his eyes. "Good morning," she whispered, smiling.

Good morning.

"I have an idea."

Rasi cocked his head.

"Tomorrow is the start of the Matthew's Day celebrations."

Rasi sighed. Matthew's Day seemed to keep getting longer. The festivities lasted a week now. *And?*

"You know how on the first day everyone dresses in disguises?"

Yes. He knew where this was going.

"I want you to come with me." She grabbed his hand as he started to turn away.

Alina.

"Oh, please. No one will recognize us. I'll wear my hair up and put on a mask. You can paint your face and wear your cloak with the hood up." She leaned around him to see his face. "I won't even make you shave your winter whiskers today. Pleeeaase?"

He couldn't believe he was even considering it. The danger was greater than any ochrid attack or mountain storm. It was a crazy idea. Finally, he nodded. *But only for the first day. Then I'm coming back.*

"Deal." She started dancing around the fire. She looked so silly Rasi couldn't help but laugh.

"Come on," she said. "Dance with me."

There's no music.

"I'll sing."

He'd heard her sing before. *I'd rather you didn't.*

She scowled. "Really?" She grabbed his hand and tugged at him until he relented. They danced slowly at first, but then she pulled away and danced faster. She laughed and danced and talked to the horses like they could answer her. Rasi grinned, unable to look away. She was perfect. He loved her more than he ever thought he could love again.

While they sat by the fire, Rasi said, *I've been working on something. May I share it with you?*

"Of course." She leaned closer in anticipation.

Rasi worked his mouth and cleared his throat. She stared intently. *Forget it.* He turned away.

She pulled him back. "No, please. Show me."

All right. Don't laugh. With exaggerated movements of his mouth, he said, "A'ena." It still didn't sound as good as he had hoped, but it was the best he could do.

Her lips curled upward. "I think it was perfect, Rasi."

He returned a half-smile and resolved to keep practicing. He'd started talking to Salient during that long, lonely winter in a desperate attempt to stay sane. His speech was slowly getting better and clearer, but he had a long way to go. Some sounds eluded him completely.

Her every step that day exuded quiet excitement. Even when he tried to close his eyes for the night's rest, she wouldn't stop humming to herself. Eventually he had to ask, *Could you tamp it down a bit?*

She snarled playfully, but then let him sleep.

They woke up before the suns rose, not because Rasi wasn't tired, but because Alina was too excited to sleep in. "If we have any hope of getting there before lunch we should leave soon."

Rasi ate a few berries for breakfast while Alina gathered her things. Soon, they were on their way. The dew was still on the ground when they reached the forest.

Once they reached the Great Plains, she stopped him and climbed from her saddle. "Get down," she said.

I don't know about this.

"You want to be recognized?"

He sighed and climbed down. She removed a small pouch from her travel bag and began to smear charred wood powder stripes on his forehead and cheeks.

You brought paint with you?

"Sure. I knew you'd come with me this time."

How did you know?

"Okay, I didn't know. I've brought paint every year."

She pulled her hair back into a tail, lifted her hood, and donned an ivory-colored mask over her eyes and nose. "What do you think? Will anyone recognize me?"

Only if you talk.

She side-eyed him. Before they returned to their horses, something caught Alina's eye. She walked to the edge of the grass. Rasi followed.

"Look, Rasi. Something strange is happening."

Rasi knelt beside her. The knee-high grass undulated without a breeze and softly grabbed at his legs. Rasi remembered a story about the Great Plains coming to life during the time of Matthew, but he didn't know what it meant. *Let's keep going.*

They mounted their horses again. Rasi lifted his hood, partially hiding his painted face in shadow. What was he thinking agreeing to this?

An annoying cramp gripped Rasi's nervous stomach. It was the closest he had gotten to Thasula in many years, and he wanted to turn back.

They rode to the main gate in the perimeter wall. Two guards stood in their elevated perch with bows slung across their chests. Rasi lowered his head as he and Alina slipped into the long line of merchants, farmers, and revelers waiting to enter. It was such a bad idea.

But it worked. They rode through the gate without attracting any notice and entered the bustling town.

The streets were alive with excitement. If Epertasians knew anything, it was how to celebrate. Alina leaned toward Rasi and said, "I told you you'd be fine. Now enjoy. Would you like an ale?"

Nothing sounded better than something cold. Once they'd stabled their horses, she led him to an ale vendor who fulfilled her order. The vendor was an old friend, but he didn't recognize her. It was the first real test of her disguise, and she passed. The ale was smooth and cold and wonderful despite not having much taste. He didn't have the heart to tell Alina that it was as bland as all but the most bitter of foods.

Alina led him to another vendor who was selling wooden knickknacks painted to look like the furry, wormlike colorfuls of legend. A little boy stood eyeing them wistfully.

"Hello," Alina said to him.

"Ma'am," the boy answered.

"What's your name?"

"Jarret, ma'am."

"And what are you today?"

"A dragon. Rarrr."

"Oh my. Very scary. Tell me, Jarret, do you know the story of the colorfuls?"

He shook his head.

Rasi leaned against a basket stall and watched. Though he knew the story, he couldn't wait to hear it told by Alina.

Before she could begin, Jarrett was joined by two other children who seemed to materialize from nowhere. She smiled at them. "Once upon a time there was a little boy named … Jarret."

Jarret giggled and puffed out his tiny chest.

"It was a time when the kingdom was very sad and afraid, for King Thadius had become very angry. Jarret lived on a farm in the west, and on his magical farm thousands of beautiful worms suddenly started growing from the ground like flowers. They were spectacular worms all the colors of a rainbow. And they were gentle. The farmer gave them to all the children in town as pets. When they slithered on the arms of little boys and girls, they were warm and they tickled." She tickled Jarret's knee and he squirmed away with a giggle. "When Jarret was given his worm, he loved it very much and took very good care of it. The Elder Three gave the creatures a name: Colorfuls."

"They live in the ground," Jarret interrupted, unable to control himself. "We have to dig."

One of the other boys asked, "Why was King Fadus angry?"

"Well, young one, King Thadius was a greedy man who didn't like not getting his own way. But Thadius had a very special son who brought hope to the people in the dark times. And one day a great fire filled the air. And when the fire passed, King Thadius had died and the young prince was the new king, and everyone was happy. That's the day the colorfuls disappeared and haven't been seen since." She surveyed the children. "Does anyone know how we celebrate that special day?"

One of the other children shouted, "Matthew's Day."

"That's right, the Day of Matthew the Peaceful."

Before sending the children to find their mothers, Alina purchased a colorful trinket for each of them. "Now, run along, children."

"Thank you, ma'am," Jarrett shouted as he ran.

She leaned against Rasi's side. *Can we consider the costumes a success now?*

He wasn't quite ready to anoint her the queen of costumes just yet.

She hugged his arm. "Come on." She led him to the stage in Cecil Park where a crowd had already formed.

A gray-haired storyteller was stepping onto the stage.

"We're right on time. He's my favorite storyteller," she whispered.

The storyteller cleared his throat and began with an even tone. "Thousands of years ago, when the rise of the dragons threatened to end the world of man, the Light of Epertase reached down from the heavens to save the people of this great land. A young warrior named Uriah was chosen to bear the Light, and from that day forward his life was intrinsically linked to the survival of Epertase and all who inhabited it.

"The Light passed to Uriah's descendants from generation to generation, never again to intervene in the trials of man. That is, until the time of King Thadius. This is his story."

The storyteller's voice grew deep and ominous. "Our tale begins on a fateful night nearly one thousand years ago. The kingdom was aflutter with anticipation of the birth of Thadius's firstborn, the possible heir to his Light. The best doctors in the land gathered in the castle as the queen struggled and strained. Her face was pale as marble and her royal blood spilled onto the floor. Something was terribly wrong."

The storyteller scanned the children with squinting eyes. They stared back with mouths open and eyes as wide as gold coins.

"From inside Thadius's soul, the Light watched his son, Prince Matthew, draw his first breath free of his mother's womb. Then the joy of Matthew's first breath was eclipsed by the sorrow of the queen's last. At that moment, the Light saw a change in Thadius's heart. The sky filled with brightness as Matthew inherited the Light that burned inside his father. It was that night Thadius began his journey into madness."

The children, and some of the adults, held their breath. The storyteller stoked their anticipation with a pause as he sipped from his tankard. He licked his lips and continued. "Thadius stared at his helpless son cradled in his arms. Instead of joy and pride, resentment oozed from his every pore. He held the child responsible for the queen's death and did not believe Matthew was worthy of the dormant Light within him. He contemplated killing his own child at that moment.

"For the first and only time in his life, a tear fell from his eye. And then, after what seemed an age, Thadius lowered his son to the cold, hard floor and left him at the mercy of the gods.

"While Matthew was an infant, Thadius consulted every skilled wizard and witch in the land in hopes of reclaiming that which he believed was still his by right. He longed to pass the dormant Light to another heir whom he deemed worthier."

The storyteller rose from his stool and paced along the front row of children. He leaned toward them while stroking his beard. The children cowered under his ghoulish glare. "When those wizards failed to return the dormant Light to him, he took their heads." The storyteller dragged his thumb along his neck. Some of the smaller children hid behind their parents.

He resumed his tale. "By the time Matthew celebrated his first year, Thadius had severed all ties. The castle staff and servants raised the young prince, filling him with compassion and a common touch.

"Thadius went on to sire twelve more children by twelve different women in hopes of changing what had already been set in stone. Even after all his efforts, Thadius couldn't change what the Light had decided. Prince Matthew, the one he considered the murderer of his wife, would one day be king. That knowledge chewed at his soul for years.

"During that time, the kingdom lost confidence in his leadership. Unrest grew in the people's hearts, so he tightened his grip. He raised taxes again and again. He forced thousands of men and boys to join his army, taking them away from their shops and farms. The people became so poor they couldn't even buy moldy bread. Hangings in the courtyard became daily events. His people pleaded with him to change his course, but that only made him angrier.

"What he saw as their treason prompted him to enact martial law upon the entire country. When his closest advisors and the few friends who remained warned him of the growing unrest, he thought they too had turned on him, and he locked them in the dungeons.

"Thadius sat alone on his throne, brooding over threats both real and imagined. He feared the neighboring kingdoms built armies in preparation for war, and he was right, though not for the reasons he thought. He was convinced that invasion was imminent, so he ordered his borders fortified. His neighbors responded in kind, which escalated the tension.

"And then Thadius declared war on them.

"When Matthew turned thirteen, Thadius began to question whether he even needed an heir at all. Soon, he had convinced himself that as long as the Light was still in him, he was immortal. He isolated himself from the world and plotted the murders of his children. Matthew alone escaped the assassins with the help of a servant whom Thadius immediately hanged in the courtyard. Matthew fled into the city.

"When he ordered an entire town slaughtered because he believed Matthew continued to hide from his assassins there, the people and some of his own army took to the streets. A rebellion swelled with a charismatic young leader at the helm.

"With the unrest at home and abroad coming to a head and a mad king vowing to never relinquish the Light, the survival of Epertase was in doubt. To save the kingdom, the Light intervened for the first time since the days of Uriah."

The storyteller paused theatrically and pointed past the rooftops to the suns hanging over the distant mountains.

"Nearly a thousand years ago today, the two suns blackened and a blinding fire saturated the air from ocean to ocean. But the flames didn't burn and quickly extinguished on their own. Thasula languished in unnatural shadows. The people feared the end times had come. Thadius, realizing the signs were an omen of the Light forsaking him, climbed atop the highest tower as the rebels stormed the castle gates.

"The mad king watched with disdain as the rebels swarmed the courtyard and began battering the great doors. Their leader was none other than Prince Matthew, his first and only surviving child."

The storyteller raised his fists and his voice. "'Treacherous boy, I will not give you my power,' Thadius shouted. 'You are not worthy.' With Matthew giving orders down below, Thadius saw his chance to end the uprising and cement himself as the one true king in the eyes of the Light and the people. He drew his sword. Thunder crackled in the sky. He shouted, 'I am immortal. You cannot vanquish me. I will kill the one who would be king,' and leaped from the tower. His bloodthirsty gaze fixated on Matthew as he plummeted toward the ground. Matthew turned away when the impact with the cobblestones ended his father's life.

"With the mad king lying dead and broken at the tower's base, a new age for Epertase began. As king, Matthew made peace with the neighboring armies and prevented a devasating war the weakened Epertase could not hope to win. He restored order to the kingdom by reversing his father's tyrannical decrees. He was a fair ruler, and a beloved one. Over his many years in power, Matthew became the greatest king Epertase has ever known. And that is why we celebrate Matthew and the mighty Change on this day."

The crowd applauded as the story came to an end. The storyteller bobbed his head. "Thank you. Thank you. But remember: no peace can last forever. We must always be on the lookout for signs of Change."

The storyteller walked toward the back of the stage, paused, and then turned back.

"Some say those signs of Change have begun anew," he said.

Alina tilted her head and wrinkled her brow. She whispered, "Did you hear that, Rasi? I've never heard that last part before. What did he mean?"

He's just a crazy old man.

Alina and Rasi spent the rest of the day enjoying the sights and performances on various stages that mostly depicted battles of the Heathen War. Alina even tried fried bat for the first time. She didn't like it, so Rasi finished it for her. They spent the night in a cozy inn on the outskirts of Thasula. His world couldn't have been better.

Before the suns rose, he kissed her and snuck out into the growing crowd preparing for day two of the celebrations.

CHAPTER 11

WHISPERS OF WAR

King Elijah watched the second day of festivities from the highest castle tower. Most years he was excited for the coming ceremonies, but that wasn't the case this year. He was certain he was being punished by the gods for his years of troubling behavior. Though once he became king he had striven to be good and just, his beloved wife was paying for his transgressions.

As he stood in the chilly air, he sensed Queen Madelyne approach from behind. Actually, he didn't sense her so much as he heard her familiar, ever-worsening wheeze. "Do you have a special someone to take to the ball?" she questioned him, playfully jabbing him in the side.

"Only the most beautiful lady in the lands," he said.

She rested her cheek on his back and wrapped her frail arms around him. "I am honored," she said.

He didn't deserve her. He craned his neck so he could see her over his shoulder. "I was speaking of Alina," he said with a smirk. She paused for a moment as though she hadn't caught his joke, but then her face lit up and she began to giggle.

"What's so funny?" he asked. "I'm serious."

"Stop that," she said, unable to contain her laughter. The strain proved too much. She covered her mouth as her laughter gave way to a deep, barking cough, the kind of cough that said the future was grim. Elijah rubbed her back. She pulled away as her coughing intensified. With a look of panic on her suddenly cherry-red face, she slumped to the edge of her bed, gasping for air.

"James," Elijah shouted.

The door cracked open. "Yes, Your Majes—Oh. I shall fetch the doctor at once."

Madelyne shook her head and gestured for James to wait. She seemed to be slowly catching her breath. Elijah spoke for her. "Just some water."

"Yes, Your Majesty."

Elijah sat next to her on the bed and rubbed her back again. Her coughing eventually subsided and her cheeks returned to their usual ashen hue. She reached for a handkerchief from the nightstand. The frilly white cloth turned crimson with each dab at her mouth.

Elijah looked into her fearful eyes and wrapped his arms around her. "I know, my love. I know."

James returned with a pitcher of water and a glass. Almost as fast as he could pour, she snatched the glass from him. Her hand trembled, splashing water onto her blouse, and she turned away, embarrassed. James gallantly pretended not to see.

"That will be all, James," Elijah said.

"Yes, Your Majesty." James bowed while backing out of the room.

Madelyne whispered, "I know you were kidding, but maybe you could take Alina tonight. She would love it. Besides, I feel I am too weak."

"I think our daughter might have met someone she'd rather not introduce us to yet. She hasn't been home for a few days." He didn't dare tell her he had been having Alina watched a little closer lately.

"I'm sure she'll tell us when she's ready. She's grown to be a very independent young woman."

"I wonder where she gets that."

Madelyne rested her hand on his. "I hope we meet this stranger soon. I'm glad to see her finally moving on after the tragedy with Blair."

"I'll try to find her today and see if she will do me the honor." Escorting Alina would give him the perfect chance to talk with her.

Elijah went quiet, stroking his wife's hair as he held her. He didn't want to burden her with what was truly weighing on him, so he said nothing. Madelyne fell asleep in his arms. He lifted her feet onto the bed, covered her with a blanket, and departed to his study.

Later in the afternoon, James knocked on the door and stepped into Elijah's study. "Your Majesty, Commander Lorca would like to see you on an urgent matter. He has a guest with him."

"By all means, send them in."

James returned with Commander Lorca, who escorted a young man through the door. The man was the opposite of Lorca in nearly every physical way. Whereas Lorca was fit and clean-shaven and wore his hair short as befitted a military man, his portly companion wore his hair long and straggly and his beard equally so. His clothes gave him the appearance of being a vagabond.

James stepped out and closed the door.

Lorca spoke without waiting to be addressed. "Sir, this is Paisel, one of your scouts from the western Wastelands."

The filthy man bowed before speaking. "Your Majesty, I have dire news."

Elijah indicated a chair across the marble floor. "Have a seat and continue, my friend."

Paisel let out a weary moan as he plopped into the chair. "Some sort of invasion force from the Infinite Sea has made landfall in the Wastelands. They arrived in a fleet of massive ships the likes of which I've never seen, stretching as far as our monoculars could see. They come in such numbers the land itself rumbles beneath them and the skies above them turn black."

Elijah sat back, nonplussed. "Have they preceded their landing with heralds or peacemakers?" he asked.

"No, sir. They are most certainly an aggressive force."

"Aggressive?"

"I took a team to see why the other outposts had gone dark. We were trying to ascertain their numbers when we were ambushed.

They moved so fast that I never got a good look at them. I heard explosions, and my men … my men are dead. Your Majesty, this is an invading army. I'd stake my life on it.

"There is no time to lose," Paisel added. "The bulk of their force has no doubt reached land by now. Your Majesty, what would you have us do?"

Elijah sat quietly, stroking the stubble on his chin. "I must have time to think about what you have told me." He hollered for James, who quickly opened the door. "Take Paisel to a guest room. Give him clean clothing, hot food, and a warm bed." He looked back at Paisel. "You have done well. Enjoy this night's celebration as my guest. See me in my meeting room at sunrise and I will have your orders. Is that understood?"

"Yes, Your Majesty."

"Very well. You are dismissed."

"Thank you, Your Majesty." Paisel exited with James close behind.

Elijah shook his head. "What do you make of this news, Lorca?"

"I think we are going to war."

"That's my fear as well."

"What do you want me to do?"

Elijah walked to the window. "I have a lot weighing on me right now. This is not a good time for a war."

"How can I help, Your Majesty?"

"I need you to accompany Alina anytime she leaves the castle until further notice."

"Does she know that I'll be doing this?"

"I'll tell her tonight. One day, Lorca, I'll tell you everything that's happening. But right now I need you to trust me."

"Always."

"You are a good man."

Lorca bowed and left the room. James entered soon after. "It's time to get ready for the ball. That is, if you're still going."

"I am." It was important that Elijah keep up appearances tonight for the sake of the people. There would be plenty of worrying for them in due time. James laid out Elijah's evening suit, and within the hour Elijah made his appearance in the Royal Hall.

Though time and time again he had requested that the citizens not trouble themselves with gifts, inevitably the main hall filled with cakes and savory pies and trinkets. He understood the people's need to follow tradition and couldn't be angry with them, but it was frustrating. He had no use for those things. As he had each year before, he would order James to deliver the leftovers to the less fortunate in the morning.

He smiled, thanking each of his guests as they entered the Hall. Many of the attendees asked after the queen, and he explained that she was busy but would be along shortly. Even though some of them probably knew it was a lie, it seemed to pacify them and move the line along.

He caught a glimpse of Alina entering across the room. She was radiant in an ivory silk dress that formed a perfect circle as it touched the marble floor. The bodice was studded with emerald buttons— too few to be considered gaudy, but enough to accent her stunning eyes. She smiled with genuine kindness to each of the guests as they greeted her. He thought how beautiful she was, and how she looked more like her mother every day. She caught him looking, excused herself, and started toward him.

He looked away, hoping she would become distracted before reaching him. A woman intercepted her to admire her gown, giving Elijah time to disappear into the crowd. He hated avoiding her, but she could always recognize worry on his face despite his calm façade, and he wasn't ready for the questioning game just yet. He was able to hide until it was time for them to lead the dance.

This time he sought her out. "Alina?" he said, and tapped her shoulder as she held court with several guests.

She turned. "Father?"

Elijah took her hand. "My beautiful daughter, may I have this dance?"

"Oh, now you want to see me?"

He led her to the dance floor, and the musicians began playing.

"You've been avoiding me all night," she whispered.

"I know. And I'm sorry. I have the weight of the mountains on my shoulders and it's getting worse by the moment."

Her courtly smile never slipped, but her eyes bored into his.

"Tell me, Father. Let me share in your burdens. I am your heir, after all."

"I know. And I do have something to speak with you about."

"Should we excuse ourselves?" she asked.

He didn't want to ruin her fun right away. There would be precious few celebrations in the days to come. "No, not now. I will visit your chambers before you go to bed, and we will speak then."

Her eyes narrowed.

"Don't let it bother you, my dear. Let's just enjoy our dance."

Reluctantly, she agreed. She moved through the steps without faltering, though her eyes never left his face.

"I love you, Alina."

"I love you, too, Father.

As the music ended, the guests applauded. Alina lifted on her toes and kissed his cheek, curtsied, and then disappeared back into the crowd.

He strained to watch her over the heads of his admirers as she passed through the room's ceiling-high double doors where Tevin stood. Elijah, seeing his closest friend, gestured for Tevin to join him in a private alcove.

"Is it true?" Elijah asked, afraid of the answer.

"I believe so," Tevin replied. "The signs are there, Elijah. The Elder Three have as much as confirmed it."

Elijah lowered his head. "When?"

"They don't know, or if they do, they aren't saying."

"So, the grass of the Great Plains coming to life was indeed the first sign as the legends have foretold?"

"It would seem so."

"Damn it."

"I know this is difficult for you, but we must move forward."

Elijah diverted his eyes, ashamed, and stared at the ground. "I don't think I can."

"You have to. I will contact the criminal. We must move fast."

Elijah swallowed a lump in his throat.

"Elijah? Yes?"

His silence was his answer. He was the worst person on the planet.

The two made their way through the Hall and into the Royal Garden. Tevin said, "If we know about the signs, then others must know as well." He looked past Elijah like something had caught his eye and nodded politely.

Before Elijah could turn, Alina asked, "What signs, Father?"

He spun toward her, startled. "As I said, I will come speak with you in your quarters. All will be explained then."

"Is this about the grass of the Great Plains?"

"I said I will speak with you later. I have business with Tevin at the moment. Now kindly leave us."

Alina huffed back into the Hall.

Once she was safely out of earshot, Elijah whispered, "How much did she hear?"

"Only what she needed to hear," Tevin answered.

"This isn't right."

Tevin shrugged. "Sometimes difficult things must be done."

The two continued through the garden, Elijah deep in thought.

Tevin broke the silence. "Is she still seeing *him*?"

"I believe so."

"You should have killed him when you found out last year."

"I know." Elijah rubbed the back of his head. "I know."

The two shook hands, and Elijah returned to the party while Tevin headed home. After the last person had left and Alina had long since retired for the night, he headed to her chambers. He had much explaining to do.

He knocked on her door before peeking his head in. "My dear?"

"Come in, Father."

He sat on the edge of her bed and she sat up beside him. He lifted a wooden figurine of a colorful and examined it before setting it back on her nightstand. She sat quietly, waiting for him to say something. He fiddled with his fingers, never looking at her.

She covered his hands with hers. "What is it? Why are you so troubled tonight?"

He hesitated.

"Father?"

"There is no easy way to say what I have to say, so I'll just spit it out. I fear for your safety."

"My safety?"

"Yes."

"Is this because of the rumors of the foreign army?"

"You've heard already?"

"It isn't much of a secret. Your scout has a loose tongue."

Elijah sighed, disappointed in Paisel. "I suppose I should make a statement to the people, then."

"Are these invaders a real threat to Epertase?"

He looked into her green eyes and saw an innocence there he had forgotten. He smiled. "You let me be concerned with the foreigners. I am quite sure they haven't traveled this far just to start a fight. No, I have more pressing matters for you to be concerned with."

"Oh?"

"You are the bearer of the dormant Light."

Alina cocked her head to the side. "I know this."

"Normally I would rule until my death many years from now, but the Elder Three have confirmed the signs of change have begun anew. The Light in you has stirred."

"Like it did with Matthew?"

"I'm afraid so."

"I don't understand. Why now?"

"I don't know. Maybe these approaching foreigners have something to do with it. Regardless, I'm worried about what could happen. You remember the stories of Thadius?"

"But you're nothing like Thadius. You're a good man."

He was saddened by her naïve belief in him. "Alina, I have made many mistakes in my life. I have tried to change, but the Light must feel I am no longer worthy."

Her lips pressed together like they had when she was a child and about to have a temper tantrum. "The Light is worthless," she said. "I don't want it. I don't want to be queen, either. Not for many years, when you die of old age."

"It is not worthless, Alina. It is what keeps us in power. It is what protects our people. It's our duty to keep them safe, to keep their souls safe, and to do so we must protect the Light at all costs. That is our purpose in life."

"I don't want it."

"It has been forewritten."

After a brief silence, she gasped as if suddenly struck with a horrible thought. "What about you, Father? Thadius died when the Light went to Matthew."

"Thadius killed himself, Alina. I assure you that I will not do the same."

She spoke quickly as she put the pieces together. "You said I was in danger. Why?"

He didn't want to answer, though he knew that he must. "There is more to Matthew's legend, things the storytellers never speak of."

She stared at him.

"The Light will be vulnerable on the day of change."

"Vulnerable? What do you mean?"

"It can be stolen."

Her forehead wrinkled. "Stolen? How?"

He looked away.

"Father, how?"

He sighed. Her glare burned through his back. He hated himself for what he had to tell her.

"Your death," he whispered.

"By the gods." Her hand went limp on his and she withdrew it.

"Since you have no offspring to take the Light, if someone kills you while the transfer is taking place, they can steal it. That is the only time your death as the active Light bearer will not destroy Epertase."

She looked like the wind had been knocked from her lungs.

"Does anyone else know?" she asked with quivering lips.

"I believe so. That's why I am putting you on curfew from now until this has ended."

"Curfew?"

"And anytime you leave the castle, you will be accompanied by Lorca and his guard. This is nonnegotiable."

She wouldn't dare argue, he was sure. She knew when his mind was set.

He kissed her forehead. "Everything will be fine, my dear," he lied. "I must take my leave. I need to speak with my loose-lipped scout." His heart broke with the knowledge of what was still to come.

Paisel was waiting in Elijah's war room and rose when Elijah entered.

"I hardly recognized you, Paisel. You clean up nicely."

"Amazing what a hot bath, clean shave, change of clothes, and a haircut will do."

"You enjoyed the celebrations, I assume?"

"I had a wonderful time, Your Majesty. Though I may have imbibed a bit too much of your ale."

"That's why it was there."

"Thank you."

"I'm quite busy, so let's get to the issue at hand. I've had your credentials researched, and by all accounts you're an exemplary soldier. Your instructors and former squad leaders speak highly of you."

"I do my best, Your Majesty."

"Though you need to keep your lips shut a little tighter. I wasn't yet prepared to address the people about the threat."

"I'm terribly sorry."

Elijah waved off his apology. "I have a new assignment for you."

"Anything, Your Majesty."

"I have created a new position for you. A promotion, if you accept."

"I would be honored."

"I want you to travel back to the Wastelands and gather all of the scouts who remain. I have ordered two thousand soldiers to your command who will accompany you on your journey. Use these men however you see fit. I want you to establish a centralized command south of Lithia and prepare to make first contact with the invading army. You are to welcome them and advise them of Epertase's peaceful intentions. Find out why they are here. Keep me informed of your progress with weekly reports. I am also sending a group of our top spies to join you. They will operate independent of your leadership and will only contact you when information is to be sent to me. Is that understood?"

"Yes, Your Majesty."

"I have had the paperwork drafted and James will have it for you when you leave. You are dismissed."

As Paisel stood, Elijah thought of one more instruction. "By the way, on your trip back to the Wastelands, detour north through Lithia and advise King Logan to prepare for war, if he hasn't already."

"I will leave immediately, Your Majesty."

"James," Elijah hollered. "Take Paisel to his horse."

CHAPTER 12

SYMBIOTS

A lina waited until she judged most of the castle residents to be asleep before she summoned her most trusted adviser, a man named Levi. He had been a loyal friend for many years, and he was one of the few men she could trust in her time of need. He arrived soon after she was dressed.

"Levi, I don't have time to explain. I'm in danger."

"Danger, Your Highness?"

"Yes. There's only one person who can help me now."

"I'll help you."

She touched his shoulder. "I know you will."

"Maybe I should get your father."

"No. Listen to me. I need you to go with me to Shadows Peak."

"Shadows Peak? You want to travel through the forest at night?"

"We have no choice. There is a man there named Rasi."

"Rasi the king-killer?"

"He's not a murderer, Levi. Trust me. We must find him. He will know what to do."

"Your Highness, I'll do whatever you command, but I don't think it's wise."

"I have to go." She slid a dagger into her bag. "Come on." She opened the door and looked both ways. All was quiet. Levi followed her through the halls and down the stairs to the first floor. He kept one hand on his sword. Together they moved through the kitchen to a back hall. A guard sat near one of the doors to the outside. His head was dropped back and his mouth agape as he nearly sucked the paintings from the wall with each snoring breath. Alina and Levi snuck past him through the door to the outside.

"Where are all the guards?" Levi asked.

"I don't know. We need to get to Allusia." Even the stables were unguarded, which was beyond strange.

"Your Highness, I didn't board my horse here tonight."

"You can ride with me."

They climbed onto Allusia's back and set off toward the perimeter wall. As they neared the open gate, Alina strained to better see. Two guards hung lifelessly over the parapet of the watch tower, dark stains trickling down the bricks below them. Blood.

Levi stared at them in stunned silence as they rode through the open gates. Alina prodded Allusia into a gallop. "We must get to Rasi."

Nothing but grass and the morning fog stood between her and the forest. Allusia was strong; they could make it. But just past the gate, a beast of a man stepped away from the wall with a long wooden pole. The pole whirled in a wide loop before smashing Alina's cheek and sending her tumbling from her horse. Levi tried to catch her, but it happened too fast. The impact with the ground took her breath.

She lifted her head to see Levi circling back. *No,* she projected at him. *Get Rasi on the back side of Shadows Peak. There's a cave at the end of a mountain path. Hurry.*

Two more strangers, a man and a woman, sprinted after Levi. He pulled Allusia's reins and kicked her into a gallop toward the Forest of Concore. Levi was quickly swallowed by the dense fog that had settled over the plains. His two pursuers returned empty-handed.

"What do you want from me?" she wheezed, still fighting to get her breath back.

No answer came, but a high-pitched cackle from behind spooked her.

She spun around, but saw no one. "Show yourself," she demanded.

The stranger cackled again, this time to her left, and she spun toward the sound.

The woman hissed, "You're mine, Princess."

Alina filled her lungs as much as she was able and screamed, "Someone help me."

No one can help you, a shrill voice answered in her head. Her knotted stomach sank to her feet. The woman and her companion approached. She remembered her dagger and slid her hand into the bag that she had tied to her belt.

Two more people approached from beside the gate. One was the big guy with the pole, and the other was sickly and wearing pointy boots.

"What have we here?" the sickly one taunted. "A p-p-princessss?" He swayed as he walked, almost like he was drunk. Each sway briefly parted his scraggly gray hair to reveal his pale, ugly face. A silver birthmark covered his cheek and part of his chest visible through the open front of his blouse.

"What do you want?" Alina cried.

She heard his voice again in her head. *Stand her up, Blogg.*

The big guy grabbed her by the hair. She clutched his thick hand as he lifted her from the ground, nearly ripping her hair from her skull. Dangling in his grasp, she kicked the brute as hard as she could in the thigh. He didn't flinch.

The fourth stranger was shirtless with his ribs standing out beneath his skin. Shiny silver splotches like the sickly one's birthmarks shifted and crawled over his flesh.

The sickly stranger, the one with the crazy voice and the stutter, the one they seemed to report to, stepped forward. He tapped the hilt of his sword at his waist with a long fingernail.

"What kind of creature are you?" Alina asked.

"I am Scorne, and I am d-d-d-d-death to all," he answered. The one he called Blogg let loose of her hair and she thudded to her knees. She peered back at him, never having seen a man so large. The same strange metallic splotches slithered across his body as well. He brought his face close to hers and grunted; his breath smelled of decaying teeth.

"We must go," Scorne announced. "Cyn, bring her along."

The woman approached, her ink-black hair heavily contrasting her pale face. She glowered at Alina for a moment, and then Alina heard another voice in her mind. *I ain't touching her. You do it, Rez.* Then the woman hurried to catch up with Scorne.

Rez, the skinniest one, looked down with disgust before turning to Blogg. *Why do I always have to touch these animals? You do it.*

Blogg grunted and shook his head. Rez glared at Cyn and Scorne as they disappeared into the fog. "At least get the horses."

As they argued, Alina slid her dagger from her bag. Rez mumbled curses under his breath. When he leaned over to grab her, she thrust the dagger at his bare chest. One of the silver splotches crawled from his shoulder to his chest just as the blade struck. Rather than flesh and bone, she felt like she had struck metal. The impact bent her wrist awkwardly. The blade fell from her nerveless fingers and stuck in the ground.

Rez's fist quivered at his side. Drool leaked from the corner of his mouth. The silver mark on his arm slid down over his knuckles. He drew back. Alina braced herself. He drove his fist forward.

CHAPTER 13

THE HUNT BEGINS

Rasi spent the day hunting, taking a swim under the waterfall, and dreaming about how perfect his trip to Thasula had been. Even though he had just left Alina that morning, he couldn't wait to see her again. Maybe there was something to her idea that he could return to Epertase and start a new, albeit secret, life. For the first time, he wasn't totally opposed.

Instead of making the long journey up the trail, he made camp near the base of Shadows Peak. Millions of tiny white pinpricks scattered across the black satin above. The moon traversed the sky while he lay awake. His racing mind refused to slow. Going back to Epertase would potentially be the most consequential decision of his life, and not one to make on a whim.

Lost in thought, he didn't hear the nearing hoof beats until his straps cautiously lifting from the ground brought him out of his reverie. It sounded like a single horse and rider coming fast. He was on his feet with his sword drawn in an instant. Had he been recognized in Thasula? If they'd discovered him, why would they only send one soldier? Maybe it was Alina, but she shouldn't be coming at night.

There was no time to hide, nor did Rasi want to. He moved in front of Salient, stretching his neck until it released a satisfying pop. *If someone wants a fight,* he thought, *they will have to come at me head-on.* His straps snapped at the air. He saw flashes of the charging horse between the trees. It was Allusia, but that was not Alina in the saddle. Instead of waiting, he sprinted toward the trees, hoping for the advantage of surprise.

The horse and rider emerged from the trees as Rasi reached them. Rasi's straps, thirsty for blood, yanked the unsuspecting stranger from the saddle and slammed him to the ground. Before he could react, one of them wrapped around his foot and hoisted him into the air.

The color left the stranger's face. His eyes grew wide. The straps wrapped his other leg and pulled them apart just enough to let the stranger know they were serious. One wrong move would turn him into a human wishbone. Rasi squatted so he was face to upside-down face with his intruder. He snarled for effect. Another strap coiled around the stranger's throat and constricted slightly.

"Please," the man pleaded. "Don't kill me." The strap squeezed a little tighter, sending a wheeze from his throat.

Rasi scowled.

Release his throat, Rasi pleaded. *I don't want him dead.*

The intruder's eyes bulged and he choked out, "Please, don't." His lips paled. Emptiness slowly replaced the fear in his eyes.

Release him, damn it.

Rasi grabbed for the intruder's throat and pried a finger beneath the strap's vice-like grip. He strained, but he might as well have tried to pull the ground from beneath his feet. *Stop, please,* he begged one last time.

Then, as if his pleas were heard, the semiconscious man dropped to the ground. The straps, not willing to give up their prey completely, fanned out around him. The stranger coughed and rolled onto his back. Seeing the hovering straps sent him scurrying backward. The straps followed like the stalking predators they were. He struggled to his knees. "Is it you?" He rubbed his throat, never taking his eyes from the straps. "Rasi?"

Rasi nodded. He would tell him no more. One of the straps brushed the man's cheek and he cowered away from it. Another one nudged his shoulder and he flinched again. They were playing with him like a cat would play with a mouse before dinner.

"My name is Levi. I'm one of Alina's advisers. She needs you, Rasi. I fear it might already be too late."

Rasi lunged forward, coming face to face with him again. The man's breath smelled of grape jam and fear.

"We were coming to see you. Someone attacked us at the main gate."

Rasi ran to Salient and vaulted onto his back. It was probably a trap, but he'd worry about that later. He grunted, digging his heels into Salient's sides.

The stranger shouted, "Hurry, Rasi."

Rasi's straps streamed behind him, as they liked to do whenever he rode fast. He shifted his weight as Salient lengthened his stride. Thank the gods for the bright moon.

They entered the tree line. Though the path was clear, branches grew across it in several places. He ducked the first branch, but he was moving too fast for caution, and it was too dark in the thick of the forest to avoid them all. A strap shot forward, batting the next limb from his path. As the branches grew thicker, all seven straps went to work, ripping and knocking the limbs out of his way. Rasi didn't slow.

He reached the edge of the forest and burst onto the Great Plains. Mentally preparing himself for battle made him feel alive, like a soldier again, and he liked it.

Riding into the open like that was dangerous, but he hoped the fog would give him cover long enough to pick up Alina's trail. He raced north toward the wall. The suns slowly burned away the fog, bringing the blur of the castle into focus. Just the sight of it made him nervous.

Near the gate, he dismounted to give Salient a much-needed rest. Two dead guards draped the watchtowers. It wouldn't be long before they were found. He crouched in the grass, looking for signs of a skirmish as the animated stalks gently tugged at his legs. Nothing. It was as blind a search as one could imagine. As he hunted for any sign of Alina, voices from the castle grounds reminded him of how risky his actions were. It was a dead-end.

When he turned to head back toward Salient, he stopped in shock. Blades of grass hoisted a small dagger as if presenting it to him. He snatched it. The emerald on the hilt assured him it was Alina's. As he searched for another sign, a section of grass parted around a faint footprint in the dirt. It was the same size as Alina's. Rasi took a step toward it and the grass parted around a larger footprint. *This must be the man who took her.* The grass parted around the next print, and the next, showing Rasi which way to go.

With Salient in tow, Rasi followed the trail, which eventually led back toward the forest. Frantic shouts near the gates made him pick up his pace. When he neared the forest, a sick feeling overcame him as he realized he might have ridden right past Alina and her abductors. He led Salient into the forest and bid silent thanks to the grass.

Following the trail now would take some real tracking skills.

His nervous straps lifted.

Or maybe not.

He slowly pulled his sword from the sheath. Had they doubled back for him? Whoever they were, they were good. Dangerous too. Who would return to the scene of the crime when they could have been long gone?

A sickly-looking woman stepped out from behind a tree. *You must be Rasi.*

Rasi cocked his head. *You can talk in my head?*

Your little girlfriend isn't the only one that can do it.

Where is she, you bitch?

She grinned. *That's no way to speak to a lady. If I told you that, then we'd both know, and that would spoil all the fun, wouldn't it? Okay, Blogg.*

Branches snapped above Rasi and a beast of a man dropped onto his straps. Rasi grunted as he was wrenched from his feet and hurled against a tree, two straps clutched in Blogg's muscular hands. His sword skittered into the bushes.

Rasi tried to shake the grogginess from his head before Blogg could attack again. But Blogg merely turned away with the straps draped over his shoulder as one might carry a bag of laundry and dragged Rasi back toward the field. The tall grass grabbed Blogg's ankles, but that hardly slowed him. It was probably more annoying than effective. The other straps flailed at the mountain of a man. He batted them away as one would an insect. He seemed as strong as the grizzly that had bested Rasi years ago. Rasi struggled to his feet, but the tug at his back just as quickly jerked him to the ground again.

A strap snagged the trunk of the last tree before they reached the open plain. Rasi smiled. He spun on his back to face Blogg and dug his heels into the dirt. The strap went taut and the big man thudded to his rear.

This was Rasi's chance. He leaped to his feet. Before he could engage the big man, the woman crashed into him. They both hit the ground. It was a race to get to their feet, and Rasi won. He punched her jaw, but it turned to hardened silver at the last instant. It was like striking steel. Pain shot from his knuckles to the pit of his stomach.

Blogg released the straps, lumbered to his feet, and charged.

"Quit following us," the woman shouted. Her metal fist moved with the speed of thought. Rasi couldn't avoid it. She struck his ribs under his armpit and he doubled over. Blogg lowered his shoulder and knocked Rasi across the dirt.

"There's nothing you can do for her now," the woman said.

Bullshit.

She grinned. *Such language for a gentleman.*

Rasi's straps lunged for her and she danced out of the way. Blogg grabbed his hair and lifted him in the air. He drove his heel into Blogg's thigh, but the strange shifting armor was there too. Blogg tossed him to the ground like he was weightless. Rasi's straps attacked. Blogg caught two of them against his chest and dropped to the ground, pinning them beneath his bulk. The others pounded his back, but his shifting metal skin caught the blows.

"Kill him, Cyn. I can't hold them for long," he shouted.

The straps strained and squealed and thrashed under him. Cyn closed in, the metal on her arm sliding over her fist and extending from her knuckle into a finger-length spike. She drew back to strike. Rasi mashed a handful of dirt into her eyes and then kicked her squarely in her chest, again striking metal, but hard enough to knock her back. He dove onto Blogg's back and shoved his fingers into Blogg's mouth. A strap slithered around the behemoth's neck, but his metal skin slipped beneath it and solidified. The metal didn't coat the soft insides of his cheeks, though. Rasi fish-hooked both sides of his mouth and pulled.

Blogg grunted and rolled from the straps. The back of his hand hit Rasi's chest with the force of a tidal wave. Rasi felt the grittiness of dirt in his mouth. Blogg rubbed his chin and repeatedly stretched his jaw like he was chewing too big a bite of undercooked meat. Blood smeared his pale cheeks from the corners of his mouth.

Rasi scrambled backward until his back met a tree. Then Cyn was upon him. He covered his face with his arms as she leaped. His straps jerked at his back, lifting him onto a branch just as she swung her metal-spiked fist.

"Come down, coward," Blogg taunted.

Rasi studied them from above. Their metal skin was quite the puzzle. He needed to solve it fast. These bastards knew where Alina was, and he planned to bleed them until they talked. He took a deep breath. *I'm coming. Don't you fret.* He crouched, ready to rejoin the fray.

As he was about to leap, something cracked the bark behind him. Pain flared in his collarbone like a bull had gored him. He couldn't breathe. He looked down at his chest, half expecting part of it to be missing. Blood oozed from a coin-sized hole just below his left clavicle. For a moment, he could only stare at it. But then instinct took over and he shoved his right hand over it until one of his straps coiled tightly against his wound. He wobbled, almost falling from his perch. A glance at the tree showed him blood dripping from the feathered fletching of an arrow jutting from the bark. His arm hung limply at his side, the pain of lifting it too much.

The fletching's Epertasian purple told him the freaks below weren't responsible. It also told him that his problems had just gotten bigger. An entire army bigger, potentially. Blogg and Cyn fled deeper into the woods.

Whoosh.

Another arrow whizzed past Rasi's head, clipping his left ear. Rasi wavered on the branch that held him. It snapped. As he fell, his straps grasped at more branches, but they were brittle and snapped as well. Before he struck the ground, his straps enveloped him like a cocoon and hardened.

Thud.

What little breath he still had exploded from his lungs.

Instantly, his straps unraveled and shot into the air, ready for their next battle. His lungs fought to expand and a high-pitched wheeze left his throat.

"Uhng … Uhng …" His chest muscles twitched and constricted. *Relax,* he told himself, struggling to his knees. *Concentrate. This will pass. Just lost my wind, is all.* His straps hovered, ready for action. He heard voices within the forest and realized they had surrounded him while he'd been busy with Blogg and Cyn.

Slowly, the invisible bands around his chest loosened. He took a deep, wonderful breath. Following his signal, Salient raced to his side.

With his good arm, he cradled his useless limb. A strap secured his wounded arm to his chest, wrapping around him like a sling. Each movement caused his collarbone to burn. He struggled to his feet, his legs shaking.

A quick glance across the plains revealed a wave of approaching soldiers. He couldn't go through them, not in his condition. The soldiers in the forest blocked his path to Shadows Peak as well.

His only chance was to head west toward Havens Ravine where he could make a stand. He grabbed Salient's mane with his good hand, but was too weak to pull himself up.

Another strap twirled around Salient's neck and hoisted Rasi onto his horse. Salient shuffled in a circle, excited, anticipating his next command. Rasi smelled the soldiers' sweat as they moved into position behind the trees.

They're good. They didn't reveal their numbers like a bunch of amateurs, leaving him little doubt that they were Epertase's finest— the Elite Guard. He knew he wouldn't get away without a lot of bloodshed, and his angry stomach returned.

One of the soldiers stepped out from the brush. "Stay where you are," he ordered. "Where is the princess?"

Another guard approached Salient from the opposite side and reached for his mane.

Salient clopped in a circle away from the soldier's grasp. Rasi scanned the enemy as they continued emerging from the trees. They were indeed good, leaving little opening for escape. Rasi's straps followed each of them. They wanted this. He gritted his teeth. Deep down, he wanted this too.

A strap lashed out, striking the soldier reaching for Salient. The man fell backward with a curse as his sword flew into the air. Another soldier pounced. A strap curled around his neck and hurled him over a thick tree branch before jerking him to a stop with an audible crack. His bladder let loose. The strap dropped the lifeless body to the ground.

Rasi kicked Salient's ribs with his heels and his stallion lunged toward the hole left in their defenses. A soldier shot into the gap and slashed Salient's thick chest with his sword. Salient, a warhorse born and bred, didn't balk. Rasi kicked the soldier's jaw as he passed. As the man fell, one of the straps snatched his weapon from his hand and passed it to Rasi. Rasi slid the sword under his makeshift sling with a grimace. He wove his fingers into Salient's mane and held on with all his strength.

The soldiers scrambled for their horses to give chase.

Rasi raced west along the forest edge with his cheek pressed to Salient's thick neck. Though each bounce sent throbbing pain through his shoulder and jaw, it was the only way he could hold on. *Push, boy.* Salient pushed harder. *Good boy.*

Salient wasn't fast, but he had a head start and that was all he needed. He snorted and strained with each stride. It was like old times. He only needed to reach one of the bridges over the ravine to give Rasi a chance.

The pursuing hooves pounded the dirt behind him. He pushed harder. *Come on, Salient, just a little farther.*

He could hear their excited breaths from behind. *I am going to kill every last one of you bastards.*

Salient's foot struck a squank's hole and he stumbled, almost dislodging Rasi from his back, but he regained his stride. Rasi knew he was pushing his friend hard, perhaps too hard, but he also knew that Salient was as stubborn as his master.

In the distance, he saw the drop-off of Havens Ravine and a bridge to the north. If he could make it to the narrow bridge, his pursuers wouldn't be able to surround him and would lose the advantage of numbers. Once again, he grew excited for the battle about to come. Fifty horse-lengths to the edge … Forty … Thirty … *That's it.* Twenty … He veered Salient north toward the bridge.

Almost there, Salient. We're gonna to make it.

From the corner of his eye, he caught a glimpse of a twirling ball and chain as it whipped past his foot. *Oh no.* He tried to yank Salient to the left, but was too late. The chain twirled around Salient's front legs, snapping bones. Rasi slammed face-first into the unforgiving ground and rolled to an agonizing stop near the edge of the ravine.

His eyes shot to Salient. His best friend thrashed on his side, trying to get up on his shattered legs before collapsing again. The bridge might as well have been on the other side of the world. The soldiers fanned out in a wide half-circle and dismounted with swords drawn. There were five of them, with more in the distance and coming fast.

Rasi struggled to his feet. His body felt as though he'd already lost, yet the battle was only beginning. Salient's struggling grew weaker. Rasi couldn't let him suffer anymore.

I'm sorry, old friend.

He pulled the sword from his strap-sling. The soldiers watched and waited, showing more mercy for his horse than they'd surely show him.

Rasi gave Salient a swift death with a well-placed plunge. He kissed Salient's snout and felt a piece of his heart die with his friend.

"Are you finished?" one of the soldiers asked.

Rasi staggered to the edge of the ravine, his left arm now dangling by his side. The strap that had been holding it had joined the others poised to strike, no longer concerned with his pain.

Another soldier feigned an injured shoulder and the rest of them laughed, but the laughter sounded forced. They kept their distance, and their wary eyes never left his straps.

"Where are you going to go now, criminal?" the jokester asked. "You don't have any more horses I can cripple."

So, he's the one.

The ravine at his back gave him a chance. If he had to fight, it was going to be head-on. He couldn't ask for anything more—except maybe two good arms.

Rasi waved them forward. *Let's see what you've got.*

CHAPTER 14

BELKE SLUG

The lead soldier, a slender twenty-something in officer's garb, shook his dirty-blond hair from his eyes and advanced. His grin had all the cockiness of youth as he twirled his sword at his side. Rasi wasn't impressed.

Someone's confidence was going to get them killed, and it wasn't Rasi's.

The show-off spoke. "Back up, men. I've always wanted a shot at the legendary Rasi."

You know me, huh? Then you should know better. Rasi lifted his elbow, draping his sword across his chest.

The other soldiers backed away as ordered. One of them shouted, "All yours, Lorca."

Lorca, huh?

Rasi's straps floated above him. Lorca seemed to ignore them, keeping his eyes locked on Rasi's. "I do not fear you, monster," he taunted.

Rasi nodded. *Let's get this over with.* He lunged forward with his sword; Lorca batted it away with his own. Rasi spun and swung again. Their swords clanged.

A strap grabbed Lorca's ankle. He gracefully slashed at it and it recoiled. Rasi swung again, and again Lorca defended. Though Rasi knew he was out of practice, battling such a young talent showed him just how much. He attacked repeatedly, only to be fended off by the kid's lightning reflexes. Even Rasi's lethal straps were unable to land a single blow without paying a price.

He was good. And fast.

A strap shot at Lorca's head, but he jerked to the side. Another one lunged forward. Lorca twirled away like a dancer. A soldier tried to sneak along Rasi's flank, but a strap grabbed his sword arm and snapped it.

Lorca laughed. "I told you to stay back."

Rasi raised his sword in time to block another assault. He countered at Lorca's head, but the slickster ducked while shoving his hilt into Rasi's defenseless gut.

Lorca gyrated away and threw a high spinning kick that caught Rasi below his wounded collarbone. Rasi groaned and stumbled back until his heels dangled over the edge of the ravine. Lorca strutted forward. Rasi teetered, his straps extended to his sides for balance.

"Where are you going?" Lorca asked.

Rasi peered over the edge, and then back at Lorca. His foe was close. Too close. He grinned.

Lorca paused. His eyes grew wide as he realized his mistake.

Gotcha.

Rasi dropped his sword, grabbed Lorca with his good arm, and dragged them both backward over the edge. One of his straps snagged the jokester's ankle and pulled him, screaming, with them. His straps clawed at the ground in a feverish panic to slow their descent.

For the first time since their battle had begun, Rasi saw fear in his young opponent. Lorca cursed him as they tumbled through the air. They both knew it wasn't the fall that would kill them.

The straps clawed at the sides of the ravine, unable to get a good hold in the hard dirt. One of them caught an exposed root, momentarily slowing their fall, but the root ripped free.

Rasi's bad shoulder slammed the ravine wall, jarring the two warriors apart. They plunked to their waists into a deep, red-tinged goop that covered the ravine floor. Lorca's sword had stuck into the wall above them. Five of Rasi's straps sank beneath the sludge, while the two remaining ones hovered above.

Grab the sword, Rasi screamed in his head. The two straps ignored him as they often did. He tried to pull his arm free, but the slime constricted like quicksand, causing each flinch of his muscles to drag him deeper.

Lorca and the other soldier struggled too, and they were pulled farther down as well.

The warm, rotten slime rose to Rasi's breastbone and then to his throbbing collarbone. He pictured his straps struggling below and begged them to stop. They were only making it worse.

The goop touched Lorca's chin before he too realized that his movements were pulling him down. Maybe the kid wasn't so dumb after all.

"Look what you got us into," Lorca screamed, his cool confidence nowhere to be found.

A roar like the cross between a whale screech and a tornado reverberated through the ravine from around a distant bend.

Lorca's face went white. "By the gods," he cried. "It's the belke slug."

The other soldier panicked. "What do we do?" he screamed.

Make another joke.

Another roar rang out before Rasi saw the creeping mountain of scaly, gray flesh in the distance. He stared in awe, having never seen the belke slug before. The front of the creature was void of any features save two vertical holes that spat snot skyward with each roar. The creature squelched through the ravine, methodically lifting its mouth above the slime with each lurch forward. Then its body puffed out like a balloon about to pop before it chomped down.

The gunk touched Rasi's whiskers. He begged his straps to stop squirming again, but they continued to ignore him as they dragged him farther down.

The beast roared again, this time close enough that Rasi smelled its stink. The top of the creature's mouth lifted above the slime again, revealing several rows of dull, grinding teeth.

The slug lurched closer and closer until it was upon the jokester. A rope thrown by the soldiers above landed next to him just in time. He grabbed it with his free arm as the slime rippled around him. "Pull," he cried.

The rope went taut. But the slug opened its mouth again and sucked the slime and the soldier in. His terrified scream was the last sound he made before a devastating crunch cut it short. Rasi couldn't watch. The soldiers above nearly lost their footing when the rope went slack in their hands.

Lorca began to hyperventilate.

Slow your breathing, idiot.

Sensing their looming doom, Rasi's two free straps clawed and scratched at the dirt walls. When one of them accidentally swiped the surface of the slime, it stuck like glue, wriggled frantically, and then disappeared beneath.

His last strap, his last hope, brushed past the embedded sword. *That's it. Get it. Get it,* he begged. By nothing short of luck, the strap touched the hilt again. *Yes, that's it.* The strap grabbed the hilt and wrenched the sword free.

Lorca slid toward the beast's open mouth and threw a pleading look at Rasi. This man didn't deserve such a death. Rasi's lone strap looped the sword in an arch like a rainbow and plunged it between the monster's snot holes. The beast released an ear-piercing screech that echoed throughout the ravine, hesitated, and then lurched forward again, the sword still impaled in its head.

Rasi's straps thrashed, dragging him down to his bottom lip in the slime. He tilted his head back to keep his mouth clear until the goop tickled his earlobes. *Stop fighting,* he begged.

Lorca whispered a foreign prayer as his legs were sucked into the creature's mouth. He didn't scream, at least not until the first crunch of bone.

Rasi wished he could cover his ears. Eventually, Lorca's screams died, and then the crunching was worse.

Still unsatisfied, the beast drudged forward.

Rasi's ears sank beneath the goo.

These damn straps.

He tried to breathe in as much oxygen as he could before—

And then the air was gone.

Concentrate. Stop struggling. He closed his eyes and pictured his straps relaxing under the gunk. *I NEED TO BREATHE. Wait, calm down. Focus.* He saw the blur of sunlight fade above as the slime dragged him lower and lower.

Stop fighting, you fools. The surface drifted farther and farther away. He felt the vibration of the creature's muffled roar. His feet slid toward the beast.

Please, he begged, *stop fighting.*

He envisioned his struggling straps hearing his pleas and lying still in the goop. His head pounded and his lungs burned, but he pushed away the urge to take a breath and concentrated. *For you and me both, please listen.*

At long last, one of the straps tugging at his back relaxed. Then another, and another, until all of them seemed to hear his pleas and stopped struggling. He felt the world fading. The warm slime filled his nose and ears. Some oozed past his lips. He was thankful he couldn't taste it, but the slimy texture nearly made him vomit.

The strap that had managed to stay above the slime tightened and pulled at his back. Instead of being sucked toward the beast's mouth, he began to drift toward the surface. *Relax,* he repeated like a mantra. The sunlight grew brighter.

Then his forehead broke through. His beautiful strap quivered and strained. The tip of his nose met the coolness of fresh air. When his mouth was clear, he gasped in a huge breath of air and slime. As he exhaled, he sank lower again. *Don't breathe,* he told himself. *Not yet.*

He looked up the beast. His strap, his wonderful strap, held a death-grip on the sword embedded in the slug's forehead.

His shoulders lifted free, followed by his waist. Then the slug opened its mouth, which lifted Rasi the rest of the way out. Rasi's dangling feet brushed the slug's blood-stained teeth. The limp straps beneath him cleared the slime and then flailed at the beast with angry, futile blows.

Once Rasi was close enough, he grabbed the sword with his good arm. His straps helped hoist him onto the sword like it was a ledge. Once balanced on the blade, he was near enough to the top of the creature's head that he could climb up using the gaps between its scales. With a sigh, he stood up and wiped the gunk from his face and eyes. Ahead of the creature was nothing but slime for as far as he could see. In the creature's wake was a barren path of slimy dirt and destruction.

Rasi took a deep breath. He slid down the slug's sloped back to the bare ground while the beast continued plodding along its relentless path, oblivious to or uncaring of Rasi's escape.

Rasi wiped his hand from his forehead to the back of his neck and then slung the thick gunk to the dirt. A new seemingly impossible task stared him in the face: the ravine wall.

Thank the gods his straps had become such skilled climbers. At the top, he plopped onto his back with his feet hanging over the edge and breathed in deep, tired breaths.

He stared at the cloudy sky. *I will bring down the gods if Alina has been hurt.* A raindrop landed on his cheek. After he rested a while, he willed himself to his feet, wondering why the other soldiers had left before the second act. The rain began to fall in earnest as he started the long walk back to Thasula.

I'm coming, Alina. I swear.

CHAPTER 15

SIMCANE

Simcane sat at the bar in Arthur's Dive as he had so many nights before. It wasn't that he liked Arthur's all that much, but it was a place he could go and not be gawked at.

Usually.

He felt the stare of the scrawny kid sitting next to him.

"Are you Simcane?" the kid finally asked, his eyes fixated on Simcane's bulky shoulder.

Simcane ignored him and sipped his ale.

"Hey, I'm talking to you," the kid said, and tugged at Simcane's tree-trunk arm, spilling some of his ale down his chin. Simcane inhaled a deep, angry but patient breath.

Marge rushed over and swiped the kid's hand away, saving him a lot of pain. "I'm sorry, Simcane honey. He don't know any better."

Simcane tapped his empty tankard on the bar and nodded for another. The bartender, Frank, stood on his toes to see over the bar.

"Here you go, big fella," he said, setting another ale in front of him. Marge and Frank had been there as long as Simcane could remember, and they had always been fair to him. For that, he tried not to cause trouble and allowed strangers more leeway than he might have otherwise.

Marge went back to cleaning tables. The kid looked down at his own empty tankard and mumbled, "Just curious, is all. I just think it's rare, such a big guy like you being a coward. Doesn't make sense. What do you weigh, anyways? Seventeen, eighteen stone?"

Simcane drank his ale without answering.

The kid kept pushing. "I don't know. Anyone who tells the heathens our secrets and then quits the military in the middle of a war can't be anything but a coward. Well, a traitor and a coward, I mean."

The kid had no idea. Simcane considered pounding the truth into him. The stump of his missing left pinky, along with the burn scars on his back, were proof of his tight lips while in the heathens' hands.

Marge slipped between the two and gave the kid a glare. "You don't know nothing," she said.

"Let him be, Marge," Simcane said.

She turned to him. "No, Sim. It ain't fair. For years, all through the city, I hear these lies and I'm sick of them. Why don't you defend yourself, tell them the truth?"

"And what's the truth, Marge?"

"Let's start with how Elijah abandoned you and your whole unit when you were captured doing his dirty work. Or how he accused you of treason after you escaped and returned, honor-bound, for another assignment."

"People don't wanna hear those stories, Marge."

"It just angers me, is all. You did three hard years before you were acquitted, and people should know that. You shouldn't let them believe you quit or were some kind of traitor. Show this child your back."

Simcane shook his head and held out his empty tankard. "Another ale, Frank."

But the drunken kid wasn't done. "Yep, I'd think a coward who fashions himself a mercenary would be out looking for our princess as we speak. Not drinking away his failures."

Marge threw her hands in the air, groaned, and huffed back to her duties. "Your pain, kid. Your pain."

Simcane studied the puny runt briefly before asking, "What happened to the princess?"

"You haven't heard? She's been kidnapped. Everybody's talking 'bout it."

Kidnapped? The kid's words struck a nerve. Not that he had ever met the princess or had any vested interest in her life, but she was going to be queen one day. As angry as he had been, he'd never hated Epertase, only Elijah.

"Yep," the kid continued without being asked. "King Elijah sent Tevin to find her this very morning. Queen Madelyne even ordered Siver to go with him."

Siver, huh? That was a name Simcane had heard before. Word had it that Siver was the queen's personal bodyguard and as good a soldier as there was. That knowledge should have put Simcane at ease, but for some gnawing reason, it didn't. He had no doubt of Siver's dedication to the queen and the royal family, but he didn't trust Tevin. That backstabber did all kinds of dirty work for Elijah. He was what the experts called a "fixer."

The kid rested his hand on the edge of the bar while he glanced around the room, probably looking for someone else to annoy. Simcane covered the kid's hand with his own and pushed himself up from his seat. The kid's face contorted. He nearly fell off his chair twisting to get free. Still pinning the kid's hand to the bar, Simcane leaned in and said, "Next time I'll rip your head off."

Suddenly, the kid forgot how to talk. Simcane released the kid's hand, gathered his tankard of ale as well as the kid's, and carried them to one of the many empty tables.

Marge brought him a third tankard. "This one's on me, hon. Don't let the little guy bother you. He's new in here and he's had a few too many." Marge had always been a sweetheart, even before their one night of drunken passion.

He laid a couple of extra coins on the table, swigged his ale, and threw on his ankle-length overcoat.

"See ya, Frank … Marge." His voice was gruff, almost hurting his throat. He flipped his hood over his head and pulled it down over his brow.

"See you in the morning," Marge and Frank shouted in unison, and he waved and walked toward the door.

Before he reached the front door, it swung open, narrowly missing his nose. Two soldiers and an officer stood in the doorway.

"Simcane?" the officer asked.

Simcane stared at the floor. "I was just leavin'." He turned sideways to squeeze past.

The two soldiers stepped into his path. Simcane stopped with an annoyed sigh.

Marge shouted from behind the bar, "No trouble here today, boys. Okay?"

"No trouble, ma'am," the officer answered. "A word, Simcane?" He held out his empty hands to show he wasn't there for a fight.

Simcane nodded.

"I am Captain Jarrah. As you may have heard, the princess has gone missing."

Simcane nodded again.

"King Elijah has dispatched my brother-in-law, Tevin the Third, to the mountains to find her and has ordered Thasula's mercenaries to stand down. There is no money in interfering. He has sent me personally to make sure you understand you are not welcome. Do you understand?"

Simcane didn't answer.

"Understand you're not welcome, that is?"

Simcane sighed. "Sure," he said, no doubt giving the officer some unjust satisfaction.

Jarrah continued, "Tevin and his men are more than capable of handling the one called Rasi without the likes of you."

Rasi? That was a name Simcane hadn't heard in years. Hell, he'd thought Rasi was dead. They were probably wrong. He'd never believed all the things they'd said he'd done. Kidnapping princesses didn't sound like something Rasi would do either.

Jarrah stepped closer to peek beneath Simcane's hood and whispered, "If you so much as move wrong, I will kill you. You are not as feared as you may believe."

The handle of a seven-inch blade slid from Simcane's coat sleeve and rested in his cupped palm. He had the drop on the captain. Jarrah glanced down at his clenched fist. The confidence drained from his face. Perhaps he realized how much he had just bitten off.

"Is that all?" Simcane growled.

Jarrah moved aside.

Simcane marched past and out of the tavern. He would not have been as forgiving when he was younger.

CHAPTER 16

UNEXPECTED FRIENDS

Princess Alina awakened on a damp, stained mattress that stank of mildew and rot. A torch hung on the wall in front of her. She had to hunch over when she sat up so as not to bang her head on the low ceiling. Her tongue found the swollen cut on the inside of her lower lip and she winced.

She reached out to touch the cold, coarse wall. Gaping cracks near the top trickled water, yet the floor appeared dry. She cautiously tasted the water then cupped her hands beneath one of the trickles to drink. As she sipped, a centipede scurried from one hole in the wall into the next.

Alina trembled and drew her knees to her chest. Her bare toes were numb with cold. She wore dirty, gray rags, more fitting for a prisoner in an uncivilized society than a princess. She shuddered to think about how she came to be wearing them. Since they were several sizes too big, she wrapped them tighter around her body for warmth.

She felt fifteen years old again, hiding in her closet from the nightmares of the monster that had killed her grandparents. If only she'd peeked out and seen him, he might not have escaped and left Rasi to take the blame. Rasi … If Levi couldn't find him, this cell would be her tomb.

She couldn't succumb to such defeatist thoughts. What kind of queen would she make if she gave up when things looked bleak?

They hadn't yet killed her for some reason, which meant she had time. She had hope.

She pulled the torch from the bracket for a better look at her prison. Her bed sat in a cubby cut into the wall of a large, round pit. She followed the slick stone wall to the top where there was no ceiling. No way could she climb out that way. The top opened into another larger room that flickered with shadows and rang with laughter.

Hunks of rotted wood littered the floor. She gathered several pieces into a pile and set her torch to it. Once the flames took hold, she scooted close to warm her hands. The welcome heat brought color and feeling back to her toes and fingers.

Exhausted, she lay on her side, drew her arms and legs to her chest, and waited. For what, she didn't know.

"Hey, Princess," someone called from above. It was the big one who had knocked her from her horse. "Bath time," he shouted.

Bath time?

A blast of freezing water dropped onto her head and doused her fire. Alina gasped. All her muscles clenched. For a few seconds, she couldn't move. She kicked the last ember away from the puddle in hopes of rekindling her flame. To her horror, the ember slowly died.

Alina stripped out of her sopping rags and squeezed the water from them. *Cold and dry is better than cold and wet,* she told herself as she spread out her rags along a dry patch of the floor. She scooted back against the wall and curled into a shivering ball, closing her eyes. If these monsters didn't directly kill her, she was sure the cold would. Her clattering teeth kept her awake.

As she lay on the dank floor, something warm, almost hot, glided across her foot. Startled, she jerked away. Another feverish touch slid across her thigh. The creature's soft fur sent tickles up her leg. She swatted it away. It was heavy, like a short, fat snake.

Bewildered, she opened her eyes to look at the creatures that surrounded her. Wriggling bodies covered in fur every stunning hue of the rainbow jostled each other to get closer to her. *It can't be.*

Several small holes formed all over the stone floor and more of the creatures slithered out. They swarmed her from her feet to her neck. Though she fought them at first, they were too numerous, and she was too tired and weak.

Though she anxiously waited for piercing teeth or constricting coils, neither came. Instead, she felt warm and surprisingly safe, like when she slept within the protection of Rasi's tentacles. Her body soon stopped shivering and her teeth stopped rattling. Were they hallucinations from hypothermia? Or could she really have been saved by creatures of legend?

Colorfuls, she thought in wonder. *Colorfuls are real.*

Since she couldn't see sunslight from her cell, she marked the passage of time by when she slept. On occasion, her captors dropped chunks of undercooked meat or half-eaten apples into the pit, along with varying insults. Her four captors took turns feeding and taunting her. It didn't matter who stood at the top of the pit, they were all equally despicable. Perhaps the only compassionate thing they did was when they gave her another torch and allowed her to build a fire again. The flames made the cold more bearable when the colorfuls weren't around. They always returned to their holes right before her captors appeared.

She had stopped begging her captors for answers. Their replies generally consisted of a rain of cold water, spit, or piss. She thought of Rasi with a better understanding of the hell he had lived through alone in his cave. Not a moment passed that she didn't dream of him coming for her, though she was beginning to fear no one would find her.

CHAPTER 17

REUNION

R asi rubbed his eyes and squinted in the flickering ray of sunslight shining through the loft. The dilapidated barn and straw bed were plenty cozy compared to where he was used to sleeping. The last thing he remembered was collapsing on the road leading to Atticus's house.

A strap floated past his face. He groaned. *I was dreaming you were a dream.* The strap pushed at his mouth. *When aren't you hungry?*

The barn door swung open. "Good. You're awake."

Good ol' Atticus.

His old friend pulled up a milking stool and sat beside him. He wore his hair in the same close flattop cut he had always worn, though now it had turned mostly gray. The scars on his cheek from a heathen's teeth had faded a little but would never truly be gone.

"Somebody did a number on you," he said. "You've been unconscious for days. I found you lying on the road."

Rasi couldn't remember much after his run-in with the belke slug. Just making it to Atticus's land was more than he could have hoped to achieve.

"I am sorry for the poor conditions, but I had to keep you in the barn in case they came looking. I've salted your shoulder. I think the infection is nearly gone, but you are putting off heat like you still have a fever. Those things on your back—they must remember me. I took far fewer bruises this time."

Though his collarbone still ached when he worked his good shoulder in a circle, he was reasonably sure it wasn't broken. A tight bandage wrapping his shoulder, his chest, and around the back of his neck helped hold his collarbone snug.

"Hungry?" Atticus asked.

Rasi's straps perked up and he nodded.

Atticus went to his house and soon returned with a bowl of cold stew.

"I could heat it for you if you give me a moment to start a new fire."

Rasi grabbed the bowl and tipped it over his face, dumping stew into his mouth and spilling it down his chin and chest. Cold or warm made no difference; food was food.

After finishing his stew, Rasi stood up and offered his hand.

"Leaving?" Atticus asked. "You need to rest."

Rasi pointed through the loft window where the tip of the castle could be seen.

Atticus leaned over for a better look. "The castle? Do you know where Princess Alina is?"

Rasi shook his head.

"Well, Elijah thinks you do. Tevin and several of Thasula's top guards have been dispatched into the mountains to find her—to find you. They know you live there somewhere, but I don't think they know exactly where. Needless to say, it's probably not safe to go back there."

Rasi nodded. He mimicked waving a sword around. Atticus smiled. "I'll leave you a new one on the porch before I go. What have you been up to? The way I hear it, Elijah was none too happy to have his Elite Guard return from your battle a few men lighter. Lorca was a rising star for him."

Rasi shrugged.

"I think Tevin's been ordered to kill you on sight."

If Atticus thought Tevin had a chance of killing him, he must be drinking again. Tevin was a coward, a spectator at best during the war. Even his wife's worthless brother, Jarrah, had joined the front lines when Epertase's victory was still in doubt. Besides, Rasi had plans for Tevin. Though Elijah had ordered Edonea's murder, it was that coward who had carried it out. If he was lucky, maybe he'd bump into him on his way to find Alina.

"Once again, Rasi, you are a wanted man. You couldn't leave well enough alone, could you?" Atticus walked to the barn doors and pulled one of them open. "Promise me you'll stay at least till tomorrow morning. You need more rest."

Rasi shrugged again.

Atticus hesitated. "Take all the time you need out here, friend. However, I must leave. I command a battalion now, and I've been ordered back from my furlough. Word has it foreign invaders have come from the western sea and have occupied the Wastelands."

Rasi glanced up. *There's life beyond the seas?*

"They move toward Lithia as we speak. We have sent peacemakers and are waiting to hear back. But they don't appear friendly. I believe Epertase is about to go to war. We could sure use a soldier like you right now."

Rasi sneered. He would never help those who had banished him, even if all was forgiven and the offer was there.

"Help yourself to whatever you need. Hopefully, our paths will cross again one day in this world." He took in a deep breath and held it for a moment. Then he added, "Or the next."

After Atticus left, the barn felt as cold and lonely as Rasi's cave. Rasi waited until he was sure Atticus was away and then limped to his friend's house. Sure enough, a sword rested against the doorframe. Rasi tried it out, twirling it, impressed with its weight and craftsmanship. Then he shoved it into his empty sheath.

The door was unlocked, which was typical of Atticus and Celia. Inside, little had changed since last he was there many years ago. The furniture was a little older and a little more worn, but the pride in Celia's upkeep was apparent.

Rasi was glad Celia wasn't home. As much as he'd enjoy seeing her again, he didn't want to frighten her. He went to the kitchen, hoping to find something to wet his lips. He settled on a half-full jug of Celia's famous almond milk. He plopped down into the nearest chair and downed the rest of the jug. Incredibly, he thought for a moment that he might have tasted it, but ultimately decided it was probably just a memory of how good it used to be. Whether he had tasted it or not, it went down smoothly. *Thank you, Celia.*

Once he'd finished, he worked his way down the hall. His obnoxious straps explored the walls, knocking a framed painting down. *Stop it,* he ordered. He rehung the painting on the nail. *Don't touch anything else.*

A pot of warm water sat next to some linen in the washroom. It was almost as if Atticus expected him to make himself at home.

After Rasi had washed himself, he lathered his beard with a mixture of wood alkali and animal fat and then hacked away with Atticus's cutthroat razor. It felt good to have some cream and use a proper razor rather than a sword for a change.

He laughed to himself while he shaved because he knew how protective Atticus was of his razor. In the service he wouldn't let anyone near it and was ready to fight if anyone so much as touched it.

Though his body still ached and his collarbone was a mess, he felt somewhat refreshed. After he finished, he returned to the main room. Sitting in the corner was Atticus's well-crafted oak desk. Rasi's back ached a little more just remembering the day he'd helped move it from the barn.

The second drawer still stuck. He chuckled. Atticus considered himself a craftsman, yet he had failed to account for the swelling of wood when he built the drawers. A slight wiggle and sharp yank pulled it free. That's where he found the ink and quill. He scribbled a note:

Atticus,

I assure you I had nothing to do with Alina's disappearance, though I promise I will find out who did. There's a lot you don't know about the night I was banished. One day, I'll explain it all.

Thank you again for your help. I pray I live long enough to repay you one day. You have been a dear friend.

Rasi

P.S. Thanks for the horse and the shave. I think I ruined your razor.

He left the note on the desk and opened the door to leave. On the other side, a woman recoiled and grabbed her chest. Rasi's hand instinctively went to his new sword, but he quickly removed it when he recognized Celia. She had a few more lines on her face and streaks of gray in her hair than when last he'd seen her, but she still had the same sympathetic gaze as always. They each stood frozen long enough for her to study his face. Then her hand left her chest and covered her open mouth. "Rasi?" she whispered.

He nodded and smiled.

Her eyes followed his straps and then worked their way back to his face. She held her arms out, inviting him in for a hug. He squeezed her tight.

"I've missed you so much." She pulled back and studied his face again. "I can't believe you're here." She touched his cheek. "Atticus told me you were still alive, but I never thought I'd get to see you again."

Atticus was deadly serious when it came to secrets, especially when they protected his loved ones. Rasi wasn't surprised Atticus hadn't told her who he'd hidden in their barn.

She cocked her head and tears filled her eyes. "I'm so sorry about Edonea. It broke my heart when she passed."

Rasi nodded, fighting back his own tears.

Celia's shoulders slouched. "You're not staying, are you?"

He shook his head.

"I wish you could."

He did too.

She held his hand. "Please be safe. I hope to see you again." She hugged him once more before he stepped away. As he backed toward the barn, he tapped his chest over his heart. She returned the gesture. He, too, hoped he'd see her again.

CHAPTER 18

THE LITHIA DILEMMA

J Elijah kissed Madelyne on her forehead while she rested in bed, and then met James in the hall.

James leaned against the wall, gasping for breath.

"Calm down, my friend."

"A scout from the Wastelands has arrived with news from Paisel. He says it's most urgent."

"Where is he?"

"I took him to your war room. He's waiting."

Inside the war room, a scrawny young man paced back and forth. Dread painted his face. "Your Majesty." He knelt.

Elijah motioned for him to stand. "What is it?"

"They're dead, Your Majesty."

"Who, son?"

"Everyone."

"Where is Paisel?"

"He's dead. The men he took with him—dead. The western scouts—dead."

"What do you mean, they're all dead? How is this possible?"

"The invaders. They're ruthless. They have weapons the likes of which we've never seen before. They're moving toward Lithia as we speak. I came as fast as I could. I barely escaped."

Elijah turned to James. "Summon my war council at once. Get them here. He turned back to the young scout. "What is your name, son?"

"Reardon, Your Majesty."

"All right, Reardon. I'm going to need you to stay here and apprise my council of the situation."

Reardon reached into a knapsack strung across his chest and removed a thick stack of paper. There was a bloodstain on the cover. "This is all of the intelligence Paisel gathered."

"You've done well. Can I get you a drink?"

"Your Majesty, I'd never impose on you, but I'm so thirsty I could drink the Infinite Sea."

Elijah poured him a glass of water. Reardon downed it so quickly that Elijah handed him the pitcher. Elijah placed the stack of papers on a long, oval table. Fourteen chairs surrounded the table with bronze-plated plaques on their backs identifying each of his commanders and their titles. Behind his chair was a wall-sized map of Epertase and its neighbors. Though he stared at it, he wasn't really looking. No king wanted to be in his war room, and he was no different. Watching his father from one of those chairs during the Heathen War couldn't begin to prepare him for the weight he now felt.

James returned. "I put out the word, Your Majesty."

"Very good. Now take that stack of papers on the table to be transcribed at once. I need fourteen copies brought here as soon as they're ready."

"Of course, Your Majesty." James gathered the papers. After feeling the weight of the stack, he added, "This could take a while."

"I know. We will still be here."

Reardon stood nervously near the door while they waited. Elijah didn't intend to ignore the young scout, but he had too many worries to engage in pleasantries.

First to arrive was Aidric. He looked Reardon up and down before turning his attention to Elijah. "Your Majesty, my battalion is ready and eager to fight whatever threat we face. Just give the word."

"Be seated, Aidric. We have much to discuss."

Atticus entered next and took his assigned seat. He was quiet.

While they waited, Aidric asked, "Any word on Princess Alina?"

"Not yet. But I have dispatched Tevin the Third to the mountains to flush out that savage, Rasi. We'll find her soon."

"Your Majesty," Aidric continued, "I do not question your decisions, but is it wise to focus all of your attention on one lead? Couldn't Rasi have simply been in the wrong place at the wrong time?"

"Was he in the wrong place and time when my parents were murdered?" Elijah was mildly surprised he didn't choke on the irony. "And what about Lorca? You knew him; he was your friend. Trust me, Aidric. I commanded Rasi during the Heathen Wars and I know what he is capable of."

"And when Tevin the Third finds him, are you not worried for your friend?"

"I sent Siver along."

Aidric's eyebrows lifted. "Oh. Very good, then. My apologies for questioning you, sir. Tevin is a gifted tracker. I have no doubt he and Siver will be successful."

"While I appreciate your concern for my daughter, we have other matters to discuss. I mourn when I'm alone. This is not the place." Elijah slid his own chair beneath the table and stood behind it with his hands firmly gripping the headrest.

Captain Jarrah entered and took his seat. He spoke without being addressed. "The mercenaries shouldn't be an issue, Your Majesty. I spoke to each of them personally."

"Very good, Jarrah."

"Any chance you would let me join Tevin's search now?"

Elijah smiled. "I know your wife is worried, Jarrah, but I am quite sure Tevin and Siver are capable of handling an old cave dweller."

Brothers Andon and Dru were the next to arrive, followed by Tate, and then the recently promoted commander of the Elite Guard, Masera. Six more commanders followed, all with encouraging words concerning the search for Alina.

After the pleasantries, Elijah cleared his throat. "All formalities are suspended for now. You may speak at will. Now that you are all assembled, we have received word that the so-called Tek army will likely attack Lithia within days."

Silence filled the room. Jarrah looked around at the sober faces. "What do we know about these Teks?"

Elijah nodded toward Reardon and all eyes turned to him. His hands shook. He licked his lips before speaking. "Uh … Yeah. Well, I just came from the Wastelands. I witnessed a Tek assault first-hand. Paisel attempted to meet with their commander and offer peace. They cut off his head."

"By the gods," Andon cried.

"They immediately attacked with noisy weapons that left bolder-sized holes in the ground and ripped our men apart. We didn't stand a chance."

This was more than anyone expected to hear. Dru asked, "How many are there?"

"Tens of thousands. Maybe more."

Atticus bowed his head.

Tate sprang to his feet and pounded the table. "Lithia is but a quarter of our size. They will be crushed."

Andon shouted, "We must help them. It is time for Epertase to go to war."

Dru nodded in agreement. "We have family there, friends there."

"As do I," Tate said.

Elijah waved his hands for calm. "This is why we are here," he said. "To discuss this matter."

Andon, still clearly agitated, shouted, "My battalion is ready for war now. It'll take us two weeks to get there. We can't wait any longer."

Elijah sighed and shook his head. "Andon, this is a time to use our heads, not our hearts. We must accept that we cannot protect the world. I agree we must help King Logan in any way we can. But a single battalion will not make a difference if what Reardon says is true. I've been thinking on this since I first received word of the invaders last week."

"So, we don't do anything?" Andon's face was red and angry. He was always short-tempered. Some said it was because his hair was kissed by a dragon, but there were plenty of redheads who didn't share his temper.

"No, not at all. I have been weighing many options. I have already offered King Logan refuge, but he has declined. He is a proud man and his soldiers will die under his command if they must. As much as I would like to fight alongside him, it would be impossible. To move our entire army, and to do it right, would take months."

"Just send a couple battalions to begin with," Tate interrupted. "We are Epertase. We are the most powerful army ever to step onto a battlefield."

"That is too dangerous, Tate. If we divide our forces, we will be weakened and unable to protect our own people. And therein lies my dilemma. I am looking to all of you for advice."

Atticus asked, "Why not send a force to Lithia as a support unit only? This unit could take supplies and weapons and help the Lith soldiers prepare for the coming threat. They could also press King Logan to accept your offer of refuge. If he refuses and war comes, they will support the front lines while remaining out of the fray. If the Liths begin to fall, our force will retreat to our front lines, bringing with them valuable intelligence."

Aidric shouted across the table, "You are writing Lithia off with that plan, Atticus."

Atticus shook his head. "No, no, no. This is a time for tough decisions. We must help them, but we must protect our land as well."

Aidric slammed his hands on the table and stood up. "Tough decisions do not mean we let our neighbors die."

Atticus stood up across from him. "No, you would just like to sacrifice all of Epertase."

"Sacrifice?" Aidric shouted. "Like Tate said, we have no equals in battle."

"That we know of," Atticus shouted in return. "We know nothing about this army."

"Enough," Elijah shouted. He rubbed his forehead. "I'm afraid Atticus is right, Aidric. I've struggled with this since I learned of their advance and I cannot come up with any way to do more. I will listen to all reasonable, and I stress *reasonable*, ideas."

"What do we know about them?" Dru asked.

"Reardon has brought with him a report developed by our western scouts. This report will be known as Paisel's Report. I have not read it yet, but it is being transcribed as we speak. As soon as it is finished it will be brought here and we will read it together."

Dru then asked what everyone was thinking. "Does Lithia stand a chance?"

Elijah frowned and looked away.

Aidric spoke up. "If this is what you decide, I volunteer to lead this force to Lithia." His eyes were angry, his face determined. Elijah expected nothing less from him and reluctantly agreed. He needed someone good in that command and there were few better than Aidric. "I will send you, but you must promise to stay well back from the front lines and return here if the Liths start to fall."

"Of course."

"Prepare a hundred men at once, Aidric. See James for a copy of Paisel's Report before you leave. When you are ready, stop back here for any last-minute instructions."

"Do not worry, Your Majesty. I will bring you the Tek commander's heart."

"Aidric, I mean it. Stay out of the fray." Elijah wondered if he'd made the right decision sending someone so passionate. "Get back to us as soon as you are able."

Andon asked, "And what will we do with the displaced Liths after this war?"

"We will do all we can. It will be difficult, but we'll find a way. We have no other choice. Liths are hard workers. They will work the farms. We will request any Epertasian family that is able to accept refugees." Elijah addressed Reardon. "Go and find yourself something to eat. We must discuss sensitive matters."

Reardon bowed and left as James arrived.

"Your Highness," James said. "The documents are being transcribed."

"Very good. Now go inform the staff to prepare a meal for us."

James bowed his way out and closed the door behind him.

Masera, a soft-spoken young man who had risen through the ranks of Elijah's Elite Guard faster than anyone in history, asked, "How will we secure the country with such an influx of refugees? The Guard is only so big."

"I know. But we will need to find a way."

Masera nodded. "You should redeploy our eastern defenses to a forward role toward the northwest. If the enemy conquers Lithia, they will move east through the Lowlands with little resistance. If they are as large an army as reported, we need to plan for a multi-front war."

Elijah surveyed the room. "Does everyone agree?"

The men at the table collectively nodded.

"I will put Andon in charge of the eastern redeployment to the Lowland border."

Andon nodded.

Dru asked, "Should we inform King Fice that we are coming?"

Elijah sighed. "It would do no good. It has been hundreds of years since we've had relations."

"We should have taken the Lowlands long before this," Dru growled. "King Fice is a virus. If anything good comes out of this war, maybe it'll be the end of his rule."

Tate whispered, "And his life, if we're lucky."

Jarrah added, "Fucking Lowlands."

CHAPTER 19

THE LOWLANDS

The classroom was typical of a Lowland school, consisting of little more than individual pieces of carpet on the dirt floor where the children could sit. During class, a window on the back wall was the only hint of the outside world. A single lecturer, called the superior, stood at the head of the room. In the summers, the air was thick and muggy; in the winters, as cold as the outside.

Seventeen-year-old Dillon shared the classroom with thirteen classmates, all of whom were his age and had been his classmates for the past twelve years. Clay, his only friend, was no longer with the class, having disappeared a year earlier after asking the superior too many pointed questions. Curiosity was the biggest crime of all.

As with each school day, this day began with a reading from the only textbook the children were ever given. Their lesson was the same one he'd heard a thousand times or more. Unlike his brain-dead classmates, Dillon had never accepted the stories as gospel as he was ordered to do. As far as he was concerned, the book was full of lies and shit.

"Read 'The Dam,'" the superior ordered, referring to the opening chapter of the Lowland bible.

Dillon, like his classmates, knew how to read, but unlike his classmates, he could read words not contained in their bible. With all other stories forbidden by punishment of death, Dillon's mother had secretly taught him the art of reading with smuggled books from Epertase. She'd never told him how she'd come into possession of the books, how she was able to read them herself, or how she had gained such insight, and he'd never asked. His mother called him special, and he knew it was true by how the other children had treated him from the time he was little.

He opened the worn-out, hidebound text to the first page. Since he read faster than the other children, he had to be careful not to finish a page before the rest. In unison, the children recited the text printed in large, bold letters:

"Recitar! The greatest land of all known lands. Seven hundred years ago, our ancestors, the knowers, told of rising water in the Northern Sea. They warned Epertasian nobles that Recitar was the lowest of all the countries of the land, including the corrupt Lithia to the west. The knowers predicted devastating floods if drastic action wasn't taken, and offered to speak to the Epertasian leaders, King Daniel and Queen Lillian. The Recitarians were ordered to flee their city and move to higher ground with no efforts made to fortify the lower lands. The knowers begged King Daniel for a different solution, but he denied their requests for 'their own good.'

"The knowers returned to Recitar with the news. The Recitarian people mourned at the prospect of losing their homes and their country. In response, they tried to wage a rebellion and demanded something be done so they could stay. However, the rebellion was destined to be thwarted as there was no strong leader to guide them.

"And then a young hero emerged. His name was Lord Fice and he was of the mythical tribe of Gildonese. He and his tribe came out of hiding to save us. It was the first time the Gildonese had revealed themselves since the Epertasian-Gildonese War. The Great Lord Fice was fearless and all-knowing. He organized an election to name a king. Impossibly, the vote was unanimous; Lord Fice was now King Fice of Recitar. When the villainous King Daniel and Queen Lillian refused to recognize his rule, he threatened to secede from Epertase at once.

"At first the tyrant King Daniel threatened invasion, but the great people of Recitar rose up and stood defiant. Daniel raised their taxes and sent soldiers to end their rebellion, but King Fice would not waver. He lopped off the heads of the invading soldiers and mounted them on pikes along the main streets of Grande Villa."

Dillon had an urge, like he always had, to shout his mother's version of the story, but he knew he'd be sent to join Clay, wherever he may be. Dillon waited for the other children to turn their pages, and the lesson continued:

"The wise and mighty King Fice ordered a great wall built along the Northern Sea. After seven years, that wall, known as the Great Dam, was finished. The elitist Liths and Epertasians laughed from their higher lands while mocking the people of Recitar. They said the dam would never hold and the Recitarians were fools to stay. To further disparage the people of Recitar, they called them Lowlanders and beasts. King Fice embraced their insults.

"Since the building of the Great Dam, the waters have indeed risen with each generation, but with their rise the Recitarians have built the Great Dam higher and stronger.

"Epertasians and Liths alike were banned from this land, this 'lowland,' with extreme prejudice. The godlike King Fice created an army in defiance of the oppressors, keeping them at bay. He and his Gildonese tribe rebuked all offers of peace until Epertase grew weary and, out of fear, no doubt, granted Recitar its freedom."

Dillon doubted that Epertase had ever feared anyone, but his mother had told him those doubts would cause him trouble, so he never voiced them. As he waited to turn the next page, he felt the superior hovering behind him. A drop of sweat, or maybe it was drool, dripped into his hair, but he continued, unfazed. He wanted to look up, but that would reveal his gift. When all the students turned their pages, he did as well.

"At first, the evil Epertasians told the Recitarians the dam would not hold, and the people would die. But, as evidence of King Fice's unsurpassed wisdom, King Daniel's men were wrong, and the dam held.

"King Daniel ordered soldiers to slaughter the women and children of the Lowlands, but the just King Fice stood strong. As

Epertasian soldiers bashed the skulls of babies with the hilts of their swords, King Fice conceded no ground."

Dillon thought about his mother's bedtime stories. He repeated to himself the truth of Epertase's legendary kindness. His mother always encouraged him to not believe the venomous propaganda spoken by their captors, as she called them. She told him of King Daniel's kindness and Queen Lillian's compassion. She rebuked the massacres that were taught in school and said, if anything, it was Fice's men who committed such atrocities on his people. Dillon often dreamed of escaping with her to Epertase and living how he knew in his mind and heart people should live. His classmates' turning pages woke him from his daze. He flipped to the next page, which began a new chapter. This was where he had to be strong, where he had to ignore the words on the page. The new chapter was titled "The State of Your Lives" and he hated it.

"As Lowlanders, you are nothing. You are worthless. You follow the great King Fice without hesitation. You will never leave these lands, nor speak with foreigners, as they will kill you on sight. Your life is to obey the dictates of our government without question or face certain death as a traitor.

"As Lowlanders you are nothing. You are worthless. You follow the great King Fice without …"

Dillon stifled a yawn. This entire chapter consisted of the same paragraph, over and over again, like a hypnotic chant. Twenty-seven times it repeated, making it hard for a distracted Dillon to find his place again. He turned the page only when the others did.

"As Lowlanders you are nothing. You are worthless …"

He would give anything for something different to break the horrible monotony of the class. Almost as he thought it, the door to the classroom swung violently open and banged against the wall. Dillon was the only student to look up. It was his mother, and she was frantic and out of breath. The other kids continued to read without as much as a glance toward the disturbance.

"Dillon, come quickly," she said, ignoring the superior's questioning look.

The superior marched past Dillon and grabbed his mother's throat. "You never interrupt my class," he said in a deep, menacing voice. "Who do you think you are?"

Dillon's mother clawed at his fingers as the color drained from her face. Dillon didn't know what to do. He looked to the other kids for help, but they continued reading, unfazed by the commotion. He rose from his rug.

"Back on the floor, now," the superior yelled, squeezing his mother's throat tighter. Dillon saw his mother's strength waning and knew he had to do something. Soon it was the superior, not her own strength, which held her up.

Instead of sitting down as commanded, Dillon moved toward the superior, who was so caught off guard that he loosened his grip. Dillon's mother dropped to her knees. She clutched her neck, gasping for breath.

"We knew you were different, Dillon," the superior said. "You cannot fool us. You and your mother are enemies to the Lowlands."

Dillon made a fist, his first ever. He glanced at his mother as she rubbed her neck and coughed on the floor.

The superior started to speak, "You will go to—"

Dillon swung his first punch. Flesh smacked against flesh and the superior collapsed, unconscious before he hit the floor.

The other children continued to read.

"What are you doing, Mother?"

"They are coming for us. They are coming for all like us."

"Why me? Why am I special?"

"You are not under his influence. You see how these children behave. They do not question like you and I do. They are brainwashed and under his spell."

"Whose spell?"

"King Fice. He sent men for us and the others like us. We must run."

Dillon grabbed her hand and led her back through the door and into the hallway. There was no other way out of the schoolhouse but the front door, so he had to take the risk. He cracked open the door and peeked out.

"They're here, Mother."

She gasped.

"We know you're in there," shouted a soldier, one of many gathered on the dirt road in front of the school.

"They're everywhere, Mother. A hundred of them, at least."

"We can't go out there," she said. It was the first time Dillon had ever seen terror in his mother's strong face.

"We will be all right. I will protect you."

Glass shattered against the outside wall. A wisp of smoke trickled through where the walls met the ceiling. Dillon grabbed his mother's hand and led her back to his classroom. All the students were staring at their open books, oblivious to the light smoke filling the room and stinging their nostrils.

Dillon shook the kid closest to him and screamed, "Get up. We have to get out of here. They're setting us on fire." The student stared at his book. Dillon went to the next, and the next, but none of them moved. It wasn't that they didn't hear him; it was that they were too afraid to deviate from the schedule.

The smoke grew thicker and darker, banking down from the ceiling. Dillon pulled his mother to the floor.

"Dillon, there is nothing we can do for them," she cried. "We have to leave."

The superior groaned as he rolled to his back. He batted his eyelids and shook his head. Dillon's mother ignored the superior, tugging her son toward the window at the back. "We have to go," she shouted.

The superior struggled to his hands and knees, still dazed. Dillon yanked his hand from his mother's. "Wait," he said, and then ran back to where the superior knelt. He drew his foot back. With a merciless kick, he sent the superior into unconsciousness again. "If these kids are going to die, then he will die with them."

He could no longer see his mother through the smoke, so he called out to her. When she choked out an answer, he followed her voice.

It was getting hard to breathe. The smoke stung his throat like razors. He reached blindly until he felt her outstretched hand.

"They've surrounded the building," she said. "I'd rather die here with you than out there with them."

Dillon collapsed to his knees. She hugged him with all her strength.

"We can't give up," he said, his voice barely strong enough to get out between the coughing. "We have to fight and make them kill us."

She regarded him sadly and nodded.

He pulled away. She held on to his shirt as he led her to the window. None of his classmates followed. He shoved the warped window outward, ripping the lock from the decayed wooden frame.

Dillon climbed out first and then helped his mother through. He turned to a waiting group of armed Lowland soldiers.

"Don't fight us, kid. It would not be wise for you and your pretty mother."

Dillon's mother began crying. It seemed they wouldn't be able to die on their own terms after all. He bowed his head and extended his hands with his palms up. A soldier came forward and held his wrists while another tied them together. Then they did the same to his mother before marching them to a line of prisoners that stretched as far as he could see.

"Where are we going?" he asked.

He glanced over his shoulder at the schoolhouse as flames kissed the sky. No one else was trying to escape from the inferno, and he shook with silent rage at the callousness of his captors.

CHAPTER 20

THE CALM

King Logan surveyed the battlefield from atop the highest castle tower. Black smoke choked the sky as the enemy army amassed beyond the hill region on the western edge of the city. The hill region was where he had sent the meat of his military. It was and always had been the best place for defending the city. They were ready.

A monocular revealed the size of the force assembled against them, and it was more massive than he had ever imagined. Though he knew his army would fight with honor, he feared he had made a grave mistake. "What manner of army is this?" he asked Carver, his personal bodyguard.

"A hardened one, Your Majesty." Carver was the fiercest soldier Logan had ever met. Every part of his being was dedicated to fighting. Even the bright red strip of hair from his forehead to the back of his neck and the spikes through his earlobes were designed for intimidation.

It was crucial for Lithia's opening salvo to damage the Teks enough to put some doubt into their minds. These Teks had likely never faced ten thousand warriors as skilled as those Lithia now presented. The longer the battle lasted, the better he would feel about his chances. The only thing tougher than defending a city from invaders was conquering a well-fortified city, and Lithia's capital was well fortified indeed.

"Carver, we should evacuate the women and children just to be safe. They should seek refuge in Epertase."

Logan's stomach turned with the knowledge that he had likely waited too long. An evacuation to Epertase of such a sizable population could take weeks, and their only hope of not being run down from behind was a long, spirited battle by his men.

He held the monocular up to his eye again and marveled at the proficiency of the Teks' movements. *When will you attack?* he wondered. "We should head back to the war room."

Carver agreed.

Soon, the evacuation began with trumpeters blaring the signal throughout Lithia. *Just give my people a few days,* he pleaded.

Logan spent most of the next three days in the war room with his top advisers, planning and waiting for the first salvo. He would know more after the first day of fighting, and they could adjust their plans accordingly.

On the third evening, Queen Lona entered the war room. She appeared weary, with puffy eyes and gaunt cheeks. Her long white hair draped over her shoulders. He took her hands.

"Please, go," he said. "Join our children and flee with our people."

"No. I saw our children off this morning, but I'm staying with you."

"There is nothing more you can do here."

"I can support my husband." She cradled his hand. "Do you think our son will actually leave? I worry about Galvin's bullheadedness."

"I don't know," he answered, unable to hide his own weariness. "I spoke to him yesterday and stressed the importance of his survival."

Her eyes brightened. "Do you think he listened?"

He looked away and lowered his head. He was sure she knew the answer, but he decided to tell her a comforting lie anyway. "Yes." He paused and turned back to her. "I'm sure he did."

Perhaps for the last time before the war began, he saw a hint of her dimples before her wan smile faded.

On the fifth morning of the standoff, Logan sent a squad of five negotiators to meet the enemy at the center of the battlefield. They carried with them a trunk of gold coins along with words of peace and a treaty proposal.

He stood with Lona and Carver on the tower, watching the meeting. Lona brought her own monocular. The small band of Lith negotiators was met by a group of armored Teks all in black.

The lead Lith negotiator rode to the fore. He offered his hand in peace. The lead Tek accepted with a bow.

After a few words, the Lith negotiator turned to the other negotiators and raised an arm above his head.

"What does that mean?" Lona asked.

"It means they want to negotiate."

"Thank the gods."

The Tek's horse awkwardly pranced closer to the distracted negotiator. Something was wrong with how he moved. Another Tek crowded the negotiator from the opposite side. "Turn around," Logan mumbled. "Oh gods, turn around."

"What's wrong?" Lona asked.

Logan didn't answer; he didn't know how. He pressed Lona's monocular down. "Do not watch this."

Lona pulled away and raised her monocular again in time to see the Tek reach for the Lith negotiator. The suns glinted off something in his hand. Logan knew what that something was. He froze, helpless. "No," he whispered.

The other Lith negotiators sat up straight, realizing they'd just been deceived. When the lead negotiator turned back toward the Tek, the Tek slashed his throat, drenching his own armor in a spray of blood.

The Lith horses spooked, rearing up on their hind legs. The Teks swarmed the negotiators as they tried to flee, dragging them from their horses and opening their throats as well. One of the negotiators scrambled free before his throat could be cut and ran back toward the hills. One of the Teks lifted some kind of long, narrow weapon to his shoulder. A puff of smoke left the end, followed by a distant popping sound. The fleeing Lith fell face-first.

Lona gasped and dropped her monocular, shattering the glass. Logan pulled her close and she buried her face in his chest. He didn't have any comforting words to give.

The Teks ended negotiations by slaughtering the negotiators' horses.

This was a different kind of enemy.

The Tek murderers ransacked the negotiators' clothing and saddlebags like savages. They opened the chest of gold coins and dumped them into the grass.

Once they'd finished, they returned to their own front lines, leaving the gold in the blood-stained grass.

What do they want if not riches? Logan wondered.

Lona started for the stairs. "I'm going to lie down for a bit." Logan followed her to their chambers. He sat on the edge of the bed and rubbed her back. Eventually, she cried herself to sleep.

He stared at her, reminded of the first time they had met. He remembered back when he was a young prince and she was a privileged daughter of the wealthiest man in Lithia. He had loved her at first sight. Thirty-four years later that love had not waned.

Logan covered her with a thin sheet and a heavier quilt. He went to his desk, buried his face in his clammy palms, and cried as well. *I've killed them all.* He lowered his head to his desk and fell asleep.

Hours passed before a knock at the door startled him awake. He glanced toward Lona, hoping she hadn't been disturbed. She stirred slightly. His hips were stiff and sore as he rose from his desk chair. He rubbed at a kink in his neck as he walked to the door.

Carver stood with a familiar visitor in the hall.

Logan's eyes lit up. "Aidric, old friend. Welcome. Come in."

"It's good to see you, Your Majesty."

"You know better than that. Call me Logan. What brings you all this way? You shouldn't have come."

"I have been sent to help you. I bring a hundred men and supplies. We are at your service."

"King Elijah has always been good to us."

"What does the situation look like?"

Logan explained what he had seen of the Tek army. He described their brutality with the negotiators. None of his words seemed to give Aidric much pause. Logan concluded by admitting to his old friend that he didn't carry much hope going forward.

"That will be enough of that talk. We have fought battles before."

"Not like this."

"Yes, just like this. They are men, are they not?"

"Well, yes, as far as we know."

"We know how to kill men. I wouldn't have been sent if King Elijah didn't believe we could win."

Logan felt a little better. "Tell me, Aidric. You didn't happen to run into our children on the road to Epertase, did you?"

Aidric wrinkled his forehead. "I did not, though the road is filled with so many fleeing Liths that it would've been difficult for me to notice them. Especially since I wasn't looking."

Lona stirred and sat up. "Aidric? Is that you?"

"Your Majesty, I didn't see you there. I didn't mean to disturb you."

"You didn't disturb me. It was time I woke up. May I get you a drink?"

"Whiskey, if you've got it."

"Sure." She poured a glass from Logan's personal stock and handed it to him. "It's good to see you again, Aidric."

"You, as well, Your Majesty."

Lona touched Logan's shoulder. "I'm going to get some fresh air." She kissed him on the cheek and left.

After she was out of earshot, Logan bowed his head. "We should have retreated."

"Well, you didn't, and it's too late now. What is your strategy?"

"I believe our best course will be the tried and true Lith way—an all-out attack. I have ordered hostilities to commence at dawn. I am tired of waiting. We will unload everything we have. You should take your men and return to Epertase. This will be messy."

"Logan, we were sent to help you, and that's what we'll do."

"I thank you, friend, but you are better served helping Epertase at this point."

"We can still do a lot of good. Let us stay and fight."

"No. I could not live with your death and the deaths of your men. It's bad enough that I may have doomed my own people. If you insist on staying, you must remain out of the fray. At the first signs of our front lines falling, I order you to retreat to Epertase. We will hold them off as long as we can."

"I'm getting tired of kings ordering me out of the fray. I was born to charge *into* the fray."

"I know you were, Aidric."

The two men shook hands, and then Aidric returned to his men outside the castle grounds.

CHAPTER 21

LITHIA'S WAR

Morning approached with a growing orange glow on the southern horizon that made the dark and menacing clouds forming overhead seem even darker. Aidric couldn't decide if rain would help or hinder the Liths' battle against the Teks. He hoped it would help since they had the high ground on the hills.

Aidric's second-in-command, a book-smart soldier and chess master named Starne, joined him at the edge of the city. Atop every hill of the sprawling hilltop region were battalions of a thousand Lith soldiers, along with archers, catapults, and giant boulders among the tents and cooking fires. It was an awe-inspiring sight.

Starne stood with his mouth agape. "I've read about the legendary battles here. It's always been a dream of mine to see the hilltop region in person, and it's every bit as amazing as I imagined."

"I've seen it many times, my friend, and it never ceases to take my breath."

"Did you know these hills are one of the two reasons Lithia's founding fathers built their capital so close to the Wastelands?"

Aidric shook his head.

"No invading army has ever been successful in trying to pass through this region. These Teks are bloody idiots."

It made sense. The thought of planning an assault through the valleys from the south or west gave Aidric a headache. The Danduke River protected the northern border. "What's the other reason?"

"Epertase. The founders of Lithia feared our numbers and the potential threat we posed, so they wanted to be as far away as possible. They hadn't yet formed as strong a bond as they now enjoy."

"Do you think the hills will hold this time if the front lines don't?"

Starne didn't answer right away. "I don't want to speculate, though I will say I'm not as optimistic as I'd like to be. The first two weeks of battle will tell us a lot about our enemy."

"Shall we go have a look at the rest of Lithia's army?"

"You read my mind."

Aidric ordered his men to follow, and then he and Lieutenant Starne led them to the base of the command hill. One look at the climb ahead quashed some of his enthusiasm. He leaned into his horse's ear. "Here's where you earn your feed, buddy." With a nudge, his horse started up the slope.

The Lith commander, a gray-haired man named Weaver, met them on the crest of the hill, and Aidric and Starne climbed down from their horses to greet him.

"Aidric," Weaver said with his hand extended. "It's good to see you again. Please tell me you brought Epertase's army with you."

"I'm sorry, Weaver, I did not. I have a small force to help with logistics. This all moved too quickly."

"That it did."

Aidric introduced Starne, and the two men shook hands. Starne studied his face. "Are you the same Weaver who escaped a heathen hanging party at the beginning of that war and killed a hundred heathens on your way out?"

Weaver chuckled. "I don't know about a hundred, but that was a lifetime ago. I take it you've heard the songs?"

"I have."

"Well, now that you've met me, has your life changed as a result?"

Starne's forehead wrinkled as if he wasn't sure how to answer.

Weaver smacked his shoulder. "I'm teasing. Would you like to have a look at what we face?"

Aidric answered, "That we would."

They left their horses and traveled by foot past the soldiers folding their tents and dousing their cooking fires. By now they all knew today was the day. The anticipation was palpable.

As the three men walked, Weaver said, "You've never seen anything like what you're about to see."

"Man is man. They all die the same."

"Yeah," he chuckled. "We'll see. You made it just in time. I just sent word to begin our attack."

"Yes, Logan said we would be starting soon."

As they crossed the top of the hill, the ground shook beneath Aidric's feet. He looked curiously at Weaver, who solemnly nodded. "As I said, like nothing you have ever seen."

Starne asked, "Why haven't they attacked?"

"If I knew the answer to that, I'd be a knower of everything."

"Should we maybe wait longer? See what they're planning to do?"

"We've waited long enough. It's time to give the first punch."

The western battlefront came into view. While the thousands of Lith soldiers readying for battle were impressive by their own right, the army of tens of thousands facing them blotted out the entire horizon. Each Tek soldier wore black, form-fitting armor from their heads to their toes and stood in perfect formation. Ground-shaking wheeled machines drove between their ranks, belching black smoke as they rumbled toward the front line. The suns drifted behind the smoke, casting the hills back into shadow.

Aidric studied the enemy. "You see how their front ranks stand farther apart than the middle and rear?"

Starne nodded.

"Those are the ones in catapult range. Fewer casualties."

Two-story-high rolling fortresses sat peppered throughout the vast army. They, too, were covered with black armor.

Starne leaned closer to Aidric's ear. "Those would be where their leaders operate."

Scattered along the front lines were strange metal contraptions about the size of horses with long tubes pointed toward the Lith forces. Starne pointed them out.

"Whatever those are could be a problem."

They were one of many problems Aidric had already seen.

At the rear of the Tek army were giant pits that should have taken months to dig. "Three days," Weaver said.

"What?"

"I see you're looking at the pits. They dug them in three days using strange machines."

"What's in them?"

"Some kind of thick, black liquid. They seem to get it out of the ground with those." He pointed to metal arms pumping up and down around the pits like giant butter churners.

What kind of creatures are these Teks?

Next Weaver directed Aidric's eyes to a mounted Lith riding through the Lith ranks. "See him? When he reaches the front, the fun will begin."

Aidric looked to the clouds as the air chilled slightly. Lightning flashed in the south, leaping from cloud to cloud, followed by a low rumble. The storm was here. "We should get the men ready," he said.

Starne nodded and stepped away.

Aidric turned back to Weaver. "We have been ordered to support you from the rear. Of course, that's not what we're going to do."

Weaver extended his hand and Aidric clasped it. "We are in this together, Weaver. Now I need to go tell my men."

"Something's gotta kill us sometime, right?" Weaver's smile was disturbing.

Nervous energy crackled among Aidric's soldiers as he rode his horse through their ranks. He shouted, "We have been ordered to stay back from the danger while our brothers, the Liths, are fighting the same enemy that will come to Epertase should Lithia fall." Sporadic boos met his words. "My friends, I cannot do that."

He raised a fist. "Any moment now, the wrath of Lithia will rain destruction on our enemies, and we will be there to join the fight."

His men erupted into deafening cheers that must have been heard as far as the enemy lines. Chants of "*Ai-dric, Ai-dric*" resonated throughout, making him proud of his decision to disobey King Elijah's orders.

A single drop of water splashed onto his hand. It seemed a fitting way to start what would soon be a nasty day.

"If the Teks break through the Lith forces to these hills, they will find us waiting, and we will show them how Epertasians fight. Men, you must fight for your fellow soldiers. You must fight for Lithia. And you must fight for Epertase."

Another roar, one that could bring down mountains, rang out. Aidric pulled his reins and his horse reared up in anticipation.

Another drop of water landed in his hair. And then another. He looked to the clouds as a drop splashed his cheek. *This'll be sloppy.* As if hearing his thoughts, the clouds unleashed a downpour of such fury that it stung his flesh. He slid his metal helmet over his head and the rain hit it with the sound of gravel on a tin roof.

The clouds seemed to stall above them as they dumped a wave of water onto the battlefield. Aidric and Starne returned to Weaver's side on the hilltop. Lith soldiers on horseback rode along the front lines with sodden Lith flags streaming from their lances.

Lith catapults on every hilltop ratcheted their arms back. Both sides of the battlefield grew eerily quiet as the Tek machines stopped in their tracks.

Weaver turned to the closest catapult. He gave a nod. The soldier manning it released the lever. The catapult clunked forward, sending a ball of fire into the sky. And then the sky turned orange as the other catapults followed suit and a thousand fireballs soared toward their targets. The Teks stood their ground. The fireballs struck with explosions that rained dirt and fire over the front lines. This Lith assault, once unleashed, was something to behold, and wouldn't end for most of the day.

Next came volleys of arrows that momentarily blocked out the sky. Aidric deflated a little as the arrows bounced harmlessly off Tek armor. It was stronger than he had hoped.

Weaver saw it too. As the next wave of fireballs struck their marks, he told the archers to stand down.

The rain extinguished the grass almost as soon as it ignited. But the catapults were effective, leaving smoking bodies strewn across the battlefield.

Despite their losses, the Teks didn't retreat. They didn't attack. They simply endured.

"Mothers of gods," Lieutenant Starne murmured.

"What do you make of this?" Aidric asked.

"I don't know."

Aidric watched the nervous fidgeting of his men. They needed something to motivate them and chase away their fears. "Join me, men," he shouted. "Line these hilltops and watch an offensive attack that would rival that of Epertase. Pay close attention to the enemy's armor. It is strong and repels the Lith arrows with ease. When we finally engage, use your shields wisely and aim your weapons true. They must have a weakness. Your swords need to find them."

As his men lined up for the show, Aidric climbed down from his horse and walked along their line, shaking each soldier's hand and reminding them to drink plenty of water. He left each man with these words: "Rejoice, for soon we will drown in Tek blood."

Some of his men stood quietly as he passed, while others engaged in pointless chatter. Some of these men he had known for many years, and his gut twisted at the thought that many of them would not return home.

Morning lumbered into afternoon. The rain eventually turned to a drizzle, but it had done its job. The grassy hillsides were left wet and slippery, which could only help if the Teks eventually broke through.

By evening the supply of fireballs had dwindled and catapult launches were more sporadic. Such an onslaught against a normal army would have been devastating, but when Aidric surveyed the enemy ranks it was apparent that the assault had barely made a dent in their numbers. This was going to get dirty, up close and personal. As night fell, the last of the catapults ground to a halt.

Aidric's soldiers slowly stood up, their chatter long ended. He turned back to the enemy and waited. His soldiers waited. The Lith army waited. The Teks waited.

The moon lurched across the cloudy sky, yet the Teks still didn't advance. Other than those callously pushing their fallen brethren aside to take their places in the lines, they simply watched. Maybe they were all bluster.

By the next dawn, constant thunder from the southern hilltop defenses awoke those who could sleep and haunted those who couldn't. The Epertasians turned questioning looks to Aidric, but he had no answer.

He turned to Weaver. "Do you think your southern forces would have attacked already?"

"Not without my orders … unless they were attacked. I've sent scouts to see what's going on."

Aidric realized things had just become more complicated.

Starne approached Aidric. "Well?" he whispered.

Aidric shook his head. If the Teks had flanked them, the southern hilltops would have to hold them off. Weaver had likely planned for such a tactic. Aidric focused on the battlefield in front of him. What were they waiting for? Did they want Lithia to charge? To retreat? To do nothing? It made no sense.

A Lith soldier shouted and pointed west toward the rear of the Tek army. Though the movements were at first subtle, they quickly escalated into a coordinated wave as the Tek soldiers parted to make way for carriages to pass between them. The horrific screeching of metal against metal grew louder and louder, like someone had awakened a thousand steel dragons.

"What are they doing?" Starne whispered. Aidric didn't know. The one thing he did know was that this was when the war truly began.

The concussive booms continued from the south, but he pushed them from his mind. He had to trust the southern commanders. One battle at a time.

Enormous snake-like cylinders on wheels rolled from the giant pits onto the makeshift roads formed by the parting Tek ranks. More smoke burped from long pipes protruding from the cylinders' tops. Webs of thick rubber hoses dragged behind them. There must have been a thousand machines and ten thousand hoses. In perfect concert with one another, they reached their destinations and stammered to a stop.

Almost immediately, the Tek soldiers seemed to lose their discipline and swarmed the rolling containers like thirsty desert rats that had found a spring. Then they returned to their posts while another group took their place at the containers.

Weaver watched the proceedings in utter bewilderment. And then Aidric had a sudden revelation. A sense of urgency filled him faster than he could get the words out.

"Now," he screamed. "You must attack now. Weaver, get the archers. Ignite their arrows. Any fireballs you have left for the catapults, launch them now."

"What do you see, Aidric?"

"They were waiting for something, right? It's those machines. They needed us to exhaust our catapults before they moved in."

Weaver's head bobbed as the pieces fell into place. "Archers," he screamed. "Knock your flame arrows." Weaver grabbed a torch and ran to the closest archer, igniting his arrow. That archer touched his flame to his neighbor's arrow, and each did the same until all the arrows were lit.

Weaver ran to the edge of the command hill where the men on the next hill could see him. He waved the torch over his head, signaling their archers. Those men began to scramble as well. They were ready, just waiting for their orders.

Weaver turned back toward his men and shouted, "We need to engage." Though his men likely had never seen such anxiety in him, he didn't try to hide it. This was too crucial. This might be their only chance to do real damage before the ground fighting began. He climbed onto his horse.

Aidric and Starne joined him. Aidric gave him a confident nod.

Before he could give the order, chaos and panic erupted from the next hilltop over. Those archers turned their flame arrows to the southern side of their hill. A low rumble filled the valley behind them.

"What's going on over there," Weaver shouted.

No one answered.

Just then, two riders approached from the rear of the command hill. Soldiers parted to let them through. "Sir," one of them screamed, stark terror on his face.

"What is it?" Weaver asked.

"More, sir," one of the scouts answered, his voice cracking.

"More what? Calm yourself."

"Sir, more invaders approach through the valleys. They're coming fast. They've already taken the southern hills."

More explosions echoed from the south, only closer. The soldiers on the neighboring hill released their boulders down the southern slope and then followed them with cries of "Chaaaarge."

"More? How many more?" Weaver cried.

"I don't know. Thousands. They will reach us soon. I've never seen an army move so quickly. We were barely able to get ahead of them to warn you. Our southern defenses fell in hours."

At that moment, Aidric realized his fatal mistake. He felt the blood drain from his cheeks.

Weaver tried to refocus his anxious soldiers. "Men," he shouted. "The fight moves to the southern valleys. Do not panic. We have the high ground." He galloped through his forces with his sword raised.

Aidric and Starne joined him. When they reached the back edge of the hill, Aidric saw what some of his men had already seen. *By the gods.* He swallowed hard. Tek soldiers poured into the valley like an invasion of ants swarming a discarded sandwich.

"Hold your ground, men. This is now our fight. Be ready to attack on my signal." He struggled to keep his voice confident though it threatened to break. One look at his men and the Lith soldiers told him that they realized the seriousness of their error, and it broke his heart.

Aidric raised his sword above his head and cried out, "It's not over, men. We can win this battle."

"Roll the boulders," Weaver screamed.

The wooden braces holding the boulders back shattered from the impact of war hammers. All five southern-facing boulders lurched forward and gained momentum.

At the base, Tek soldiers tried to scramble out of the way, but their numbers were too thick, and the boulders plowed through them, leaving temporary voids that were quickly filled by more Teks.

Aidric glanced at the crest of the neighboring hill where Tek soldiers ripped through the Liths like a wildfire. The speed at which these Teks moved and killed was ungodly.

The battlefield west of the hills erupted into deafening explosions tenfold louder than any created by the Lith fireballs. The hill shook. Some of Aidric's men nervously glanced back. "The fight's in front of us now, men. Do not be concerned with what you cannot control. The Liths will do their jobs. We must protect their rear by stopping this advance."

Aidric kicked his horse and charged down the hill. His men howled as they charged alongside him. The Teks rushed the muddy hill, navigating the slick terrain with apparent ease.

Before Aidric reached the fight, a deafening boom popped his eardrums. Mud and body parts hurled past him. He didn't slow or even look to the damage. A whistle whined above, followed by another bone-jarring concussion to his rear. Death screams echoed from his men. *What manner of weapon can cause such devastation? Ka-boom. Ka-boom.* Two more.

The explosions devastated the hillside along with his men. Their dying screams were almost more than he could stand. Hot bursts of air and blood slammed into him with each blast. As much as he wanted to retreat and regroup, he couldn't turn back now.

Unwavering, Starne rode beside him. He pointed to several machines being dragged by the Teks and yelled, "We're being destroyed by those before we're even in the fight."

"Just keep moving," Aidric yelled back. "Endure. Endure."

As Aidric neared the advancing Teks, their front line stopped and lifted strange, iron tubes which they braced against their shoulders. Smoke puffed from the ends of their instruments like they were filled with japsy weed.

Rat-tat-tat-tat. Dozens of his and Weaver's men crumpled to the ground, their shields and armor peppered with pebble-sized holes. They were being massacred and Aidric didn't know how to stop it. "Keep coming, men," he shouted.

The front line of Teks dropped their tube weapons and drew swords. Aidric's horse collided with the wall of Tek soldiers with enough force that it nearly threw him from the saddle. He swung his sword like a madman. Each blow sent ineffective sparks into the air. Metal shrieking against metal polluted the air as his soldiers collided with the enemy. The Teks were everywhere, swallowing them into their masses. Men screamed and cried in agony.

Aidric whirled his sword with all his might. His weapon struck a Tek helmet. Though it didn't penetrate the armor, the force of the blow knocked his foe down. But that Tek was immediately replaced with two more. As hard as he fought, there were just too many of them and they swarmed him. His horse's front legs buckled under their weight. With no more room to swing his blade, he used the hilt to pound every helmet he saw, but it didn't do any good.

He thrashed against dozens of armored hands as they grabbed and tugged and beat at him. His upper lip split. The fingers on his left hand snapped beneath someone's boot. His sword was knocked out of his grasp. As he was dragged from his saddle, he locked eyes with one of the Teks. He didn't see a soul. The Tek turned away in what Aidric could only imagine was indifference. A sword plunged into his horse's chest.

The Teks' armor hissed and spat moist air from vents near their necks. Before Aidric disappeared beneath the sea of black, he reached for a small, glistening hose that stretched from one of the Tek's shoulders to his helmet. The Tek pulled away, but Aidric had already grabbed hold of the tiny hose. Bitter black liquid splashed like a severed artery into Aidric's eyes and mouth.

The Tek soldier's head jerked to the side as if he were unable to control his body. He pushed away from Aidric and retreated as others pulled Aidric to his knees.

That's when Aidric heard the most sickening clunk. The sound of a sword piercing armor was as distinct as it was devastating. It was a sound he had heard many times before, only it had always been he who delivered it. He didn't need the cold sting of the steel sliding between his ribs to tell him that his battle was over. He grunted and bit his tongue. The many armored hands released him to move on to their next fight.

He looked to Starne. His friend's helmet had been knocked free and his armor was stained with blood, but he still fought valiantly. For only an instant, the two men made eye contact. Starne shouted something, but the clashing metal and screams drowned out his words. Aidric read his lips. "I'm coming, Aidric. Hold on."

Aidric tried to push to his feet, to help his overwhelmed friend. The Teks ignored him like he was inconsequential, like they knew he was already dead. Unable to hold up his weight, he plopped back to his rear.

He watched helplessly as a Tek soldier approached Starne from behind. They were everywhere. Aidric reached for his friend and tried to warn him, but instead of words filling his mouth it was gurgling blood. The Tek's blade burst from Starne's chest. Aidric flinched with the blow. When the Tek yanked his weapon free,

Starne collapsed to his knees. Even from so far away, Aidric could see his friend's eyes glaze over. Starne wobbled and then fell onto his face.

Aidric looked away just in time to see a blade eviscerate Weaver farther up the hill. Another Tek stopped in front of Aidric, blocking his view of Weaver. He held a war hammer. Unable to fight back, or even lift his arm, Aidric lowered his head in defeat. He hated himself for what he had done to his men. He deserved this. The Tek drew the hammer back. Aidric thought of Starne's wife and family and wondered …

Clunk.

Aidric opened his eyes to a bright, cloudless sky. The sounds of battle had been replaced with a ringing in his ears and faint moans of the dying. He tried to sit up, but the pain in his side was too great. He turned his head to see the battlefield. Broken and battered bodies littered the hillside around him. They'd never stood a chance.

He breathed through his nose because his jaw hurt too much to move it. The air was thick and putrid. Vultures pecked at the flesh of the men around him. Some of the men were still alive but too weak to fight them off. His stomach turned. Vomit and blood sprayed from his nose and through the gaps where his front teeth had once been.

He saw Weaver lying on his back, both arms across his stomach, holding his guts in. His face was pale and covered in beads of sweat. His short, rapid breaths were as fast as a hummingbird's.

Aidric tried to get up again. The pain was crippling, but his men still needed him. *I'll find help,* he silently vowed.

As he straightened, a rush of pain ripped through his lower back. When it finally dulled, he started up the bloody, mud-covered hill.

He convinced himself that reaching the top of the hill meant salvation for his dying friends, and that drove him onward. But with every painful step closer to the top, reality gnawed at his gut. It wasn't the rivulets of blood oozing from his many wounds that worried him, nor was it the puddles of rain water and gore that he had to be careful not to slip in. It was what he heard over the ringing in his ears. Or, more accurately, what he didn't hear. Instead of sounds of combat, the Lith battlefield was quiet. He needed to see why. Surely the fight wasn't over already.

His weakness pulled him back to his knees. He crawled forward, climbing over bodies along the way. It took him hours to reach the top. What he saw there confirmed his worst fears.

Hundreds of Lith soldiers lay bloodied in the matted grass and churned-up mud. Women and children who had refused to evacuate the city searched the sea of carcasses for their husbands and fathers and brothers and sons. Grown men sat and sobbed in the face of such devastation.

He wondered if the same scene was being repeated on the western battlefield as well. Given the earie silence, he thought he knew the answer.

Aidric wobbled at the sheer magnitude of their failure. He puked again. This time there was more blood in his vomit than before. He rolled to his back, exhausted. From beside him a soldier looked back with death's cold stare.

By Aidric's side was a small, dark puddle no bigger than a footprint, and it burned with a tiny flame. It was the same black liquid that had sprayed from the Tek's neck during the battle. Was this what the Teks had dredged from their pits?

He heard a sound and turned his head. An old woman approached. Her dress, arms, and face were smeared with red. She leaned over Aidric and mumbled something, but Aidric still couldn't hear very well over the ringing in his ears. She crouched closer so he could see her mouth. "Can I help you?" she mouthed.

He nodded weakly. She was a big woman, strong, and she lifted his arm over her shoulder with little trouble. His wound tore at itself. He winced. She carried him to a horse-drawn wagon full of other dying men. An elderly man, maybe the woman's husband, helped lift Aidric into the wagon next to a lifeless soldier. The elderly man mumbled something to the woman before the two of them pulled the dead soldier from the wagon.

Aidric whispered, "My men are on the other side of the hill. Help them, please."

He strained to hear her reply. She gently brushed the back of her hand along his cheek. "You'll be all right," she said.

She started to walk away, but he summoned enough strength to grab her dress. "I need to get to King Logan."

She shook her head. "My dear boy, the city is lost."

He closed his eyes.

CHAPTER 22

DEADLIER WITH AGE

Z affka looked over the carnage of the Lith battlefield with pride from a high window in his rolling fortress. His soldiers had performed well, as always, and the civilization known as Lithia hadn't stood a chance.

With the battle over, his soldiers cleared a path through the dead for his approach to the capital city they called Reigal. By the time the fortress reached the edge of town, the city was theirs.

The streets were mostly empty save for grieving women and children who had either refused or were unable to flee. The Lith castle lay ahead, a trophy of sorts for the Tek commander. Hundreds of Tek soldiers stood guard around the castle to prevent any of the royal family from escaping before Zaffka got to greet them.

Alone in the room, Zaffka turned to his command table. Resting on the table was his jet-black suit of armor. The time had come to get his hands dirty. He dragged his fingers proudly along the red stripes painted on the neckpiece.

He slid his legs into the boots first. The soft insulation felt warm against his bare flesh. The next sections of his armor clamped around his knees, thighs, and groin, fitting together like puzzle pieces. Then he lowered the chest piece over his head and onto his shoulders, meticulously fastening every clamp to leave no gaps. His helmet was last. With the blood tube from the chest piece secured to his helmet and the suit's vascular system complete, he took a step. His legs and arms hissed.

Zaffka turned to his prized possession, a magnificent work of art encased in glass. It was perfect in every way. He unlocked the gold clasp and opened the lid. With something approaching reverence, he grasped the hilt of his sword and lifted it from its cushion. The first time he had held the weapon years ago, he'd known it was unlike any sword ever made. The blade was thin, yet not brittle, and weighed less than a sparrow. It cast a faint blue glow and was said to cut through anything made by man. At least, that was what its previous owner had bragged before Zaffka removed his head. Legend said the sword was created by two parts smithing skill and one part witchcraft. Zaffka didn't care how it was made; only that he now possessed it.

The proud commander slid the work of art into its special sheath and strapped the sheath to his back.

The time was near.

He was ready.

Except now he had to piss.

General Rayles met him at the fortress base. "The enemy castle has been surrounded, sir. Shall I send the word to overrun it?" he asked.

"No, no. I will lead the assault."

"Very well, sir. Your transport awaits."

A band of bodyguards accompanied Zaffka and Rayles to the Lith castle and a soldier with a single red stripe on his armored neck greeted Zaffka at the main entrance.

"No one has left since we arrived, sir. We believe the king is still inside."

Zaffka nodded. "Did you search for underground passages?"

"Sir?"

Zaffka turned to Rayles. "Relieve this man of his burdens."

Rayles drew his sword. Zaffka walked away as the soldier dropped to the ground. Rayles hurried to catch up.

"You're still going in, sir?"

"I find them," he answered in Epertasian.

Rayles grinned. "You have been practicing. Very good, sir."

Zaffka's bodyguards led him and Rayles through the castle's main entrance. The walls were bare. Empty crates littered the floor, giving the impression the castle had been robbed. Epertasian words were painted on the bare walls. Rayles asked Zaffka what they meant.

"Die, Tek demons. There is nothing for you here."

Rayles smirked. "When will these fools learn we care not for their possessions?"

Zaffka ordered the soldiers to clear each room and line any survivors along the front wall. He scanned the foyer, eyes lingering on the grand staircase. "If I were a king in this castle, I would be up there," he said. Rayles led the way up the dark staircase and into a long, bright gallery.

At the opposite end stood a single warrior who wore a sword at his waist, a shield on his forearm, and the arrogance of a man who knew how to kill.

Zaffka nudged Rayles aside. "Who are you?" Zaffka asked in Epertasian. "Are you king?"

The man answered, "I'm Carver. And this is as far as you go."

Zaffka scoffed at the funny red-haired man. He drew his sword. Carver did the same.

Zaffka took a deep breath, huffed a bored sigh, and then charged. Carver responded in kind.

Zaffka pointed both of his arms forward. Thunder exploded from cylinders along his forearms, first from his left, then from his right. One projectile missed its target by a squank hair and shattered chips of rock from the farthest wall. The other slammed Carver's shield, knocking him off his feet. Carver stared for a moment at the smoking hole in the center of his shield and then tossed it aside.

"Why not face me head-on, coward, instead of using your witchcraft?"

"Oh, my friend, that wasn't witchcraft. That is called gunpowder."

"I don't understand your filthy language."

Carver dusted himself off and stood up. Zaffka leaped and swung his sword. Carver ducked. The sword sliced through the stone wall with ease. Carver's eyes bulged just like all the previous warriors who had seen the sword's power right before they felt it.

Zaffka chuckled. "Now, that's witchcraft."

Carver shrugged as if unimpressed. He lunged with his sword. The blade ricocheted off Zaffka's armor. He squatted, and in one fluid motion he swept Zaffka's legs while shoving him to his back. The impact jarred Zaffka's sword from his hand. His armor hissed and spurted as he scrambled to put distance between him and Carver. Carver dove at him, heaving his own sword at Zaffka's head. Zaffka spun away, impressed with Carver's skill.

The brave defender of the castle lunged at the Tek again, but struck air. Zaffka shoved his knuckles against Carver's leg. Carver's eyes widened as he realized his mistake. Zaffka's arm recoiled with a concussive boom. The Lith warrior fell to his back, clutching the gaping, bloody hole in his thigh. Carver didn't make a sound.

Zaffka strolled past him to retrieve his sword and then stood above him. He removed his helmet and clipped it to a clasp on his chest piece. "Not bad," he said in Epertasian. He took a couple of deep, agitated breaths. "Where king?"

Carver tried to lift his sword, but Zaffka stomped his arm back to the floor.

"You'll never find him. He's far away by now."

"No matter," Zaffka snarled. He raised his blue sword with both hands. "We find him. Eventually. Why he leave you?"

"I insisted."

"Very well."

Zaffka drove the blade down through Carver's chest and into the stone floor beneath him. With an air of arrogant pride, he watched

Carver twitch. Slowly, the life left the Lith warrior's body. Once the twitching had ceased and Zaffka could gain no more sick pleasure, he grunted and wiggled his sword until it pulled free of stone and armor and bone. Zaffka sensed Rayles standing behind him.

"Round up everyone," he ordered. "Locate the tunnels and send search parties through. Find the royal family and execute them."

"Yes, sir."

They walked down the stairs into the throne room. "You and I will leave for the area known as Havens Ravine in the morning. That is where the real battle will take place. The Epertasians will fight hard to protect the city they call Thasula." Zaffka sat in the king's throne.

"It suits you, sir."

Of course it did. Zaffka sneered at the queen's throne beside him. He gave it a good shove with his foot, knocking it over. "That's better."

"After we feast on the food of this city, we will be ready to move out. The workers have already begun digging for black blood."

Zaffka nodded. "Is our advance team ready to go to Recitar?"

"Recitar, sir?"

"The Lowlands."

"Ah, yes. I have ordered them to enjoy the spoils of war here for the night and then start their march in the morning."

"Are we still on schedule?"

"Yes, sir."

"If the Epertasians are as dumb as these Liths, we will have our treasure in no time."

"It's all coming together, sir."

"Of course. Now send me in a new wife and leave us. I have a strange craving for one with fire hair."

"Right away, sir."

CHAPTER 23

LACTNEE
WAREHOUSE

S imcane knelt in the high grass of the Great Plains as the blades tickled his thick calf muscles. The clumped dirt at the forest's edge stank of dried blood and easily crumbled between his fingers.

"Is this where Rasi was first seen, Jasper?" he asked one of his seven hired hands.

"That's the word from my source in the Elite Guard. He said Rasi was struck by an arrow and fell from that tree." He pointed.

Simcane ground the dirt some more before flicking it into the breeze. He squinted and wrinkled his forehead.

"East," he muttered.

"Sir?"

Simcane rubbed his chin.

"Sir?" Jasper asked again. "Why east? Tevin has gone south to the mountains where Rasi is said to live. Shouldn't we as well?"

"We're not chasing Rasi. We are searching for Alina, and she has been taken east. Look at these tracks. Now why would Tevin ignore this and …" He trailed off.

"Rasi might have left these tracks to throw someone like us off his trail."

"Yes, I suppose."

"But you don't believe that, do you, sir?"

I just don't know. Simcane grunted. "These tracks mean Rasi had help, and I don't see someone living alone in the mountains for so long suddenly enlisting help to kidnap a princess. We will follow where this trail leads. If Shadows Peak and Rasi are what we seek, we will find them soon enough."

Simcane climbed onto his horse, Eko, and surveyed the landscape one more time. Something didn't feel right. In his experience, if something felt wrong, he'd best be leery. The band of mercenaries gathered and followed him east.

The trail led straight to the town of Parsons.

He turned to his hired hand Bach. "Somebody here must know something. Put out word to the vagrants. Two bits for any information."

"Why the vagrants, sir?"

"Because they are the only ones who truly know what happens at night in the city. Also, they'll tell you anything for two bits."

"Aye, sir," Bach answered, and the mercenaries dispersed.

Simcane made his way into a quaint but crowded pub at the edge of town. Sometimes listening was more fruitful than looking. He absorbed the condescending glares of the high-class clientele while paying them no mind. After all, their disdain wasn't going to quench his thirst.

The seated customers at the bar left little room for his bulky frame and made no effort to create any. Simcane crammed between two snooty men and waved the tender over.

"Ale," he ordered. The tender seemed to ignore him, turning away to speak to another patron. Simcane leaned over the bar and grabbed his shirt. The tavern silenced. The bartender froze.

"I'm looking for information. We can do this nice or not so nice."

The tender stammered, shaking like a man about to piss his drawers. Having made his point, Simcane released the man's shirt. When he looked around, the other men in the bar quickly looked down at their drinks. "I'm looking for the princess and any information that could lead to her whereabouts," he shouted.

The uppity patrons stared at their hands. Simcane upped the ante with silver, but a couple of bits didn't sway men of privilege as much as the men he was used to associating with. He thought wistfully of Arthur's Dive.

By late afternoon, Simcane had lost track of how much he'd drunk. The tender delivered yet another ale with a look of disbelief, perhaps not used to men consuming such quantities, at least not while remaining vertical.

"Just the drinks, not the stares," Simcane muttered, and the tender diffidently turned away.

Simcane downed most of the ale before Jasper burst through the front door, attracting everyone's curious eyes.

"Simcane," he shouted. He ran over and leaned close to Simcane's ear. "I found a vagrant who said there's a lot of strange activity of late in the warehouse district."

Simcane stood up and shoved his hand into his bag, which caused the tender to flinch. He tossed several coins for the ale, plus an extra one for an undeserved tip, onto the floor behind the bar. He and Jasper left, the stares of the crowd following them all the way to the door.

The vagrant Jasper had found met them outside. He was covered in dirt and alcohol-stink and his clothes were in shambles. His hair stood up like the feathers of a diseased peacock. He waved his arms and flapped his mouth in incessant ramblings, revealing he had more fingers than teeth or smarts.

"Hey, hey," the man shouted. "Where'smyreward. Huh? Huh? Huh?" His mouth seemed to move faster than his brain. Simcane told him to calm down.

"Hey, man. TheLactneewarehouse. Lottaactivitylately. Yeah. Way too much for the holiday season, that is. Someone even kicked Tom and Alice out. Canyoubelievethat? They've stayed there during the holidays for years."

"Lactnee?" Simcane asked.

"Youdon'tknowLactnee? Everyone knows about Lactnee. You heard of Lactnee boards, right? Most of Thasula was built using them."

Simcane didn't remember hearing the term, but had grown tired of the conversation and halfheartedly agreed.

The vagrant glared at him suspiciously. "You heard about the Great Conflagration, haven't you?"

Simcane hadn't the patience for a history lesson. "Of course, I have. Get to the point."

"Well that's where it started. They say a clumsy worker started the fire with his weed stick."

"Why do I care?"

"Because the warehouse is abandoned now, left for the rats and the less fortunate."

"You mean like you?"

The vagrant wiped his nose and smirked. "I mean, like Alice and Tom."

"I want you to take us to it tonight," Simcane said.

"Sure thing, but it'll cost ya."

Simcane tossed a bag of coins on the ground. The man scooped it up. "This is more than two bits."

"Are you complaining?"

He shoved the bag into the front of his pants. "Nosir."

As the suns set, Simcane's team of mercenaries returned one by one, each with little or no information. The Lactnee Warehouse was their best lead. They mounted their horses and followed the vagrant who rode his—no doubt stolen—spotted jackass.

The warehouse district was a town in itself, full of the hard-working men who made and transported supplies to all the venders of Thasula and other towns. Simcane had been through the area a couple of times many years before, but a lot had changed since then.

The homeless man pointed down the road to the burned-out building of Lactnee. "That's it."

"Where is everyone? I've never seen it so ..." Simcane fished for the right word. "Dead," he finally said.

The homeless man, so full of knowledge, answered, "The workers take a long holiday for Matthew's Day and don't return for several weeks. Most of them travel to their hometowns with their families."

Simcane looked down at the man, who sat proudly upon his jackass. "And you? Not enough jobs for you to work?"

The man gave him a look that said "don't judge me."

"How do you know this 'activity' is what I seek?" Though he asked, he could not envision a better place to hide a princess.

"I saw the strangers last night. Creepy. One of them's big as you. Probably as dumb, too." He backed his donkey out of reach and showed his missing teeth.

Simcane jerked Eko to the side and forward a couple of steps before dismounting.

The toothless informant rode off into the shadows between a couple buildings.

Simcane turned to his men. "Leave your horses here. We will approach on foot."

Bach asked, "Should we circle around to the rear?"

"No," he answered. "As little light as there is out front, I am sure there is even less around back. I prefer to see my enemy in front of me. Besides, we are not expected. We will walk through the front door and do our work."

Hugging the walls of the factories and warehouses, they snuck closer and closer to Lactnee.

"Stay alert, men," Simcane said. "A kidnapper of princesses will likely be skilled."

Simcane and his mercenaries reached the front of Lactnee as night set in. Four of his men crept past the doorway and crouched next to a pile of waterlogged wood, careful not to be seen through any of the many holes in the walls. The foundation creaked and swayed in the slight breeze.

Simcane waved his hand and Jasper crawled to the rotted door. He glanced over his shoulder, waiting for Simcane's command. Simcane gave a nod. Jasper stood up, drew back his foot, and bashed the door open.

He burst inside with Bach on his heels, but Bach stopped short of the door as though he sensed something. He stood up straight, turned, and nodded toward the road behind Simcane. "Uh, boss?"

Simcane turned to see a white-haired stranger on the opposite side of the road. *Pretty good,* he thought. *Sneaking up on me is not easy.*

The stranger cocked his head. "I've heard that b-b-b-before."

Simcane lowered his brow. "Are you the one we seek?" he asked.

The stranger took a step forward. "I sure hope s-s-s-sooo."

Simcane opened his arms and shed his cumbersome fur, exposing his muscular chest. His waistband held a blade that reached past his knees and curved like a crescent moon. He intertwined his fingers and bent his knuckles backward in a cacophony of cracks. Then he extracted his blade. "Come on, criminal. Let's get this over with."

The villain cackled and shuffled from foot to foot like he was dancing. "Are you sure that is w-w-w-what you want?" He stepped to the side and revealed a motionless figure lying on the ground with a rope around his neck.

Simcane scoffed. "If you expect me to fear a man who slaughters vagrants, you are mistaken."

"But I k-k-killed his donkey, too."

Simcane flicked his hand at his side.

Jasper balked at the order. "Fan out? Sir, there is only one of them."

"Fan out, I said. There are at least four." Simcane darted his eyes side to side while fidgeting in a circle. "They are surrounding us as we speak." His men drew their swords with shaky hands. Good help was hard to find. Simcane ordered them into a defensive half-circle and hoped for the best. "Come out, creatures," he yelled. "I smell your stink."

"One behind you, sir," Jasper warned. "Big as a house, this one."

"I know. I saw him. There are more. One east and one west."

Simcane's hired hand Shiloe asked, "What are they?" His sword quivered in his unsteady hand.

The lead one shouted, "I s-s-s-smell the fear in your men, Simcane."

"You know my name, heathen. What is yours?"

"I am d-death to all. I … am … Scooorrnnne." His words trailed off like a sick song.

Simcane had heard whispers of a group of killers led by a man named Scorne. There were four of them, three men and a woman, and they called themselves symbiots. If this man was indeed Scorne, then the big one was Blogg, and the two in the shadows were Cyn and Rez. Based on the lurid tales of their exploits, he'd been expecting the symbiot leader to be much more imposing than the stuttering scarecrow before him.

"Well, Scorne, I am not impressed."

"Maybe you should b-b-be." Scorne calmly sauntered closer to Bach.

"Sir?" Bach held his blade trained on the freak. His eyes shot from Simcane to Scorne, and then back to Simcane again.

Simcane butted between the two men and stood chest-to-face with Scorne. Scorne backed away, drool spooling down his chin. Simcane stepped back with a snarl. He heard shuffling feet, but saw little more than a blur of black hair whipping past and just as quickly disappearing into the shadows. Shiloe's sword clanged to the stone. He clutched his throat and dropped to his knees. Blood squirted between his fingers as he gasped for air. He collapsed to his side. A river of red surrounded his convulsing body, filling the imperfections of the street and seeping into the cracks. A black-haired woman stood at the opposite side of the road with a murderous grin, fresh blood dripping from her arm. Cyn had revealed herself. That left one more in the shadows.

Simcane steadied himself. "Fight or die," he shouted to his remaining men.

The mercenaries bunched closer together. Two enthusiastic members of his team leaped at Blogg, who lifted his giant broadsword in time to block both swords with one blow. Their combined steel was no match for his strength, and the impact slammed both men backward.

Scorne grinned. "You've brought amateurs. Th-th-this will be a pleasure. I've heard of you." He slid his sword from his sheath.

"Good," Simcane muttered.

Scorne leaped.

Simcane raised his curved blade and deflected Scorne's attack. He aimed a kick at Scorne's gut, but struck metal. The impact still pushed Scorne away.

Scorne rebounded and swung his fist. Simcane batted it away with ease, knocking Scorne to the side. In one fluid move, Scorne twirled and drove his sword forward. Again, Simcane blocked his blade.

Simcane's team of mercenaries wasn't faring so well against their opponents, especially after Rez finally showed himself and joined in the melee. Enough messing around. Soon he'd be alone against these freaks if he didn't act fast.

Scorne lunged again. Simcane dropped his blade and shoved Scorne with both hands. A thunderous boom exploded from his fingertips, sending a blast of air into Scorne's ribs. The freak slammed into the factory wall on the other side of the street, nearly busting through.

Simcane wobbled under the growing weight of the air around him, his thighs quivering under the strain. He hated using his gift.

Rez, having finished off his foe, dove in and swung his blade. Simcane dropped to his knees as the blade whiffed past his head. He took up his sword and rammed it at Rez's exposed chest. The freak's metal skin shifted to deflect the steel. Rez thrust a knee at Simcane's jaw. Simcane absorbed the blow to catch Rez's knee. With all his weight, he drove the freak to the ground.

When Simcane tried to bounce up, Cyn was on him like a swarm of frost beetles. Pain shot across his back. His chest jutted painfully outward. He glanced over his shoulder. She grinned with her head cocked sideways. Her metal skin protruded like the long blade of a knife along the contour of her forearm. She licked his dripping blood from it.

She leaped forward. He rolled to his back and heaved his open hands at her with a grunt. A shockwave collided with her face, flipping her backward head over heels. Blood exploded from her nose.

The air thickened even more around Simcane. He pushed back to his feet on trembling legs. His chest surged with each breath. He needed time to retreat, to recover. He peered at his men as they moaned in their own blood in the street.

A sword plunged toward his head. He grabbed the attacker's wrist and twisted, feeling bones break in his grip. Rez squealed and yanked his arm away. His metal skin slithered around his broken wrist and hardened like a cast.

Simcane rose to his feet. He sensed an attack from behind, but was too late to avoid the massive fist that crashed into his temple, spinning him into the wood pile next to the building. His vision blurred. He needed to retreat. "Get up," he willed himself. His four attackers approached in a cautious half-circle.

The big one feinted at him. Simcane threw his arms in front of his face and a boot slammed into his defenseless stomach.

He fell against the building. His hand bumped a chunk of wood. He grabbed it. The crushing air was letting up now. Simcane could stand, but he wasn't yet right.

Just another moment, he thought.

"More?" Scorne mocked.

"All you can give, heathen," he replied.

Rez attacked first, sword in his good hand.

Simcane swung the wood with both arms, shattering it against Rez's metal jaw. He wished the wood were stronger and Rez's chin weaker. Rez was still conscious.

Blogg's massive fist pounded Simcane's rib cage.

Simcane grunted as the wind left his lungs and he fell back onto the scattered rotten wood. As he struggled to stand again, Cyn dove onto his back with a howl. Her metal fist bashed his skull over and over. He tried to shake her from his back, but she held firm.

He twisted away from the wood pile. She rode his back like she was taming a wild horse. She struck the back of his head again, sending white flashes across his vision. He couldn't take much more.

"Rrraaahhh," he screamed as he drove his weight backward, smashing her against the warehouse wall. Her body went limp and she let go of his back.

Simcane wobbled to the side. Blogg was there to meet him. He grabbed Simcane's head with both hands. Simcane heaved his elbow into Blogg's face, breaking the symbiot's grip. He tried to step away, but Cyn was back on her feet and both she and Blogg closed in. Blogg cocked his fist.

"Wait," Scorne screamed. Cyn, Blogg, and Rez stopped. "S-S-Simcane, you fight hard. It is a shame that this is where you end."

Keep talking. I'm almost back.

Scorne smiled as he sauntered past Blogg and Cyn. "B-b-b-back? You're not almost b-back. You're almost d-d-dead."

Simcane glowered at his enemy. "I haven't"—*huff, huff*—"gone anywhere yet." He looked down at Scorne's fist. Metal slithered around the symbiot's knuckles and then rose to a point.

Just as Scorne moved, Rez leaped in from the side, as if the two men were in sync with each other.

Simcane clasped his hands together and heaved them with all his might. His hammer fist collided with Rez's cheek, hurling him against the wall. Simcane turned toward Scorne.

Too late.

The scream that left his lungs was one he had only heard from his opponents before. The world went black from his left eye. He grabbed his attacker's forearm with both hands. Scorne wiggled and twisted; Simcane's head twisted with him. He fell to his knees, still clutching Scorne's arm.

Wait, wait, wait, he screamed in his head. *Don't move.*

Scorne laughed. The bastard pressed his foot to Simcane's forehead, strained, and tugged his weapon free. Simcane's head snapped back. He collapsed to his rear. The vitreous from his eye mixed with his blood and trickled down his cheek. He covered his ruined eye with the palm of his hand.

Scorne stepped back, admiring his work. "Let Rez have him," he cackled. "Payback for the arm."

Blogg put his arm around Cyn, and she shrugged it off. "I don't need to watch this," she said. She joined Scorne as he returned to Simcane's dead and wounded men. He leaned over the still-writhing Jasper and yanked his head back by his hair. Jasper begged weakly for his life. Scorne paused, as if considering his pleas, but then jerked his free arm upward, ripping a gash across Jasper's throat.

Simcane cringed. He pressed his hand harder over his wounded eye, trying in vain to stop the throbbing. Scorne and Cyn moved to the last of Simcane's living mercenaries.

Rez's leg stepped into Simcane's view. He reached down, cupped Simcane's chin, and guided him up to his knees. "Look me in the eyes when I speak to you," he said. He started to laugh. "Oops. I forgot." He released Simcane's jaw, allowing him to crumple to his heels.

Rez pointed his sword at Simcane's nose. Blogg chuckled. Rez drew back his blade.

Simcane thrust his hand at Rez's leg, sending an air burst into Rez's knee. The loud boom was followed by a deafening crack and Rez's knee bent backward. He cried out and grabbed his leg. Simcane shoved him to his rear.

Blogg straightened up, confused. Scorne turned back with blood smeared across his face. Cyn covered her mouth.

Simcane forced himself back to his knees. He stretched both arms out to his sides. Rez lifted his head and stared uncomprehendingly at Simcane's chest.

Simcane swung both arms at once. The metal on Rez's face scrambled to one side then back to the other in a confused blur. Simcane's hands stopped short of Rez's ears. Another thunderous boom rang out. Rez stiffened and then his arms dropped limply to his sides. Blood trickled from Rez's nose. He swayed and then fell to his side.

Cyn screamed.

Simcane's muscles twitched under the heaviness of the air. He didn't have much time. Somehow, he pushed to his feet again. His first step was clumsy, like he walked on sand with legs made of hemp. His bloody, throbbing eye socket reminded him what was at stake. He strained to reach for the stars.

Scorne, Cyn, and Blogg charged as one. He waited with his weary fist in the air for them to get just close enough. Cyn leaped first, cursing in the heathen tongue.

Simcane drove his fist into the ground. The shockwave crashed into his enemies. Wood and debris pounded the side of the Lactnee building. The symbiots were thrown against the building on the opposite side of the road, with Scorne crashing through the door. Simcane couldn't fight the weight pushing him to his back. Even taking a short, shallow breath was torture, but he fought for it, sucking in as much air as he could. When he had enough, he whistled for Eko.

Across the road, Scorne stumbled from the shattered doorway of the warehouse. He shook his head like he hadn't yet regained his wits.

Eko trotted to Simcane's side, between him and Scorne.

"Down, boy," Simcane whispered.

Eko bent his front legs, lowering his chest to the ground. Simcane rolled to his side. Too weak to get on, he entangled his hands in Eko's mane. "Go," he whispered. Eko began to run with Simcane bouncing along the hard ground. Each jarring jolt hurt like falling from a roof. He lifted his head enough to look for pursuers.

Cyn chased him on foot, unbelievably closing the gap between them. He decided if she caught him, she deserved her glory. But Eko wasn't finished and pushed harder, lengthening the gap between them until Cyn gradually lost ground and gave up the chase.

CHAPTER 24

IMPOSSIBLE PROMISES

E lijah stood in the doorway of his war room with a queasy feeling in his gut. Before he could muster the strength to enter, he paused to consider the magnitude of the coming days. This was his second time in the room in recent days, and it never got easier.

He made his way to the wall-sized map behind his chair. One by one, his top commanders entered and took their seats. They weren't as jovial as last time, gearing up for the looming war. There were no pleasantries or idle chatter, only serious faces and tense gazes.

Elijah waited until everyone was there before he spoke. "Men, everyone knows why we are here. War is upon us." Some of the officers nodded in agreement. Elijah saw no benefit in softening his next words. It was best to be blunt. "If you haven't yet heard, Lithia has already fallen."

Gasps met his statement. The officers looked to each other in disbelief.

Elijah continued, "Lithia's army, as powerful as it was, fell in less than a week."

"A week?" Dru interrupted. "How is that possible?"

"Our enemy uses weapons unlike any we have ever seen. They create explosions that leave craters in the ground. They wear armor that repels sword and arrow alike. And their numbers were ten times those of the Liths."

"And Aidric?" Dru asked. "What has he reported? Why isn't he here?"

Elijah bowed his head. "We have not heard from Aidric. We believe he and his men have fallen as well." He allowed the sting of his words to settle. It would help the men be sharp in their planning.

Elijah spoke again. "Those who served with me during the Heathen War will remember how we defeated those mongrels in the great final battle. I have no doubt that same strategy will be successful again. A head-on, full offensive with all our resources, I believe, is our best approach. No army has ever withstood the full might of Epertase."

"Your Majesty," Atticus said, "I have studied Lithia's military for many years, and forgive me if I am wrong, but wasn't that the same strategy Lithia used? Considering how quickly they were annihilated, why do you assume it will work for us?"

"That is a good point and one I have wrestled with. We are only now getting sporadic reports from Lithia's front line. From what I am able to piece together, it sounds as though they were too greatly outnumbered. Our numbers are greater and we'll be able to spread the invader's front line thinner. If we can thin their numbers with our initial assault, we can give ourselves better odds. As I see it, this is our best chance for victory."

Dru and Tate agreed.

"What about drawing them into ambushes?" Jarrah asked.

"It's too risky," Dru answered. "If we funnel them into ambushes and it doesn't work, we would be faced with their armies already inside our borders."

"I agree with His Majesty," Tate said. "Epertase is not Lithia. Our superior numbers will prevail."

"How long do we have?" Jarrah asked.

Elijah turned toward the map and pointed to Lithia's western border. "As I said, we are receiving only sporadic reports on the battle. All we know for certain is that the enemy attacked on two fronts. They moved with such speed as to catch the Liths completely off guard and they could not counter in time. We believe the smaller of those two forces are moving toward the Lowland border from the northwest. The Lowlanders will not likely put up much of a fight. We must stop or slow that advance to have any shot at victory in the bigger battle to the west." He pointed to Havens Ravine on the map. "I want to draw their larger force there. That is where we will make our stand."

Atticus asked, "Sir, have our eastern defenses redeployed yet?"

Elijah ran his hand along the map. "Andon should have them near New Arc in the north within the next two days."

"Would you like the Elite Guard to join in the fight?" Masera asked.

Elijah waved him off. "No, no, no," he said. "You need to protect the castle in case another threat arises."

James rushed into the room, clearly agitated. With his head down, he hurried to Elijah and whispered that the queen needed him right away. The look on James's face told Elijah the gravity of the summons, and he excused himself from the table.

The captains and servants alike sat quiet with their heads bowed. Everyone knew what it meant.

Elijah hesitated a moment before exiting. "As of now, all war protocols are in effect. Mark today's date as the first day of the war against the Teks."

The planning was in his officers' capable hands, at least for now. He would check in on their progress when he had a chance.

He raced to Madelyne's room, pushing the door open with a stomach full of dread. "My love," he shouted.

The court physician sat close to where she lay, the floral bedding swallowing her frail body. He rose and bowed, then placed a solemn hand on Elijah's shoulder. "Your Majesty, there is nothing more I can do. The queen's lungs are bleeding and soon she will drown."

Elijah shook his head. He refused to accept it. He eased down next to her and lifted her delicate hand in his.

The physician stepped out.

Many years had passed since Elijah had allowed himself the weakness of tears, but he could feel them building up, eroding the dam of his resolve. Madelyne was his life, his everything.

"Do not mourn, my love," she whispered. "I am the luckiest woman in the land. You are a good man."

He pulled his hand from hers and turned away, ashamed. "No, I'm not." He pressed both hands over his face. "You made me a better man, but my soul is evil." He couldn't fight the tears any longer.

"Shhh," she whispered. "That's not true." An awful coughing spell interrupted her, quickly followed by gurgling sounds like she was being held beneath water. She struggled to recover her wind and her composure, and then said, "I need you to promise me something."

"Anything, my love. Anything."

"Promise me you'll find Alina ... that you'll protect her for all eternity. Please find my little girl." She coughed again. This time when she moved her hand from her mouth, her chin was bathed in blood. "I know Siver is skilled and that you sent him with Tevin, but ..." She trailed off, too weak to finish.

Elijah grabbed a handkerchief from the nightstand and dabbed the blood away. "I can't lose you," he said. "I need you." He put his head on her lap. She stroked his hair. It killed him to think he'd never feel her touch again. "Maddy, you're all that's good in me."

"Now it'll have to be Alina." Her hand slowly slid down his back to the bed.

"No, no, no, please don't go." He tried to lift her hand back to his head, but it wouldn't stay. "Please."

She gurgled a final breath.

He held her hand, never wanting to let go. "I'll stay with you while you walk through the darkness of death. I won't leave you, my love."

Her cheek was already cool when he finally pressed his own against it. In some naïve way, he hoped his own heat would somehow keep her from truly leaving. As he held her close and thought about her last words, a new resolution filled him. He brought his lips to her ear and whispered, "I swear to you, my love. Alina will be freed. And she will one day be queen of Epertase. You have my word. I have done evil in this world, but I will make amends. I owe you that."

CHAPTER 25

MENDING

Several miles east of the warehouse district, in a field of crops, an old farmer worked his fingers raw as he had every day of his life. With the cold season rapidly approaching, Homer's land needed to be plowed for the winter wheat crop. He worked alone, as he had for the past fifty seasons. Having a barren wife meant he had no children to lighten the burden.

His old oxen struggled to pull the plow through the hard ground. One of them, his strongest, became stuck once again. This was getting to be a habit. He put his shoulder to the ox's hindquarters and pushed. Neither the oxen nor the man were as strong as they once had been, and getting stuck provided plenty more problems than it had in years past. For years he'd been promising himself to purchase new oxen in the spring, but money was always the deciding factor and he was forced to pray the old pair made it through.

He wasted most of the afternoon digging and wrestling with the mud before his exhausted oxen finally broke free. Though the air was frigid, he was drenched in sweat. It gave him a shiver. With his already soaked handkerchief, he wiped the sweat from his brow and leaned on his plow.

He scanned the field, disheartened by the amount of work yet to be done, and took a frustrated breath before climbing back onto his plow. Just as he lifted the reins, he noticed movement on the dirt path that ran along the edge of his land. To his surprise, there was a horse—a great beast of a horse—clopping wearily along as if lost.

A fine horse to be out here alone, he thought. He stepped away from his plow. *Wait a moment ...* Something dragged behind the stallion. He strained to focus his bleary eyes. Not something, someone. He started to jog toward the path. "Irene," he shouted over his shoulder.

His wife stepped through their front door. "What is it now, Homer," she asked, annoyance dripping from her voice. "I'm trying to cook—" She stopped mid-sentence when she saw the horse and its burden; her eyes were much sharper than his.

As Homer closed in on the horse, he quickened his pace. "Whoa, boy," he said, and grabbed the reins. He petted the stallion's chest to let him know he had done well.

A pale, limp cannon of an arm hung along the horse's side, thick fingers entangled in the mane. Homer yanked at the long hair until the man's black-and-blue hand fell free and thudded to the ground. The man lay motionless except for the occasional faint rise and fall of his chest. Dried blood and bruises covered large portions of his body.

With his shoulder, Homer shoved the big man to his side like he was a stuck ox. Dirt, grass, and pebbles were embedded in the raw meat of his side and legs. The road wore skin and blood like a trail to where his misery began.

Homer lifted the man's head from the ground. His first sight of the bloody, empty eye socket made him turn away in horror. He covered his mouth, hoping not to spill his stomach. "Someone sure did a number on you," he mumbled through his fingers.

Irene ran to Homer's side. "By the gods. Is he alive?" she asked.

"Barely. But he won't be for long. We need to get him to the house, but he's too big to carry." Homer quickly scanned his field and a plan started to take shape. "Stay with him while I get Shelby and her sled." He hobbled with his sore, overworked knees across the field to his barn.

Maybe he shouldn't have left Irene with the broken man, but he imagined there was no other voice that could sooth a dying soul as well as hers.

At the barn, Homer hooked his horse Shelby to a metal sled and covered it with worn-out Lactnee boards as a rudimentary stretcher. He hurried back across the field with Shelby in tow.

"Help me pull him up. He's a big one."

Irene tugged at the man's arm, but wasn't much help at first. The two struggled and strained until the giant of a man lay half on the sled, half in the dirt. As hard as they worked, that was as far as they could get him.

Homer gave his horse a light slap on the rear. "Slow now, Shelby," he whispered. Irene sat up on the sled next to the dying man, caressing his head while whispering encouragement into his ear.

At the front stoop, Homer said, "We're not going to be able to get him into the house without help. Get some blankets. Keep him warm. I'll get Doc Eckels." He limped into the barn and then burst through the open doors on his fastest mare, a blazing one he called Dakota.

He didn't slow until he reached the small town east of his farm. It was more of a street with a couple of shops and pubs than an actual town, but it was much closer than Thasula or Parsons, which were his only other options. Besides, Doc Eckels was a good man.

Doc Eckels was a small, unassuming man with spectacles and a neatly trimmed, salt-and-pepper mustache. When he spoke, Homer had to really listen closely because he didn't use much volume. He immediately agreed to help, grabbed his kits, and followed Homer back to the farm. They found Irene on the porch, dabbing a damp cloth across the big man's forehead and dry lips.

"He's getting worse," she said. "He's been moaning."

After a great deal of effort, the three were able to get the hulking, unconscious man into Homer's house and onto a bed. Half a day passed, maybe longer, before Doc Eckels emerged from the bedroom with his head held low.

Homer eagerly met him in the hallway. "Well?"

The doctor whispered, "He may live, but not because of me. I suspect he may simply be too stubborn to die. He wouldn't have lasted this long otherwise. Regrettably, I could not do anything for his eye. I was, however, able to treat his wounds and force some herbs down his throat, which may be just enough."

Homer rubbed the back of his head. "What can we do?"

"He is exhausted and needs to rest for at least a few days. I hate to ask, but he really shouldn't be moved and …"

Irene snapped, "Of course he can stay here. What kind of people would we be if we put him out like that?"

Doc smiled at her. "Irene, if everyone were as caring as you, I would hardly be needed. But I have to tell you something before you make any decisions."

"Go ahead, Doc," Homer said.

"I recognize your guest from when I practiced in Thasula years ago. He is a very dangerous man and no doubt involved in something very treacherous out here. His name is Simcane, and he is a mercenary. Any man or even group of men who could have done this to him should be considered extremely dangerous. Keeping this man with you may put you in danger."

Irene appeared puzzled and said, "And what would you have us do? Throw him into the streets to die?"

"No, no, ma'am. I only mean to inform you, is all."

"Thank you, Doctor," she said, sounding a tad annoyed. "He will be welcome here as long as he needs."

"I expected nothing less, my friends. Homer, are you still fighting with those fields out here all alone?"

"Of course. Till my dying day, I suspect."

Doc shook his head. "You two be careful. I will check back tomorrow." He reached into his bag. "If he awakens tonight, which I highly doubt, give him this herb, and another in the morning, and each time he eats until they're gone."

Homer held out his open hand. "Thank you for coming out, Doc. We'll see you in the morning." The two men shook hands and Doc Eckels left for home.

CHAPTER 26

THE LAIR OF THE ELDER THREE

For more than a thousand years, the mysterious lair of the Elder Three had sat undisturbed in the center of Thasula near the castle. Very few Epertasians had been allowed entry, and Rasi had not been one of them. For all he knew, his soul would leave his body if he walked uninvited through the doors. But he had little choice. Alina's trail had been cold for days and the mysterious Elder Three may be his last hope.

It made him nervous to be so close to the castle, especially with a fresh target painted on his back, but it was necessary. He hid under his cloak and kept his head down.

A set of double doors stood as tall as the entire front of the building with hoop handles that could fit over Rasi's head. A glimpse around assured him there were no prying eyes as he slipped inside. The dark entryway seemingly stretched on forever despite the building looking no bigger than a quaint cottage from the outside. It smelled old and dingy like he imagined a tomb would smell. His steps left footprints in the dust.

Torches burned with bluish flames along the wall and he wondered what kind of magic fueled them. As he followed the winding hall, his gums began to tingle. The inside of his mouth grew warmer and warmer as he edged farther and farther. A million tiny nerves exploded like swarms of stinging insects dancing between his teeth. The shock sent him to his knees. His saliva turned to cotton as though he'd been lost in the Wastelands without water for days. He licked his suddenly cracked lips, but had no spittle to wet them.

Wait. He licked his lips. *What kind of sorcery is this?* he wondered.

Then he formed his first articulate word in many years, and it was wonderful. "Alina," he said.

He stuck out his tongue and strained with crossed eyes to see it. He stood back up. A slight breeze at his back nudged him forward.

He continued through the hall until he reached another set of doors not quite as large as the main doors. The doors creaked and groaned and opened without his touch, as if someone had been expecting him. He ran his finger along the edge of the door. It was smooth and cold. For the first time in years, his old shoulder wound didn't ache when he moved. He felt young and strong. His next step lifted the hairs on his neck as well as his straps.

"Come in, Rasi," a chorus of voices echoed from within.

He entered what appeared to be his cave on Shadows Peak. He squinted and wrinkled his forehead. They must have seen the confusion in his face because all three of them said in perfect unison, "You only see that which you know best or desire most."

They were identical in every feature, down to the matching wrinkles in their faces and sagging skin on their necks. Their dirty white hair joined their equally dirty beards to brush the stone floor. Their arms were sticks, poking from the drooping sleeves of their robes. Their feet hovered above the ground. When they spoke, they spoke as one. "You seek she who has the Light."

"Yes, I do." He still couldn't believe he was hearing his own voice and hardly recognized it.

They answered though he hadn't asked, "Your missing tongue returns in our home because none who is broken can be so here."

"And these creatures on my back? Why do I still bear them?"

Their answer was crushing and final. "They are not broken. They are part of you."

Rasi stepped forward, confidence growing. "Do you know where Alina is?"

"Ahhhhh," they echoed and trailed off in a hush. "We do not."

Rasi turned away, frustrated. His straps coiled, ready to rip the place apart. "Then am I wasting my time here?" he shouted.

"The Light chose you by choosing her. You must find her before it is too late."

"That's why I came to you. I've lost her trail."

"Go to the town of Parsons. Seek the man with punishment in his name."

"Enough with the riddles. Just tell me who to find and I'll find them and kill them. Please."

"We do not see his name. We cannot tell you that which we do not know. You ..." They paused and looked past him. "You must leave now. You have been seen. You cannot go back the way you came."

Rasi looked over his shoulder. The doors had quietly closed.

In unison, they lifted their fingers and pointed toward a blur of rock on the farthest wall. They said, "You must go through that exit if you hope to survive."

Rasi walked toward the wall, but stopped short, sensing they had more to say.

They added, "Do not come back here uninvited. We cannot promise you will survive our second meeting." They lowered their soulless gazes to the floor while their images faded into little more than ghosts of statues.

Rasi poked the rock wall with his finger and it sank like the wall was made of bread dough. He closed his eyes and took a deep breath, not sure if freedom or pain awaited him. Then he dove at the wall. His stomach turned. But when he opened his eyes, he found himself outside again with his back against the solid wall of the lair.

His mouth tingled, ice-cold this time. He breathed out and dark ashes rose like burning paper from his mouth. And, as quickly as it had come, his tongue was gone again, replaced by familiar emptiness.

Rasi looked around the deserted alley. Just beyond on the main road, soldiers' unattended horses were tied to a trough. He crept to one of them, careful not to be seen. While the soldiers were preoccupied waiting for him to leave through the front of the lair, he leaped onto the horse and fled east.

He had never visited the town of Parsons, though he knew from his pre-Heathen War studies that it was an interesting town. Not one of the men living there had joined the military during the war. King Cecil had once wondered aloud if it was because Parsons was made up of some of the most affluent citizens living in the very same neighborhoods as some of the poorest. Even if the rich wanted to fight, which there had been no indication that they did, they feared leaving their homes to the mercy of the hungry would mean they'd return to nothing. The poor didn't join because they were terrified of giving up their jobs in the warehouse district and having nothing to return to. King Cecil always worried that the poor in Parsons would one day have enough of the inequality and rise up. But they never did. And the royal family could never understand why.

The late hour and holiday season meant few places were open. He passed a crowded pub and kept walking; a busy pub was too risky. A few dark doors farther along sat a small cottage with a single lighted window. As he got closer, he read the sign: Parsons Eatery.

Perfect.

He was hungry, but more importantly, he sought information. If he couldn't find what he needed in the eatery, he'd be forced to take his chances at the pub, and he wasn't too keen on that prospect.

His straps squirmed beneath his cloak. If anyone looked closely enough, they would no doubt see them fidgeting. Rasi spotted a corner booth mostly hidden in shadows. With his hood up and head lowered, he took a seat there.

A waitress delivered a loaf of bread with a glass of warm water. He was weary and happy to fill his belly, even though the bread was hard.

"What do you want?" she asked.

Rasi held up a chunk of bread and shook his head.

"That's it?"

He nodded, his eyes fixed on the table.

"Very well," she said and moved on to the only other customers.

Two men at a center table sipped from their tankards and ordered, "Meat. And lots of it." Their behavior and increased volume left little doubt of what was in the tankards or how long they had been at it.

As if the gods were on Rasi's side, it wasn't long before one of the drunkards ran his mouth. "Did you hear about the commotion out east?" he asked his friend.

His buddy shook his head with a mouthful of meat.

The drunk continued with slurred speech, "You've heard of that mercenary, Simcane?"

His friend nodded.

Rasi's attention piqued. The Elder Three had said to seek a man with punishment in his name. He'd been caned more than once in his youth. It was too good to be a coincidence. All he needed now was for the men to keep talking.

The one drunk continued, "Well, someone roughed him up but good and left him for dead. Two days ago, Doc Eckels was summoned out to some old-timer's farm to treat a stranger who was pretty close to death, the way I hear it."

"And how did you hear it?"

"I don't know. Doc must have told someone who told someone. You know how secrets are around here."

"Why would Simcane be all the way out here? The money's in the big cities."

"Who knows? When was the last time you read a book on how nearly indestructible, psychopathic mercenaries behave?"

"When was the last time I read a book?" They laughed. "I'll tell you this much. I wouldn't want to meet the man who put a whuppin' on that Simcane fella, that's for sure."

Rasi picked up his small bag, dropped a piece of silver on the table, and slipped out the side door largely unnoticed. He waited in the shadow of the alley beside the eatery. He needed more information, but not a commotion.

An hour passed before the two drunkards spilled through the front door into the dark street.

Rasi was on them in a flash. His straps lashed out and lassoed the neck of one before he could shout for help. While the drunkard clawed at the strap, it hoisted him into the air like a hunk of meat dangling on a hook.

Another strap slammed the other drunkard's face, knocking him stiff before he hit the ground. Rasi scanned the street for witnesses. Seeing no one, he dragged his prey into the alley.

The strap lowered the drunkard face-to-face with Rasi. A low rumble emanated from deep inside his chest.

Drop him, he screamed in his head, and the strap unraveled from around the drunk's neck. The man scurried until his back met the wall of the eatery. Rasi moved closer, his straps fanned out around him.

"Wait, wait, wait. What do you want?" the drunk cried.

Rasi knelt and wrote two words in the dirt with his index finger. WHERE SIMCANE

The smell of urine touched his nose. Rasi was disgusted by the man's weakness. No wonder no one in this town had joined the war.

The drunk rambled, seemingly unable to spill his guts fast enough. "Some farm … outside of town. That way." He pointed south. "That's all I know, I swear. Please don't kill me."

Rasi put his finger to his lips. He backed away, looked around again for witnesses, and then disappeared into the shadows.

CHAPTER 27

A FOOL'S ERRAND

During their long, unfruitful search for Rasi through the mountainous region, Tevin's men had grown more skeptical after every failed "lead." The treacherous climb of Widows Run without any payoff made keeping them from mutiny almost impossible. Especially Queen Madelyne's personal bodyguard, Siver, because unlike the others, he wasn't there for gold. Tevin had stalled them for as long as he could before finally leading them to the base of Shadows Peak, which anyone worth their salt should have known was the mountain with the most promise.

Siver knew. He'd always known. His subtle glares when he thought no one was looking told Tevin as much. That he'd let the charade go on for so long was his most surprising failing.

The hairs on Tevin's neck tickled from the building static of a looming storm.

"It's going to get bad," Siver said.

"Yes," Tevin answered. "We should hunker down here, get some sleep, and then head up in the morning. The men are exhausted."

"Whatever." Their mutual disdain for each other briefly knitted their stares together before Tevin turned away. This might be the night he'd have to kill Siver in his sleep.

Still playing the part, Tevin looked past Siver and added, "We may be fighting Rasi real soon."

He started to walk away, but Siver stopped him. "That is what we're doing here, right, Tevin? Looking for Rasi and Alina?"

Brant lifted his eyes from his knapsack.

Tevin smirked. "Of course. Why else would we be here?" He turned back to the others again. "Find some cover and set up camp. These mountain storms can be brutal. As soon as there's a lull in the storm, we'll head up."

At the first drop of rain, Tevin draped his heavy fur over his head. The pupil-constricting flashes of lightning seared his eyes, accompanied by simultaneous deafening thunder. If it was this bad at the base, he could only imagine what it was like higher up.

Then the fist-sized hail began to fall. Tevin found a separate overhang where he could still see his men, especially Siver. With his back against the wall, his knees pulled to his chest, and his fur draped over his forehead, he watched.

As the night passed, the thunder and lightning eventually slowed, though hail still blistered the ground. Tevin lost sight of Siver at some point. Though he fought to stay awake and keep an eye out for the most dangerous man of the bunch, his exhausted mind played games. While convincing himself he could fight sleep, his heavy eyelids betrayed him. The first bob of his head startled him awake. By the second bob he was out cold.

Tevin was nine years old again, shy and friendless. While the other children played on their school break, he hid and put colors to paper like he often did. But soon the older children came looking for him. The bullies always found him. Their first method of torture was to take his doodles. He lunged for them, but the lead bully yanked them out of reach.

"Please, give them back," he begged.

"Two, four, five, six, Tevin's grandma is a witch. Six, five, four, two, Tevin's mother is one, too." One of the kids poked Tevin's ribs with a blunt stick.

"Stop it," he whined.

The lead bully teased, "My mom said your grandma is a freak. *You're* a freak." They all laughed.

"No," he cried. "You lie."

"Are you going to cast a spell on me, witch's kid?"

The bully raised his fists. Tevin always hated the beatings, but not nearly as much as their venomous words. He cowered from the punches that normally followed, but this time the blows didn't come.

"Get away from him," a child's voice said.

The bullies backed away as if called by their mothers. The lead bully stuttered, "Your Highness, w-w-we were just messin' around."

Tevin's savior, the young prince, pushed past the bullies, taking Tevin's drawings back on his way through. He took Tevin by the arm and escorted him through the group to safety. As Tevin passed the other kids with Prince Elijah at his side, he stood a little straighter. He was suddenly untouchable, special—almost brave. That was a new feeling for him.

Elijah examined his drawings with a smile. "You're very good at pictures," he said. "You're safe now. The others won't bother you anymore. What's your name?"

"Tevin, Your Highness. Tevin the Third."

"Call me Elijah. You can sit with me tomorrow while we eat."

"Thank you."

"Prince Elijah," a pretty young girl called. When Elijah looked over, she blushed and turned to her giggling friends.

"Coming, Madelyne," Elijah answered.

Tevin looked down to see Elijah's extended hand. He shook it.

"What do you think they want?" Elijah asked.

Tevin had no idea; as far as he knew, none of the girls even knew his name, much less called him over before.

"It's a pleasure meeting you, Tevin." Elijah turned and ran toward the group of girls. They squealed and ran off, so he chased them.

The daylight started to darken as though the suns were dying. The playground faded before his eyes until it and all the kids were lost in nothingness.

Paralyzed by fear, Tevin stared into the black where the face of a tiny skull, almost too small to see, appeared in the distance. It grew larger as it floated toward him. Another one appeared at his side, startling him. Then another. At first, he thought they might belong to the bullies. "What do you want?" he whispered.

The skeletal faces answered with screeches of pain that hurt his ears. Covering them did no good.

One by one the skulls shot toward him like arrows before just as quickly pulling away. Though he somehow knew he was dreaming, he couldn't wake himself like he could with other night terrors. Maybe this one was different because Siver had finally opened his neck and this was the other side.

One of the skulls hovered in front of him again, appearing out of nowhere. "Teeeeevinnnnn," it moaned with a strangely familiar voice before fading back out of sight.

"We're coming, my little warrior," the skull to his left whispered. *Little warrior?* "Grandma?" he asked. "Is it you?"

Another skull shot out of the darkness. "It's your tiiiimmmme," it screeched.

Something nudged his ribs. He brushed the annoying offender away, but it nudged him again, only harder. He opened his eyes.

Siver stood over him and was about to kick him again. "Hey," Siver shouted.

"What?"

"You were dreaming or something. It's time to go. The storm's broke."

Tevin's sweat-soaked clothes clung to him. He parted his matted hair away from his eyes. It was dawn. The men were already packed up and waiting. Tevin gathered his pack, strapped his sword to his waist, and joined his men at the base of the mountain path.

The trail was barely wide enough for a horse. "We should leave our horses here," Tevin said. "We don't want them getting spooked and taking us over the edge."

Siver nodded. They tied their horses to a tree and started up the mountain on foot. Tevin walked alone ahead of the group. Siver's rotten morning breath announced his approach from behind. "This is it for me," he whispered. "I'm done with your games. If we don't find Rasi today, I am on my own."

Tevin focused on the path. One wrong step could be fatal.

Siver trailed him closely. He whispered, "If you've wasted our time and the princess has been harmed, I will report your incompetence to the queen at once … Or I'll simply kill you myself."

With his back still to Siver, Tevin smirked and then hastened his march. They were close now.

The air grew thinner the higher they climbed. Brant struggled to keep up and stopped with his hands braced on his knees. "Hold on," he huffed. "I need to catch my breath."

Tevin didn't slow. He only shouted back, "Then you will be left behind."

CHAPTER 28

A CANING

Homer sat reading his favorite author in his favorite wicker rocking chair on his front porch. By habit, his middle finger pushed his reading spectacles with the broken right arm back up his nose for the fiftieth time.

Little did he know, Irene had been watching from her rocking chair on the other side of the porch for the last forty-nine. "Will you just get a new pair of spectacles, already?" she groaned.

"Why would I do that? These are fine. They don't bother me."

"Well, they're driving me nuts." She huffed, shoved her yarn and needles into her knitting basket, and got up. "It's getting chilly," she said. "I'm going inside."

Homer sat wondering how he could have messed up so badly by just reading his book. "I'll be in shortly," he answered.

He shivered and wrapped his blanket tighter around his shoulders. He surveyed the landscape for any signs of movement. Two days had passed since Doc told him about his guest, and he had been unable to sleep more than a few winks since. He dreaded the possibility of such a big fella waking in anger, so much so that an old rusty knife sat on a flimsy table at his side. Every so often he peeked at it just to make sure it was still there.

Homer had many doubts about keeping such a fearsome hulk in their home, but when he hinted they should send him elsewhere, like a hospital, Irene made her compassionate opinion clear. So, with no other real option, he was afraid that sleep would elude him until the mercenary was on his way.

"Honey?" Irene shook him. "Honey?"

Homer sprang from his chair and fumbled for his knife, knocking it to the warped wooden floor. "What is it?" He blinked the sleep from his eyes.

"Our guest is awake," she said. "I'm sorry for startling you." She went back into the house while Homer gathered himself, rubbed his eyes, and then picked up his knife from the floor. He folded it onto itself and stuffed it into his front pocket.

Irene stood at the end of the hall in the doorway to the bedroom where Simcane slept. Homer squeezed past her. The headboard was mostly hidden behind Simcane's back and the sagging mattress appeared moments from failure.

Simcane's voice was dry and scratchy when he asked, "Where am I?" Homer was shocked at how gentle he sounded.

Irene stepped past Homer and Homer reached for her shoulder. "Don't get too close, honey," he said.

She glared back at him and mouthed, "Stop it," before sitting on the edge of the bed beside Simcane's legs. "You're with friends," she said.

He looked around the room with uncertainty.

"How do you feel?" she asked, gently touching his hand.

"Tired," he answered.

"Are you thirsty?"

"Very much so." He licked his cracked lips as if the mere mention of a drink had subconsciously directed his tongue. "Do you have any ale?"

"I could get you some water."

He nodded. "Water would be fine." His stomach rumbled.

Irene smiled. "I'll make some breakfast, too." She mouthed to Homer, "Be nice," as she passed, and squeezed his forearm for emphasis.

Homer leaned against the doorframe and stared through tired, bloodshot eyes at the hulk of a man. "I've heard about you," he said.

Simcane raised an eyebrow.

"I've heard what you do. For a living, I mean."

"Is that so?" Simcane scratched the back of his head. "Everyone needs to get by."

"I need you to tell me something with honesty." He looked down the hall to make sure Irene wasn't within earshot. "Are my wife and I in danger?"

Simcane stretched his arms above his head with a grimace and a moan. "Not from me."

He tried to swing his legs over the edge of the bed, but then he winced, coughed, and lay back against the headboard.

Homer put his hand on the big man's shoulder. He felt guilty for his apprehension and prejudices. "Relax," he said. "You don't need to go anywhere right now. You're our guest and you need to rest." Homer leaned against the doorframe again. "So, what's it like mercenary … ing?"

"Keeps me in ale."

"You know, when I was younger, I considered selling my sword for a living. I was pretty nimble for my size. In fact—"

"Homer," Irene called from the kitchen. "Could you help me carry?"

"Be right there." Homer leaned closer to Simcane. "We'll pick this up later."

Simcane closed his eye.

In the kitchen, Irene handed him a tray with a plate holding a huge pile of eggs, potatoes, and two slices of ham. She grabbed a glass of water and started down the hall.

Homer trailed her. "You didn't make such a good meal for me yesterday morning."

She glanced back. "Stop it. You said you weren't hungry." As she walked, she added, "Don't go talking our guest's ear off, either."

Homer hesitated. "What are you talking about?"

"You know what I mean." She reached the doorway to Simcane's bedroom and flinched, dropping the glass of water. She covered her mouth.

Homer shoved the tray of food at her and squeezed past. A stranger sat in the corner chair beside the open window next to Simcane's bed. The ceiling crawled with blood-red tentacles unlike anything Homer had ever seen. With a cautious eye on the tentacles, Homer stepped forward, as any man would, to protect his home.

"Who are you?" he shouted as he dug into his pocket for his knife. He fumbled to get it open and pointed at the stranger. "Why are you in my house?"

"Wait," Simcane shouted.

But it was too late. One of the straps lashed out, swatting the knife from Homer's hand with enough force to knock him into the dresser.

The intruder stood up, shooting Homer an intimidating glare.

Simcane motioned for Homer to stay where he was. "Rasi? Is that you?" he asked.

The stranger nodded once.

Simcane sighed. "Stay calm, Homer. I don't think Rasi is here for you." Then he asked Rasi, "You ever think of knocking?"

Rasi stood silent.

"You know you've scared these poor people to death."

Rasi's stone face didn't change.

Simcane shook his head. "It's been a long time since I've seen you. Not since the war, I believe."

Rasi nodded again.

"Are you looking for Princess Alina, as I am?"

Rasi nodded a third time.

"I didn't think you were one for mercenary work."

Rasi stared, emotionless.

"Well, I think I almost found her. If she hasn't been moved yet, I think she is in the Lactnee building in the warehouse district. Give me a moment to get dressed and I'll go with you."

Rasi walked toward Homer, who stepped in front of Irene. Simcane swung his legs over the edge of the bed and grimaced again.

Rasi ignored him as he continued through the doorway and into the hall. Simcane shouted after him, "Those savages keeping guard over her aren't to be taken lightly, my old friend. There are at least three of them and they are as hard as iron."

The front door slammed. Homer rushed into Simcane's room with Irene on his heels. She rubbed her shoulders and hurried to close the window.

"You have just met the legendary Rasi," Simcane said. "As you can see, he is a man of few words."

Something sparkled on the chair where Rasi had sat. Irene picked it up.

"What is it?" Homer asked.

"Silver? Two bits?" she answered.

CHAPTER 29

THE DAY OF CHANGE

Alina awakened on her moldy mattress, gaunt and hungry. The natural hue of her skin was long gone, replaced by a sickly tone. She had developed a deep, unproductive cough, left three fingernails lodged in the walls, and could no longer tell how long she had been in the hole. Her only indication that it might be night was whenever the lifesaving colorfuls returned.

The small chunks of raw deer and squank rarely dropped into the pit weren't enough to sustain her for long. She had lost any hope of being rescued.

Blogg stood at the edge of the pit. "Tonight's your night, Princess," he shouted. He tossed an animal leg down that, like previous meals, was more bone than meat. More than anything, she didn't want to give him the satisfaction of seeing her desperation, but she was starving. She snatched the meat from the ground. While he watched her with sick pleasure, she threw a fresh piece of wood onto her glowing embers.

With each puff from her cheeks, the embers grew brighter, a small but wonderful flame taking hold of the wood. As she piled the last remaining chunks of wood onto the fire, the flames flared into warmth.

She put the bone in the fire and waited impatiently for the meat to cook. With a small stick, she raked her feast out of the flames to the floor. She almost burned her lips as she ripped a chunk away with her teeth. Three bites. That's all she got. It did little to ease her hunger.

"How was your last meal?" Blogg shouted.

She hurled the bone across the pit.

Cyn appeared beside him. "It's time," she said.

Alina's skin crawled.

Blogg disappeared and then returned with a wooden ladder that he dropped into the pit. Alina backed against the opposite wall. He climbed down first, followed by Cyn.

"Go ahead and get her, Blogg," Cyn said.

Alina screamed, "Stay away from me, monster," and flailed at his face and chest. She wanted to scratch his eyes out, but she wasn't strong enough.

He continued to laugh while clutching both of her wrists in one hand. As he lifted her from the ground, she kicked his groin, but he seemed not to notice her weak assault. He threw her over his shoulder.

"Quit playing with her, Blogg," Cyn said.

Blogg carried her up the ladder while she kicked and thrashed to no avail.

The pit opened into a well-lit room. Alina squinted and tried to shield her eyes with her hand. Blogg lowered her onto a table. The metal slab was like ice on her back through the thin rags she wore. He held one of her hands down while she clawed at his face with the other. He shook away her fingers like a dog about to sneeze. Cyn tied her wrist to the table with some kind of pliable metal band. Alina tugged against it, but it dug into her wrists until she couldn't stand the pain. She tried to kick Blogg while he tied down her other arm, but her attempts were worthless. He moved to her legs and held them down while Cyn cinched restraints on them as well.

Scorne appeared by her head. His ugly face interrupted her view of the ceiling. "Hi, P-P-P-Princess," he hissed. An oozing sore on his cheek leaked milky pus. "You are in for a s-s-surprise tonight."

"Please," she begged. "Let me go. I will give you anything you want."

"What could you possibly offer me that my current employer couldn't?"

"I am to be queen, future ruler of the free world. I have unlimited resources, riches beyond your dreams."

"Used to be f-f-future ruler," he said with a cackle.

Alina turned her head from his decaying breath. She was in a dungeon, or a basement. She could see no windows, only a stairwell in the far corner. She wondered how deep beneath the world's surface she actually was.

Is someone above us? Will they hear my screams?

No, Scorne answered inside her head. She'd forgotten he could do that too. She considered screaming just in case, but didn't think she had the strength.

Scorne called out, "It is time. Come out and f-f-f-finish this. I grow tired of her whining."

She whipped her head from side to side until she saw a shadow emerge from the stairwell. She screamed, "Who are you?"

The figure stepped into the light. Her heart shattered.

"Alina, don't be afraid."

"Father?"

Elijah approached the table, his face twisted with pain. He looked like a man who carried the world on his shoulders, and someone had just piled another world on top of it. He glared at Scorne. "What have you done to her?"

"Your Majesty, she was a terrible prisoner. I d-d-did everything I could just t-t-t-to keep her alive."

Cyn came down the stairs. Alina hadn't seen her go up. "The suns are growing black," she shouted.

"You must d-d-do it now," Scorne insisted.

A tear ran down to Elijah's chin and then dripped onto the table beside Alina. "I am sorry for doing this, Alina. I love you more than the world, as did your mother."

"Sorry? What are you going to do? Father?"

He drew a knife from his waistband.

"Father, no. Why?"

Scorne grabbed her cheeks. Slobber dripped from his lower lip. "You s-s-s-stupid wench. Don't you see? Your greedy father doesn't want to give up the throne just yet. That means you have to d-d-d-d-die. Just like his parents before you."

"What? What does he mean, Father?"

Elijah answered, "I've done things in my past that I'm not proud of. Over the years I have tried to make amends, but I can never erase what I've done."

"You can now. You don't have to do this."

"It'll all be over soon." He raised the knife over his head with both hands gripping the hilt. Scorne stared into her eyes as if waiting with sick pleasure to see the life going out of them. He licked his lips and then dragged his sleeve across them.

Alina closed her eyes. "Please, Father, don't do this." She strained one last futile time against her restraints.

Scorne shouted, "What are you waiting for? Do it now or I—" A grunt replaced his words.

She opened her eyes. Scorne's grin faded into something that would be worthy of pity if it wasn't on such a monster. He grasped his side and staggered away from the table. His metal skin scurried to cover a bloody wound.

Confused, she turned her head to her father. Blood dripped from the blade he held at his side. His face was full of infinite sadness. "I could never hurt you, Alina. I think I knew that all along ..." He hesitated. "At least, I hope I did."

With one hand on the table, Scorne glared at him. He cocked his head, licked his red fingers, and then snarled at the taste of his own blood. Elijah lifted his blade in defiance.

"I s-s-see fear in you, coward," Scorne said. Metal slithered around his knuckles. He pounced, heaving his fist forward. Elijah drew back his blade, but Scorne was too fast.

Alina screamed, "No."

Scorne connected with Elijah's cheek, sending the king sprawling to the ground. She heard her father's knife—his only chance—slide across the floor beneath the table.

She stretched her neck so she could see him. He scrambled across the floor on his hands and knees.

"Come back here and face me," Scorne said as he stalked him across the floor.

Elijah sprang to his feet as Scorne closed in. Elijah punched him, but shattered his own knuckles against Scorne's metal-coated jaw. The metal on Scorne's arm pooled at his elbow and extended into a hardened point. Alina screamed for her father. Elijah reached for Scorne's throat, catching only air as the symbiot spun. Scorne's elbow plunged into its target, sinking between Elijah's ribs. Elijah froze. The determination on his face changed into hopelessness. Elijah's chin dropped onto Scorne's shoulder.

Scorne leaned his head back and kissed Elijah's cheek.

"Please," Alina cried.

Scorne twisted his elbow, eliciting pained grunts from Elijah. Then he ripped the weapon free.

Alina cried out.

Scorne stepped away and Elijah dropped to his knees. *I'm sorry, Alina,* he whispered in her mind. *Be strong, my little butterfly.*

"I can hearrrr you," Scorne said in a sing-song voice. He shoved Elijah to his back and straddled him.

"I'm getting good at killing kings," he said.

Alina cried as she watched helplessly.

Scorne cocked his metal-coated fist back and hammered Elijah with it. Elijah's feet bounced from the ground with each blow until they lay flat and twitching. Scorne didn't stop. Alina looked to the ceiling, trying to tune out the heart-wrenching sounds without success.

Cyn and Blogg surrounded Scorne and Elijah to watch.

When the sounds of the beating ended and Alina built enough courage to look at her father again, she saw what no daughter should have to see. Elijah lay on his back, breathing in shallow, rapid gasps. Blood bubbled from his ruined mouth and nose with each dying wheeze. He choked and coughed, sending blood spitting into the air. Scorne was nowhere to be seen.

"Monster," Alina sobbed. She turned her head away from her father's broken body. Scorne startled her, standing smiling at her side. He raised his knuckles to his lips and licked them, staining his tongue bright red. He took a deep, quivering breath and his lips trembled. His eyes rolled back into his head and his body shivered in apparent ecstasy. *No death is quite as sweet as that of a king's.* He turned toward Alina. *Except maybe a princess.* He flashed his yellow teeth.

Something heavy crashed to the floor above, followed by someone screaming in anger. Scorne looked to the ceiling and tilted his head.

Alina followed his eyes. She took a chance. *Rasi? Is that you?*

CHAPTER 30

NOTHING &
EVERYTHING

Rasi stood outside of the Lactnee warehouse. The streets were empty. The suns grew black as if in the throes of an eclipse. He wasn't trying to hide, abandoning stealth entirely. He was there for blood, and if his enemy saw him, it made little difference.

The doorway had three pieces of waterlogged wood stretched across it with bright new nails holding them. Rasi yanked the wood from the frame.

It was dead inside. The mostly empty warehouse smelled of glue and chemicals and faint whiffs of burned wood, even after all those years. The interior was colossal, much larger than the exterior fascia would lead one to believe. Bird nests littered the open rafters. A small bird, maybe a sparrow, dove for Rasi's head and swooshed past in a rush for the outside.

The ceiling was more hole than roof, allowing the rapidly dimming sunlight to cast plaid patterns onto broken-down coal-burning machines. He couldn't believe no one was here; he'd thought he was so close.

It was empty.

It was a dead-end.

It was over.

He slouched, defeated, and dropped to his knees on the soggy wood. He had no other leads. He pictured Alina's face, hoping whatever foul acts her kidnappers had subjected her to were quick and painless.

The mere thought of her suffering laced his despair with frustration and building anger. He would find whoever had hurt her and return that pain on them a hundredfold. Growing rage pushed him back to his feet. He shed his cumbersome cloak, exposing his bloodthirsty straps. They lashed out, overturning one of the massive coal-burning machines. He ground his teeth and flexed his muscles eagerly. His rage poured out of him with a roar that reverberated through the vacant warehouse.

As he struggled to calm his quivering breaths, he heard the most wonderful voice in his mind.

Rasi? Is that you?

Alina? He was suddenly breathless.

It wasn't empty.

It wasn't over.

She was near.

Where are you?

By the gods, she answered. *I don't know. I'm in a dungeon. Or ... or ... a basement.*

Someone else answered in Rasi's head. *Yes, Rasi. We are in the basement. Come see us.*

Old wooden crates lined the walls. *Where is the door?* He crashed his fist through a stack of crates and then kicked them into splinters. "Aaaaaahhhhh," he screamed, loud enough that the gods must have heard.

Almost at the brink of insanity, he saw the faintest speck of brass between the crates stacked against the farthest wall. The dim lighting struck it perfectly as if beckoning him. It was a doorknob. And it was everything.

I'm coming, my love.

Rasi's straps ripped away the crates. He crashed through the door, tearing it from its hinges.

The one called Blogg stood at the bottom of the staircase. Rasi's chest heaved. He had hoped for a second shot at his big foe. Blogg drew his broadsword.

"I got him, Cyn," the lummox said.

From atop the stairs, Rasi scanned the room for more threats. The woman stood across the room, poised to attack. Her eyes flicked to the side, and Rasi followed her line of sight. That's when he saw Elijah lying in a bloody mess in the corner. Why was he there?

Then he saw Alina lying half-naked on a table like a sacrifice. Rasi's rage burned even hotter. *I will kill you all.*

He marched down the stairs, darting his eyes from Blogg to Cyn to Scorne then back to Blogg again.

The lummox backed away slightly. Maybe it was to let Rasi get to even ground, or maybe he saw something in Rasi that he hadn't seen when first they met at the Forest of Concore, and it gave him pause. Whatever it was that made Blogg back away, it didn't matter. Caution wouldn't help him now.

There wasn't time for posturing. Rasi leaped from the middle of the staircase. Blogg swung his sword like a lumberjack with an axe, but Rasi's straps entangled his arms, shunting his swing aside. They twisted until the big man's sword fell from his hands. Rasi's momentum slammed him into Blogg's chest, but the monster didn't move.

It was at that moment that Rasi realized his mistake. Damn him for letting his rage control him. He knew better. Blogg wrapped his vice-like arms around him. Rasi's straps engulfed the villain's powerful upper body and constricted. One of them slithered around his throat, but his metal skin hardened beneath it. What Rasi wouldn't give to have a healthy Simcane along right now.

Cyn leaped from behind. A strap caught her in the chest, flinging her into the staircase. Rasi glanced at Scorne, who stood at Alina's side. For the moment, the murderous freak appeared more concerned with Rasi than with her. That was all Rasi could ask for.

Blogg squeezed so hard Rasi feared his spine would snap. He tried to take a breath, but there was no room for his chest to expand. The straps tightened around Blogg's chest, but as Rasi weakened, so did they.

Rasi drew his arms back and clapped his hands against Blogg's ears, but the behemoth hardly flinched. Unable to catch his breath, Rasi dropped his chin onto Blogg's bulky shoulder. He scanned the room for some kind of advantage and found one. It was Blogg's sword waiting on the floor like a gift from the gods.

Rasi concentrated on his straps, praying they would listen. He closed his eyes and envisioned his straps grabbing the weapon. *Concentrate.*

By some miracle, they listened, or at least one of them did. It unraveled and reached toward the blade, which lay just out of reach. Rasi wheezed as he tried to inhale. The strap strained and stretched less than a hand-length away. Rasi struggled to lift his head. It was no use.

But then another strap shot toward the stone stairwell behind him and stiffened, pushing against it. Blogg stumbled backward just enough for the other strap to curl around the sword.

Exhausted, Rasi let his arms collapse to his sides. He heard Cyn giggle from her new spectator perch on the stairs.

Rasi summoned his last bit of strength. What he was about to do was going to hurt. A lot. He jerked his head back and then drove it forward. At the same time, his strap swung the sword hilt toward the back of Blogg's skull. Blogg's metal splotches scrambled to defend his forehead. Rasi's head collided with the metal, ripping a gash across his own brow, while the strap bashed the back of Blogg's unprotected skull with the hilt. Rasi wished it had been the blade. Blogg's cocky grin morphed into a surprised grimace. He loosened his hold and Rasi fell to his back. Blogg staggered and dropped to his knees.

Cyn dove from the stairs, not waiting to see how her partner recovered. Metal slid down her arm and pooled into a razor-sharp edge from her elbow to her wrist. She was fast, too fast, and before Rasi could react, she slipped past his straps, slicing his back while they grabbed air.

Rasi grunted, his back burning like fire. Cyn circled around for another lightning pass. His straps lunged blindly, entangling her legs and crashing her head-first into the stairs.

Rasi turned back to Blogg, who swayed on his knees. Cyn bounced to her feet. Three of Rasi's straps hovered and hissed while she stalked side to side, looking for an opening. The straps mirrored her movements.

This was Rasi's only chance.

Blogg stared past him with blank eyes. He rubbed the back of his head and his hand returned bloody.

Rasi reached into his waistband at the small of his back, drawing a dagger with an emerald on the hilt.

"Blooooogg," Cyn shrieked. She leaped at Rasi, but his straps enveloped her like a spider's web. She thrashed to free herself, slashing and stabbing with her metal skin. The straps paid the price, but they held firm.

Blogg's metal skin scurried over his body as if unsure of where to defend. The strap still holding Blogg's sword swung around again and slammed it into Blogg's side. The metal successfully deflected the blow, but left other areas exposed. Rasi plunged Alina's dagger into his chest.

The hulking monster let out a wail. Cyn echoed him, and the straps hurled her back against the stairwell.

The symbiot crumpled into a heap. Rasi reached for the blade, but Blogg's metal skin liquefied and pooled into a silver puddle near his feet. Rasi stepped back and the glob followed him. Leaving the dagger, Rasi retreated as the silver liquid released a high-pitched squeal then hardened and corroded to a brownish hue.

"Keep him busy," Scorne shouted to Cyn. Then he turned to Alina.

Cyn babbled angrily in some kind of heathen language. Her metal skin pooled along both her arms and legs, rose from her skin, and melded into razor edges. She pounced. Rasi's straps met her attack. She hurled herself recklessly into their web, swinging and slicing indiscriminately at them. Blood sprayed from some of them while the others grew more hesitant.

I'll rip out your throat, murderer, she screamed in Rasi's head.

Her flailing got her close enough to land a surprising punch on his cheek. It felt like he'd been hit by a horseshoe. His ears rang and vibrated through the back of his head. His legs went limp momentarily and he tumbled backward. Two of his straps braced against the floor to stop his fall and then pitched him back to his feet.

Cyn swung again, but Rasi crouched beneath it and drove his fist upward. She was too focused on attacking to see it coming. He struck her chin. It was a beautiful sound. She dropped. His straps grabbed her feet and slung her across the floor to hit the wall.

Rasi turned to Alina.

CHAPTER 31

A CHANGE BORN OF FIRE

As the battle between her lover and her captor raged, Alina wrenched her neck to see her father lying in his own blood. His legs no longer quivered, and his chest barely moved. She turned her head toward Scorne.

The freak still held his side, blood leaking through his fingers. He started to collapse, but caught his elbows on the table, just managing to keep himself upright.

"Your coward dad cut me deep," he said. Unable to hold himself up any longer, he dropped to his knees and bounced his chin on the sharp edge of the table. "Umph," he grunted, and spat out the tip of his tongue. He slumped out of Alina's sight.

She heard him gag and then what sounded like a bucket of water splashed onto the floor. "I hope it hurts, murderer," she said.

His hand plopped onto the table with Elijah's blade. He pulled himself up again, fresh blood dripping from his mouth. "Keep him busy," he shouted to Cyn. "Is that your savior?" he asked Alina. "The one called Rasi?" He laughed, then coughed, then grimaced.

She turned away, but he kept talking. "You should be more p-p-p-particular in your choice of heroes."

He leaned over her to see her face. Blood dripped onto her cheek. As Cyn leaped from the stairwell at Rasi, Scorne whispered into her ear. "Oh, my dear Princess, you d-d-d—You d-d-don't know. The one you know as Rasi is no savior at all. In fact, he helped me when

I k-killed your g-g-g-g—" He paused, took a frustrated breath, and then tried again. "Your g-g-grandparents."

"I have little doubt that their murderers were you and your friends."

"Oh yesssss. I do not d-d-deny my most b-brilliant work. I only feel it prudent that you know about your so-called savior's p-p-part in it. That night, he b-b-battled the guards so I could slaughter the king and queen."

You lie. Rasi would never.

"Ah, yes, Princess. You should ask him about that n-n-n-night. If your end wasn't so near, that is."

She failed to hold back a tear, surprised she had any tears left at all.

"Now I will be k-k-king," he whispered, and let out a crazed giggle.

Rasi slung Cyn against the wall and ran toward Alina, but he was too far away.

She turned her head to look at her father's broken body. Scorne raised his blade into the air.

Elijah's final breath sucked all the air out of the room. Scorne hesitated. And then, as suddenly as the air had left, it exploded back with a blinding inferno. The fire engulfed everyone. Alina braced for the scorching pain that was sure to follow. But instead of burning, every nerve in her tired body tingled as the fire passed through her soul. She opened her eyes to an exquisite wall of dancing orange and black flames. Everything seemed so calm and beautiful.

Scorne recoiled and Rasi fell to his knees and covered his face with his arms as the flames consumed him.

"Rasi," she cried.

As quickly as the flames appeared, they dissipated, sucking back into the basement walls. Rasi rubbed his eyes. He was alive.

Rasi, get up, she screamed in his head.

He looked at her with dull eyes.

Scorne wobbled next to the table, having not yet recovered his senses either. He reached out blindly with his knife hanging from his hand.

Rasi shook his head and then charged. He grabbed the wrist of Scorne's knife hand and pulled it down while driving his other hand against Scorne's elbow. It snapped. Scorne howled and pulled his injured arm away, his knife clanging to the stone floor.

Rasi tackled him beside the table. The pair hit the ground, and all Alina could see were Rasi's straps flailing. The sound of flesh striking flesh reached her.

Cyn shot past the table carrying a lead pipe.

"Rasi, look out," Alina screamed.

Alina heard a sickening thud followed by a grunt. "Nooo," she screamed. Cyn squatted and lifted Scorne, cradled in her arms. She carried him up the stairs.

Rasi? Alina pleaded. *Answer me, please.*

Rasi's hand thudded onto the table next to her head. *I'm here, darling. Just a little woozy.*

He pulled himself to his feet, wobbling as if drunk. *I've gotta catch them. I can't let them escape.* His hand slipped and he hit his shoulder on the table. *I'm all right,* he told her. *Just need the room to stop spinning.*

"You can't go after them like that. You need to free me."

Rasi vomited beside the table. One of the straps gently caressed Alina's cheek.

She smiled at it. "Let me up," she said.

Rasi ducked down and then returned with Scorne's knife. Leaning heavily on the table, he moved around it to free her arms and legs. She sat up and wrapped her weak arms around him. "I love you," she said. "Are you all right?"

He nodded. He might have been lying.

"Rasi, I need to see my father. Are you sure you're all right?"

He motioned for her to go ahead.

She climbed from the table and ran to her bloody, broken father.

"Father? Please don't die," she cried, and wrapped her arms around his neck. She rocked back and forth, holding his head to her bosom, weeping. "I love you, Father. Why did you do this? I didn't even want your throne."

Rasi staggered to her side and used her shoulder to keep from falling. *I'm in no condition to fight,* he said. *We need to get you to safety before they come back.*

"I can't leave his body here."

He tried to kill you, Alina.

She looked up with teary eyes. "He's still my father," she snapped.

She pressed her forehead to her father's and sobbed.

Please, Rasi said. *We have to leave.*

She pulled her head back and stared at her father. "I love you, Daddy." She kissed his cheek and slowly lowered his head back to the ground. Her legs shook when she stood, and Rasi grabbed her. She didn't know if he was helping her or if she was helping him.

Together they struggled up the stairs. Rasi grabbed his cloak and wrapped it around her shoulders. Then he checked for enemies outside the door. With the streets clear, they hobbled to where Rasi had stashed his horse. *I know where we can go. It'll be safe until I can return you to Thasula.* They rode south.

CHAPTER 32

BIRTH OF A
WIZARD

evin and his band of mercenaries quietly approached what was believed to be Rasi's cave. "Once inside, fan out," he ordered. He played the part well as he drew his sword, knowing all along that Rasi wouldn't be there. "Prepare for battle. Rasi is a hardened soldier and will not be taken easily."

The smell of mold wafted from the cave ahead of them. Ink bled into the suns. It was happening.

Siver ignored Tevin and pushed past him. "Rasi," he shouted. "Come out and surrender."

The cave was dark and empty, just as Tevin had expected. Tevin's torch highlighted a wall where thousands of vertical lines were etched in meticulous columns. Siver ran his finger along one of them. "A long time to be out here alone."

Cold, gray ashes and a chunk of rotten meat littered a fire pit at the cave's center. At the back, thick spider webs stretched from ceiling to floor, forming a curtain that proved no one had ventured deeper in a long time.

"Damn," Tevin said.

He sensed Siver step behind him. The mood had shifted. The others watched the two men with uneasy stares. They would have to be blind not to see what was happening now.

Siver cleared his throat. "Why are we here?" he snarled. "It's not for Rasi, so what is it?"

Tevin gripped the hilt of his sword. With the suns now completely black, the torches were all the light they had. Tevin expected to see skulls again. He looked down at Siver's hand; Siver had already partially drawn his sword. He backed away toward the webs.

"What does he mean, Tevin?" Brant asked.

The game was up. "You are all very stupid, you know?" Tevin started to pace, eyes trained on Siver. "Siver's right. We have not been searching for Princess Alina or Rasi at all."

Siver's upper lip curled. Brant moved to block the cave's mouth.

Tevin continued. "Elijah knew there would be much outcry for Alina to be found. We had to satisfy the masses by hunting for Rasi so that the plan could proceed. You don't even know how hard it was for me to continue parading you all around these mountains like babies. Every passing moment, I expected one of you to have an original thought, but you never questioned me. Why would we go to Widows Run before Shadows Peak? My gods, you're idiots."

He pointed the torch at Siver. "And you. Why did you play along all this time? You disappoint me. The great Siver. My gods. I mean, I can see the others ignoring the obvious since gold was involved. But you?" He shook the torch. "When the queen ordered me to take you along, Elijah and I couldn't have been more ecstatic. We laughed at everyone's blindness. Elijah knew you would not rest until you found Alina, and the queen removed you from the game for us. I was going to kill you in your sleep before we left, but this is better."

"Then why didn't you kill me after we left? You've had plenty of chances."

"I figured a good swordsman would be valuable against the creatures we might encounter, so I let you live. I wanted to kill you last night, but I fell asleep before you."

"What's your endgame?" Siver asked, venom oozing from his voice.

"Why, that's simple. It's for Elijah to remain king, of course. The suns' very blackness reveals that the prophecy is being fulfilled as we speak. Alina will die so that Elijah may continue to rule."

Brant cleared his throat. "Should I kill him now, Tevin?" he asked.

Siver peered over his shoulder. "You're a part of this too, Brant?"

Brant shrugged.

Tevin smiled. The other soldiers backed up against the wall. Everything was changing so fast that they didn't know which side to choose.

Brant readied his sword, not nearly as tired as he had pretended earlier. Like a good warrior, Siver backed toward the wall so he could keep an eye on both of them.

Brant attacked, impatient and eager. Siver engaged him in a spark-inducing battle lasting mere moments and ending with Brant's head on the cave floor.

Siver shouted, "The queen will double your reward for Tevin's treacherous head." That did it. The others crowded alongside him, blocking Tevin's escape.

Siver grinned. "I guess you should have chosen a better warrior as your ally, Tevin."

Tevin looked to Brant's head on the floor. "I suppose you're right."

Siver nodded toward him. "Kill the traitor," he said.

The men stepped toward Tevin with murder in their eyes, swords in their grips. Tevin's back met the wall of webs.

He lifted his hilt defensively above his shoulder with the blade draped across his chest. They mimicked him as they methodically closed in.

Tevin considered himself an average warrior at best, and it had been a mistake to assume Brant's skills would match the now headless mercenary's bravado. This was going to be a tough fight.

One of the soldiers pounced. Tevin's blade clanged against his. The next soldier used the opening to attack. Tevin retreated into the webs.

A low rumble lifted from the cave floor like the start of a mountain quake, freezing them all in their tracks.

Siver shouted, "Ignore it. Just kill Tevin before it's too late."

The rumble grew into a thunderous roar like another mountain storm within the cave. The noise was deafening. The men shoved their hands over their ears.

And then, as quickly as the thunder began, complete silence replaced it. All Tevin could hear was his own heart beating. No one moved. He felt a slight tickle of air on the back of his neck. His ears clogged.

With a sudden, violent explosion of heat at his back, the air and spider webs were sucked from the cave. The soldiers' torches snuffed, leaving only a sliver of light from the edges of the suns. Tevin planted his feet against the surge, his long hair tickling his cheeks. The vacuum stole everyone's breath.

His panicked opponents grabbed their throats as they stumbled against the cave walls. Tevin told himself that he only needed to be calm and endure. The stories of the Change said it would happen fast.

The air returned with a blast of all-encompassing flames, bursting into the cave as if breathed from a dragon's snout. Tevin turned away, but the fire was everywhere. It enveloped him, only it didn't burn. Siver and the others dropped their swords and fell to their knees with their hands shielding their eyes.

"It is done," Tevin shouted, his voice strong and godlike over the oven roar. "The Light shall never leave Elijah, and I will stand at his side forever."

"What have you done, traitor?" Siver yelled.

The flames tingled beneath Tevin's flesh. Siver stood up after realizing they didn't burn. The others continued to cower.

And then the inferno was sucked from the cave and the black ink drained from the suns. Tevin and Siver locked eyes.

Tevin's blood boiled within his veins. He dropped his sword and stared at his open palms. Something was wrong. His face grew feverish. The left side of his brain went numb. His tongue swelled until it seemed too fat for his mouth. As drool trickled from the corners of his lips, he realized he was powerless to stop it. He made a fist with his right hand, though he had no strength. He tried to lift his fist, but was unable to raise it above his waist. He tried to take a step and his right leg dragged along the dirt.

What is wrong with me? Why doesn't Siver attack? Instead, the warrior stepped backward as if afraid.

Tevin dropped his chin to his chest. A faint orange glow emanated through his clothes. The soldiers, still on their knees, crawled backward like they'd seen a god. *And maybe*, he thought, *they have.*

"A printheth dieth thith night," he whispered. The pressure built in his head until he was sure a vessel was about to burst. Blood dripped from his nose.

The mountain rumbled beneath his feet again, only this time he felt like he was causing it. He peered at the other soldiers as they tried to get to their feet, staggering to the wall for support.

The cave walls and floor cracked and shifted. Blasts of steam vented from the newly formed faults in the ground. Pebbles and rocks and debris lifted and floated around Tevin. He reached out, picked one from the air, and studied it. Then he grinned, dropped the pebble, and lifted his gaze back to Siver. He'd never seen so much fear in such a hard man before.

He nodded. The floating pebbles pelted the others with stinging velocity. Covering their faces, they backed toward the entrance. The mountain cried like a volcano about to erupt. A chunk of the outside path ripped away and disintegrated into the sky.

With pain still ripping through his skull, he half-smiled. The right side of his face didn't work. He wondered if he was having some sort of stroke and this was his end, though something about it didn't feel like an end. It felt like a beginning. He'd never felt so much power and weakness at the same time. Maybe Elijah's Light was rewarding him, awakening something special within his soul. He saw his grandma again, and she looked happy.

Despite his fear, Siver swallowed hard and charged. Tevin called more pieces of the crumbling mountain from deeper within the cave. First, a small rock whiffed past his head and blasted Siver's shoulder. Siver continued charging against the unnatural wind.

Tevin trembled. A crash echoed from behind. Siver leaped forward with a hate-filled cry. Rocks, dirt, and chunks of mountain whipped past Tevin's head just as Siver swung his sword. The rocks and debris slammed into the warrior, sending him tumbling back toward the mouth of the cave. Siver clawed at the ground, but tornado-like winds dragged him past the entrance.

Brant's body and his severed head were carried on the wind from the cave. The other men scrambled for handholds on the cave wall as the wind lifted their feet from the ground. Tevin stood solid, the wind whipping around him like he was a tree planted firmly in the rock. One of the soldiers lost his grip and shot screaming into the abyss.

Tevin dragged his right foot forward a step. He lifted his good arm. The soldiers begged for their lives as they tumbled nearer the edge. Siver tried to pull himself around the outside of the cave entrance, away from Tevin's wrath, but the wind was too strong.

Tevin casually flicked his wrist, sending soldier after soldier out of the cave and over the cliff until only Siver remained. Siver begged the gods to end Tevin's witchcraft, but he might as well plead for the suns to die.

"Face me without your devil's magic," Siver screamed.

Tevin limped toward him. His arms extended as his feet lifted from the ground. Another wave of heated air exploded behind him. The blast slammed Siver with the force of a tidal wave. The warrior wailed as his clothes burned away. His exposed skin blistered and charred. With no more life left to hold on, his hands released, and his scorched carcass tumbled over the edge.

Tevin looked around. With his enemies vanquished, the world suddenly calmed. His feet met the ground again. The throbbing in his head was gone. He made a strong fist with his previously weakened arm.

He felt different.

He *was* different.

He smiled. "I like this."

And then he collapsed.

CHAPTER 33

RECOVERY

Irene served Homer a bowl of oatmeal for dinner. "Isn't this more of a breakfast food?" he asked.

"Not if you eat it at dinnertime."

"I know. I mean, why?"

"You're spoiled. I just didn't have time to make anything else today."

Homer blinked at her. He had spent most of the day calming the animals. They'd been terribly spooked by the suns turning black and the flames that didn't burn. He had been a bit spooked himself, if he was being honest. But Irene had never come out to help. "You didn't have … Ah. I understand."

"What?"

"Nothing."

She rolled her eyes. "Fine."

Homer couldn't let it rest. "You spent all day with Simcane again, didn't you?"

Her face lit up like she'd been waiting for him to ask. "He has the most fascinating stories. I could listen to them for days."

"You have."

She lovingly tapped his shoulder. "Nonsense. I'll join you after I serve our guest." She hurried back toward the kitchen.

Homer called after her, "He'd better be getting oatmeal, too."

She looked back with an ornery grin.

"Oatmeal sounds great," Simcane said from the hallway. He leaned against the wall, filling the hallway with his bulk. His size was truly stunning.

When Homer caught himself staring, he turned away so as to not offend. Simcane coughed and staggered. Irene rushed to his side, though she wouldn't be much help if he were to fall. Homer hurried over as well.

"Simcane," Homer said, "are you sure you should be on your feet already?" He tossed Simcane's arm over his shoulder and couldn't help thinking that the injured man's appendage was like a thick tree branch—with all the tree's weight behind it. "Let ... me ... help ... you," he grunted.

Simcane limped to the table and sat in Homer's chair. "I am a fast healer," he said. Realizing where he had just sat, he tried to push back to his feet. "I'm afraid I've taken your chair. I'll ..."

Homer pressed on the giant's shoulder. "Nonsense," he said. "Sit." He took a seat across from Simcane. Irene placed a steaming bowl in front of their guest and hurried back to the stove to prepare her own.

Homer noticed a small red dot growing on the bandage covering Simcane's eye. He didn't seem to realize. Homer cleared his throat. Simcane looked up from his bowl. Homer pointed to his own eye and handed Simcane a handkerchief.

Simcane dabbed the bandage, saw the blood, and turned away. "I'm sorry. I ... I ..."

Homer nodded. "All is well, friend. The strain of doing too much must have caused a little bleeding."

Simcane held the handkerchief against his bandage with one hand and his spoon with the other. Irene took her seat. After they finished eating, she gathered the dishes. "You two must have been hungry," she said. "I almost don't need to wash these." She went back to the kitchen.

Homer asked, "Do you think your friend has had any luck? The one with the tentacles, I mean?"

"Oh, Rasi?" Simcane shrugged. "I can only hope. After meeting the princess's abductors myself, I'd say he is probably her only chance."

"If I may ask, why were you looking for her? I mean, was it the money?"

"The money?" Simcane paused with a look of surprise. He half chuckled and half grunted. "No, not really. I think it's because I saw a special kind of hope in the young princess. Something in her that would be, I don't know, good for Epertase. A kindness; an evenhandedness. Someone I would be willing to fight for as I did her grandparents." He looked to the table as if ashamed. "But I failed."

Homer imagined he didn't speak those words often. Neither man spoke again for several minutes.

Simcane finally broke the silence. "I'll be leaving in the morning."

"Leaving?" Irene hollered from the kitchen, obviously eavesdropping. "You are welcome here as long as you need."

Simcane smiled. "I thank you, but I still have business to attend."

"I see," Homer answered. After a pregnant pause, he clapped his hands together, startling the big man. "We shall move out to the front porch for a nightcap."

Simcane nodded. His arms shook as he pushed against the tabletop.

Homer reached for him. "Here, my big friend. Let me help you."

The unlikely friends staggered through the front door onto the porch. Irene followed closely behind with their drinks. Simcane sat in Irene's rocking chair and the wood creaked like a weakened tree on a windy day.

"I picked up some ale at the market this morning," Irene said. She handed it to Simcane.

"Thank you, ma'am."

She handed Homer a glass of water since he wasn't much of a drinker.

"Well, I'll leave you boys," Irene said. "I'm going to get some sleep."

Simcane tipped an imaginary hat. "Goodnight, ma'am."

Irene kissed Homer on the cheek. He lightly smacked her butt as she walked away. She shook her head as she went into the house.

Simcane looked into the darkness of the field and asked, "Do you not worry out here in the middle of nowhere with such dark nights?" He sipped his ale. "How do you protect yourself?"

"Heh. Who'd want to hurt an old man like me? I haven't made too many enemies over the years." He'd never much thought about it. "Besides," he added. "There are a few wild dogs that hang around here at night. I feed them sometimes. In fact, I'm surprised we haven't seen them yet. They sleep under the porch. No, I'm not too worried out here. The dogs will let me know if anyone's coming long before they're actually here."

The two continued with mostly small talk while Simcane nursed his ale. After a while he turned his empty glass upside-down. He said, "I think that's my cue. I should get some rest." He stood up.

"I guess time has gotten away from us."

Simcane smiled. "I feel better already." He straightened, his bones crackling like musical instruments. Homer went to help steady him, but he gently brushed Homer's hand away. It seemed important to him to do it on his own.

With Simcane in his room, Homer crawled into bed beside Irene, careful not to disturb her. His head had no sooner hit the pillow when a barking frenzy erupted out in his field. He hadn't heard the dogs lose their barking minds like that since Doc Eckels made a rare late-night visit after Irene had come down with pneumonia.

Homer sprang from his bed. His little toe slammed into his nightstand. He groaned.

Irene sat up, rubbing her eyes. "What is it?" she asked.

"Shhhh. Someone's coming." His old rusty knife sat on the table. After slinging his shirt over his head, he snatched it up. *Why don't I keep a sword handy?* he wondered. He grabbed Irene's shoulders as she met him at the foot of the bed. "Stay in here no matter what you hear. I'll be back."

He limped into the dark hallway and hurried through the front door. The partially hidden moon illuminated his empty field. Balancing on the heel of his injured foot, he hobbled down the steps. The dogs were too far away for him to see what they were barking at. Homer wasn't sure what he'd do if he were to actually find an intruder.

"Homer," a voice whispered from behind, causing him to almost stab himself in the leg. He twirled around with his knife outstretched.

"Who's there?" he whispered.

"It's me." Simcane's hulking shadow hunched by the porch.

"Simcane?" Homer relaxed. "You scared me to death."

"Shh. Don't look at me. Go back into the house. Act satisfied that you didn't find anything. Don't come out again until I come for you." Simcane ducked back into the darkness behind the bushes. Homer stumbled back into his house. Irene stood by the table. She was trembling. His heart pumped against his ribcage with a force he was sure anyone within earshot could hear.

"Who's here?" she asked.

"I don't know." She hugged him and he whispered, "Everything will be all right."

The silence outside was almost more than his old heart could stand. Then he heard the dogs again, and they were getting louder. He'd had enough waiting and whispered, "Stay here."

Irene's eyes bulged. "Wait," she whispered. "Where are you going?"

"I'm taking a peek."

Each creak of the old floor momentarily froze him in his tracks. He reached out to open his curtains a speck.

The front door swung open. Irene shrieked. Homer flinched. His stupid, worthless knife hit the floor. He couldn't move. Or breathe.

Simcane shouted from the porch, "Quick, Homer. Out here." Homer rushed out with Irene plastered to his back.

A single horse crossed the field toward them, a barking escort challenging its every step. Simcane limped to the edge of the field and waited. The horse carried a long-haired man with a woman draped across his lap. The man's dancing tentacles revealed his identity.

"Rasi," Homer muttered. "Does he have the princess?"

Simcane led the horse to the porch. "We need a doctor," he shouted.

Homer helped him lower the woman to his shoulder. Irene went to Rasi. He was barely conscious.

"Let me help you," she said. Rasi limply grabbed her hand.

"Simcane," Homer said. "Take her in the house. I'll help Rasi."

Rasi fell forward before Homer could get to him. Irene tried to slow his fall, but with his straps he weighed as much as Simcane. Homer grabbed under his arms, and together they dragged him to the steps. One of the straps coiled around a porch post and helped pull him onto the porch.

Dried vomit decorated his chest.

Simcane emerged from the house and helped carry Rasi to the bedroom.

"I'll fetch Doc Eckels," Homer shouted. He raced to the door and disappeared into the night.

Sometime later, Homer returned with Doc Eckels in tow. Homer had spent the return trip trying to prepare Doc Eckels for encountering Rasi's unique physiology. The good doctor had seen just about everything and had taken it in stride, but Homer was afraid those ornery tentacles would test his limits.

Irene met the two men in the hall with a finger against her lips. She whispered, "Rasi's in and out. He refuses to leave her side. I fear his head is badly hurt."

Doctor Eckels scooted past her into the room.

"Where's Simcane?" Homer asked.

"He left after you did. He said he would keep watch and I haven't seen him since." Homer felt a little safer knowing the big mercenary was on guard.

Irene and Homer sat at the table, waiting, while Doc Eckels worked. Homer considered having the good doc take a look at his black-and-blue toe, but figured even if it was broken, there wasn't much that could be done for it.

Irene made some hot tea and gave a cup to Homer. It hit the spot. It was morning before Doc Eckels exited the bedroom with his medical bag. He rubbed his slightly swollen, cherry-red cheek. "Those tentacles are quite dangerous," he said. "I had difficulty convincing them that I was there to help."

Irene wet a rag and took it to him.

"Thank you," he said.

"How are they?" she asked.

"They need rest. I encouraged the silent one to move into the other room where he could lie on the bed, but he won't leave her side." He pressed the rag against his cheek.

Homer slid a chair out for the weary doctor. "Have a seat, Doc. Something to drink?"

"If it wouldn't be too much trouble."

"Hot tea or tornment juice?"

"Tea will be fine, thanks."

Irene returned with a mug and the pot. She topped off Homer's mug. "Is the princess going to be all right, Doc?"

"It's hard to say. She is dehydrated, exhausted, and malnourished. She'll need fluids when she wakes up. The vitamins in tornment juice would be especially helpful. Her recovery will take time. I've cleaned and dressed her wounds and checked for infection. Right now she needs rest more than anything."

Homer nodded. "And Rasi?"

"Oh, yes. Rasi has sustained a serious blow to his head, but I think he's out of danger now. He also has many lacerations along with some muscle damage, though the muscle damage appears to be old."

Doc shook his head. "He must have had a rough life, judging by all the scars he wears. More than I've ever seen on one person, that's for sure. Unfortunately, his cuts were too old to stitch, which will add more scars to his impressive collection."

"Thank you, Doc. We'll take care of them."

The front door swung open. Simcane's hulking body filled the doorway. "Are you ready to leave, Doc?"

Doc Eckels nodded.

"All's clear. I assume everything you have seen here tonight will remain under locked lips?"

"Yes, yes, of course."

Homer escorted Doc Eckels to the door. "Thanks again, Doc. Just bill me and I will make things right. I may need to make payments, but I'll do my best."

"Nonsense, Homer. I'm happy to help the royal family in any way I can."

They shook hands and Doc Eckels joined Simcane out front.

Homer slipped down the hall to the bedroom where Rasi sat in the chair and the princess slept. The door squeaked as he opened it. Rasi looked up.

"Just checking on the patients," Homer whispered. "You can relax, friend."

Princess Alina lay motionless beneath the sheets. Homer had never been so close to any member of the royal family and he was taken aback by her vulnerability.

As innocent as a mourning dove, he thought.

CHAPTER 34
PAINFUL TRUTHS

In between nodding off, Rasi watched Alina sleep from the chair at the foot of her bed. She looked like an angel. His headache had subsided, though his coordination still felt off. As a test, he closed his eyes and touched his finger to his cheek. The problem was that he was trying to touch his nose.

Alina groaned and stretched and opened her eyes. Rasi rushed to her side. His straps crowded her, each trying to caress her cheek and make sure she was well. *Leave her be,* he ordered. They ignored him. Alina smiled weakly, pushing them away. "I'm doing better," she whispered.

Rasi leaned forward. *You're safe.*

"Where are we?"

On a farm near Parsons. Are you hurting?

She shook her head.

We made it. We're going to be ok.

She looked at him for a second, and then her eyes filled with tears and she looked away.

What is it? He fumbled his attempt to caress her arm. Undeterred, he took her hand. *I'll never let anyone hurt you again.*

She pried her hand from his, leaving his open palm resting on the bed. She must still be tired.

Alina? I tried to save your father. I tried to find you in time. I'm sorry I didn't get there sooner.

She sat up, scooting back to lean on the wooden headboard for support. With a soft touch, she lifted his chin so she could see his eyes. There was something different to her gaze, something he'd never seen in her before.

What? What is it? he asked. *Please, talk to me.*

"I need you to be honest with me."

Anything.

"I've never pressured you to talk about your past."

He started to turn away, but her hand guided his chin back. *I don't want to talk about Edonea.*

"No, not that. About something else."

What?

"Maybe, in some way, never asking about the night my grandparents were murdered allowed me to ignore what the people say. But I cannot ignore it any longer. I need to know the truth." Her hesitation filled him with dread. "I believed you when you told me you would never hurt them. But where were you that night?" she finally asked.

And there it was: the lightning bolt of a question he'd always feared she'd ask. Her question brought back his overwhelming guilt. Intentional or not, he had drawn the guards away that night while attempting to kill her father, and there was no way he could tell her that.

His face must have told her everything she needed to know. She covered her mouth and turned away.

Alina, I—

"Were you there?" she interrupted. "That bastard Scorne said you helped him. Is that true?"

Rasi shook his head, silently pleading with her not to go down that path.

"I didn't want to believe him, but everyone always said it was you, that you were there that night. Is everyone lying, Rasi? Do I not know you as well as I believed?"

There wasn't an honest answer he could give that would be any comfort to her. He wanted to crawl into his cave and hide forever.

"Did you lead the guards away so Scorne and his sick friends could kill them?"

Rasi's heart broke. *It's true I was in the castle that night. But I did not—*

The devastation on her face stopped him cold and he struggled not to cry. A lifetime in the rashta pit would have been less painful. *I wasn't helping those monsters. I would have given my life for the king and queen. I loved them like my own family.*

"Then why were you there? What could you have possibly been doing in the castle?"

That was the second question he'd prayed she'd never ask. How could he tell the one he loved that he'd wanted to kill her father? And if he did tell her, it would only lead to more questions with horrible answers.

He shook his head. *Please, Alina, I can't answer that.*

A tear rolled down her cheek. He reached to wipe it away, but she pulled back and wiped it with her own hand.

Rasi pictured Elijah's cold, callous eyes the night he was banished. He thought about Edonea and what terrible things Elijah had Tevin do to her. Maybe he should tell her everything. Tell her the things her father had done. Nothing else could satisfy all her questions. She'd believe him. She'd understand. To not tell her the truth would protect Elijah and Elijah didn't deserve to be protected.

But Alina did. He bowed his head. *You just have to trust me.*

"No, Rasi," she snapped. "Not anymore. You have to tell me the truth. I'll listen."

Rasi turned away with a weighted sigh.

"Rasi?" Her voice had strengthened. "Why were you in the castle when my grandparents were murdered? What aren't you telling me?"

He took a deep breath. He didn't want to look at her because what he was about to say would hurt her to the core. But she needed to see the truth in his eyes. *Your father killed my wife.*

She stiffened; her face drained of every bright spark that made her. Any innocence she still held on to, Rasi was taking away with his confession, and he'd rather die than do that to her. She put her hand over her mouth and let out a whimper, one he'd never forget.

"My father? Why?"

He wasn't a good man, Alina. It is true I struck him on the night I was banished, but I had good reason. He had threatened my wife. After I struck him, he sent Tevin to make good on those threats. Your father had a very dark side. He's the one who took my tongue.

"Oh, gods, Rasi." She touched his arm.

I'm forever sorry for the pain my words bring you. Though he hesitated, he knew there was no turning back. *You wanted to know everything.*

"I deserve to know everything."

On the night your grandparents were murdered, I was there to kill your father. I wanted revenge. I didn't know anything about Scorne or what he was planning, and I've regretted what happened every day of my life since.

Shock stole her voice, leaving a silence that would cripple the gods. She gagged like she might vomit. "Why didn't you tell me? All of these years, you kept these secrets?"

You loved him, Alina. I saw it in your face when you spoke of him. No daughter should know such secrets of their father.

"If what you say is true, he was a monster."

I'm sorry.

"I never dreamed he could do anything like that. Did you know he had Scorne throw me in that pit?"

No one could have known he was capable of such evil.

"Wrong," she snapped. Her hand fell from his arm. "You knew. You were the only one who knew what he was capable of. Yet … Yet you let me live with a monster. When he kissed me on the cheek, you knew he was a monster. When he comforted me after Blair died, you knew he was a murderer. I've always believed you to be my protector. I felt safe in your arms, but again and again you let me go back. Look what he was able to do to me because you didn't tell me of his evil." Her tears were flowing freely now.

He bowed his head to her chest, desperately hoping to feel a comforting touch. He felt nothing in return.

"Rasi," she said. "I need time to think. To be alone."

He jerked his head back. *Alina, wait. What are you saying?*

"I need you to leave me alone while I make sense of everything that has happened."

Please don't say that. You're all I have. I need to stay with you, to protect you.

"But you haven't protected me, Rasi. All these years you could have ended my nightmares by telling me about my father."

You loved him. You wouldn't have believed me.

"I would have believed you till the end of time. I love you, Rasi. But you must leave me now." Her words were like ice.

Out of the corner of his eye, he caught a glimpse of Homer standing in the doorway. *Get out.* His straps slammed the door shut with such force it buckled.

"Do not be mad at him, Rasi. He did nothing wrong."

Alina, I am deeply sorry. I never meant for you to be harmed. I would have told you long ago if I ever thought your father could sink so low. I knew he was evil, but I never believed he would hurt you. I swear.

"Rasi, I have a kingdom waiting for me. My mother is sick. She needs help."

I'll help.

"No. I have much to do. You only confuse my thoughts right now. You may not have heard, but an army approaches from the west, and I need to help her now that my father is gone. I need to get home as soon as I'm strong enough to make the journey. Please leave me. Don't make this harder for me than it already is."

Rasi stood up. *Very well, my love. I will make things right, I swear.* He knew what he had to do.

"Please, just go."

Homer pressed his back against the wall to make room for Rasi's angry departure. As Rasi passed him, two of his straps stiffened and postured in front of Homer's face before Rasi called them back. *It's not his fault.*

Simcane stood in the living room. "Rasi, I will see that the princess arrives home safely. You have my word."

Rasi barely acknowledged him, and his straps overturned the table as he stormed through the room and out the door.

CHAPTER 35

RETURN OF THE NEW QUEEN

As the days passed, Alina regained more and more of her strength. By dinnertime on the third day, Homer had finished fastening a new handcrafted leg to the broken kitchen table and was righting it when Alina came from the bedroom.

He bowed. "You're looking better every day."

"Thank you. I feel better."

Irene and Simcane came from the kitchen carrying four plates of ham and potatoes. Alina ate well, a good sign of her improving health. Simcane chewed with his mouth open, something Alina tried desperately to keep from seeing.

"Are you sure you're ready to travel, Your Majesty?" Irene asked.

Alina covered her mouth with her napkin to hide her chuckle. "Oh, Irene, you're mistaken. The proper way to address me is Your Highness. My mother would be Your Majesty."

Irene looked down at her food. Alina looked around and saw the top of Homer's head. Even Simcane had stopped chewing and stared at his plate.

"What is it?" Alina asked.

No one answered.

Alina raised her voice a little. "Answer me. What has happened to my mother?"

Irene stood up and made her way around the table to put her arm around Alina's shoulder. Alina's heart dropped into her stomach.

Homer lifted his head. She saw pity in his expression.

She wasn't going to accept their silence as an answer. "What happened to my mother? Tell me now."

Irene's voice was soft and soothing. "I am so sorry, child. I am afraid your mother has passed. The papers say she succumbed to the sickness in her chest."

"Passed? That can't be."

"I'm sorry, but it's true."

Simcane and Homer both nodded, still unable to look at her.

Tears filled her eyes, but she fought them back and shrugged away from Irene's comforting touch. There wasn't anything in the world she wanted or needed more than comfort right now, but she couldn't let them see her weakness.

"But she was doing better," she whispered.

"I know," Irene answered. "Sometimes we don't see these things coming."

Alina searched for something to fill the hole that had just ripped through her heart, and settled on resolve. It was the only thing she could find. "I must leave at once," she said, and wiped her eyes. "Homer, Irene, thank you for your generosity." She stood up and turned away. "I'll need a horse, which I'll return as soon as I am able. Simcane, if you're coming with me, prepare to leave right away."

Irene's hand hovered near her shoulder.

Alina paused, closed her eyes, and whispered, "There will be no pity in this house for me." She turned back toward them. "Do you understand?" She took in each of their sad gazes. It felt like she was at a funeral. "I must accept what cannot be changed if I am to be queen."

Irene tilted her head. "Child, you must take time to grieve."

"I don't have time to grieve."

Irene approached Alina with extended arms, but Alina stepped away.

She was the queen now. The burden was hers alone.

"I'll prepare a horse, Your Majesty," Homer said, bowed, and left for the barn.

She wished he wouldn't call her that. "Irene, I'm sorry for my rudeness. Your hospitality has been immeasurable and will not be forgotten. Thank you for all you have done."

"We would always be of service to you."

Simcane followed Alina outside. Irene stood in the doorway to see them off.

Simcane mounted Eko as Homer brought another horse from the barn. "This is Caesar, Your Majesty. He's a fine steed."

"I'll treat him as my own," she answered, and climbed onto the saddle. "Thank you again."

Alina nodded with a sad smile to Irene and then started for the road. After shaking Homer's hand, Simcane hurried to catch her.

It was a long, sore, and uneventful ride to Thasula, but eventually the bustling capital city came into view. It was the first time Alina allowed herself a real smile since her ordeal had begun.

Simcane peeked over his shoulder. "There she is, my queen," he said. "Your home."

She rode up next to him, leaned closer, and gently tapped his knee. Her look said thank you better than her words could.

"I know, my queen. I know."

They reached the busy Main Street that led to the castle. It was lined with soldiers. Each quietly bowed as they recognized her. Most of the crowd was too busy with everyday tasks to notice her at first, but Simcane was so large and intimidating that it was only a matter of time. A young child no more than nine years old spotted her and hurried into the street. "Your Majesty," he shouted, drawing all eyes to her.

She politely waved as others started to line the street. As word spread that the lost queen had returned, people poured from their homes and shops to get a peek. They applauded and bowed as she passed, shouting warm welcomes such as "Hail to the new queen" and "The gods be thanked for your safe return." She was home. This was where she belonged.

She continued waving to the adults and blowing kisses to the children. An ivory flower landed on the street in her path. Then a red one followed. By the time she had traveled the length of two shops, flowers carpeted the pavement.

"Thank you," she shouted. "I love you all."

"And we love you," a man shouted back. The crowd cheered again.

The closer she got to the castle the thicker the number of soldiers grew. The city felt on edge. Masera and several of his guards met her at the castle gate.

"Your Majesty," Masera said with a grin. "Welcome home."

"Thank you, Masera."

"I am truly sorry about your parents. Your mother was as kind as any queen has ever been. And your father was an honorable and decent man."

Alina gave Simcane a sidelong look. "Yes, he was," she answered.

"We have good news concerning that matter."

"Oh? And what would that be?"

"We have apprehended the chief suspect in your kidnapping and the king's murder."

Scorne? "Who is this suspect?" she asked.

"The outlaw known as Rasi, of course."

She gasped. "Rasi?"

"Yes. He rode into town last moon carrying your father's body."

"And that makes him guilty?" Her voice cracked.

"Your Majesty, he killed Lorca. He was seen when you disappeared. He's wanted for the murder of your grandparents. He may also have murdered Siver and Tevin, who were searching the mountains for him. They haven't returned, and our messengers have been unable to locate them."

"So, if Rasi were guilty of the highest crime in the land many times over, why would he simply ride into town knowing it would mean his death?"

"As I said, he has been wanted for many years. Perhaps he cracked under the pressure. I don't know why men like him do what they do."

"Where is he now?"

"In the dungeons awaiting trial."

Simcane interrupted. "May I ask how you got past those lethal tentacles on his back?"

It didn't seem like an outrageous question to Alina, but Masera's brashness wilted. "What do you mean?" he asked. "They were harmless. They didn't even budge while the scoundrel was … uh … how should I say? Interrogated."

Alina's hand covered her mouth. *Monsters.* "He is to be released at once, Masera. Take him to my chambers and make sure he is harmed no further."

"Your Majesty, is that safe?"

"Take him to my chambers now, Masera, or you will be relieved of your position."

"Yes, Your Majesty. At once." He was confused but loyal.

He flicked his wrist at one of his men, but Alina halted him. "No. I want you to take him personally, Masera. I want to be assured he won't be harmed further."

"Very well." Masera regarded Alina as though he feared she had cracked under the pressure as well.

In a calmer voice, Alina added, "I'm sorry to be so stern, my friend, but Rasi is not whom you seek. I will tell all later, but I assure you he is innocent."

"I have no interest in doubting you, Your Majesty."

Masera's loyalty wasn't her concern. Why Rasi was there felt more pressing. What could he have been thinking to risk so much?

"Is there anything else?" Masera asked.

"Yes, Masera. I have one other task for you."

"Anything, Your Majesty."

"I'll have Simcane draw a map. I want you to have two bags of gold taken along with this fine steed and a strong, healthy workhorse back to the farm from which I came. Also, find two of the strongest oxen in Thasula and take them as well. You must entrust this task only to someone in whom you have the greatest faith. Inform your men that a rebuff from the couple who live there will not be accepted, that this is a gift from Thasula, the royal family, and all Epertasians. The husband and wife there are to be treated with the highest respect. If they have any requests, your messengers should move mountains to complete them, whatever they may be. Is that understood?"

"Of course, Your Majesty." Masera bowed his head and tugged his horse to the side, opening a path. "Your home awaits you."

CHAPTER 36

PLANS CHANGE

Masera unclasped the manacles around Rasi's wrists and stepped back from Alina's chamber door. Rasi shifted nervously and nearly knocked a vase of tulips from the hall table. He swallowed a hard, dry gulp of nothing before he found the courage to knock.

"Come in," Alina answered.

The door felt heavier than it should. It must have been guilt that weighted it so. Inside, Alina sat across the room at her vanity with her back to him. Her hair was tied into a bun, leaving the back of her neck exposed. Rasi wanted to go to her and kiss her soft neck, but she was as likely to slug him as she was to return the affection. Her mirror hid behind hand-drawn diagrams of strange machines and maps of enemy troop placements.

Masera stepped in behind him and the straps poised above. One of them nudged Masera's shoulder as if goading him into a fight.

"Your Majesty," Masera called, ignoring them. "I will be right here in the hall if you need anything."

"That'll be unnecessary, Masera. Thank you."

Masera eyed the straps with a narrow stare as he backed out and pulled the door closed.

Hello, Rasi whispered.

She hesitated and then turned around. He hadn't seen the damage his interrogators had caused, but judging by the horror on her face when she saw him, it couldn't have been good.

"By the gods, what did they do to you?"

It's nothing. I'll be fine.

She raced over and gently touched his swollen eye. He fought the urge to wince.

"This is unacceptable," she said. "I'll summon those guards and—"

Rasi shook his head. *There is no need. I will heal. Nothing is broken.*

Her finger outlined the contour of his face until her silky palm cupped his cheek. He leaned into it and closed his eyes.

"Why did you come back? You knew what they would do."

Your father needed to be home.

"You could have been killed."

I wasn't.

"There was no need for such risk. I would have sent men to retrieve his body."

I felt I owed it to your people. His eyes met her emerald gaze and it weakened his knees. *To you.* He covered his mouth with his fist and coughed. This time he was unable to hide the wince of pain.

Her hand fell to her side and she turned away. "Rasi, you're free now," she said, without turning back. "I will issue a full pardon and inform every town crier of your complete innocence in all crimes of which you're accused. You don't need to hide in the mountains anymore."

I don't want to hide in the mountains. I don't want freedom. I only want you. He stepped closer and touched her shoulder.

She shuddered. "Why do you make this so hard? I have work here that is bigger than us. I cannot think about you right now. I haven't the energy."

Rasi struggled with what he had to say next. He pressed his palm to his forehead and ran his hand to the back of his head. The right words were as elusive as a fleeting dream. When she turned back toward him, he took in her powder-soft cheeks and lost himself in her rose petal lips. It pushed him forward. Against every promise he had made to himself, he told her, *I've come back to lead your army to war.*

Her eyes widened. She shook her head slowly, unsure of how to answer. Or maybe she knew exactly how to answer, but didn't want to.

Gentle words wouldn't do. *I have a gift for killing, Alina. I hate that it's true, but it's all I've known since I was young. When I met you, I was reminded of the goodness I have inside, and that's what I want to have again. But if your kingdom is in danger, I will help even if I have to be the man that I fear ... the man that I hate. I love you, and that's all that matters.*

"I don't even know you anymore, Rasi."

Yes, you do, Alina. Everything good you felt about me is still true.

"I don't know if I can ever believe you again."

I know, but I can't live without trying to earn back your trust.

She walked to her desk and traced the top with her first finger. Rasi waited on the edge of a cat's whisker. After an eternity of silence, she turned back. "What do you need to prepare?"

A thousand doubtful thoughts chased away the eagerness. Deep down he had expected her to decline and had convinced himself that "no" would have been great. Anxiety and excitement and fear rushed through him at once. His heart fluttered and his face went hot.

I will need intelligence, whatever your father has collected. I need our current troop deployments and war plans. Set up an immediate meeting with all available commanders for as soon as they can get here.

"I have been told that most of them have left for the front lines."

I will meet with whoever remains.

A tap on the door followed by a man clearing his throat interrupted their conversation.

"Yes, James," Alina said.

"Your Majesty, Aidric has requested an audience. He said he has critical information about the advancing army."

"Send him up."

"Your Majesty, he is badly injured and in the infirmary. He just arrived last night. The nurse accompanying him said he shouldn't have even tried to make the journey, but he insisted. He said his information is too crucial to trust with messengers."

"Then why am I just now being informed?"

"He's been in and out of consciousness, Your Majesty."

She hurried toward the door.

Rasi and James followed her down to the infirmary at the rear of the castle's first floor. The familiar lingering stench of a dead animal left sweltering in the suns for days took Rasi back to a bad place.

"James, who are all these men?"

"They're some of the wounded from the Lith battlefield."

"Why have they come this far to be treated? It must have taken them a week or more to get here."

"Doc said they arrived on the same wagon as Aidric. He said they needed more care than could be delivered at the emergency tents."

The first cot inside the door held a boy no older than sixteen. He lay motionless, his unblinking eyes fixed in death's stare. Where his body met the cot, his waxy skin bore plum blotches where blood had pooled underneath. He'd likely been dead for hours. One of his arms was missing and the empty shoulder socket swam with maggots. The boy's other arm stood stiff in the air like he had died in the act of reaching for something.

A nurse slowed as she moved from one cot to another when she noticed Alina. She bowed. "Your Majesty, it's good to see you safe."

"Thank you. What happened to this boy?"

"We don't know for sure. He made the trip without incident, but overnight his heart stopped. His infection must have been far more severe than we thought."

"Why did he even travel so far? Couldn't they fight infection at the battlefield infirmaries?"

"He's one of ours. He insisted on being near his mother. She's ill and couldn't make the trip to Lithia to be with him."

"Where is his mother now?"

"She just left with his brother. I'm sure she'll be back for the body soon."

"Please give her my condolences when she returns."

"Of course, Your Majesty." She stood quietly next to Alina.

Other soldiers who needed the skills of Thasulan doctors filled every cot. One young man bit on a stick as two nurses held him down. Horizontal lines drawn with dates across his calf revealed how quickly the redness had risen toward his knee. A doctor sterilized the skin above the redness. There weren't enough sticks in the world to prepare him for what was coming. At least there was an empty whisky glass beside him. The first swipe of the saw was the worst. Alina turned away.

Rasi looked away as well. Images from the Heathen Wars that he had spent years trying to forget crowded his mind as fresh as if they had happened yesterday. For the first time in many years, he felt the dread of an oncoming battle.

Other nurses and doctors worked to cut away dead tissue and stem the tide of infection at seemingly every turn. Their aprons and face masks were covered with bloody fingerprints and splotches. Though it seemed like barely controlled chaos, Rasi knew it was a far cry from the carnage of a battlefield infirmary tent.

Alina appeared dazed as though she'd been whacked in the head with a rock. Rasi followed quietly, nudging her along. As painful as these sights were, they were crucial for a queen to see before leading men to such a fate.

Rasi asked, *So Lithia fights as we speak?*

Her stoic face when she glanced back chilled his bones. "Lithia fell in less than a week."

Rasi struggled to not show his horrified shock. Losing Lithia so quickly was devastating. He had intended to develop his strategy based on intelligence from the Lith front, but perhaps the only lesson was that Epertase couldn't possibly win.

Alina turned to James. "Put a call out to the medical professionals throughout Thasula at once. Have the festival tents constructed in the Royal Garden as an additional infirmary in case more wagons arrive. Ensure that the monasteries are ready as well."

"Right away, Your Majesty." He turned to leave, but she stopped him. "Oh, yes. Gather all my father's military documents pertaining to the Teks and deliver them to a guest room at once. Take Rasi there when he is ready."

"Of course, Your Majesty."

It was at that moment Rasi saw something had changed in her. Seeing her giving orders befitting a wartime queen while fighting back tears made him sad and proud at the same time. He'd always known she would make a fine queen. He'd often said he would die for her. Now he may get the chance.

She asked the nurse, "Do you know a man named Aidric?"

"Yes, Your Majesty. I'll take you to him."

As they walked, Alina's gaze took in each wounded soldier. At the far end of the room, a man with bandages wrapped around his head lay on his side with his back to them.

"Aidric?" Alina said softly after the nurse pointed him out and went back to her duties.

Aidric strained to roll to his back. His face between the blood-stained bandages was a balloon of purple and black. Alina sat next to him and touched his swollen hand. She whispered, "It's me, Aidric. Alina."

He turned his head toward her voice like a blind man. He had a bandage over one eye and the other was swollen almost shut. "Your Highness? I'm so glad you're safe." His front teeth were missing.

"I'm just fine, Aidric. I'm more worried about you."

"They say I've lost my eye." He choked back tears.

Alina lightly caressed the side of his head. Sometimes a touch was worth more than words.

"I failed Epertase, Your Highness."

She leaned back so he could see her through his swollen eye. "Nonsense," she said. "Never speak like that again, Aidric. You, and men like you, are the reason we have a kingdom at all."

She picked up a cloth from his bedside table and dipped it into a basin of water before dabbing it across his crusty, cracked lips.

"I have much to tell you, Princess."

Rasi half expected her to correct how he addressed her, but she didn't.

"We will stay all night and listen if that's what we must do."

Rasi pulled a chair near the bed. Aidric strained to see him. "Who's with you?" he asked.

"A lot has happened since you've been gone. This is Rasi. He's going to help us."

"Rasi? The king-killer?"

Alina sighed. She went on to explain Scorne's confession, and her father's death, leaving out his participation in her kidnapping. She told of how she had known Rasi for many years and trusted him as much as anyone in the world. Rasi felt good to hear it, even if she might be overselling her confidence in him.

Aidric was either too weary to care or simply accepted her assurances. "It's good to meet you, Rasi."

For the next several hours, Aidric explained how the Teks had conquered Lithia so quickly. He described their explosion-making machines and strange mechanical suits of armor. Rasi paid especially close attention to Aidric's description of the black liquid in the pits and coursing through their suits.

Recounting everything took a lot for Aidric in his weakened state, and he eventually fell asleep mid-sentence. Knowing he had gained as much information as possible from the man, Rasi excused himself. Alina stayed by the wounded warrior's side with his hand in hers.

James escorted Rasi to his guest room. For most of the day, Rasi studied the files and scribbled-upon maps that were sprawled across his bed and a cherry desk. One folder amid the pile of paperwork read "Paisel's Report" on the cover. Rasi sat and began reading it. He leafed through it five more times before the day ended.

By the next morning, his studies had invigorated him. He was an artist who had been kept from his craft for many years and then suddenly given the canvas of the world. This was where he excelled. This was why he'd been born. Elijah had been right—he was no farmer.

He studied until his eyes blurred and weights hung from his lashes. Several times, he nodded off only to wake up with a paper stuck to his cheek. The bed beckoned him from across the room. He tried to remember when last he'd slept well. He stretched his stiff back with a groan.

The more he studied Elijah's war plan, the more he was convinced it was flawed. One only needed to read the reports of Lithia's fall or listen to Aidric's words to see as much. This invading army was strong and unwavering, relentless and remorseless. How could Rasi tell Alina that the Teks may well be unbeatable? He sat at the desk and rubbed his temples raw.

A knock at the door gave him a welcomed break.

"Rasi?" Queen Alina's soft voice put his agitated straps at ease. *Come in, Alina.*

"Simcane is here to speak with you."

Rasi stood up. *By all means, bring him in.*

The hulk of a man limped into the room. "Rasi, my friend."

They shook hands. *Alina, ask him what I can do for him.*

She did.

"I am here for the war effort, of course," he answered.

Alina continued to speak Rasi's thoughts for him. "Surely, mercenary work pays better than soldiering."

"Indeed," he answered. "But it's not as steady as I'd like. Besides, I like the idea of fighting under our new queen's command. Something … honorable about it, I suppose."

"How are you mending?"

"My body heals as we speak. I will be right soon enough. Well, most of me. Doc said these don't grow back." He playfully tapped his gray eyepatch, a constant reminder of his dedication to Alina.

"Well, I may actually have something requiring your special set of skills. How do you feel about working behind enemy lines?"

Simcane grinned. "Like old times, I suppose."

Rasi led him and Alina to the map on the bed. For the next several hours, he detailed his plan as Simcane sat quietly and listened. When Rasi finished, Simcane looked up with a smirk. He only had one thing to say. "When do I leave?"

Rasi and Alina shared a smile. "Immediately. How many men do you need?"

"If they're the right men, six should do. Any more and it'll be hard to keep undercover."

Rasi turned to Alina. *Who do we have?*

"Jarrah knows most of the local mercenaries."

Simcane groaned. "Jarrah?"

She looked surprised. "Is that a problem?"

"No, no, Your Majesty. You're right. Jarrah knows most of us. I just think he's a weasel."

"Well, you don't have to marry him."

"You make a good point."

"I'll have Jarrah head up a search for Epertase's elite." She looked back to Simcane, "Where do you want to meet your team?"

He shoved papers away from the map to study it better. "Well, Your Majesty. Since time seems to be an issue, I'm going to have to trust your judgment in choosing my team." He scanned the southern portion of Lithia and then pointed to an area south of the Lith town of Pataska. "I will meet them there in three moons. There is a large church at the northern edge of the Boke Forest. It's been abandoned for years. It's out of the way and perfect for our meet."

"Very well. Rasi, do you need anything else?"

Yes. Are the commanders gathered yet?

"They are."

Order them to the war room.

Alina and Simcane left.

Rasi pulled his hair back and tied it into a tail. Alina had left a new uniform hanging on the back of the door. The lightweight cloth pants fit comfortably to his knees, open along the inseam for better movement. One leg was the color of indigo while the other was ivory with a black outline of a dragon emblem on it. The vest was similar except the indigo and ivory were the reverse of the pants. After much coaxing, Rasi eventually guided each of his straps through the seven holes that Alina's seamstress had cut into the back. The fit was perfect and reminded him of the pride he had felt when he'd first donned such clothing as a teenager. With a foot on the chair, he wrapped the leather straps of his boots up to his knees. Once dressed, he took a swig of water and then headed for the queen's war room.

Queen Alina paced in front of the giant map. She cocked her head and smiled when she saw Rasi enter. "My, aren't you handsome."

He joined her at the map. *Some of your father's commanders are not going to be happy to see me.*

"You leave that to me." She sounded confident, but appeared nervous.

Are you ready? he asked, and flashed her a comforting smile. *Take a deep breath. We'll get through this together.* Rasi ordered his straps to lower to the floor so as to not make his introduction more challenging.

He turned to the entrance. His eyes hardened. His jaw clenched. He caught Alina's concerned look out of the corner of his eye, but he didn't acknowledge it. For many years he had refused to let her see the side of him that she was about to see because he was afraid it would scare her away. He took a deep breath in through his nose.

The double doors swung open. Dru, Jarrah, and Masera entered, engaged in idle chatter. Atticus followed close behind.

Dru casually turned his head toward Rasi and his eyes widened. He drew his sword and advanced around the table. "You," he shouted.

Rasi ignored him like he was a bee without its stinger. His straps, however, sprang to life. Masera grabbed Dru from behind, stopping him short of the straps' reach, and saved him a broken bone or two. Dru's stunned gaze shifted to them.

Alina shouted, "Dru." Then she lowered her voice. "Please, sheathe your sword." She went to him and placed a comforting hand on his sword arm. One of the straps draped gently over her shoulder.

"Not all you have heard about Rasi is true." She held out an inviting hand toward Dru's chair. "Please, have a seat, my friend."

Jarrah glared from the entrance.

Dru hesitated, his eyes still trained on Rasi's straps. Alina continued, this time addressing all of them. "As your queen, I want you …" She paused. "No … I need you to trust what I have to say next."

Tate arrived late as usual and stood next to Atticus and Jarrah in the doorway. "What's going on?" he asked.

"We have a new commander," Atticus answered with a grin and a wink toward Rasi.

"Great. Who wants something to drink?" Tate snapped his fingers. When his assistant rushed over, he said, "Ale for everyone, please."

Rasi shook his head.

Tate squinted as though he'd never seen anyone refuse ale before. "No worries," he said. "I'll drink his."

Each man took their seats. Jarrah's blistering stare didn't fade. He would be the toughest to convince.

Before Alina spoke again, she purposefully looked into the eyes of each member one by one. "I am placing Rasi in command of the military from this moment onward," she declared.

Atticus nodded, obviously pleased. Dru and Jarrah grumbled under their breaths. But not Tate; he didn't appear to give two shits one way or the other.

Alina continued, "Rasi was a great soldier in my grandfather's army and served with my father in the Heathen Wars. Some of you fought with him. Over the last several years, he has more than earned my trust and respect."

Dru shook his head in disbelief.

Atticus said, "A wise choice, Your Majesty." He turned to the others. "I, too, have known Rasi for many years—since we were boys, as a matter of fact. I will vouch for him with every ounce of my honor."

"Atticus," Masera said, "If you vouch for him, then I trust your judgment as well as the queen's. I say welcome, Rasi."

Jarrah shifted uncomfortably in his seat until he couldn't stomach it any longer. He stood up, knocking his chair back with a screech of wood along the polished stone floor. "Where's Tevin, Rasi?" he shouted.

"He has yet to return," Alina answered.

He pointed at Rasi and screamed, "The truth is, he's not coming back. Is he, Rasi? You killed him, didn't you? You killed my brother-in-law."

Rasi stood emotionless. He had no interest in engaging in crazy accusations, nor did he care much if Tevin were indeed dead.

Jarrah kicked his chair over and stormed around the table, appearing ready to throw punches. Rasi welcomed it, and so did his bored straps. Jarrah had a pain-saving epiphany at the last moment and stopped just out of the straps' reach.

Atticus eased Jarrah off the proverbial ledge. "I'm sure Tevin will return soon enough. He probably hasn't heard the change in circumstances just yet. Trust me."

"I don't know about this, Atticus. I know you two were friends, but you've heard what he's accused of doing. We don't even know for sure that he didn't kill King Elijah."

"We do know," Alina snapped. "I was there. It was a lowlife named Scorne. If you want to unload your anger on someone, I suggest you find him when this war is ended."

"And your grandparents? I suppose that was Scorne too."

"Actually, yes. Rasi is completely innocent of all charges."

Jarrah righted his overturned chair and sat down with a huff. "Just watch your back, Rasi."

One of Rasi's straps snapped at the air. Rasi didn't think he needed to worry much about his back.

Tate's assistant returned with a tray of tankards for the commanders and passed them out. Tate made sure he got Rasi's.

"Gentlemen, are we all finished with the bravado?" Alina asked, scanning each of their faces. "Good. Now, let's get started. I'm pleased to have such respected commanders leading our military in this time of need. I am sorry to take you from your preparations, but a few things have changed since my father gave you his orders. I have become aware of some concerning facts regarding our enemy."

Atticus leaned forward in anticipation.

Alina continued, "If you haven't heard, Aidric has returned from Lithia and is mending in the infirmary."

Approving nods and smiles circled the table.

"He has brought us much intelligence on our enemy, and his experiences concern me. I believe my father's strategy is flawed and we need to make immediate adjustments."

Jarrah spoke up, "Your Majesty, it's too late for changes. The Teks approach the Lowland-Lith border as we speak. Andon is already there preparing. We have a week at most before they obliterate the Lowlanders."

"That does complicate our plans. Moving entire armies in such little time is impossible. However, we have taken our limitations into account in our revised plans."

Tate stopped drinking long enough to say, "I hope these new plans take into account how quickly Lithia fell."

"They do. Rasi has developed a new strategy that I believe in wholeheartedly. It is our greatest chance for victory, as far as I'm concerned. I have already started setting the plan into motion."

Rasi looked to Atticus. Alina spoke for him. "Atticus, Rasi needs you, along with Masera and the Elite Guard, to escort me to the Lowlands where I will meet with King Fice. Once finished, you will continue to our northern front lines while Masera and I return home. Since Commander Andon is already at the northern Lowland border near New Arc with the eastern forces, he will operate in conjunction with you." She turned to Dru. "Commander Dru, you and Commander Jarrah are to head for Havens Ravine and await Rasi's and my arrival. As each of you leave, James will give you a copy of our new strategy and your orders. Learn them. Study them. Then destroy them. Is all understood?"

The men nodded.

"You are dismissed."

As the men started to leave, Alina pulled Jarrah to the side. "I know you are upset, but I thank you for trusting me. We will find Tevin. I'm sure he'll be fine."

"I'm putting a lot of trust in you."

"I know you are. That's why I'm putting additional trust in you. I have another task that I need accomplished before you head to the ravine."

"Anything, Your Majesty."

She explained his assignment.

"I will find only the best warriors for Simcane, Your Majesty."

He bowed and left the room with a lingering glare toward Rasi.

After he was gone, Alina turned to Rasi and whispered, "Did you kill Tevin?"

I wish.

She sighed.

CHAPTER 37

THE GILDONESE

Queen Alina, Masera, Atticus, and a small number of the Elite Guard arrived at the southern Lowland-Epertase border. There were no roads leading from Epertase to the Lowlands and no easy way to get there.

The farther they traveled from Thasula, the more desolate the countryside became. Instead of quaint cottages and small towns built around a single main street, the most they saw was an occasional stone hut, usually near a stream or some other kind of water supply. If anyone lived in any of the huts, they didn't make themselves known.

Alina's party stopped at a wall of overgrown brush that stretched in both directions for as far as they could see. It appeared to be mostly thorn bushes, intentionally planted to act as a barrier to prevent any Lowlanders from accidentally bumping into an Epertasian. Or so Alina had been told.

Alina pointed west. "Can we go around?"

Masera held a monocular to his eye. He looked east first and then west. "I see no way around, Your Majesty."

"Then we have no other choice."

Masera lifted his arm above his head. "We're moving forward," he shouted.

Three soldiers dismounted from their horses, drew their swords, and began hacking away at the brambles to create a path barely over a horse wide. When they grew tired, another three took their places.

Trio after trio hacked their way forward with Alina and the others creeping behind.

"This will take forever, Masera," she said.

His eyebrows lifted. "It is what it is, Your Majesty."

"How do you suppose Andon's battalion got through here?"

"Probably the same way. Though there may be passage through New Arc."

"We should have gone there."

"It would have taken us too long to get that far north."

The thorns drew lines across Allusia's sides. Alina used some of her water to dampen a cloth. She leaned to the side of Allusia's neck and dabbed at the many scratches and gouges. "I'm sorry, girl. We'll be through this soon."

Hours of painstakingly slow progress passed before one of the soldiers finally reported the bramble seemed to be thinning.

Alina stood up and balanced on Allusia's back for a better look. "He's right," she said. "I see the end." That motivated her tired men enough that they increased their efforts until they reached the other side.

Once through, the soldiers marked their entrance with red handkerchiefs to help them on their return.

The first sign of Lowlander life they came upon was a small farm. Well, Alina assumed it was a farm, though the barren fields showed no evidence of actual farming. An old man sat on the porch of his run-down brick house at the property's edge. His porch leaned to the side, threatening to crumble with so much as an ant's breath. Alina waved, but he didn't return the gesture. Perhaps he didn't see her, but more likely he didn't care.

Houses became a more frequent sight while their conditions hardly improved. Alina didn't see a single curtain, flowerbed, or color of any kind that might indicate cheerful inhabitants. Everything was gray and dull and dead.

They reached the first semblance of a road that was little more than a dirt path cleared of brush. Atticus studied his map. "As best I can tell, we're getting close."

Finally, they saw a town ahead. "Is that Grande Villa?" Alina asked.

"If I'm reading the map correctly."

A rock ricocheted off Masera's shoulder and he instantly grabbed for his shield. Alina looked toward a dirt mound off to the side where a filthy little boy stood. He smiled with no teeth and held out his middle finger. One of the archers said, "I could end his miserable life, if you'd like."

Alina shot him a stern look.

"I'm just kidding, Your Majesty." He bowed his head and added, "Kind of."

Masera turned to his archers and pointed three fingers to the left and then three fingers to the right. The archers dismounted and jogged to the rear of the buildings on both sides of the street.

As Alina and her party entered the town, Lowlanders of every age seeped into the streets to have a look at the outsiders. The children pointed and giggled, presumably at the Epertasians' funny-looking clothes and majestic horses.

Three children no more than twelve years old puffed on weed sticks as they stood outside of a wooden shack. The sign above the front door read "Hore Hous" in a childish scrawl. One of the kids tossed his weed stick, squashed it with his bare foot, and disappeared through the doorway.

Horses seemed in short supply, as evidenced by the number of asses trotting along the dirt streets and carrying packs of who knew what. If someone had an ox in these parts, they'd likely be considered rich.

As the crowds grew courage and closed in on the foreign party, Masera placed his hand on the hilt of his sword. "Be ready, men," he whispered. The other members of the Elite Guard quickened their pace and surrounded Alina. Masera rode to her side.

"My gods, Masera, these people live in filth. How can they live like this so close to the wealth of Epertase? It's not right."

"Your Majesty, these people choose to be segregated from the kingdom. They chose it a long time ago."

A little boy, probably five years old, made his way to the front of the crowd. He shoved his finger into his nose, dug around, and then stuck his findings into his mouth. He was parentless as far as Alina could tell, and more dirt than skin showed on his face. He was barefoot and shirtless with protruding ribs. Alina wanted to give him some silver, or a sandwich, but she feared it would cause a riot. Everyone appeared hungry.

"And him, Masera? He chose this life?"

"Point taken, Your Majesty."

More and more people filled the streets as her party ventured deeper into the town. A loud clank from one of the shops startled her jumpy soldiers. *Everyone take a breath,* she said in their heads. *React, but don't overreact. We don't want trouble.*

She wondered how they had gotten as far as they had without being approached by any authority. *Do they even have lawmen or soldiers here?* she asked.

"We know very little about this place," Atticus answered.

Since her ability to communicate telepathically had never been tested on Lowlanders, she had concerns whether she could be heard by the crowd. Though, even if they did hear her secret conversations with her men, she wasn't sure they'd understand.

The crowd thickened until the road clogged with people, bringing them to a standstill.

Masera turned to Alina. "Your Majesty," he whispered, "it's not safe here. This was a bad idea."

Alina ignored him and motioned to a small girl in the crowd. "Come here, young one," she said.

The little girl squeezed through the front line of people and scuttled boldly between the horses. She looked up, her brown eyes full of redness and innocence.

Atticus grabbed Alina's arm. "Careful. She's got the funk eye. It's highly contagious."

Alina brushed him off. "We have medicine for that." She leaned her head closer to the girl and whispered, "Where do the leaders address you?"

The girl stood silent.

Alina tried again, "Where do you listen to your king speak?"

The little girl turned and pointed to an open field with a broken-down stage. Alina reached down and brushed the little girl's dirty cheek and the girl shied away.

"Masera pushed to the front. "Step aside," he shouted. No one moved.

"We should just ride through 'em," one of the soldiers said.

Alina ignored him.

And then the entire crowd parted at the same exact time. Alina quickly saw the reason. Several riders appeared in the distance. Even from so far away, she could see there was something strange about them. They were tall, lanky riders whose feet dragged in the dirt. The young girl vanished into the crowd before the people retreated into their stores and homes.

Masera raised his monocular to his eye.

"How many do you count?" Atticus asked.

"Maybe seven, I think," Masera answered. "It's hard to tell since they're riding like a rope."

"A rope?" Alina asked.

"Straight and single file."

Masera stayed on one side of Alina while Atticus moved to her other side. "Your Majesty," he whispered into her ear. "Stay near us and be ready to retreat. This could get tricky."

Two of Alina's Elite Guard made their way to the front.

"Who are they, Masera?" she asked.

"I don't know, but I can tell you what they are. They're Gildonese. And they are fierce warriors."

"Gildonese? Here? I thought they were of fables."

"No. There aren't many believed to be alive in the world, but they are very real. And very dangerous. Stay close to me, and whatever you do, don't stare into their eyes."

The strangers closed in, appearing more frail than fierce. Their gangly bodies seemed to glide fluidly in their saddles independent of their horses' gaits.

Alina stared in awe. And stared. And stared.

Masera poked her ribs. "Don't look into their eyes, Your Majesty."

She shook her fuzzy head and looked away. It felt like she had been asleep and awake at the same time.

Within a couple of horse-lengths, the pale strangers stopped. Five of them were shirtless with flat chests and protruding ribs. The other two wore torn slivers of dull gray fabric across their chests which partially hid their tiny breasts. None of them wore much armor, only small plates on their backs and shoulders, appearing more suitable for acrobatics than war. From a distance, their height was impressive; up close it was startling. Each Gildonese must have been at least a man-and-a-half tall.

They waved their hands gracefully as they swayed on their horses, like ripples on a pond.

Soothing. Hypnotic.

"Alina," Atticus shouted.

She shook herself again.

One of the females with hair the color of fire poking from beneath her helmet rode past Masera's horse and grunted. Her eyes were cold, completely black, and deadly. She didn't speak. Alina turned away.

The Gildonese surrounded them. Her men turned nervously, trying to keep an eye on each of them.

Masera whispered, "Remind me again why we came with so few numbers?"

We couldn't look threatening. We must gain their trust, which is why I had to come personally.

The lead Gildonese's horse brushed against the lead soldier's. The soldier's upper lip curled and he tensed for a fight, which Alina was sure was what these strangers wanted.

She opened her mouth to speak, but the lead Gildonese cut her off. "Why are you here?" His voice quivered with a soft, almost feminine, pitch.

Alina answered, "We are here—"

"Epertasian," he interrupted, his voice cracking with excitement. He paused for a calming breath. His voice lowered to its original pitch, only now his tone was more deliberate. "Epertasian colors are not welcome here." He squeezed his steed between the guards and moved closer to Alina. Her soldiers froze, seemingly powerless to stop him.

She looked up into his dead, black eyes. She should have been afraid, but something about his gaze calmed her. She heard his voice again, though his lips didn't move. *Look into my eyes. Gaze into the blackness. Your mind is open to my ...*

Alina's head filled with a dull sound like sandpaper smoothing rough wood. Atticus nudged his horse against the Gildonese leader and waved his hand in front of Alina's face. She jerked her eyes away.

The leader glared at Atticus. "You are rude, Epertasian. I only wanted to speak with the whore for a moment."

Atticus opened his mouth to defend her, but she waved him off. Insults wouldn't be acknowledged. She addressed the Gildonese. "Do not try to put me under a spell, stranger. I will not have it."

He tilted his head to the side, apparently surprised that she spoke so directly, maybe even a little impressed.

Alina noticed the female had captured Masera's gaze. "Masera," Alina shouted.

Masera jerked his head around. He gripped his sheathed sword and nudged his horse against the stranger's. These creatures were dangerous indeed.

The Gildonese leader nodded his head toward the rooftops and chuckled.

Alina looked upward. Three Lowland archers had taken perch on the roof on both sides of the street. The stranger snickered. "Speak quickly," he said. "Time is not with you."

"I'd reconsider your present course," Masera said.

The Gildonese's voice deepened. "And why is that?" he asked.

Masera nodded back toward the rooftops. The stranger guided his eyes upward again. This time, his archers stood with their bows at their sides and Epertasian soldiers at their backs with knives at their jugulars.

The Gildonese's pitch rose again. "What business have you here?" He took a deep breath and then said in painfully slow, rambling speech, "If you are here because of the western invaders, I assure you that you needn't worry, as our King Fice is well aware of the threat, and we are quite capable of defending ourselves against any tyranny, including tyranny from our Epertasian neighbors." His words were almost peaceful in their anger.

Masera laughed. "What, your eight thousand or so men?" He turned toward Alina. "This freak is delusional."

"Masera, show respect," she snapped. "We are here uninvited." She nudged Allusia forward past her guards. "Sir, I only wish to address the people of the Lowlands. I believe the threat we both face has the potential to end all of our ways of life."

He sat atop his horse, pondering her words. He repeatedly tapped his upper lip with his long, skinny index finger. "Very well," he answered before turning to one of his comrades. "Announce a town meeting to begin at once in the town square, where we will give these foreigners ample time to say their piece before we escort them back to their luxurious and pampered lives in Thasula."

"Sir, I want every Lowlander to hear my words, not just the ones in this field."

"Silly woman, they needn't be here to hear your words as long as I am near, and I will make certain your words spread like a scaffe infestation, which is about what they're worth. You have my word." He spun away and trotted toward the field that was already filling with subjects. Alina and her men followed close behind.

CHAPTER 38

KING FICE

Alina followed the Gildonese to a makeshift stage that wobbled and creaked. The people filling the field spoke to one another with the same cold, unemotional tones that combined to sound more like a steady buzz than conversation.

Atticus and Masera ushered Alina onto the squeaky stage. She looked out over the filthy crowd, amazed at how fast they had gathered. There wasn't a hint of curiosity in any of their faces, not even the children's, despite that they looked up at the first outsiders they may have ever seen.

As she prepared to speak, the lead Gildonese motioned to the crowd and the audience hushed. He glowered at Alina. "I shall introduce you now." He turned back to the silent, somewhat dazed crowd. His voice quivered as he bellowed louder than even the windiest herald, "Lowlanders. This so-called Queen of Epertase has words that she would like to present to you for your consideration as the Epertasian kingdom would once again like to control your every action, and if this woman's words are heeded, you will be saying farewell to your freedom." He bowed his head, shot a smirk toward her, and moved to the side of the stage.

Alina scowled at him before stepping forward. "I am Alina, queen of Epertase. King Elijah, my father, has passed on. I am here to open the relations between our two countries and discuss a matter most grave." The Lowlanders didn't react in any way, and she wondered if they even heard her. She glanced at the Gildonese leader beside the stage. His lips moved, yet she heard nothing with either her ears or her mind.

She continued, "Neighbors, Lowlanders, Recitarians. A threat has emerged to our west, one that has traveled many miles over the vast seas with the sole purpose of our destruction. This invading army kills all in their wake. They are heartless and violent. But I am here to tell you all that they are not invincible. We can defeat them, but it will be hard. It will take all of us coming together. We need your soldiers. We need your support. I did not send a messenger to deliver this news, nor did I stand back and allow you to be exterminated. Instead, I traveled a long distance to demonstrate my dedication to you and my support for everyone who breathes the free air. Not just the people of Epertase, but all of the people across this great land."

The crowd seemed indifferent, unfazed by her predictions of death, but she continued just the same. "What I ask of you now, I realize, is a great sacrifice, one that I have no right to ask. But I give you my word. If you trust me, when this war has ended, I will make things right for you. I will give you everything you have now and more. Your children will have education. Your families will have food and clothes, and all the things you need to live a peaceful existence. But more importantly, if you do as I ask, I can give you life."

The Gildonese leader climbed back onto the stage with one fluid step. He brought his hands together in slow, methodic claps. When he stopped, the claps continued to beat like a drum in Alina's head. He addressed the people again. "These words may sound straightforward coming from what I could only imagine is a serpent's tongue, though I have not seen it to confirm for myself, but we must keep in mind that she is, after all, Epertasian, and surely she has some other motive than simply saving us poor, pathetic Lowlanders. What might this great sacrifice entail?"

There was no easy way to say what needed to be said next, so she decided to be blunt. "I am asking you to abandon your homes and live in peace in Epertase. Do not listen to this Gildonese." She shot him an icy look. "Where is your King Fice? I should like to speak with him."

The crowd didn't react—not a moan, not a boo, not a cheer, nothing. She could have told them it may rain tomorrow and receive the same response.

The Gildonese leader grinned. "Lowlanders, I have told you no lie, as the true desire of this queen has now been presented to you." He glared back at her, and she felt his calming sway. She shook it off and looked away.

Slowly and smoothly, his shoulders lifted in an elegant shrug. "If your ancestors were unable to dupe us into rejoining the mighty Epertase, then why do you think we will up and move for you? We are quite capable of self-defense, as our ongoing freedom from your tyrannical empire clearly proves."

"Good sir, we have not shown aggression toward you for many years, if ever." She directed her attention back to the crowd. "I do not expect you to leave your homes for me. Indeed, I do hope you are willing to help us in our time of need. But be aware of and take this into consideration: Our survival will directly affect your survival. I do not expect you to do this for me, I expect you to do this for yourselves … for your children." She pointed west. "That smoke you have gone to bed to each night and awoken to each morning for the last several days, the very smoke that draws nearer each passing day, that, my friends, is your neighbor Lithia. Even as I speak, she burns."

Their faces remained stoic and she couldn't fathom why. "Do they hear me?" she asked.

The Gildonese leader's lips curled upward. "They hear every lie, whore."

His use of the word "whore" had more sting to it than it rightly should have. There was something unnatural indeed about his venomous speech. Alina walked to the edge of the stage and scanned the emotionless crowd. "We can win this war." She received nothing from them. It was useless.

The Gildonese leader turned to the docile crowd and back to her. "They have made their decision. They wish for you to leave and never return."

"What kind of spell do you hold over these people?"

He merely smiled.

Alina huffed to the back of the stage, where she was met by Atticus. He helped her down and onto her horse. She whispered, "All that can be done is return home and watch for the convoy of Lowlanders to arrive."

"And if they don't? What are my orders?"

An ache filled her heart. "Oh, Atticus, I believe they will do what's necessary. If they don't, we will be forced to alter our plans."

"That will prove fatal to Rasi's overall strategy."

"What choice do I have, Atticus?"

His answer was cold like a good soldier's should be. "In war, sacrifices need to be made."

She glowered at him. "I will not be the death of these people. That is not how Epertase behaves. These people will leave, I have faith. Or else they will fight."

"And they will die."

"But not at our hands."

"Very well, Your Majesty."

She had done her best, and in that she took solace.

"Lady?" the Gildonese leader's voice squeaked from behind. "A moment of your time?"

"I think we are quite finished here, sir," she replied without as much as a glance in his direction.

"I do believe you will want to hear what I have to say." Alina was surprised to turn and find the Gildonese leader beside her. His ink-black eyes sat level with her own eyes though he stood and she was on horseback.

Masera crowded his horse between the two. "You can talk from there," he said. Another soldier moved his horse behind the Lowlander.

The Gildonese leader looked hatefully at Masera and the other soldier. With the fluidity of a ripple in the water, his arms lifted outward and then whipped around. Though his movements seemed to flow with the speed and effort of a gentle wave, Masera and the other soldier were unable to react in time. His open hands struck their chests with a powerful whack, knocking them from their horses.

Atticus closed in. Masera bounced to his feet, anger quickly replacing the surprise on his face. Alina waved them off. "Easy, both of you. I will hear him out. Lowlander, you have my attention, but my patience is thin."

He bowed his head as if humbled and muttered, "Alone."

Alina struggled with how to answer.

His dark eyes met hers. It was like looking into a calm ocean at night. He said it again. "Alone." She couldn't see how it would hurt.

Masera white-knuckled the hilt of his sword. "It's a bad idea, Your Majesty."

She wanted to answer him, but couldn't make words for some reason.

Atticus crowded her other side and nudged her forcefully. "Alina," he snapped.

She blinked and looked around in confusion.

"The queen will speak with you," Atticus said. "But not alone."

The Gildonese leader looked at each of the soldiers, crinkled his nose, and then relented. "Very well. I find it amusing to hear your demands as my friends ..." He lazily extended his arms.

Alina turned to see that the six other Gildonese had somehow surrounded them. Masera and his soldiers pulled their swords. Alina gestured frantically. "No, Masera."

"But, Your Majesty ..."

"We will let them speak. Sheathe your weapons."

Though they hesitated, her men did as commanded. The Gildonese leader licked his teeth while he waited impatiently. His fingers scratched the patch of clear scruff on his bony chin.

"As I was saying, we could have killed all of you ten thousand times by now if we had so desired, and I'm still deliberating on whether to let you live. And while we speak of it, don't think we couldn't kill your entire invading army near New Arc if that was our wish."

"Then why don't you kill the invading Teks if you're so powerful?"

"Perhaps we will."

Atticus scoffed. "He's delusional."

The Gildonese leader cocked his head to the side. "Maybe."

Alina had had enough. With her eyes focused on the ground, she said, "Say your piece. I've grown tired of listening to y—"

"King Fice," he shouted, "ruler of the Lowlands, has sent a message."

Alina's patience was now paper-thin. "We don't recognize your King Fice any more than we recognize you as a negotiator."

"That may be, but the people here do, and that is what matters if you are to succeed in your phony attempts at diplomacy."

"Very well. What does Fice have to say?"

"It is *King* Fice, whore." He lowered his head for a moment, sighed, and then lifted it again. "I am sorry for that. It is just that the Great King Fice demands respect, and he is concerned about losing his power and wealth if he follows your request. He would like some kind of—"

It was her turn to interrupt. "He will lose his life if he does not."

He sighed again. "That may be true, but the Great King Fice would gladly sacrifice his people before he sacrifices his power, and he—"

Alina bit her lower lip. "Where are we going with this?"

"You are very rude. It is simple. He only wants your guarantee that he will be restored as leader of the Lowlands when this war is over and not be interfered with by royal Epertasian whores."

"Or else w—"

"I am not finished. I will not be interrupted again, or I will gut you and feed you to your crying men bite by fucking bite. Now then,

King Fice also requires a servant's room full of gold and silver for his troubles. Before you answer, understand these are not requests, but demands that you must accept if you truly care for these people, as you insist you do, though I do not understand why."

"I do not respond to extortion."

"Then you will cause many to die."

Alina paused before asking, "You will evacuate tonight?"

The stranger grinned. "But of course."

"And your soldiers? Will they join the fight?"

"And leave King Fice unprotected? I think not."

She wondered if he even had soldiers. "Where will you and King Fice go?"

"That is not information that you should be privy to, but know the Gildonese have survived many years without help from Epertasian scum, and King Fice will be fine wherever we all may go."

She pondered his offer, then nodded once, yanked at Allusia's reins, and returned to the others.

The Gildonese leader walked away, leaving his horse wandering the street. The other Gildonese stepped from their horses and joined him.

She addressed Atticus with a caring hand on his shoulder. "The plan is in motion. Be safe, my friend, and I will see you soon."

"I will put the Tek cowards into the ground, my queen."

She knew he would do his best. She took in his face, hoping this wouldn't be the last time she saw her loyal friend.

Once the Gildonese were out of earshot, the crowd in the field started to disperse. A teenage boy passed with the same blank look as everyone else wore. Alina reached for him, snagging his oversized shirt. "Young boy?"

He stopped and looked at her as though he hadn't known she was there.

Alina pointed at the Gildonese. "Who is that tall man?" she asked.

He looked at her like she had just asked what her own name was. "Why, that's King Fice, of course," he said, and then made his way to the "Hore Hous."

CHAPTER 39

MERCENARIES

Simcane waited in a tree within Boke Forest at the outer edge of Pataska. Because mercenaries weren't the loyalest of people, he'd arrived a day early yesterday to prevent anyone getting the drop on him. Having the upper hand put him in a good mood, and he decided a feast for his coming guests would be a nice welcome.

The doe he had been watching crept closer, stopping repeatedly along the way with its ears perked as if catching his scent. *Keep coming*, Simcane pleaded. His mouth watered as it approached the base of his tree. *That's it. Just a little farther.*

The doe wandered beneath him. Simcane held his breath and leaned forward. Just as he let go of the tree, the doe flinched. Simcane grabbed air. The doe's bushy white tail bounced and zipped in and out of the trees until it was out of sight. Surprised, he stood up and dusted himself off. *How did it know?*

The answer came by way of a deep snarl from behind. A better, more efficient hunter had arrived. Since Simcane wasn't built for speed, he turned to face the creature.

King of beasts, huh? We shall see.

The hungry lion pounced.

Simcane thrust his hands forward and sent a blast of air at the creature's exposed chest. The lion yelped, more stunned than hurt, and landed on its back. Simcane wrapped his arms around the creature's neck as it scrambled to its feet. The beast thrashed and bucked. Simcane squeezed with all his strength. The fight didn't last long. With the lion's limp body at his feet, he stood victorious over the creature.

He grunted. "Though it's not the tender meat of a doe, meat is meat, I suppose."

Since the lion was too heavy to carry, he gutted it on the spot. The fresh pile of entrails started the clock. He wasn't interested in trying his luck against an opportunistic bear or pack of wolves, so he quickly dragged the carcass back toward camp.

The first of his guests was putting a fresh log on Simcane's campfire. The man was a strange-looking fellow who sat as tall as a normal man stood.

As Simcane approached, mindful of making enough noise to announce his arrival, the man rose to his feet, not the least bit concerned. Simcane dropped his game to the ground. It was rare that he had to look up to make eye contact with another.

"Gildonese?" he asked.

His guest nodded.

"I'm Simcane. It's a pleasure." Simcane shook his hand, surprised at the skinny Gildonese's strength.

"I am Eldon of New Arc and I am pleased to make your acquaintance, Simcane, as I have heard many great things about you and look forward to serving under you in this mission for the soul of Epertase."

"I did not know any Gildonese still lived, let alone in Epertasian or Lith territories. It's definitely an honor to know you. Are you hungry?"

"I live a simple and private life, and yes, I am always hungry."

Simcane tossed another branch onto the fire. "If you don't mind me asking, how did that weasel Jarrah ever find you?"

"The one called Jarrah once sought me out when he was in New Arc doing work for King Cecil when the former was a young up-and-coming soldier, as the great king wanted to know all manner of beings who lived inside his borders. I made a name for myself long ago before I took to retirement, so it isn't uncommon for young ones to seek me out."

"I'd never heard of you."

"I do not take offense to your words, as my days working for gold were probably before you grew hair in your nether regions. And you are right, Simcane, the one called Jarrah is indeed a weasel."

"I meant no offense."

Eldon nodded with closed eyes.

"Do you have family, Eldon?"

"I do not. I have heard tale of my kind living in the Lowlands, but have never ventured there to find out for sure. That may be for the best, as when more than a few Gildonese gather in a pack, it can bring on unhealthy urges."

Simcane had heard such legends before.

Eldon leaned over to better see Simcane's catch. "A lion? Very impressive. May I help you prepare it for eating?"

Simcane held out his open palms. "Be my guest."

Eldon was talented with a knife, and the lion was skinned and ready to cook in no time. The meat was rich and tough and tasted a little like pork might if eaten off a blacksmith's floor. Each bite made Simcane long for the elusive doe.

As the two talked, Simcane realized they had more in common than he would have guessed. Both had lived hard lives and neither had much patience for those who didn't know what it was to struggle. The Gildonese grew on him very quickly, almost unnaturally.

One by one, the rest of the team started to arrive. First was Thairen, a battle-hardened warrior with a solid reputation. Simcane had heard that while in the service he'd volunteered for every dirty, sneaky, dangerous mission he possibly could. More scars than clean skin made him easily recognizable to anyone who'd heard his legend. It had been said that Thairen was harder to kill than most. His V-neck blouse under his open albino tiger fur showcased a poorly healed puncture wound in the soft flesh beneath his Adam's apple. It looked like someone had tested his legend recently.

Simcane approached him. "Thairen, it is good to meet you. I've heard excellent things about your skills in battle."

"I don't care." He left Simcane's hand dangling.

Seeing no weapon, Simcane asked, "Where's your sword, soldier?"

"No swords, only knives," he answered as he lifted his fur wrap, revealing blades along either side of his waist.

Eldon asked, "Why knives and not swords?"

"I like to be close to my kills."

"Closer than a sword?"

The closest thing to a smile that most people would see on Thairen's face cracked his lips. He walked to the uncooked portion of the lion carcass and tore off a chunk of raw meat. Blood oozed between his teeth with each bite. "Ummm, lion," he groaned.

"Where are you from, Thairen?" Simcane asked.

Thairen turned and headed toward the church.

Eldon and Simcane shared a look, not quite sure what to make of their newest guest.

Next to arrive was an old friend of Simcane's. Though he only stood to Simcane's gut, his heart was twice as tall. The whole left side of his face and half of his head were hairless and heavily disfigured by burn scars.

"Willum, it's been awhile. How have you been?"

"Well, Sim. Very well."

"I am pleased to have you join us. How long since we last made company? Thirteen, fourteen years?"

"I don't know, Sim. How long has it been since you lost your taste for war and abandoned the Epertasian army for Elijah's jail?" Willum smiled an ornery smile.

"Oh, yes. Back in the Heathen War, I believe. Back when you were young." He returned his old friend's smile. "And still had your looks."

"I am surprised you can even see my burns. Did you anger a woodpecker?" Willum extended his hand and Simcane grabbed hold. "Good to see you, friend."

"Lion's meat?" Simcane offered.

"Nah. I brought my own food."

"Still not eating meat?"

"I use animals, not eat 'em."

A well-dressed, white-haired, scholarly man with a bow over his shoulder and a quiver strapped to his back arrived next. He said his name was BJ the Keen, leaving little doubt of his confidence. Simcane knew very little about him. His long, narrow face and kind amber eyes portrayed a trust that had surely lulled a few of his victims into complacency.

Gillian, a battle-tested field doctor who prided herself more on her medical skills than her combat ability, and Joseph the Priest arrived separately shortly thereafter. Gillian introduced herself as a failed abortion, which caused Joseph to laugh. Her cold stare caused him to stop.

Joseph wore a long black coat with a narrow white clergy collar.

"So, you're a priest, huh?" Simcane asked.

"No, why?" he answered, and snagged a piece of cooked lion.

Each warrior came highly recommended, and with his first sight of them as a group, Simcane was pleased.

After everyone had a chance to indulge themselves in dinner, Simcane gathered them for a meeting. Everyone except Thairen, as he'd disappeared. Simcane resigned himself to tracking him down later and filling him in on the details.

Once Simcane had finished, everyone found spots on the floor in the church and went to sleep. Everyone except Simcane. He went outside and watched the fire burn down to embers. The scenery of the stars felt right for sleeping, even if it was a mite cold.

They headed out before dawn.

The smell of death wafted throughout Lithia's capital city. Nearly every open field sported six-foot-long mounds of dirt in meticulous rows or new mounds being created by those still alive as wheeled carts delivered more bodies.

The only Teks Simcane and his team encountered were workers more concerned with setting up their metal machines than hassling a few traveling grifters. Simcane was amazed at the many giant, hastily erected pumps that plunged up and down into the ground.

"What do you think they're doing?" Willum asked.

"That must be what pulls the black stuff from the ground. They're probably getting ready for their Lowland battle, I suspect."

"Should we make a stop?"

Simcane shook his head. "These aren't part of Rasi's plan."

Simcane's team reached the main street leading to the castle. It was named Pontius Way after the capital's founder and was the street Simcane had grown up on. Any hopes he'd had that it might have been spared were quickly squashed. The sight of it broke his heart and filled him with enormous guilt. He never should have left for Thasula and higher paid work so long ago. Maybe, had he stayed, he could have helped his friends King Logan and Queen Lona.

The distant sight of the broken and deserted castle was almost more than he could stand. Strange gray and black flags replaced Lithia's flags on each of the castle's three towers. In the destruction he saw Epertase's future.

Their arrival at the castle perimeter wall brought on the hardest part of the mission yet. From there they needed to move by foot, which meant he had to say goodbye to Eko. He caressed his friend's mane and leaned into his ear. "You have been a loyal steed. I thank you. If I can, I'll come find you when this is over." He pressed his forehead to Eko's neck and then slapped Eko's hindquarters, sending him back the way they had come. The others, except for Thairen, followed his lead with their own horses. Thairen simply walked away from his without a word or even a pat. Simcane wondered if he'd be just as happy eating it.

As the team continued toward the castle, a disgusting sight came into view. Five bodies hung on display from makeshift gallows at the entrance to the courtyard. Simcane's knees weakened. He grabbed his mouth and started to run toward the bodies while his stomach weighted down his feet. "No, no. It cannot be."

At the first body, he slowed with his hands pressed to his temples. He looked to the others and then back to the bodies. He fell to his knees and covered his face with his hands. Willum stepped beside him and put his hand on Simcane's shoulder. "I'm so sorry, Sim. I know what they meant to you."

The first body was King Logan's eldest son, Prince Galvin. His face was bloated and purple, proving he had fought until the end. Logan's daughter, who was Simcane's age and a frequent childhood playmate, hung not far from Galvin. Simcane touched her cold, stiff foot. He almost threw up. Her face hid behind her curly, coal-black hair. "Lilliac, I'm so sorry I wasn't here for you." He wiped his flowing eyes.

King Logan's other son, his youngest child at twenty-nine, was the third body hanging in the row. Simcane didn't recognize the other two people, but their long dresses indicated they were likely servants.

"Hey, Sim," Willum said. "I don't see King Logan and Queen Lona, so maybe they got away."

Simcane appreciated Willum's effort, but nothing could fill the void torn in his heart.

Thairen, without a care in his miserable body, plowed past Galvin, shoving him aside as if he were merely a deer hanging in a slaughterhouse.

Eldon grabbed Thairen's shoulder. "You should show more respect, young warrior, for these bodies were people before."

Simcane looked up with disdain.

Thairen yanked his shoulder away from Eldon. "What is done is done," he said coldly. He reached out to push Lilliac aside.

"Touch her and I'll remove your arm," Simcane snapped as he rose to his feet.

Thairen paused and cocked his head, as if debating whether he wanted to try his luck. Then his arm fell back to his side. "What would you like us to do, then, Sim?"

"We will take a moment here and cut them down. And you will do so with respect."

Thairen's eye roll wasn't lost on him.

BJ asked, "Should we bury them properly?"

Simcane lowered his head and turned his back to them. "We haven't the time. We'll burn them." It wasn't a fair end for his friends.

As smoke from the fire drifted toward the castle, Simcane hoped the Teks inside choked on it.

He led his team to a candy shop once owned by the Shawvers, a sweet older couple who were never stingy with their candy when Simcane was growing up. He hadn't thought of them in years and hoped they were all right. "We'll stay in here until dark. Then we'll go to the harbor."

Once inside, BJ offered Simcane a piece of chocolate.

"I'm not much in the mood for anything right now," Simcane said with a scowl. "Unless it's enemy blood."

CHAPTER 40
BEHIND THE ENEMY

At nightfall, Simcane's team decided splitting up into small groups was the best way to get to Danduke Harbor without being discovered. It would be a tragedy if all of them were caught. Simcane, Joseph, and BJ chose to enter at the front of the castle past the makeshift gallows. Willum and Gillian traveled to the west. Both Eldon and Thairen insisted on heading off alone. When Simcane asked Thairen which way he was going, he answered, "Don't worry about it," and walked off. When he asked Eldon, the Gildonese pointed to the wall and then effortlessly scaled it.

The lack of Tek guards was unsettling because it implied they had no interest in holding the castle. Simcane's group only came across two Teks, and they were more concerned with their ale than with guarding anything. They were easily avoided.

Thairen was already waiting at the pier, leaning against a post beneath a torch and picking his teeth. As Simcane passed him, he caught a glimpse of Thairen's face and stopped for a better look. His cheeks were smeared with blood.

Simcane shook his head and rubbed the back of his neck. "I don't even wanna know."

"That's probably best."

BJ asked, "What'd you do with whoever that blood belongs to?"

"Oh, don't worry about them. They won't be found any time soon. I just wouldn't drink any well water from here on out if I were you."

Simcane couldn't tell what bothered him most: That Thairen killed so easily, or the sick grin on his face as he talked about it. Gillian and Willum arrived next. They reported little activity and an easy trip.

The harbor was a ship graveyard with the larger boats either heavily charred or sunk with only their masts poking from the water. Willum gave Simcane a concerned look.

Simcane winked. "Worry not. We didn't come for the bigger ships anyway. We only need the small two-seaters, and I see a few of them."

Eldon arrived last, carrying a dead Tek on his shoulder. Once on the dock, he put his mouth over the guard's lips and sucked. His face turned bright red and his neck veins bulged, but he didn't stop until the guard's ribcage popped and his sternum collapsed. Eldon straightened, wobbled, and then righted his balance with the help of a post. He lowered the Tek into the water, and the body sank like a bag of gold.

Thairen grunted as he passed Eldon. "Nice trick. You kiss all your kills?"

Eldon's jaw dropped and his head spun toward Simcane. The look of shock on his face was priceless. "I did not kiss anyone," he said.

Simcane patted his shoulder. "You just have to ignore him sometimes."

Thairen jumped into one of the boats.

Eldon's stunned gaze moved to Gillian as she walked along the shore. "You don't think I kissed that dead man, do you?"

She ignored him and climbed into another boat. BJ approached to join her. A push of her leg sent the boat floating out of BJ's reach. "Uh-uh," she grunted. "This one's full, Bartholomew James."

BJ threw up his hands, flabbergasted.

"What?" she snapped as she floated farther away. "You don't think anyone knows your name?" She leaned against the prow, interlocked her fingers behind her head, and stretched her feet to the stern.

Eldon, BJ, Joseph, and Willum filled two more boats. Simcane stood at the end of the pier and motioned Thairen back.

Thairen's shoulders dropped. "Why?"

"We're sharing."

"Go with someone else."

"There's not enough boats. And no one else wants to ride with you." He pointed over the water to a boat floating at the opposite side. "Unless you want to swim to that one."

"But Gillian ..."

Simcane felt his eyes roll. It was like babysitting. He joined Thairen and shoved off from the pier.

Rowing from the harbor to the river wasn't nearly as challenging as listening to Thairen grumble about having company on "his" boat.

Once out of the harbor, Simcane stood in the boat to better see over the tall embankment. Though it was too dark to see the Tek soldiers, he could see their campfires. Hundreds of them followed the contours of the river for as far southwest as he could see.

He sat back down. "There'll likely be patrols along the bank. We just need to get past their camps before sunsrise."

Thairen's knee wedged against Simcane's back and he pushed. "Why don't you ride somewhere else, like in the water?" he mumbled.

Simcane's middle finger was his answer. After catching the slow current, he lay along the bottom of the boat, told Thairen to shut up and do the same, and pulled the cowhide tarp over their heads. The others did the same.

Simcane's fifth peek of the night revealed a dull glow on the underside of the clouds, which meant it would soon be too bright to continue so out in the open. They hadn't cleared the Tek camps yet. It was time to improvise.

He shoved the tarp away and whispered, "We need to ditch the boats and swim along the embankment from here."

The icy water took his breath as he eased into it, careful not to make a splash. Once the others were in the water, they scuttled the boats. Quietly, they dog paddled toward the bank.

Though he'd prefer not to be so close to the Tek side of the river, anywhere else was too dangerous. At least the high embankment gave them cover from patrols.

Simcane barely breathed for fear he would be too loud. Thairen's grunts while he swam proved he didn't share the same concerns. With luck, they might just make it. Simcane had long ago learned not to trust luck.

As they floated down the painfully slow current, the Tek chatter from the embankment grew louder. A group of them approached the edge. Thairen giggled and Simcane jabbed his ribs below the water. This wasn't a game.

They used protruding roots from the embankment to pull themselves closer while keeping their heads barely above the water. They waited while the Tek patrol stalled directly above them. If a single Tek peered over the edge, the mission would be violently over. One of the Teks cleared his throat and then spat a thick wad of phlegm into the water beside Simcane's ear. Thairen grinned. Simcane couldn't figure out what was so funny. A weed stick fizzled in the water behind them. *Just get moving,* Simcane willed them.

Their chatter stopped suddenly and one of the Teks shouted, "Carpe, quianpe." Simcane lifted his eyes, expecting to see eyes staring back, but instead saw a hand pointing out over the water. He followed it to one of the boats that hadn't sunk and had gotten hung up on something. *Damn.*

Some of the Teks ran off while at least one of them stayed behind. At best, they were simply curious and were looking for a boat to ride out and investigate. At worst, they had gone for reinforcements.

Thairen's grin now nearly split his cheeks. "Don't wait up," he whispered, and reached for a protruding root higher up.

Simcane shook his head vehemently.

"If we stay here, his friends will come back and we'll be found. And we'll have lost."

Simcane bit his lower lip. *He's right. Damn him, he's right.*

Thairen leaned closer to his ear, "Besides," he snickered. "I need to do something about this churn. It's driving me crazy."

Simcane lifted his arm above the water. A thin, pulsating film of pink-tinged slime covered his arm like a second skin. *Churn.* Vile, disgusting creatures that existed for no other purpose than to be flattened out by smooth rocks and cooked alive under magnified sunlight. It had been among his favorite pastimes when he was young. At that moment, it probably would have been again.

He hadn't noticed the churn at first, but now that Thairen had said something, he couldn't think of anything but. Each steady pulsation was another bite from their microscopic teeth. He knew how it worked. First, they'd chew on his dead skin, which is part of the reason he hadn't felt it right away. Next, they'd get to the new skin underneath and blood would start oozing from everywhere, which would attract even more churn. And then the real pain would begin.

"We have to have patience," he whispered, mostly trying to convince himself. Thairen rolled his eyes, but stayed put.

Simcane's legs throbbed, telling him more churn were hard at work down there. Since churn had a talent for getting under clothes, he cringed to imagine what was happening to his manhood. Thairen fidgeted—he wouldn't be contained much longer.

"Wait," Simcane snapped.

It was too late. Thairen pulled out of reach and grabbed the protruding root to pull himself higher. Simcane ordered him to stop, but he might as well have commanded the water to stop flowing, or the churn to stop eating. Thairen scaled the embankment. The lone Tek above shouted, grunted, and then fell into the water behind the team. His sliced-opened throat attracted more churn.

Thairen peeked back over the edge. "Simcane." He pointed west. "Their water supply is just up ahead. That's why they're still here. You can make it. I'll buy you time."

Simcane grimaced. "No. Wait for us." He sank his hands into tangled vines in the muddy wall.

"No time. They're coming. And they bring their machines." He disappeared.

Simcane slipped and tugged and climbed until he pulled his thick body over the top of the embankment. The rest of his team had beaten him and were lying in wait in the knee-high grass. They lifted their heads just enough to see Thairen charge the approaching enemy like he had an army at his back. There must have been twenty or thirty Tek soldiers. They were caught off guard and without their armor, staring in amazement at the charging lunatic.

Fire flashed from the long cylinder of one of their wheeled machines, followed by a monstrous explosion of dirt and fire near Thairen's side. But the rushing maniac wasn't fazed. He didn't slow, closing the gap between himself and the enemy in a flash. The machine fired again, but missed as Thairen zig-zagged.

The Tek soldiers drew their swords; Thairen readied his knives.

"We should help him," BJ said, and started to push to his knees.

Simcane grabbed his shoulder and lowered him back to the ground. "We can't. They've already sent for more reinforcements, no doubt. We could save Thairen, maybe, but it would be at the cost of our mission."

With a squeal of delight, Thairen leaped into the Teks.

Simcane's team clawed away the churn from their arms and legs and crotches. Simcane wished he had time to torture the cursed creatures, but suffocating out of the water would have to do. His flesh from head to toe was raw and dotted with specks of oozing blood. It hurt like the worst sunburn.

He looked away from Thairen for a moment to the Tek water supply ahead. The enemy forces there had abandoned their posts to investigate the commotion.

Thairen was right—the crazy bastard's plan was working. He grunted and screamed as his knives carved enemy flesh. There was nothing subtle about his aggression, only raw fury and skill. He spun away from a lunging sword, and then drove his knives into another attacker's chest. Sprays of blood rained over him like a shower, and he loved it. It looked like he was dancing. Another Tek swung his sword, but blood squirted from his neck before he could finish his assault.

More Teks—armored Teks—rumbled and hissed toward the battle.

A sword slashed Thairen's back, but the madman didn't flinch. Even from so far away, Simcane could hear laughter. And it didn't come from the Tek soldiers.

Thairen disappeared within their swarm for a moment before leaping free.

Now run, damn it.

All he had to do was flee, but he circled back and leaped into the fray again. He seemed to enjoy the lopsided fight. A sword plunged into his gut. Instead of pulling the blade free, he grabbed the Tek's hands and he pulled the sword deeper into his own stomach, smiling the whole time. The tactic, however painful and stupid it might have been, brought him closer to his assailant. With a wide swing of both arms, he drove his knives into the sides of the Tek's neck. Then he ripped the blades free.

Thairen stumbled back from his prey to catch his wind. He grasped the hilt of the sword lodged in his gut while the Teks watched in stunned silence. With a grunt, he yanked the blade free and dropped it. His hand extended toward them and he gave a "come on" gesture. They surrounded him.

Simcane didn't want to see any more. "Let's go." With the Teks occupied, he and the others crawled in the tall grass along the edge of the embankment until they reached the hand-dug trench of the Tek water supply.

"We haven't much time to distance ourselves," he said. "They'll search every bit of this land."

Willum grinned. "That Thairen sure is insane."

Simcane looked up from cleaning away the last of the churn from his legs and snapped, "He's reckless. Let's not waste his sacrifice."

"If we follow their water supply, we should be behind their forces within days."

"Do you think they drink from this water?" Gillian asked.

"Sure. Drinking and bathing, probably. If the filthy animals even bathe, that is. Why?"

"No reason." She dropped her pants and, turning her back to the men, thrust her pelvis forward. Simcane couldn't see how she did it, but she sprayed a stream of piss that would make any man proud into the waterway. If he hadn't just seen her bits with his own eye, he'd think she was hiding something.

BJ shook his head. "That's very mature," he said as he pressed his spectacles farther up the bridge of his nose. "Are you finished?"

She squirted out one last drop and pulled up her pants. "Quite," she said with a smirk. She backed into Simcane's stonewall chest and peeked up at him. "I'm sorry, sir," she said. "It won't happen again."

"Hmph," Simcane grunted. "Well, what are the rest of you waiting for?" he asked, dropping his own britches and adding to the water supply.

CHAPTER 41

LOWLAND
PRISON

Atticus and Andon had traveled to the western edge of Grande Villa where they could better view the Tek army on the other side of the would-be battlefield. The enemy front line was positioned within catapult range, mimicking their Lithia strategy. So far, so good. The sea of black-clad soldiers and rumbling machines hunkered down for the long fight ahead. Atticus marveled at their coordinated movements and meticulous attention to detail as every soldier moved in concert, as if they were all fingers on the same hand. If they held true to their Lithia strategy, they would wait for the Epertasians to attack first. Rasi's plan counted on it.

Andon's men took over the abandoned town, moving wheeled catapults through the narrow streets while fortifying their troop buildup for a new kind of fighting he called urban warfare. Atticus took in their nervous looks. The amassing Tek army was something to behold, and he couldn't blame them for their increased anxiety. More and more he heard their questioning whispers and saw their long, focused stares across the battlefield. With the enemy in place, it was time to tell them.

"They look nervous," Atticus said.

Andon nodded. "Well, that's what we wanted, wasn't it?"

"Yes. We needed them to look the part in order to sell it."

Andon called for his lieutenants. Once they gathered, he informed them it was time to reveal the plan to the men. He turned to Atticus. "Time for you to head north."

"That it is. You have three nights to evacuate."

"Yes, sir."

"Remember, don't let the Teks see what you're doing. Leave everything behind. The catapults, the oxen, everything. Retreat from the rear first and use the dead of night and the buildings as cover. Wait until the third night to pull the front lines. They'll never know as long as you keep it calm and methodical."

"Do you think they'll give chase if they see us?"

"I doubt it. They've fortified their forces for our attack. By the time they realize we are retreating and receive new orders from their leadership, it will be too late."

Andon offered his hand. "Good luck, Atticus."

Atticus took it. "And you, as well."

He rode slowly through the town, shaking hands and offering his gratitude and encouragement to every man he came across. After he made it through the town, he headed north to the Great Dam. By evening after the second day of travel, the Great Dam came within view.

Hundreds of Epertasian soldiers and architects had worked night and day to build three castle-high trebuchets made of thick tree trunks that had been milled from a forest outside of New Arc. Boulders that had been dragged in on wagons by an army of oxen were secured in the slings, ready to soar. Atticus was proud of his men. It usually took weeks to build one of those contraptions from scratch, and here they had made three in a fraction of the time.

"Commander Atticus," one of the builders greeted him. "Good to have you back." The others turned to see him.

Atticus relaxed in his saddle. "Good to see you, men. How goes the trebuchets?"

"We are just working through our final checks, sir."

"Will they achieve our objective?"

"And then some, sir. These are the largest and most powerful ever created, to my knowledge."

"Very good. And where's Lieutenant Crawford?"

The soldier pointed to the dam.

"Keep up the good work, men." Atticus rode to where Crawford sat on his horse, marveling at the massive wall of stone and concrete. From the base, Atticus couldn't see the top as it appeared to touch the sky, nor could he see either end as they stretched for miles. He was amazed that such a magnificent creation was made by man and not formed by the gods. He shook hands with Crawford. "What're you doing over here, Michael?" he asked his lieutenant.

Michael rode to the wall and dragged his finger along a deep and winding structural crack. It wept, and he touched the tears. "Taste it, if you want."

"There's no need. I'm going to assume it's salty."

Michael nodded. "As salty as the Infinite Sea. But that's not all. If you walk very far along the wall, you'll find tons of these cracks. Also, the ground is littered with large chunks that have already broken free."

Atticus couldn't believe his eyes. "The dam was going to fail anyway?"

Michael nodded solemnly. "Maybe not today, but sometime in the not too distant future."

"So, the Lowlanders were on the brink of destruction?"

"It looks that way, sir." Michael pursed his lips in disgust. "No one deserves such leaders."

"No, they don't. Shall we head back?"

As they rode back to the working men, Michael asked, "How goes the Grande Villa deception?"

"Is that what we're calling it now?"

Michael nodded.

"By morning Andon's men should be clear of the town."

"Those dirty Teks have no idea what they're in for. Do you think their armor floats?" He smirked.

"We're counting on the opposite."

While they were examining one of the magnificent trebuchets, a soldier shouted, "Commander." He pointed toward the barren land from where Atticus had recently come.

Atticus squinted to better see. A lone woman staggered across the field. Atticus and Michael rode to her. She wore only a large fruit sack with holes cut out for her arms and head, and her bare feet were bloody. She looked like she hadn't eaten for days and her exposed skin was mottled with reddish blotches from the cold. Her dark hair could house birds.

"Who are you?" Atticus asked.

"Mister." Her gaze didn't rise above his feet. "I need help." Her voice was soft and weak and broken. She was hard to understand through her swollen lips, and Atticus strained to make out her words.

"Go on," he said.

"I have escaped a Lowland prison."

"Prison? Where?"

"In the town." She pointed in the direction of a winding dirt path. "It isn't far by horse."

Michael said, "The Lowlanders were supposed to evacuate everyone. They did not release you?"

"No, sir." Her gaze dropped to the ground.

"Why were you in this prison? What crime did you commit?"

"No crime," she said, and for some reason Atticus believed her. "Hundreds of us were gathered up and locked away. We didn't do anything except fail to fall under the spell of King Fice. There are children and babies in there. My son is still there."

Michael asked, "If you weren't guilty, why did your leaders do this to you?"

"I heard whispers while they led us to jail. They called us sacrifices to the approaching enemy."

Atticus glanced at Michael, who wore the same look of horror that he imagined was on his own face. "How did you escape?" he asked.

She turned away.

"It's all right. We're here to help."

For the first time, she looked up. Heavy bruising on her swollen face indicated her imprisonment hadn't been peaceful. "I snuck out when one of the guards fell asleep on top of me."

Atticus saw the shame in her hazel eyes. She bowed her head again.

"Please help my son. I'll do anything for you. They've had their way with me many times." She hesitated and breathed in an unstable breath. "If it would help, I guess you could as well. If you'd like, I mean."

Atticus gently reached down and touched her shoulder. "Michael, take this woman back to our camp. Get her aid and food and something warm to wear. Give me your lantern. I'm going to the prison."

"But, Atticus, you might not make it in time."

Atticus curled his upper lip and crinkled his nose like he'd smelled something foul. "Then I'd better be able to swim."

Michael passed him the lantern. Atticus kicked his horse into a gallop over the overgrown dirt path. Traveling by lantern and moonlight slowed his progress greatly, but by dawn he reached the outskirts of a town. He was cutting it close.

An old, empty blacksmith's shop sat beside a dilapidated stable. Rundown shops and saloons were at every turn. A general store, ransacked with smashed windows and shattered doors, stood next to a law enforcement house. Atticus could only guess what they considered law. At the far end of the strip he saw his destination: a sprawling windowless structure two stories high.

Any society that needs a place so big to keep miscreants doesn't seem like a society worth saving, he thought.

He found it sadly comical that in this miserable town the main road led not to a prominent castle or bustling town square, but to a prison. He wished he had japsy weed and more time to really show the gods what he thought of that devil's town.

As he neared the prison, he saw very little activity at the front gate. He decided to approach on foot anyway. His horse could use the rest.

An out of sight post next to an outhouse was the perfect place to leave his horse. He reached into his saddlebag and withdrew a hunting knife that was as long as his forearm. Up close and personal was the way to go for this mission, at least in the beginning.

A guard sat at the entrance with his back to Atticus. An empty bottle of whisky lay by his feet. He was breathing heavy, though he might have been snoring. Quietly, Atticus opened the guard's throat, almost decapitating him in his adrenaline-fueled exuberance. If he had been sleeping, it was a helluva wake up. Atticus dug through the guard's pockets while he still twitched on the ground until he found a key.

The long, winding hallway inside echoed with moans and blistering howls and laughter from tortured souls. The decomposing body of a young man rested on his stomach with his head awkwardly twisted to face Atticus. His last moment of agony was frozen on his face. A puddle of water, or maybe piss, surrounded him. Three severed fingers lay at his side. It wasn't a prison anymore, if it ever truly was.

Atticus pulled the front of his shirt over his mouth and nose, though it did little to stop the stink of blood, death, and feces. *These Lowlanders are as evil as the people we fight against, I believe.* His heart sank with a sudden realization. *And in trying to save them, we've unleashed them on Epertase.*

A guard exited a cell and wiped blood from his hands onto an already bloodstained rag. He hadn't seen Atticus yet. His sick grin told terrible stories of what he was doing inside. That grin faded when he looked up. Without thought, Atticus hurled his blade into the guard's chest. He stepped up to the fallen guard and yanked his blade free. The guard's haunting stare matched the poor dead boy's, and it made Atticus smile. The dead man's pocket yielded a second master key. Atticus took it just in case. A look into the cell made him wish he hadn't killed the guard so quickly. He said a silent prayer for the dead inside.

Each cell in the first hallway revealed more of the same. It felt hopeless. He reached a thick steel-and-wood-framed door secured by a padlock. It seemed odd to see a padlock there. A padlock held everyone inside regardless of whether they had a key. Even the guards weren't expected to escape. The door groaned like an old war hero with achy bones, opening into another long hallway. More cells lined both walls. The fearful whimpers gave him back hope of finding survivors.

The first cell held women and children who recoiled from the bars when he approached. How could children commit crimes worthy of such a hell?

In the far corner of the cell, in a space purposely left open by the crowd, a mother rocked back and forth with a limp infant held to her bosom. Atticus had seen enough atrocities to know she was in shock and the infant was dead.

Two of the women stepped forward. Their aggressive postures said that they'd had enough.

"It's all right," Atticus whispered with his hands up. "I'm here to free you." He swung the gate open and stepped to the side. "You two," he pointed to the two bravest. "Are you strong enough to free the others?"

They nodded. He handed them the second master key. "Open the rest of these cages. After you do, go southeast to higher ground as quickly as possible. Head for Epertase. You don't have much time."

In the next corridor, Atticus found even more cells. He opened the first, which was packed with men, some alive, some dead. He started to tell them that they were free, but laughter from farther down the hallway silenced him. It was two approaching guards, too preoccupied bragging about their latest atrocities to notice Atticus.

Atticus slipped into the cage with the prisoners, held his finger to his lips, and pulled the door nearly shut, careful not to let it latch.

The footsteps came closer.

Fitting in would be difficult because of his officer's clothes, but he put his back to the bars and bowed his head just the same. He only needed them to get close. The guards stopped at the cell. He could feel their breath and smell the alcohol on it.

"What's this?" one of the guards asked.

Atticus furtively slid his knife from his waistband.

"You," one of the guards shouted, and poked his shoulder with a club. Where did you get those clothes?" The guard's pocket jingled as he fished for his keys.

Atticus spun and drove the cell door into them, pinning them to the neighboring cell. While the guards struggled with their footing, Atticus jammed his blade into the first guard's chest.

Before the other guard could react, a pair of puny arms reached through the cold bars of the neighboring cell and wrapped around his neck. The guard flailed and clawed at the arms, but a second pair grabbed him through the bars. Cheers erupted when Atticus plunged his blade into that guard as well.

Atticus opened each cell and gave the occupants orders to flee to higher ground. One of the stronger-looking men picked up one of the guard's swords with a vengeful scowl. He led the way.

Atticus turned his attention toward the next hallway door.

"Sir?" someone called out from behind. It was a teenage boy from the cell he had just opened.

"What is it, boy? I'm in a hurry."

"Was it my mom? I mean the one who sent you. Was it her who saved us?"

Atticus nodded.

"They didn't hurt her, did they?"

Atticus hesitated, not sure of how to answer. "She's safe," he finally said.

The kid gave him a relieved smile. "She said she would free us."

Atticus patted his frail shoulder. "That she did. That she did. Now get to high ground. You haven't much time."

The kid turned to join the crowd, but Atticus called to him. "What's your name, son?"

He spun around with a new sense of purpose on his face. "Dillon," he said. "My name's Dillon."

"Nice to meet you, Dillon."

The kid bounced, unable to control his excitement, and rejoined the fleeing crowd.

Atticus continued down hall after hall, up to the second floor, and then eventually back down. Though none of the six other guards he came across had wronged him personally, he slaughtered them all just the same. His search eventually returned him to the outside door with the dead guard still lying beside his chair and empty whisky bottle.

Atticus stepped from the stoop into toe-deep water. It had begun. The wave that would level the town couldn't be far behind. One last look at the prison filled him with guilt. Though he and the others had freed as many prisoners as they could, the prison was a maze of corridors and hidden cells, and he couldn't help but fear he had missed some innocent Lowlander victims. The more he thought about it, the more he was sure he had.

The water was rising fast, already covering the tops of his feet. Cartographers would be busy for years changing the maps after what Andon and his men had done that day. He only wished he could see the looks on the Teks' faces as the wave plowed through them and turned Grande Villa and the rest of the Lowlands into a new lake. They could call it Lowland Lake. Or Tek Cemetery. That last one had a nice ring to it.

The water was up to his calves by the time he reached his horse. With the reins free of the post, he kicked it into a sprint, quickly catching up with the fleeing prisoners. A roar like a tornado echoed in the distance behind them.

"Keep moving," he shouted. Those too weak leaned on those stronger. It was a glimpse at the kindness some of the Lowlanders were capable of, and it reassured Atticus the risk was worthwhile. As he and the dozens of former prisoners reached higher ground, they looked back and watched the town flood. Since they were closer to the outer rim of the Lowlands, they wouldn't get the brunt of the wave, though he was confident that the Teks had. The water rose above the stores and shops, and eventually the prison. Dillon stepped up next to him.

Atticus took his hand and pulled him onto his horse behind him. "Let's go find your mom, kid."

CHAPTER 42

HAVENS RAVINE

Rasi arrived at Havens Ravine as the southern skies began to glow with the orangish hue of dawn. He was in awe of the mighty Epertasian army amassing on the Great Plains. The grass, so alive and vibrant just a few days before, was now brittle, brown straw. In the distance, he saw the northern edge of Concore Forest and the faint outline of Shadows Peak beyond. Even as the suns rose, Thasula remained hidden in gloom.

He peered into the ravine and thought of Lorca. Though he couldn't see the belke slug, he knew from his earlier encounter that the beast lay in wait and would reveal itself when food tickled its slime. He only hoped it was Tek food and not Epertasian.

A deceptive calm rested on a knife's blade as the soldiers had yet to see what made the noises they'd heard all night long: Distant thunder not made by storms, viper hisses of strange machines, and drumming feet in perfect coordination. Though loud and incessant, the noise could not prepare the men for the sight of the enemy army.

Throughout Rasi's ranks, the older soldiers shared wisdom learned from years of hard living and the Heathen War with the younger ones, some of whom were no older than thirteen. Other men kneeled and prayed to their gods. Some tried to show strength in front of their sons or fathers. Some of them were bested by their nerves and they vomited. A few men—the minority—stood excited and eager for the bloodshed ahead.

Rasi turned back to the enemy, an almost endless sea of armor-clad foreigners preparing to destroy all that he knew. In the faint light of dawn, across the distant span of the ravine, he saw the enemy's battle-hardened ranks and knew the fight would be long and hard and messy.

To his right sat his queen, his lover, his friend, upon her beautiful mare. On one hand, he was sad that she insisted on being there. The atrocities and violence she was about to witness would haunt her until her dying day. Yet she would have it no other way.

On the other hand, he admired her strength. Her will was to die for her people, with her people, if she must. That her death was a real possibility broke his heart. She put too much faith in her safety because of the Light within her, and nothing Rasi said could change her mind. That no Epertasian Light bearer had ever died without an heir was more likely luck than divine providence.

Her legs trembled in her stirrups. Rasi pretended not to notice, but she caught his glance and moved away. There was no shame in what she was feeling. He felt the same. He was just more experienced at hiding it.

Dru rode to the front bearing good news. "Word has just arrived, Rasi. The northern Tek army has been obliterated by Andon's floods. Your plan has worked. There will be no northern wave and we didn't lose anyone."

Rasi nodded, measured in his reaction. The floods were only his opening gambit. The real fight was about to begin. He looked past Dru to the incredible Epertasian army standing in wait. With Alina in tow, he rode out to address them.

Rasi made eye contact with Dru and nodded once. Alina rode up next to him.

Dru's horse pranced as even it seemed to anticipate the carnage that awaited. Dru shouted, "Epertasians. As you stand here and wait for war, you should know that the first battle has already been won." His impassioned voice prompted roars of approval.

That was good, Dru, Rasi thought. Lithia's fall wasn't a secret, and a morale boost was most welcome. *Give them a taste of victory now. Let them know this enemy isn't invincible after all.*

Dru bobbed his head, struggling to contain his zeal. His horse strutted side to side. "We have come here this day to face a conquering army—an army that has traveled many moons with a single, violent purpose. We have done them no wrong, yet these animals are here to bring us death. We are facing the gravest threat we have ever known." He pointed toward the invaders. "Look across that ravine." His voice cracked and wobbled. "Each of you, look at our enemies' faces and see their hatred. When you look at these creatures and deliver cold death by your blades, do not have pity, as they are monsters that deserve retribution. Drive your swords deep into their rotten hearts and twist with the pleasure of knowing you are on the side of the righteous. Know they want to kill your wives and children, and it is up to you to stop these murdering swine. Each one you kill is a blessing. Do not mourn them any more than you would mourn a lowly frost beetle crushed underfoot." Venom thickened in his voice.

He stopped to catch his wind. "These creatures are not invincible. They bleed like all animals. They drown like all animals. Now let them drown in blood."

The answering roar rivaled that of the Tek machines.

Dru's chest lifted and fell with his rapid breaths. "This battle we face will not be the end of Epertase, but the beginning of a new world. You must have faith in the soldier beside you, as he will put his faith in you. You must believe in Commander Rasi's strategy, as it is strong and true. Those of you who fought beside Rasi during the Heathen War know his value in combat and leadership. Those of you who have lost trust in him must know he has the confidence of all your leaders. He has been proven innocent of his crimes and we will win because of him. With Rasi to lead me, I am eager for this fight. I am not afraid. We have been free for many generations, and when we awaken after this war has ended, we will be free still." His face glowed red with passion. "And we will have sent a message to any invading armies across the mighty oceans. We will not be conquered. For we are Epertase."

The soldiers' howls could have been heard by the Tek masters in their homeland on whatever shit continent spawned such putrid evil. Rasi hoped they couldn't sleep tonight having realized they had sent their people to slaughter. Dru spun his horse away from the men to face the enemy. Rasi did the same, and then looked over his shoulder. He gave a nod.

Dru raised his sword into the air. "For Queen Alina." Twenty thousand cheers in perfect harmony lifted the hairs on Rasi's neck.

Rasi turned his head toward Alina, who stared back with fearful eyes.

My queen, it begins.

The natural prewar instinct of doubt seemed to settle into Alina. *Should we send peacemakers first?*

Rasi didn't reply. He understood that deep down she knew the answer. A slight breeze ruffled his hair as the battlefield went eerily silent. Even the birds and rodents seemed to have fled.

Dru's sword swept downward in a glittering arc.

A single ball of fire streaked over Rasi's head like a comet. He pointed to it.

This is our peacemaker, Alina.

The calm of the battlefield was suddenly and violently shattered by a single explosion behind the Tek front line. A handful of Tek soldiers rolled on the ground to smother the choking flames.

And then on cue, the rickety creak of a thousand catapults ended with jarring thumps. A thousand fireballs lit up the dawn sky like a third sun rising. Alina covered her ears. The fireballs engulfed the enemy and kindled the grass along the front line for as far as Rasi could see in either direction.

Without mercy, a second and then a third wave of explosions pounded the Tek forces. Rasi watched, in awe of the might of the Epertasians. Not since the opening battle against the heathens had such might been imposed.

Cries of wounded Teks could barely be heard over the explosions. Their dead lay in the burning grass with smoke trickling from gaps in their armor. Other Teks callously shoved their charred comrades into the ravine before replacing them at the front.

The pungent odor of burned flesh rode the cool breeze past Rasi's nostrils. He let a guilty smile adorn his face. The birds returned, or at least the vultures.

While the catapults rained death, Rasi lifted his arm above his head. His men watched intently. They cut through ropes that held back giant, twisted arms on tightly wound coils. They snapped and whipped the arms forward. Their payloads of chain shot twisted and twirled through the air. This assault was Dru's idea. The pairs of iron balls connected by lengths of chain were designed for use in naval battles to disable enemy ships. They had never been used as designed, but they were proving effective against the armored Teks, shredding pathways of death through their ranks. That Dru was a bright one. If he lived through this battle, he had a brilliant military career ahead of him.

Alina turned to Rasi, her fingers still plugging her ears. *There's no end to them. Every one we kill is replaced by two more. We cannot maintain this offensive for long.*

This is only the beginning. Your army is plenty resourceful. You know our strategy.

The Teks appeared to dance in the fiery light of the inferno as they tried in vain to extinguish fires and dodge spinning bolas. Rasi studied them intently. Their every movement was important to how he would move forward. Their armor was strong, stronger than he had imagined, and their resilience sent a small bit of despair into his gut.

The legendary Epertasian onslaught continued throughout the day and into the night. The second dawn of the offensive was dulled by dark clouds. The muted sunslight gave Rasi his first good look at the damage they'd inflicted. Right away, he realized it wasn't enough. Alina kept looking at him, and he tried to hide his concern behind a hardened stare. But there was no hiding that the Tek numbers appeared as thick and plentiful as they had at the beginning. And now they were mad. The battle was about to get messy.

"Rasi, our attack has done nothing," Alina screamed over the explosions.

Our attack has done fine, he lied. *You must trust me now. I need you to order an end to our attack.*

She froze. Her mouth dropped open. "Already. That's it? There's still too many of them. We'll be overrun."

We must stick to the plan. Order the ceasefire.

She hesitated. He gave her a stern look that said there was no more room for arguing. She reluctantly turned to Dru and called for the ceasefire.

Dru raised a horn and pressed it to his lips. The signal was repeated by other horns along the front line. The catapult barrage slowed to a stop. The moans of wounded Teks and the squawks of scavenger birds were all that broke the disquieting silence. Rasi rode to the ravine's edge for a closer look. *Let's see what you have.*

The Teks were disciplined. They had stood firm during the incredible Epertasian onslaught, and now they waited to make sure it was over. Rasi had seen the most hardened heathens wilt under such pressure. The Teks continued rolling the dead and mortally wounded into the ravine before falling back into line. Others seemed eager to attack, but stayed the course.

Rasi sat on his horse, his stomach having its own war with itself. The brisk day dragged on, yet no retaliation came. Alina returned from a visit to the tents and shifted back and forth on Allusia's saddle. She rubbed her hands together as though washing imaginary blood from them. Her eyelids were puffy. While rations of dried meat passed from the rear to the front, she nervously asked Rasi what the enemy was waiting for.

They're waiting to see if we're finished.

"Then let's show them we're not."

Patience. It's still early. There is a lot of blood yet to be shed. Maybe you should fall back and get some rest.

"No. I have told you; I'm staying with my people."

They're still your people in the rear.

She glared at him.

Dru came up alongside them. Even he showed doubts. "Where's their response, Rasi?"

Rasi shook his head. He looked toward the many old, wooden bridges that spanned the ravine. The Teks made no move toward them.

The wait seemed worse than actual combat could possibly be. He had forgotten how he always suffered such prefight anxieties until his angry stomach reminded him. *Maybe they're waiting until night.*

Dru handed him a fresh water bladder and some jerky. Afternoon slogged into evening. And then the ocean of Tek soldiers swayed like ripples of silk from the back through to the front. Distant puffs of smoke rose into the air.

Rasi watched.

Alina watched.

The Epertasian army watched.

The sea of Teks parted, forming large pathways stretching from the rear to the front lines. The soldiers' movements appeared well-choreographed; their steps flawless. Distant puffs of smoke grew larger and nearer, accompanied by a low rumble.

The first sight of their smoke-belching, wheeled machines was stunning. They were bigger than any horse-drawn carriage and covered in the same black armor as the soldiers.

One of the rolling monsters advanced close to the edge of the ravine, let out a thunderous hiccup, and squealed to a jerky halt. A final blast of thick, black smoke puffed from several chimney-like pipes along its roof. Throughout the Tek forces, the other machines found their places. The sky blackened from the smoke.

A horn blared like the bellow of the belke slug from the first machine. It was followed by equally deafening howls from all the machines. Rasi plugged his ears.

When the horns fell silent, the Tek soldiers swarmed the machines like bees. For the first time they didn't seem disciplined and patient, thirsty for whatever the machines carried. They climbed up the sides and ran along the tops until the machines were buried beneath them. Long, rigid hoses extended from the machines' underbellies and stretched up to the swarming Teks.

This was what Rasi was waiting for. *That's it,* he told Alina. *Aidric spoke of their need for the black blood. That is why they waited to attack; they needed their thirst quenched first. Now's the time, Alina.* Rasi lifted his arms and his straps high above his head.

Another wail rang out from the metal monsters pouring smoke from their stacks. *They're feeding,* he marveled. *My gods, they're feeding.*

Alina's eyes lit up. She raised her arms to mimic Rasi.

He looked to Dru over his shoulder, and Dru pressed the horn to his lips again.

Rasi waited. The timing had to be perfect. Let them feed and drench themselves in the black blood. Aidric had said it burned like japsy weed.

Wait.

The Teks danced with ungodly delight while their suits drank the blackness. As the liquid spilled out, they worshipped it, bathed in it, swam in it. They were in ecstasy. Their offensive was about to begin, and they were drunk on bloodlust.

Alina stared daggers through him. She was ready now.

Waaaiiit.

The enemy troops slithered against each other, consumed by their feeding frenzy. Rasi grinned. When not even a hint of the machines could be seen beneath their armor, he let his arms and straps drop.

Now.

Alina did the same. Dru's instrument let out another ear-piercing note.

The catapults launched a new wave of fire into the air. As the flaming balls soared over Rasi's head, the swarming Teks froze in terror. They'd been caught. And they knew it.

Explosions erupted all around the metal monsters. The Teks scattered like roaches, but they were too slow.

And then it happened.

One of the missiles landed close enough to its mark that a blinding, beautiful fireball kissed the sky. Rasi felt the heat on his face. It was warm and comforting and satisfying. When the smoke cleared, the wheeled machine was little more than twisted metal. Dead Teks littered the ground around it. Then, farther down the line and deeper, another machine sent a fireball to the sky, followed by another. Teks sailed through the air, some of them in flames, others in pieces.

Ka-boom.

Another and more wonderful blast erupted deeper within their ranks.

Keep it coming.

Alina screamed, "It's working." She turned to Rasi. "You're a genius. You've done it." He'd rarely seen her so excited. Though he knew the battle was far from over, he didn't want to take the small victory from her.

Additional equally impressive explosions filled the landscape as Teks scrambled to find safety from the deadly infernos. Epertasians laughed and pointed and celebrated their success.

Rasi signaled the archers. Riders with torches rode along the line of archers, igniting their arrows. Once the row of archers had flaming arrows knocked, they released. Though the arrows didn't penetrate the Tek armor, it ignited their glistening sheens of black blood. They rolled on the ground, desperately trying to put out the flames.

Rasi's heart slammed his breastbone with the force of a battle-axe. More wheeled machines exploded. Rasi's straps snapped at the air. The ground war was close. He gritted his teeth.

Alina, while they're in chaos. Now's the time for attack. Order it.

Rasi raised his right hand into the air. *Stay on this side of the ravine when we cross the bridges.*

"Dru," she shouted. "Prepare the advance."

"Of course, Your Majesty." He put the horn to his mouth.

Alina, on my com—

He didn't finish. The ground shook. His ears popped and a blast of scorching air knocked him from his horse. He thudded to the ground, nearly sliding into the ravine.

He lifted his head to focus on his frantic army. They scattered, searching for refuge from the strange projectiles in the air. A crater nearby was strewn with dismembered bodies. Another explosion, this one deeper within his forces, threw body parts skyward. Rasi looked around. He lost his breath. His stomach knotted. *Alina?* He couldn't see her.

Explosions racked his forces in every direction. An Epertasian soldier knelt in front of him, terror on his blood-splattered face. His lips moved, but Rasi only heard a dull, constant ringing. He tried to shake away the fog and focus on the soldier.

The soldier screamed, "What do we do, si—" Blood sprayed from the back of his head and he collapsed face-first onto Rasi's chest. His body quivered as he died. Rasi shoved him aside and twisted to face the Tek front line.

Small puffs of smoke trickled from the ends of long, cylindrical instruments aimed from their shoulders. He rose to his knees. *Alina,* he mentally screamed, but she didn't answer. His horse staggered past, blood trickling from its ear. The explosions were relentless. Rasi pushed himself to his feet and grabbed his horse's mane. Epertasian bodies flew through the air.

The Teks in the front row raised their death instruments to their shoulders. *Pop. Pop. Pop.* Small bursts of smoke rose from their weapons. Rasi threw his hands in front of his face as his horse let out a wail, then fell to its knees.

A hand grabbed Rasi's shoulder and spun him around. Several straps wrapped around the assailant's neck before Rasi realized it was Dru. The straps relaxed.

"Commander Rasi, we need to stay low and withstand their assault."

Rasi grabbed Dru's shoulders. "A'ena?"

"I don't know. Allusia raced past me a few moments ago. The queen was not with her."

Rasi breathed angrily through his nose. More devastating explosions erupted amid his forces. The Epertasian first salvo had been impressive, but this was something else altogether. He wished Aidric had stayed conscious longer so he could have asked him more questions.

He caught a glimpse of the front line of Teks as they raised their death instruments once again. He tackled Dru to the ground an instant before another series of pops rang out. More good soldiers dropped in an instant. Even their shields were of no use.

The Tek weapons were incredible. Ruthless. Devastating. It wasn't a fair fight.

Rasi shoved Dru away and ran along his front line. He frantically gestured for them to get low. Dirt pelted him from another explosion. Farther along the front line, brave leaders did the same as Rasi, urging their men to the ground.

The Epertasians hunkered down as best they could as the destruction continued throughout the night, laying waste to Rasi's forces. He felt helpless to defend them. Even retreat would be deadly. Once everyone was down, Rasi crawled along his front line, searching for his love.

Dru raced past him again on horseback, fearlessly barking orders along the way. "Stay low to the ground," he yelled. "Dig holes if you can. Hide inside the craters left by their explosions. We must endure until morning."

Each relentless, fiery concussion was followed by new waves of agonized screaming. Blood splattered Rasi's face as another nearby soldier fell. Any soldiers trained in treating the wounded moved from crater to crater, tying tourniquets and removing mangled limbs.

The night was brutal, the enemy unyielding.

The soulless eyes of the fallen stared back at him, making him sick with himself. He had led these men to such an end before the real fighting had even begun. The belke slug roared from the ravine below, no doubt enjoying its bounteous meal. At every brief lull in the Tek attack, Rasi pushed to his knees, constantly in search of Alina.

Epertasian blood flowed past his feet in streams, slowed only by dams of corpses. The stink of death saturated the air and he feared he would never be free of it. The hair on his arms matted together in clumps of gore, some dried and some still fresh. He didn't even know if some of it was his own. He sucked in lungfuls of air while watching the Teks prepare for their next wave. It had been a brutal night, and the morning was shaping up to be even worse.

Dru, now on foot, grabbed his shoulder. The right side of his face was bloody and burned. His ear was gone. "We're being slaughtered," he screamed. "We need to advance."

Rasi shook his head. His men were falling by the hundreds, maybe thousands, but if he attacked now, he was sure the slaughter would be even worse. He wasn't ready to give up the catapult barrage just yet.

"If we stay, there won't be enough of us to mount an offensive later."

He was right.

"We can't endure much more as it stands. Their long-range weaponry is too effective. We must advance. I know these men. They will fight hard."

Their heart wasn't what Rasi questioned. He needed more time. Charging this soon went against all his meticulous plans, but what other choice did he have? He looked into the eyes of his men; they were eager for the fight. Then he looked back across the ravine. The Teks were just as eager. All along the front line hundreds of shoulder-mounted cylinders puffed smoke again and hundreds of Epertasians fell.

Rasi nodded his head once. What had he done?

Dru blared the horn with all his might. Then he screamed, "Chaaaaaaaarge," until his voice broke like a pubescent teenager's. A collective battle cry reverberated from his men. They crawled from their craters to begin the march and the ground rumbled with their footsteps.

All along Havens Ravine, the bridges filled with Epertasian warriors, met in the middle by their Tek counterparts. The bridges creaked and swayed and threatened to crumble beneath their weight. Teks and Epertasians alike hurtled over the sides, only to be replaced by more warriors.

Rasi raced to the edge to see if his men had survived the fall. Under each bridge, soldiers were getting mired in the maddening belke slug slime. The creature had finished a pass and turned to suck up its new trail of slime. Its hunger was insatiable.

Rasi waved frantically at the lead archer until he caught his eye. He flashed five fingers three times and then motioned to the ravine. Fifteen archers accompanied their commander to the edge. Rasi pointed at the belke slug. The archers peppered the creature with their entire quivers, leaving enough arrows protruding from its back to make it resemble a porcupine. The creature howled and turned away.

Dru ordered groups of men to rescue those in the slime. "Leave the Tek bastards," he added.

The front line of Teks bustled with activity. They wheeled hundreds of small, horse-sized catapults to the edge of the ravine, forming a wall of sorts. The metal catapults cocked back collectively and then sprang forward, hurling armored Tek soldiers across the ravine. Rasi watched, helpless, as they soared over his head, swords in hand. Thin, white, almost translucent material billowed out from their backs and slowed their falls. The human catapults sent wave after wave of Tek soldiers.

And just like that, the battle moved to the Epertasian side of the ravine.

Other Teks raced to the edge. They pointed weapons that were like their death-making sticks, only larger. A chorus of clanks rang out and pairs of metal spears rocketed from the ends and embedded into the dirt and rock of the Epertasian side. The spears were attached to chain ladders.

Dru pointed and screamed, "They're coming across. Knock out those chains."

Epertasian soldiers rushed to the spears and dug at the ground, but the anchors were set too deep. The first waves of Teks reached them, met by their swords. A lot of Teks fell, but more of them reached firm ground.

It was all falling apart. Rasi joined the battle at the edge, madly swinging his ineffective sword at their superior armor. His straps hurled screaming Teks into the slime below. More and more Teks poured across the ladders, too many to hold back, but Rasi and his men held their ground.

As Rasi fought off a swarm of Teks, he glanced to the wooden bridges, where the Teks were pushing the Epertasians back. One of the bridges in the distance had collapsed beneath their weight.

Rasi staggered back to catch his breath. He scanned the battlefield, trying to estimate how much of his army had already perished. More Teks flew overhead, white cloth bubbling out from their backs and catching the wind.

On the enemy's side, the explosion-making machines grumbled forward like gigantic snails and repositioned for a fresh wave of attacks. Rasi could only hope they wouldn't fire with their own men in their sights, but from what he knew about their brutality, he likely hoped in vain. He needed to trust his plan. If his strategy was sound, and Simcane was as good as his legend told, he'd have a chance. He only hoped he would still have an army left to fight.

CHAPTER 43

INFILTRATE

Simcane stood with his team atop a sand dune and beheld an unimaginable sight. Following the water supply trench had led them to their goal. The Wastelands, once a barren desert where only the hardiest creatures like fishers or hylocks could survive, now resembled a strange, new civilization.

His team stood in awe alongside him. The campfires stretched over the terrain for as far as he could see, only broken by large circles of blackness. "Those are the pits," he said. The first pit was below him near the bottom of the dune. "I'll get this one."

Giant, tree-like towers spewed raven-black ink from long tubes into enormous basins. The basins were connected to the pits by fat hoses strung across the ground. Strange and fantastic metal creatures rolled between the tents and bonfires and carried the black blood from the pits in the direction of Havens Ravine.

There was no time to waste. Every load carried away fueled the fight against Epertase. Simcane gathered his team. "May the gods see us through our mission and grant us mercy if we are to stand before them this day in the afterworld. May the fires we make here tonight be celebrated all the way in Havens Ravine and beyond. Good luck."

Without a word, Eldon glided down the sandy hill like he had wheels on his feet. He disappeared into the night. BJ and Simcane waited atop the dune while Joseph, Gillian, and Willum headed south.

Simcane knelt next to BJ. At the bottom of the dune next to the pit, three tiny orange dots flared like fireflies. "Weed sticks," BJ whispered.

The guards didn't have armor and their black-stained clothing was more fitting for workers than soldiers. One of the weed sticks hit the sand and then was snuffed out by a sandal.

BJ quietly knocked an arrow, drew it back, and waited. It hovered just above Simcane's head. Simcane's open right hand hovered near his ear. "Wait," he whispered.

Then he saw a tall, lanky shadow projected onto a tent from the light of a bonfire.

With Eldon in place, Simcane closed his fist. "Fire at will," he whispered. A whoosh of air rushed past his face. A dull thump was followed by a grunt and a gasp. A worker stumbled to the side, purple fletching protruding from his back just below his shoulder blade.

With the grace of an angel, two skinny arms clutched one of the other two workers by his head. Even high on his perch, Simcane heard the snap. The final Tek of the trio turned to run, but Eldon was on him like a lion. Blood sprayed from the Tek's mouth as he too fell dead. One by one, Eldon dragged the dead guards to the black pit and tossed them in. They quickly sank. Then, like a calm ocean wave, he vanished back into the darkness.

Simcane said, "Be careful, BJ." He shook BJ's hand. "See you at the farthest pit."

"I'll be there."

BJ disappeared into the night.

Simcane scooted down the dune on his butt. An army of tents filled with sleeping Teks waited to spoil the party only a few horse-lengths away. He would have enjoyed killing each one of them as they slept, but he was a good soldier and his mission trumped vengeance.

Faint concussions echoed from the direction of Havens Ravine. Simcane hugged the pit as he worked his way around to the front where a wheeled machine slept. It seemed as good a place as any to hide and give his team time to get to the other pits. The machine was cold and lifeless.

An unsuspecting Tek stepped around the front of the machine and into Simcane's path. They both froze. The Tek seemed to have forgotten how to yell. Simcane thunked his head with a fist. As Simcane lowered the unconscious Tek into the black pit, he heard another group approaching. They talked and laughed, complacent in their guard duties. They hadn't seen him yet. Simcane hurried back to the machine and squatted between it and the back of a tent. After the men passed and were out of sight, he started around the machine again, but the metal creature's head gurgled and choked and screeched like it was trying to clear a hairball. A steady grumble followed as the machine rattled and shook.

With nowhere to go before the racket woke the others, Simcane dove beneath it. Individual grains of sand vibrated and tumbled over each other like millions of ants swarming a discarded treat.

A pair of sandals stepped to the monster's side between it and the pit. "Knock mei a sul ock."

Another set of feet joined the first. "Com de so laffe."

The two Tek workers yanked at levers along the beast's side, exposing a long tube from its belly beside Simcane. A set of hands reached beneath. Simcane held his breath. He was confident he could kill a few of them, but not a thousand. He wasn't crazy like Thairen. The Tek felt for the tube without leaning his head down to look. The tube was just out of reach. Simcane nudged it close enough for the Tek's fingers to brush it. Simcane breathed again. Once they stretched the tube into the pit, they cranked the levers again and fed their beast its black tonic.

Simcane crawled close to their feet as they waited. He needed some kind of distraction so he could climb out unnoticed.

And then, as if on cue, a column of fire ignited in one of the pits to the east. From Simcane's limited view, it looked like the entire world had been set ablaze. Shrill alarm horns blared throughout the camp.

Simcane slithered from beneath the machine, his prey distracted by the orange glow. The machine shook and cringed and bounced. A satisfied screech combined with the black liquid spurting from the couplings told them the beast was full. Simcane was now within an ochrid whisker behind them as they yanked at the levers and frantically closed the valves. One of the Teks pulled the tube from the pit and retracted it back into the machine's gut with the black blood still dripping from its end.

Simcane engulfed him in his tree-trunk arms. The Tek hardly had time to tense up, let alone scream for help. He squirmed and kicked and let out a wheeze. The racket of the machine was the perfect cover and the dying Tek's companion remained oblivious to the struggle behind him.

Simcane flexed. The Tek grunted and his spine snapped. His body stiffened briefly and then went limp, his head falling against Simcane's chest.

The other Tek turned and gasped. Simcane heaved his partner's lifeless body at him, knocking him to the sand. He closed the distance and crushed the man's throat. An image of Princess Lilliac flashed through Simcane's mind. Killing the Teks felt good.

With no time for finesse, Simcane tossed both bodies into the pit, splashing dark goop on his face and lips. It was thick and bitter. Smearing the muck from his mouth with his forearm, he watched the bodies in the black lake as they sank like they were in quicksand. His pulse quickened; his chest heaved in rising excitement. It was only a matter of time before he was spotted, so he needed to work fast.

Another eruption of flames tickled the sky to the north. *Eldon.* He smiled. His team was doing well. Now it was his turn. He fished a clump of japsy weed from his waist bag and rubbed it between his palms. The spaces between his fingers glowed orange, prompting him to rub faster. His palms heated. Japsy weed was a strange plant in that flames could be started in one's hands because the oils from it temporarily coated the skin. It was almost ready when a blast of searing pain slammed his shoulder, sending him sprawling to the ground. Damn him for being so sloppy.

His shoulder burned as though he'd been struck by a scalding battle hammer. He spun his head toward the metal beast's tail where a single Tek stood, frantically fiddling with the end of a cylindrical weapon. Simcane dug through the sand until his hand brushed his japsy weed. With it between his palms again, he scrubbed his hands together while the Tek aimed his noisy weapon.

Simcane only needed another moment. The Tek's instrument flashed. Simcane closed his eye and thrust one hand toward the weapon. The Tek's projectile met his air blast with a boom, sending a tiny, flattened lead ball harmlessly into the sand.

Simcane rubbed his hands together again.

The Tek dropped his weapon and drew his sword. The orange glow in Simcane's hands turned white as he kept his eye directed on his charging foe. The Tek raised his sword. With a subtle swipe of his foot in the sand, Simcane broke the trail of black blood leading from the pit to the machine. Then he dropped the japsy weed on the trail that led to the pit. He smiled before diving beneath the machine.

The Tek stopped in his tracks while the trail of fire lurched toward the pit. Then he crouched to see under the machine, looking at Simcane like he was the worst hider in the world. Simcane covered his head with his arms. The creeping flame reached the pit. The air around them sucked toward it before exploding into a wall of flames. The Tek batted at his burning skin and tried to flee, but the scorch was too intense, and he crumpled to his face. Simcane scrambled away from the vicious heat as the tiny hairs on his neck and arms singed. Along the tent line, Teks raced past, more to escape the heat than to do anything about it. Not that they could have.

Simcane crawled out from under the machine, its bulk shielding him enough to make the heat bearable. In the confusion, one of the frantic Tek soldiers collided with him, said something in Tek, and then continued about his business.

The head of the metal beast lay open and empty, so Simcane slipped inside. Two metal seats faced small slits at the front of its head, and he sat on one of them. The seat was a frying pan and getting hotter. He yanked the door closed as a Tek worker, apparently one of the more observant ones, leaped onto the machine. He glared through the door's window and reached for the handle. Simcane grabbed the handle on his side and held it as the Tek wrenched at it from the other side. His puny arms were no match for Simcane's strength. The worker shouted what he assumed to be Tek curse words.

One of the Tek's strange weapons sat between the seats. Simcane wedged it into the door handle, effectively locking it. He smiled at the frustrated worker.

A metal lever rested at Simcane's right side and another sat along his left hip. He thrust the left lever forward and the machine jerked to the left. The right one jerked him right. He shoved both handles forward. The machine vibrated and roared before lurching forward. The ride was slow, the vibrations violent and bruising.

He shifted from cheek to cheek on the hot seat until the machine moved far enough away from the fiery pit to be comfortable. Trying to rid himself of the painful kink the enemy's weapon had caused in his shoulder, he worked his arm in circles. Each movement felt like something foreign rubbed against the bone beneath his skin. Though he was in pain, the wound wasn't a bleeding one. As with all other wounds he'd absorbed over the years, this pain too would pass.

The Tek hanging on to his door eventually gave up, leaped free, and ran back to the camps, no doubt to tell others what he'd seen. Blazing pits filled the horizon, surprising him at his team's efficiency.

With both levers jammed all the way forward, Simcane eventually passed another raging pit. His attention focused ahead, he didn't notice the figure running alongside his door until a rock hit the window, followed by muffled cries of "Simcane." He pulled the levers back and the metal beast stopped. With a grin, he freed the door handle and opened it.

"We've been chasing you forever," Eldon said. "Can we get a ride?"

Simcane leaned out and looked around. "We?"

"The others will be here soon. Their legs do not move as fast or nimbly as mine."

Gillian arrived next, followed by Willum and BJ. She held three Tek worker uniforms. "Look what I found in an empty tent. Think they could come in handy?"

Simcane nodded.

"I don't have one for anyone as fat as you or as tall as Eldon, though, and Willum's going to look like a kid in his daddy's clothes."

Fat? She really knew how to dig a guy. "Where's Joseph, by the way?" Simcane asked.

Gillian answered coldly, "He didn't make it."

Willum added, "We had just ignited the final pit when a Tek got him from behind with one of their long-range weapons. Hit him right in the head. He was dead before he hit the ground."

Simcane winced and shook his head. "It's a shame."

Gillian climbed in beside him. "He wasn't much of a fighter," she said. "He probably should have been an actual priest instead."

Eldon climbed in beside her, making it a tight fit.

Gillian tilted her head slightly as she examined Simcane's shoulder. "Did they get you too?"

"Looks that way." He wondered if she was judging him like she had Joseph.

"Mind if I dig it out so it doesn't get infected?"

Simcane shrugged.

She produced a knife. "This is gonna hurt."

"What else is new?"

She began digging. She was right—it hurt like scalding water. Finally, something hit the metal floor of the machine with a clank. She shoved a rag against the wound. It still burned, but already felt better.

Willum and BJ climbed onto the top of the machine and donned the Tek clothes while Gillian stripped down inside the cab. Seeing her pants drop for the second time, Eldon turned away. His face reddened. She chuckled.

Next stop: Havens Ravine. Simcane shoved the levers forward.

CHAPTER 44

TEVIN'S WRATH

Inside Rasi's cave high on Shadows Peak, Tevin opened his crusty eyelids. The floor was cold against his back. At first, he didn't recognize or remember where he was or how he had gotten there, let alone how long he had been unconscious, but flashes of Siver and Brant and the others slowly reoriented him to his mission. His head hurt like the worst hangover he'd ever had. The suns' brightness stung his eyes. He shaded them with his hand and squinted.

He squeezed his right fist, making sure he hadn't lost the strength in it again. He remembered the all-encompassing fire that had changed him to his core. He couldn't wait to tell Elijah about his newfound gift.

He stood up and took a step, and his legs burned with power. He took another step, and an unfathomable energy crawled beneath his skin. He felt stronger than ever before. He *was* stronger than ever before.

The cave was mostly quiet except for a distant thunder echoing from Thasula's side of the mountain. He listened closer. The rumbles came too regularly to be thunder. They sounded more like explo—*Oh no. The war. Elijah.*

His feet barely touched the narrow path on his way to the bottom. As he ran, his mind wandered to a time when the school bullies had mocked him. He wished they could see him now. Or that he could see them. Oh, how they'd pay.

Lost in his daydreams, he reached the base of the mountain.

"Irackne," someone shouted, startling him.

There must have been a thousand men clogging every open spot of land in the valley. They wore odd, hissing black armor and perplexed expressions.

"Hello?" Tevin said. "You must be the Teks. Reinforcements, I presume?" He looked past them toward Widows Run as his mind whirled. "If the battle is already waging behind the mountain," he mused aloud, "and the early reports were that your friends approached from the west, where are you guys from?" He shook his head as the pieces fell into place. He waved his finger. "Ah. Tsk, tsk, tsk. Very sneaky. You made landfall on the southern beaches, didn't you? I wonder, does Elijah know you're coming?" Tevin extended his hands to his sides with his palms up. An orange glow grew from his chest, bright enough that he couldn't see his own hands anymore. He cocked his head.

Only one of them found the courage to step forward, and he had to order three others to join him. The four moved with slow, hesitant steps. They screamed some sort of heathen gibberish as if trying to intimidate him. Tevin couldn't help but snicker.

"Slock tei," one of them shouted. "Slock tei," he yelled again when Tevin didn't react. They stopped short and lifted their odd, stick-like weapons to their shoulders. "Ick lock talley fol," the closest one commanded. He poked Tevin's shoulder with his weapon and then quickly retreated to the others.

Tevin smiled as they squinted against the orange glow. "It's like looking at the suns, huh?"

The soldier's voice rose in excitement, "Ick lock talley fol." Tevin saw every slight wrinkle and subtle bulge of their index fingers around the tiny levers of their weapons.

The ends of their weapons flashed. Tevin flinched, expecting pain or even death to follow. But pain didn't strike him. Death didn't come. He smiled.

Four lead marbles thudded to the rocky ground. The Teks' faces faltered.

"Is that all?" Tevin mumbled.

The Teks screamed more of their gibberish, though what they said didn't much matter.

They'd better be praying, Tevin thought.

They nervously fumbled with their weapons as though they'd forgotten how to work them. One of the men finished whatever task he was attempting and pointed his noisemaker at Tevin again. Tevin braced for the thunder. He imagined the heat of the suns.

But this time thunder didn't come. Instead, the soldier dropped his instrument like it was on fire. The soldiers next to him dropped theirs as well. Each of the four weapons glowed red.

Tevin waved his hand experimentally. Their light moans were the first sign something was wrong. They began clawing at the armor around their necks. Their moans turned into agonized wails loud enough for Elijah's army to hear as their armor began to glow red like their weapons. Their brethren watched in horror; Tevin watched in ecstasy. The struggling Teks crumpled and writhed in pain. One of their friends rushed over and emptied his water bladder onto the nearest suffering soldier. The water hissed and steamed when it met the glowing red armor. Their skin sizzled within, sending a foul, putrid stench into the stale air.

For only the briefest of moments, Tevin pitied them.

When their screams finally died and smoke rose from their gaping mouths, he grinned. At that moment, he realized something about himself. Watching the horror of the suffering men should have bothered him in some way, but it didn't. He was glad to have done it and looked forward to frying every godforsaken one of them.

He eyed the dead a final time and told himself he would never give in to the weakness of pity.

He glared at the Teks, who froze with fear. "You will all die," he said, though he doubted they understood him.

They charged. The ground shook.

Tevin burned with rage. The valley filled with a deafening howl from high above. Some of the charging Teks stopped to look upward while the others lowered their heads and continued their attack.

The first Tek to reach Tevin raised his sword and shouted as he swung it. A horse-sized rock dropped on him with a satisfying splat. At that point, even the bravest of them froze. Their eyes lifted toward the mountaintop. There was nowhere for them to go. Tevin didn't have to look to know the mountaintop was crumbling. Panic washed their faces. Boulders, some as large as cottages, pounded their ranks. The Teks screamed and wailed as the raining rocks crushed the meat of their forces.

The mountain swayed and shook and then burst apart at the top like a glass vase hurled against a wall. The ground rattled as the avalanche bore down on the rest of the Teks. Their screams were like sweet music.

Tevin remained unscathed as the rocks broke apart above his head and piled over and around him without ever touching him. The suns went dark behind the increasing pile, with only a sliver of the sky still visible. And then the rubble blotted out that light as well. As quickly as the thunder and rain of rocks had begun, everything turned black and silent.

Now how do I get out of here?

CHAPTER 45

HOPELESSNESS

Rasi leaped into the Teks like a fearless madman. This was what he did best; this was where he felt most alive. Around him swords struck shields and armor and flesh with a sickening din.

A Tek screamed, driving a war hammer toward his head. Rasi shifted to the side, letting the hammer divot the ground. It was a costly error. The Tek knew it. Rasi knew it. Only one of the two smiled. Rasi bashed his sword hilt against the hard steel of the Tek's helmet, sending the dazed enemy to the dirt. Rasi then drove his blade downward with all his strength, piercing the strange black armor. It took the perfect angle and perfect thrust, but it found its way true to his foe's heart.

Rasi hadn't time for celebration. He swung his sword around with abandon. His straps lashed out, pummeling steel helmets and chest plates. Many Teks fell; even more of them kept coming.

A strap twirled around a Tek helmet and squeezed with all its might. The Tek clawed at the tentacle, but it only tightened its grip. The strain sent blood rushing to Rasi's face. He groaned and his muscles and straps trembled. A second strap wrapped around the first. They quivered. A bone-jarring pop rang out in concert with the Tek's high-pitched yelp. The straps let loose of the crushed helmet. Their victim, limp inside his suit, collapsed to the ground.

Rasi whirled around and smashed his sword into the armored chest of another attacker with little effect. A steel gauntlet grabbed his ankle. Rasi shook his leg, but couldn't break free.

Another Tek came at him from behind, wrapping metal arms around his neck. He finally shook his ankle free and whipped around, but the attacker on his back only squeezed tighter. Another hand grabbed Rasi's blade and shoved it downward. Rasi squeezed the hilt with all his strength, but a punch to his biceps made his fingers go numb and his sword, his lifeline, slipped out of his hand.

His straps fought the enemy swarm, but the coordinated Teks grabbed them and pinned each strap to the dirt until Rasi was forced to his back.

He grunted and groaned; his muscles strained. "Raaaahhhh," he screamed and tried to sit up. A fist cracked his cheek, knocking his helmet off. Rasi saw a white blur. Dirty metal fingers grabbed his hair and pulled.

Metal bodies piled onto him, crushing him flat to the ground again. The veins in his temples bulged. A trickle of blood dripped from his nose. His straining might have broken something in his head. He wiggled an arm free, but another Tek immediately pinned it to his side.

He couldn't give up, not now, not yet. He braced for an end that didn't come. Where were their blades? Where was his honorable death?

An Epertasian soldier slammed into one of the Teks, knocking him from Rasi's chest. The lone soldier was no match for the swarm and quickly succumbed to a filthy Tek's blade. Everywhere Rasi looked, he could see his army falling. They were dying in droves, and he realized he had led them like cattle to slaughter.

Beyond the massacre of the Great Plains and over the Forest of Concore, he saw a sight that ripped out his heart, a sight that sucked any hope of victory from his gut. For in the distance, the top of Shadows Peak, the top of his home, crumbled away. Only a Tek weapon could cause such destruction. His mind shot to the attack on Lithia. Had they flanked his army as they had King Logan's? Had they come by sea to take Thasula while his back was turned? If they had, this war was as good as over. He wondered if the outcome would have been different if he'd had more time to plan. Surely, he wouldn't have left the south so exposed. Now all of Epertase would pay for his mistake.

Alina was gone.

Epertase would fall.

He had lost.

And it was all his fault.

He relaxed in his enemies' grips, buried beneath their mass of cold black metal. He closed his eyes.

A chunk of his hair ripped from his skull and he moaned. The cold feel of metal filled his mouth and he tried to bite the intruding thumb, almost breaking his teeth. The Tek thumb fish-hooked his lips and tore his cheek, flooding his mouth with blood.

A knee drove into his groin. Someone twisted his left foot, threatening to snap it. The thumb in his mouth pulled out only to be replaced by a metal forearm against his throat. A twist of his head to the side shifted the pressure from his windpipe, but not the hurt.

He heard nothing but their foul, foreign tongue and laughter. *What are you waiting for?* he screamed in his head, anticipating cold steel piercing his heart at any moment. His sternum compressed beneath his chest plate under their weight. He could no longer expand his lungs. His senses faded.

I'm sorry, Epertase.

CHAPTER 46

HAPPINESS IS DYING

Rasi woke up in a lush theatre chair in the middle of the grandest concert hall he'd ever visited. The feather cushions enveloped him in comfort and security. The plush curtains in front of an old, rotted stage were pulled aside, showcasing a performance of some type. He could only make out blurred outlines because a blinding light shone from behind the stage. He looked around at all the empty chairs. It seemed odd that he was alone for such an obviously important performance.

He squinted toward the stage again and saw his breath plume in front of him. A terrible shiver washed through him. The blinding light dimmed, as if what came next was more important for him to see. The outline of a single dancing figure slowly formed. He struggled to make out her features, but could only see her dress.

Her dress. Stunningly red and familiar. The frilly skirt formed a perfect circle around her on the stage, and every time she moved it flowed with her and became a circle again when she stopped. A snake slithered with less grace. She leaped into the air with the smoothness of smoke before landing with equal elegance. As the light faded, her long, dark hair captured his gaze. It swayed hypnotically as though floating in water. She spun toward him like an angel. He saw her face.

For a moment, he felt sick to his stomach. It wasn't possible. *How could she be here?* It had been many long, hard years since he'd last seen her, yet here she was as young and beautiful as the day they were married.

Edonea?

While her movements were breathtakingly flawless, her face wore an expression of infinite sadness. Rasi looked around for answers, but the hall was still empty. He felt her loneliness and wanted to cry.

He needed to shout to her, tell her that he was coming, that he loved her and missed her, but he had no tongue.

She turned toward him. Her eyes widened and she smiled. He felt like an adolescent again, in love for the first time. She gestured for him to join her on the stage. He wanted to, more than anything, but something pulled at his back and held him down. He was tired of fighting. He was ready to be happy again. *Maybe,* he thought, *death isn't so bad. I'm coming, my love. I'm co—*

BOOM.

She looked at him with fear in her eyes. With a gasp, she ran to the side of the stage. He reached for her, but she was too far away. She quickly returned with a blanketed bundle.

BOOM.

The stage grew darker, fading into the neverworld. She stared at him with incredible urgency, holding the bundle out as if to say, "Take him." She peeled the blanket away. Rasi strained to see what she tried to show him. Her image faded.

No, wait. He squinted for a better view.

The blanket held a baby.

The blanket … held his son.

Oh gods …

BOOM.

Though he didn't see the explosions, he heard and felt them to his bones. Each blast made Edonea harder and harder to see as she faded along with the stage, and then the entire hall around him. He was alone again on his back with nothing above him but the darkest night.

Am I dead? The pain in his groin suggested otherwise. Cracks of the smoke-filled sky appeared as the Teks panicked and disengaged from the pile.

BOOM.

He could breathe again. The knee pulled away from his crotch; the elbow lifted from his neck. He could move his arm.

He sat up. A Tek jumped onto his chest, pinning him back to the ground.

"*Locknei*," the Tek screamed. "*Locknei*."

The Tek raised Rasi's own sword into the air. Rasi pushed at him, but the Tek shifted his weight and Rasi's hands slid off the slick, blood-covered armor.

BOOM.

A wave of heat seared Rasi's chest, blasting the Tek off him. The tension on Rasi's back lessened as the Teks holding the straps fled like they'd seen angry gods descending from the heavens. The straps sprang into the air. Rasi rolled to his stomach and pushed to his feet.

Dru stood, surrounded by dead Teks, next to a smoking, wheeled weapon and said, "They called this a 'cannon,' whatever that means."

"Where?" Rasi slurred.

Dru pointed to one of the bridges where the Teks had pushed the Epertasians back. "They brought it with them. I borrowed it. Though I think that was the last of its projectiles."

Rasi nodded his appreciation. Dru nodded back.

Something glistened across the ravine and caught Rasi's eye. A shiny ball of metal launched from a cannon directly toward Dru's back. It didn't move with the velocity of the exploding projectiles, but it wasn't slow either. Rasi waved his hands frantically and pointed, but by the time Dru turned his head, it was too late.

A pliable metal net enveloped him, knocking him to the ground. The more he fought, the tighter it became.

Rasi raced toward him. Another Tek intercepted him and they both tumbled to the dirt. Rasi grabbed an abandoned sword. One of his straps strained and ripped at the Tek's helmet until it whistled and hissed and pulled free. Rasi swung his blade from his knees and took the man's head.

He looked to Dru, who kicked and thrashed as he was dragged toward the edge of the ravine.

More nets were launched across. Rasi watched helplessly as other Epertasians were captured and dragged toward the edge.

Rasi ran after Dru. He'd never make it in time. Just then, he caught sight of a bloodstained silver mare galloping along the ravine's edge. Its rider whirled her sword over her head like a soldier as she raced toward the net.

Alina, no.

Desperate to save Dru, she dove from Allusia's back as the net disappeared over the edge. Rasi's knees went weak. He shoved his sword into his sheath and darted to the drop-off. Alina dangled from the net on the opposite wall, somehow still hanging on, as the Teks heaved her and Dru up.

Hang on, Alina.

Rasi searched for a way across. His first instinct was to use the ladder bridges, but he had to be smarter than that. The enemy would release their end if he tried to get across that way, and he'd be stuck in the slimy muck below. His only hope was to cross one of the bridges, which would take time he feared he didn't have. There was no other choice.

He climbed onto Allusia and kicked her toward the nearest bridge. Tek soldiers tried to cut him off. His straps bashed them out of the way.

Rasi skirted the edge of the ravine as he closed in on the bridge. Then the explosions began again. His earlier suspicions were confirmed; the Teks would indeed shoot at their own soldiers. Their projectiles devastated pockets of warring fighters, both Tek and Epertasian alike. The ground rocked as the explosions came closer and closer to him. They were aiming at him.

He was near the bridge when his ears popped again. A blast of heat and dirt and blood slammed into him. The concussion tumbled him from Allusia and over the edge. He didn't think as much about the fresh pain in his side or the burning in his eyes as he did about the horrible belke slug that might soon return.

But instead of falling to the slime, he jarred to a stop with a painful tug at his back. He wiped the blood from his eyes and peered over his shoulder. The bottom of the bridge rested above him as he hung by his straps, his wonderful straps. Plank after rickety plank, they swung and grasped and pulled. Faster and faster, he was carried to the other side beneath the oblivious Teks.

Out of the corner of his eye, he saw Alina and Dru dragged to the top of the ravine wall, hoisted by a line of Teks. *Faster,* he told himself and his straps. When he reached the opposite side, his straps flung him over the edge. Instead of attacking him, the Teks were busy stripping away their armor.

Like a candle out of wick, their precious armor died without its black blood to fuel it. That explained everything. There was a reason they had charged before their machines could annihilate the Epertasian defenses from afar. They were vulnerable, and more blood wasn't coming. He might have kissed Simcane had the big man been standing before him.

He glanced at Alina and Dru. As long as the Teks didn't kill them on the spot, there was a chance.

They bound Dru's and Alina's wrists and tethered them to a growing line of captured officers. They led them behind a two-wheeled mechanical horse deep within their ranks.

I'm coming, Alina. Rasi turned to a semi-circle of approaching Teks. Though they were now in their skivvies, they still had their swords. Rasi was as excited as a kid on Matthew's Day. He drew his sword. *Where are your fire-making weapons?*

Rasi charged. There was no more conscious thought, no more pity, no more fear. All that remained was a bloodlust he had never experienced before.

His sword danced in his hand while his straps defended him with an effective combination of accuracy and recklessness. Teks fell around him; he didn't slow. He'd fight their whole army alone if that's what it took to save Alina. Their blood, their bright red blood, sprayed his face and matted his hair as he laid them out before him. Each blow was precise and fatal. This was the kind of war he was trained for.

The enemy kept coming, while Dru and Alina pulled farther away until he couldn't see them anymore.

After a dozen or more Tek soldiers fell, they wised up and stopped attacking with such abandon. They stepped back to assess this crazy, tentacled freak who slew them single-handedly. It was good timing—he was exhausted. His hands rested on his knees. He sucked in precious air. The last thing they should have done was give him a break. His sword dangled from his hand, ten times heavier than when he'd begun his assault, but it didn't matter.

While he waited for their next advance, several Teks wheeled out a line of cannons and aimed them at him. They seemed proud that they'd distracted him until their weapons arrived. He was proud of the bodies in his wake.

CHAPTER 47

JOINING THE FIGHT

Simcane's ride toward the battle was violent; the machine obviously wasn't built for comfort. His team bounced around the metal cab, while Willum and BJ held on for dear life up top.

The constant vibrations rattled Simcane's teeth until he worried about them falling out. The metal seat was as unforgiving as a rock and his ass hurt. His back hurt. Hell, his everything hurt.

Ahead was a small group of Tek soldiers presumably marching toward the ongoing battle. Simcane pushed his door open and yelled for Willum and BJ to get low before closing his door again.

The Teks cheered with their arms raised as he drove by.

Gillian snickered. "Idiots. They think we're delivering black blood to their brethren, when in fact we're delivering death. And they cheer us for it."

Soon, they reached the back of the Tek army and another pit of black blood. Machines like the one Simcane drove had their pipes extending into it. A look farther south revealed several more. At least they were lightly guarded.

Gillian asked, "Do you think they'll ever run out of that stuff?"

Eldon answered, "I do not know anything in this world that isn't finite."

"I mean, before they kill everyone in Epertase, stupid."

"Oh. Well, I would hope so, or else we have been wasting our time."

Simcane pulled the levers back, jolting the beast to a stop. "You know what you need to do."

Gillian nodded. "More fire, huh?"

"Yep."

Gillian climbed over Eldon's lap, intentionally burying her knee in his crotch. His eyes turned to saucers. Simcane shook his head.

"Why'd she do that?" Eldon whined once she was out.

Simcane threw his hands up. Between Thairen and Gillian, he was worn out.

BJ and Willum climbed down. Along with Gillian, they ran toward the pits where armored Teks waited in lines. Simcane and Eldon watched Gillian through the side window. As she passed the unsuspecting Teks, she discreetly rubbed japsy weed between her palms. Once at the pit, she tossed the japsy weed and continued on her way as if this was just another day in the army. The Teks watched, confused. An inferno erupted from the pit with mile-high flames.

Simcane grinned and set the mechanical beast back in motion. No one tried to stop him.

The rear lines of the Tek army parted for Simcane's machine, still not connecting it to the chaos raging behind. Eldon's lips curved upward. Eventually, Simcane reached a section of Tek soldiers who, instead of parting, waited eagerly for their precious black blood so they could rejoin the battle. He could hardly wait to see the looks on their faces when he drove by without stopping. He jammed the levers to the floor and the beast accelerated like a turtle.

Just keep moving to the front, he thought. *Don't draw any unnecessary attention.*

After passing seemingly endless ranks of armored Teks, Havens Ravine came into view. The fighting was fierce, and Simcane couldn't wait to join his brothers. With more and more Tek soldiers rushing toward him and Eldon, he couldn't resist any longer. He yanked the right lever halfway back and veered the mechanical beast into a line of them. They stampeded each other to get out of the way, but their ranks were too thick. The machine jerked and rocked, but it was made well and didn't get bogged down on the bodies. Simcane bounced against the ceiling and then hit the seat in a losing battle against the turbulence.

Eldon rode the thrashing waves like he was on a boat and had already gotten his sea legs. He watched Simcane tumble around, fighting back a giggle.

"This is this funny to you?" Simcane snapped.

"Not at all. I'm just wondering what it is you are doing."

It didn't take long for the Teks to wise up and begin climbing onto the rig. "Do this," Simcane said and wedged the door handle again. Eldon found a metal rod behind his seat and did the same on his side.

Simcane continued through the ranks, his vessel covered in Tek soldiers. He nodded toward the ravine. "What do you think? Give 'em a ride?"

Eldon craned his neck until he could see past the swarm of soldiers clinging to the front of the mechanical beast. "Sounds like fun."

A few of the Teks on Simcane's side saw what was coming and dove off, allowing him to remove the wedge from the handle and swing his door open. He punched a Tek who took the opportunity to try to climb in and knocked him under the wheel.

"All right. Jump," Eldon said.

Simcane grabbed both edges of the door. But before he could take the leap, an explosion cratered the ground in front of them. Dirt and rock pelted the machine like marbles hitting a shield. The impact threw Simcane back into the cabin and onto the floor.

The front dropped forward and bounced, and then rocked with such violence even Eldon lost his footing and knocked into him. The next bounce tossed Simcane's injured shoulder against the unyielding metal floor. He grunted and winced. Eldon gracefully righted himself. Simcane pulled himself back to his seat, but another blast slammed his head against the ceiling, wrenching his neck.

He tried to gather his wits as the machine careened toward the edge. "Are you jumping?" Eldon asked.

"I'm trying," Simcane snapped. Another jolt rocked him forward. He couldn't right himself. At one point he was facing Eldon instead of the outside, and the Gildonese appeared greatly disappointed. That damn machine was giving him a worse beating than any Tek could.

With an annoyed sigh, Eldon unceremoniously pushed Simcane out the door. Simcane briefly felt weightless before hitting the ground and rolling to a painful stop. He looked up to see Eldon step effortlessly off the machine as it and the Teks too stupid to jump free rolled over the edge. Eldon's sword was already drawn, and he felled two Tek soldiers in a blink.

From the ravine, a ground-shaking *ka-boom* preceded a fireball.

Simcane pushed to his feet and drew his sword. He scanned the battlefield until his eyes landed on a bridge where a line of Tek soldiers stood next to their fancy wheeled weapons. They pointed them at a single Epertasian with red tentacles waving above his head.

"Eldon," Simcane shouted.

Eldon looked up from his flawless killing.

"See that man with the tentacles?"

Eldon plunged his sword into one unarmored Tek, removed it with a spin, and lopped off the head of another. "Yes."

"Help him. He means everything to this fight."

Eldon bowed and then took off at a sprint. His movements were fluid like a feline's. Any Teks in his path met their deaths at his blade without slowing him.

As he passed one of the smaller wheeled machines, he snatched it up with one hand and heaved it toward the bridge without missing a step. The machine plowed into the Teks that were threatening Rasi. Using the diversion, Rasi charged, his straps whipping other Teks into the air.

Eldon finished the final two and ended chest-to-face with Rasi. "I guess you're important or something," he said.

Rasi shrugged.

Eldon reached out to touch one of the straps and it smacked his hand. "Interesting," he said.

Simcane joined them and they stared out over the massive Tek army. As hard as Rasi's men had fought, it was a simple matter of numbers, and Rasi didn't have enough. Despite the seven new columns of smoke from the burning pits in the west, Rasi looked resigned.

"Should we cross the bridge?" Simcane asked.

Eldon and Rasi looked back. While the Epertasians fought valiantly, the Teks were already too thick over there. All along the ravine the Epertasians had lost the bridges. On the Tek side, more enemy soldiers were closing in.

"I guess this is it," Simcane said.

Rasi shook his hand and then Eldon's.

"It was a solid plan, Rasi. It looks like they just did too much damage at the beginning."

Rasi nodded. He lifted his sword.

But before the Teks could attack, an ungodly roar echoed from the north. Every eye, Tek and Epertasian alike, turned in that direction.

Epertasian flags waved high above a charging army of thousands of fresh Epertasian soldiers. Their beautiful battle cry grew louder and more intimidating with every hurried step. Atticus and Andon led the way.

Battle-weary Epertasians reached deep within to find renewed vigor while the Teks lost theirs. Tek battle horns blared through their ranks.

On the Epertasian side of the ravine, the once confident and merciless Teks panicked and tried to retreat across the bridges and ladders. The chaos gave the Epertasians the advantage. They gave chase, led by Jarrah on horseback. They ran the Tek scum down from behind. The same scene played out at every crossing.

Once Jarrah cleared the nearest bridge, Rasi waved him over and commandeered his horse. He kicked it westward while the Tek army turned their attention north.

Simcane raised his sword to the Epertasians on the other side of the ravine. "No mercy," he shouted.

They cheered in reply.

The Teks had likely never faced such a talented foe without their full complement of armor and their boom-making machines. There was no doubt they would fight on, but there was also no doubt of who was ultimately going to win.

CHAPTER 48

ZAFFKA

Sweat poured from Rasi's pores and soaked through his uniform. Pushing Jarrah's horse as hard as he could be pushed, Rasi weaved through the Tek ranks as they mostly ignored him, their focus locked on the northern advance. The ones who did take notice were easily tossed aside by his straps.

The hulking, multistory command fortress was ahead. With all its power and terror-inducing looks, it wasn't much for speed. Rasi rode harder. Dozens of Epertasian officers walked behind it, tethered to the rear by chains. Future slaves, perhaps, or prisoners to be interrogated. He could only imagine what torture methods Teks might use.

A look along the line revealed Alina and Dru weren't among them. Perhaps they were inside and the interrogations had already begun. The thought was too painful to entertain, so he thought about how he would have no mercy on their captors instead.

Tek guards rode two-wheeled machines along either side of the marching prisoners, whipping those who fell out of line. Rasi galloped toward them, his straps poised for their next taste of blood. When one of the Teks saw him coming, he waved for two guards to deal with him. Rasi didn't slow. His straps assured they never got close, leaving them bloodied in the dirt beside their machines.

The captive Epertasians cheered despite their exhaustion. *Just hold on,* he willed them. The remaining two Teks fled into the machine after two large doors in the rear lowered like drawbridges to admit them.

As Rasi reached the line of marching prisoners, one of them shouted, "They took the queen inside."

Rasi climbed from his horse onto the lowered doors. That they hadn't closed them suggested the Teks wanted him to come inside. There was a long hallway, empty of soldiers, housing the two abandoned wheeled machines. The hall led to a poorly lit spiral ladder, barely wide enough for Rasi to climb. He expected an ambush at the top. What he got was more like a welcoming party. The two Teks he had followed backed away with lowered weapons. Rasi studied them as he cautiously finished his climb to solid footing. They raised their hands as if in surrender and nodded toward a set of double wooden doors.

What kind of trap was this? He pointed to the brass hoop handles on the doors and they nodded again. With sword in hand, he braced for the inevitable blast from the other side. He pulled the door open.

"Come on in," an old, grizzled voice commanded from within the room. It was the voice of a man accustomed to being obeyed.

Rasi stepped into a magnificent chamber as big as a ballroom with a ceiling nearly as high as the fortress itself. The floor was carpeted in plush scarlet fibers that felt soft under his step. The walls were lined with granite statues standing nearly as tall as the ceiling. They were of armored soldiers, and Rasi wondered if they were legendary Tek warriors. He pulled the door closed so no one could sneak up behind him.

At the opposite end of the room, an old man leaned against the leg of a statue that bore his likeness. He wore black Tek armor from his neck down with the thin hilt of a sword poking above his right shoulder. He took a toke on a weed stick and then snuffed it on the statue before tossing it into a bin.

Rasi took in the room. Not far to his left stood another Tek, younger and without armor. Behind the younger Tek, Dru dangled from leather straps tied around his wrists. His toes brushed the ground. Barely conscious and too tired to lift his head, he drooped forward, a string of blood hanging from his lips.

Alina was next to him, chained to the floor like a dog with a collar around her neck. Her eye was swollen and purple. Rasi's jaw tightened, almost breaking his teeth.

The old man walked to her and said, "Forgive my Epertasian. I learn recent." He lifted her chin and tilted his head.

Alina leaned around him and shouted, "Rasi, he has weapons on his ar—"

The Tek bastard backhanded her with his gauntleted hand. She crumpled to the ground. Rasi felt the blow as if it were given to him. He breathed deeply through his nose, drew his sword, and stepped forward.

The old man chuckled. "Rasi, huh? Since you here, you must be worthy. That's why I allowed you entry." He then spoke in his native tongue.

The other Tek turned toward Dru and swung his sword at the leather straps, freeing the Epertasian to fall face-down on the ground. Rasi took another unsure step.

The old man wagged his finger. "Easy," he said. "Ignore Rayles. I am Supreme Leader Zaffka. We fight now. If you defeat me, you go free." He removed his helmet from a clasp on his chest and fastened it over his scarred head.

Dru struggled to his knees. "Rasi?"

Just hold on, Dru.

The old man looked over his shoulder. "He, however, should be punished."

Panic gripped Rasi's chest. He sprang forward, but there was too much space between them. Zaffka spun with deceiving speed, drew his sword from his back, and drove the glowing blade deep into Dru's chest. Then he slid the blade back into its sheath.

Alina screamed.

Rasi stopped in horror, his eyes locked on his dying friend.

Dru stiffened momentarily, and then collapsed onto his face again.

Zaffka turned back with a glare. "Now you know stakes, warrior."

Rasi stared across the room into Zaffka's eyes, and Zaffka lowered a tinted visor to hide them.

Rasi's straps snapped like whips. Zaffka's armor hissed. The two charged. The Tek commander extended his left arm. Rasi heard a thunderous blast as the Tek fired some kind of projectile at him from a contraption on his forearm. Blood sprayed from the end of one of Rasi's straps.

Zaffka quickly stuck out his other arm and fired another blast, but Rasi jerked to the side and it merely grazed his chest.

Zaffka deflected Rasi's sword thrust with his armored forearm, and Rasi lowered his shoulder and slammed into him. They tumbled to the ground, Rasi's sword thudding out of reach. Losing his sword mattered little; it wouldn't help against the armor anyway. Zaffka rolled to one knee just out of reach of the straps and fired another shot.

It clipped Rasi's thigh. He ignored the pain. A strap wrapped the wound. Rasi pounced. Two of his straps grabbed Zaffka's wrists and pulled his arms out wide. Rasi grabbed the Tek's helmet with both hands, attempting to wrench it off, but it was either on too tight or he didn't understand the fasteners. Zaffka kicked him in the balls, sending him to his knees.

To Rasi's frustration, the straps hurled Zaffka across the room to collide with a statue. *No. I need him close.*

Zaffka shook his head and staggered to his feet. He slid the bluish blade he had killed Dru with from his back. Rasi picked up his own sword again.

They ran at each other. Zaffka swung his blade. Rasi parried, but Zaffka's blue steel sliced through his sword like it was made of water and continued just over Rasi's head. His straps darted out of the way. Rasi dropped his useless sword.

He swept Zaffka's leg, almost breaking his foot on the armored boot. Zaffka fell. Rasi dove at him, but Zaffka's blade arced from the ground in a wide, looping swing. Two of Rasi's straps wrapped around one of the statues and yanked him backward out of range.

He planted his feet. His straps strained. He strained. The statue wobbled and tilted forward. Rasi pulled harder. The gigantic stone figure tipped toward Zaffka. The old man struggled to his feet. As the statue tumbled, he swiped his sword blindly above his head, slicing the statue in half, both pieces of granite crashing on either side of him.

He lunged and swung at Rasi again. A strap grabbed his wrist. He fired another shot from his forearm and missed. The battle raged with each man giving and taking in deadly competition. Rasi's face bled; his muscles ached. Zaffka sucked in air and danced away as if stalling. He complimented Rasi's warrior spirit and Rasi spat on him. Zaffka backed away, laughing.

Rasi lunged again. For the first time in the battle, instead of driving forward, Zaffka retreated and tumbled over a broken chunk of granite. As he fell, he swung his sword. Rasi's straps batted his arm away. His magical blade slipped from his hand and landed in the plush carpet beside his face. Rasi sat on top of his heaving chest and grabbed Zaffka's helmet again. This time his straps pitched in, and together they ripped it free.

"Rasi," Alina cried. "Behind you."

Rasi's straps lashed out and knocked the sneaky Rayles to the ground.

Rasi reached for the blue blade and raised it high above his head.

Zaffka whispered, "In my day, boy …," pant, pant, "I'd have killed …," pant, "a freak like you." Then he wheezed and coughed.

Rasi curled his upper lip. *Well, it's not your day.* He tensed for the killing blow. But something stopped him before he delivered his strike. It was a sinking feeling in his gut, a feeling he had learned to listen to over the years. It was Zaffka's cough. Something had changed in it. The corners of the Tek commander's lips curved upward as his cough melded into laughter.

Rasi hesitated.

Zaffka's eyes went to Rasi's waist. Rasi followed his gaze. His heart sank. *He got me.* He drove the blade downward and Zaffka flinched.

He didn't feel the blast to his gut as much as he felt Alina's scream. The impact kicked him back violently from his foe.

The blue sword slipped from his hands as Rasi sailed backward and the world slowed around him.

Instinctively, one of his straps snatched the magical sword from the air and whirled it around as the Tek commander sat up. Zaffka's eyes widened. Rasi hit the floor. The tip of the blue blade went in one side of Zaffka's armored chest and then emerged from the other. Like a true warrior, he didn't make a sound.

Rasi wrapped his arms around his bleeding gut and curled into a ball. With all his strength, he lifted his head enough to see Rayles rush to Zaffka's side.

Rasi summoned his deepest reserves to sit up despite the worst cramping he'd ever felt. He couldn't let Alina down, not when they were so close to victory. He pushed at the ground, somehow making it to his feet. Blood puddled beneath him. A strap wrapped his gut and tightened. He doubled over and almost collapsed. The strap holding the blue sword set it at his feet like a trophy. Rasi winced, bent over, and picked up the weapon. He had to fight for every breath.

He glanced at Alina still chained to the floor. He staggered to her and sliced through her restraints. Then he turned his attention to Rayles. It was almost over now. The Tek knelt beside his commander, staring up at Rasi. He stood up and held his open palms out in surrender.

Perhaps Rasi's intentions were written in his narrowed eyes because Alina shouted, "Rasi that man surrenders. He's our prisoner now."

Though Rasi didn't want to listen, he knew in his heart that she was right. He knew killing the unarmed Tek would not bring back Dru or the tens of thousands of other Epertasians and Liths, and that the Tek officer should be tried and hanged in Thasula's town center for all to see. He looked at Dru, dead on the floor. He looked at his lover's battered face and his heart broke again. He stared into her eyes and feared she would never be safe again if he allowed this man to live.

Alina shook her head and mouthed, "Mercy." He saw kindness and innocence in her and he loved her for it, but he also knew he needed to protect her from those very qualities. It was his lot in life to do what was necessary even when it was hard.

He sighed. *I'm sorry, Alina.* He twirled and thrust the cursed blade through the Tek's black heart.

Alina gasped and turned away. "Rasi, why?" she cried.

It's what he deserved.

He reached for her hand, but she pulled away. "We are better than the Teks," she said. "We show mercy; that is what makes us Epertasians."

I told you that you didn't want to see this war. I told you to stay back, but you refused. I did what I needed to do for your kingdom, for your people, for you. I would do it all again a thousand times.

She turned back to him. Her eyes hid behind tears. "You don't understand. It isn't that we had to kill. We are in war, I understand that. But we can't kill in cold blood. There has to be some respect for life."

I kill, Alina. You knew that when you accepted my offer to lead your soldiers. You needed me to save your kingdom, and that's what I've done.

"I know and I am grateful, but I've never seen you so ..." She searched for the right word. "Heartless," she finally said.

This is who I am.

"No. It's not, Rasi. I've seen your kindness."

And now you've seen my wrath.

Somewhere deep within, he wanted to apologize, to tell her that he was just angry and didn't mean his words, but that wasn't true. He did what was needed and, damn it, she should see that.

She bowed her head. Rasi coughed and then wiped the gore from his chin so she wouldn't see how badly he was hurt.

She walked to the door and waited without looking back. Rasi swung the door open into a hallway full of Tek soldiers. Rasi entered first, scowling at them and daring them to come forward despite knowing he had no more fight left.

They lowered their swords, bowed their heads, and slowly parted. It was as Zaffka had promised. Win and go free. The fortress jerked and jostled to a stop. Rasi led Alina down the narrow stairwell.

A sea of Epertasian soldiers met them at the rear doors. Atticus rode to the front. "Your Majesty, the Teks are on the run. Your plan has succeeded."

"You mean Rasi's plan."

Rasi turned away, having no need for praise.

Solemnly, Alina said, "Atticus, we've lost Dru."

He bowed his head. "Damn. Do you want me to tell Andon?"

"No. I'll do it."

"Where's his body?"

She pointed into the fortress. "Send soldiers up the stairs at the end of the hall. They'll find Dru there. Take any Teks they find into custody. And then burn this godforsaken machine to the ground."

Rasi tried to hide how badly injured he was as he walked away, but he wasn't a good actor and one of the soldiers noticed. He grabbed another man and rushed to Rasi's side. They draped his arms over their shoulders and helped him onto a horse.

While Alina addressed the soldiers, Rasi quietly headed back to Havens Ravine where the Epertasian army had set up medical tents.

Rasi rested his head against the horse's neck as he rode. When Epertasian soldiers saw his straps, they cheered and shouted his name. His straps danced above, soaking in the adulation.

That evening, after his wounds were dressed and against the advice of the doctor, he snuck away under the cloak of night. It pained him to leave Alina in such a way, but he couldn't face her again. Not then. Maybe one day she would understand why he'd done what he had. Or maybe one day he would understand why he shouldn't have. But this wasn't that day.

CHAPTER 49

LEANDER

Four moons had passed since the battle, and any Teks who could be found had been rounded up. Atticus met Alina outside the newly built prison camps that stretched across the vast farmlands.

"Your Majesty, it is good to see you," he said.

"You as well, Atticus. What are the numbers?"

"We count twelve thousand, give or take. Countless thousands more have escaped to their boats and put to sea."

"Have any of the prisoners resisted?"

"Actually, no. They have been model. But there's something else. You won't believe this, but they've sent a spokesman who has miraculously learned our language in the time he has been here. He is young and very cordial."

"Really? I would like to meet with this man."

Atticus waved his hand. One of his soldiers left and then returned with a stocky young man. His hands were bound behind his back. He knelt before her, gorgeous blue eyes lowered to her feet. His hair was dirty blond, thick, and curly.

"Rise up, sir," she said. "What is your name?"

"Leander, ma'am."

"Where did you learn our language?"

"I've been studying books since we arrived. Also, your guards have been helpful since we've been in your camps."

"Impressive. Well, Leander, what have you to say?"

"Queen, my fellow soldiers and I ask for your mercy. I will not try to excuse what we have done, but you should know that the soldiers you keep here were forced to serve at a young age and do not ..."—he searched for the right word—"harbor ... ill will to you and your people."

"Leander, I appreciate your words. However, you have killed many innocents."

"We were obeying orders. We had no choice."

"That doesn't erase what you've done."

"I agree." He hesitated. "But if you can find it in your heart to give us mercy, you will not regret it."

Alina pondered his words. "I have actually come here today prepared to give your people a sentence. I have no desire to kill you, yet we haven't anywhere to keep such a large force here in Epertase. We will not be known for our prisons. And therein lies my dilemma. After much deliberation with my council, I have decided to exile you to the southern islands of Torick, where you will be free to pursue your lives however you see fit. But you will start your civilization from nothing. And if we find that you prepare for violence again, we will attack and destroy you. That is the only way I can see to show you mercy and exact justice for what you've done to my people. You will not build ships, and you will never leave."

"You are a just queen."

"Leander, I charge you with leading your people from this day forward. I am trusting your word."

"We have no desire to go home in disgrace, ma'am. I vow that from this day forward we will abide by your demands and live in peace on your islands." He bowed his head. "I thank you for sparing us."

"We will be watching you, Leander."

Alina wondered if every soul in Thasula was in attendance for the celebrations in the Royal Garden. Outside the castle walls, the streets were packed with people hoping for a chance to attend such an auspicious occasion.

Children chased each other through the crowd with wooden swords and strips of red cloth tied around their necks.

"Stop, you filthy Teks," one shouted. "I am Rasi."

"No, I am Rasi," another child screamed.

Alina grinned, overwhelmed with the pride of knowing these were her people and they were safe once again. The slow, steady transfer of Leander and his men to the Torick Islands was proceeding without incident, and life within Thasula was returning to normal. She hadn't seen Rasi since they had left the Tek fortress, but she hoped he would come to the celebrations to receive his honors.

The crowd quieted when she stepped onto the stage. She gave them a warm smile. "Epertasians, Liths, and Lowlanders. We came together in our mutual time of need to defend our world from tyranny, and we have come away victorious."

She scanned the crowd, as she had a hundred times since she'd arrived, hoping Rasi would be there. But each time she looked she was more disappointed than the time before. "We are here this day to celebrate our warrior heroes who have led us in our struggle. We will also remember those who have fallen and mourn them as we should. As we mourn the losses, we must remember that their sacrifices were not in vain, that their deaths gave us back our freedom."

She praised many soldiers including Jarrah, Andon, Tate, and Masera. She spoke of Dru's bravery and Atticus's undying loyalty. She told stories of Paisel's tragedy and thanked Aidric, who sat in a wheeled chair in the crowd, out of his infirmary bed for the first time.

She called Simcane and his team forward. The vibrations of the crowd's applause could be felt through the floorboards as first

Simcane then BJ, Eldon, Gillian, and Willum stepped onstage to accept their awards.

Once the applause for Simcane's team died down, she told the story of what they had done, though their legend had already spread and the people could probably recite the story better than she. She spoke of Joseph the Priest and Thairen, vowing Epertase would never forget their sacrifice.

She asked Simcane, "And where do you go from here?"

"Oh." He paused. "I owe an old man a great debt."

"Then I will know where to find you if ever I have the need."

"I hope you never have the need, Your Majesty." He bowed, as did his team.

Alina ended her speech with an announcement that a week of celebration was to begin at once in honor of the heroes of Epertase.

Her closest adviser, Levi, helped her down the stairs at the back of the stage. "Shouldn't you tell them the rest of the news?" he asked. "The people, I mean?"

"No, no, not yet," she answered, and gently rubbed her belly. "It's still early. We'll keep it secret for now."

"Very well. And Commander Rasi?" he asked. "Have you heard from him?"

She scanned the crowd one last time, lowered her head, and turned away.

"Does he even know?"

She shook her head.

CHAPTER 50

A NEW
BEGINNING

O n the outskirts of Thasula near Atticus's home was a small
field of wild grass and weeds with a small patch of bare
earth. At the edge of the patch grew a single maple sapling.
Its frail, leafless branches drooped sadly as it tried to build enough
strength to survive the coming winter. Atticus and Celia stood arm-
in-arm near their house.

"Farewell, my friend," Atticus said, offering his hand.

Celia wrapped her arms around Rasi and squeezed tightly. Rasi
didn't have the heart to tell her how much it hurt his still healing gut.
The doctor had said it would hurt for a while and that he was lucky.
Every time he stood, he didn't feel so lucky.

"I'm sorry for all you have been through," Celia whispered, and
kissed him on his cheek. "Thank you for saving our country." She
pulled her head away and looked into his eyes with kindness. "You
are always welcome here."

Rasi nodded. He knew that he was.

She took Atticus's hand and they walked back toward their home.
She glanced over her shoulder one last time before disappearing
inside.

Rasi stood motionless. A bundle of seven long-stemmed, freshly
cut roses wrapped in a plain tan cloth nestled in his arms. He told
himself to go to the tree, but his legs refused to move. He looked
around for an excuse, but he was alone like he'd always been.

The invisible wall crumbled with his first step. Every step forward against the regret and fear that held him back took more and more strength. But he pressed onward. By the time he reached the maple, he was almost on his knees.

Though the tree branches looked weak and sickly, the trunk was strong and gave him hope that it would stand for many, many years.

A wooden plank leaned against the trunk. Carved in the wood was an epitaph:

Here lies a most beautiful and kind woman with her unborn child. Her name was Edonea and she was a friend. She will be missed by all who knew her. The Year of Matthew 988-1012

Rasi dragged his finger gently along the letters before collapsing to his knees. The grave site was freshly trimmed and well maintained—a tribute to Celia's hard work and love. It was a patch of beauty in an otherwise ugly field.

Rasi fell back on his rear. He felt like an incredible weight had been lifted. He let loose tears that flowed like the waterfalls by his home on Shadows Peak. He didn't try to stop them.

Edonea. This is hard for me. I'm going home to Puimia now to see my parents and I won't be coming back. I need to tell you something before I go, something very difficult for me. I have thought about both of you every day since the day you died. But it is time for me to move on, to live again. I will never stop loving you, but I need to tell you goodbye, and that is why I'm here. If there are gods above, I will see you both again one day, and I long for that meeting.

It was a stunning day with not a cloud in the sky, perfect for sitting with his wife. He sat in silence for most of the day, at one point even falling asleep. But eventually he knew he had stayed as long as he could. He needed to begin his journey home. He gathered enough strength to stand up.

The roses dressed the head of the grave nicely. He lightly kissed the wooden plaque and started to walk away. Then he paused and turned back to the tree. *I love you both and always will.*

Rasi turned away and looked to the road ahead. The world before him was somehow brighter, offering a new life and a new sense of hope. He mounted his newest gift from the royal house, a black beauty of a stallion worthy of a king. The likeness to his old friend Salient was uncanny and he took a moment to remember him.

He smiled, turned his horse eastward, and headed home.

END

EPILOGUE

RETURN OF A GOD

O n the eastern edge of Parsons was a tiny town full of average people living average lives. As a whole, the people of Silo had no particular goals in life, but rather embraced their peaceful, slow-paced existence. For as long as Silo had been a town, the people had been largely oblivious to the happenings throughout Epertase, and they liked it that way. In fact, only thirty of the three hundred eligible men who lived there had volunteered and fought during the Tek War, and even fewer of them in the Heathen Wars before that. Twelve of those men had survived the Teks, and their return home marked the biggest event in Silo's recent history. The town threw celebrations for seven nights and seven days in honor of their brave warriors. The men were treated like immortals, revered by all.

Dordan was one of those warriors. He was the rare Silo citizen who had traveled throughout Epertase even before the war, and was considered worldly by Silo standards. A month had passed since he had fought in the great Battle of Havens Ravine, yet mundane tasks like a visit to the local meat shop still brought him praise and admiring gazes. Children chased his horse through the main drag whenever he ventured through town, overwhelming him with the attention. He was never fully comfortable with the title of "soldier," let alone being called a "hero." The flattery and attention embarrassed him almost to the point that he wished he had never joined the fight.

The biting air foretold a harsh winter on the horizon. Though Dordan had seen many beautiful places on his travels, he always returned home to Silo. He loved living within a day's ride of the ocean. He was just contemplating a walk on the beach as he fetched water from the well when two riders on horseback appeared on the road at the far end of his family's fields.

"Now, who could that be?" he whispered. He watched as they crossed the field toward him.

One of the riders was a woman. She rode a brown mare that had specks of white on its snout as if someone had splattered its face with paint. The other rider, a boy, rode a dull, plain-looking black steed with gray blotches. They shouted Dordan's name, and he realized it was his neighbor Betsy and her brother.

Dordan set his two pails of water down and took a step toward his visitors.

"Dordan, come quick," Betsy shouted before she reached him. "You are needed at Al's shop."

In all the years he had known her, he'd never seen her so agitated. "Calm yourself, Betsy. Tell me, what is the matter?"

She slowed her steed, along with her breaths, until she and her brother were beside him. "A stranger arrived before dawn. He ransacked Al's store and now he won't leave."

"What does he want?"

"We don't know. He hasn't spoken a word since he arrived. Al is afraid. He asked us to fetch you."

"Does anyone know this stranger?"

"No one. Al figured you might."

Me? "Where is the marshal?"

"He went into the store and has not returned. We fear for him."

Dordan swallowed hard. The downside of hero status was that he was counted on in times of trouble, and deep inside he wasn't convinced he was the right man. But it was hard to say no when Betsy looked at him with such faith.

"Very well. I will fetch my sword …" After a pause, he added, "Though I likely won't need it." He wondered if he was trying to convince them or himself.

Dordan turned for his horse, tripping over one of his pails and spilling water on his leg. He looked back, embarrassed, and swiped at his cold, wet pants. Betsy turned away, likely to keep from offending him with her giggles.

Dordan ran to the barn and grabbed his sword from where it hung on a hook inside the door. He shouted toward the house as he readied his horse, "Mother, I'm going to town. I will return as soon as I can." She didn't answer, probably too preoccupied with cleaning to hear. He didn't bother to tell her again. He rode alongside Betsy and her brother toward Al's shop.

He arrived to find a crowd of worried bystanders waiting outside the store. When Al caught sight of Dordan, the shop owner hurried to meet him. "Thank you for coming, Dordan," Al said. "The marshal entered and has not returned. I didn't know what else to do, so I sent for you."

"You did the right thing," Dordan said, trying to sound brave. "This is likely a miscommunication." He fastened his sword belt around his waist, careful not to reveal his shaky hands. "I will return shortly, and I will bring the marshal and our new friend with me." He dismounted and hesitantly headed for the storefront with all eyes on his back.

With a nervous gulp of air, he stepped through the door. The oil lamps on the wall had been extinguished, and even though the suns were out, unnatural shadows filled the room. The shelves were bare, all the produce scattered across the floor in every aisle.

"Hello?" Dordan called out. In the dark, he stepped into tree sap. "Ugh." He checked his sole. The sticky sap stretched from his boot to the floor and stuck with each step.

He looked down each row until he came to the last. The town marshal lay face down in a puddle of partially coagulated blood mixed with tornment juice. He was breathing but unconscious. The slight shaking of Dordan's hands increased. He grabbed the hilt of his sword, not to ready himself for a fight, but to steady his hand.

Dordan knelt beside the marshal and shook him. "Marshal?" The marshal didn't answer.

"Who are you?" a nasty, crackling voice asked from the other end of the isle.

Dordan nearly pissed himself as he fell to his rear. He refocused on the darkness. Hidden in the shadows at the back of the store was the faint outline of a man. His glaring eyes and the dull, white glow around his hands were all that broke the darkness.

"My name's Dordan," Dordan answered. He wondered how he found himself in such predicaments and considered retreating to the street and the safety of numbers. But fear of being perceived a coward was a great motivator. In fact, it was the only reason he had enlisted to fight the Teks in the first place. In slow, non-threatening movements, he stood up.

The man spoke again with a voice that would scare the gods. "What do you want?"

"I am here to help you," Dordan answered, his voice timid and weak.

"Am I in Thasula?"

"Thasula? You're about as far away from Thasula as you can get."

The man's eyes strained and he looked at his hands. "How did I get so far away?" he asked himself. "I don't remember anything after the—" He trailed off and lifted his gaze.

He stepped forward where Dordan could better see him. Dordan was stunned that a man who exuded such intimidation could appear so frail and disheveled. His tattered shirt exposed his entire dirt-covered chest. With his beard and long, straggly hair, Dordan thought he looked more like a vagrant than someone to fear.

Yet Dordan backed away from him.

When the man walked past the marshal and through a ray of sunslight, Dordan noticed red stains mixed with the dirt on his bony chest. Dordan's back met the store window. The stranger's cold glare as he passed him lifted the tiny hairs on Dordan's neck. He stank of sweat and death. Dordan held his breath and froze, too afraid to even grab his sword.

The stranger stopped near the front door and turned back. Dordan swore his eyes glowed a dull red.

"What happened to the war?" he asked.

"It's over," Dordan answered. "We've won."

"Hmph." The stranger looked at the floor as if in thought.

"Queen Alina and Commander Rasi led us to a glorious victory," Dordan offered. If all the stranger wanted was news of the war, Dordan could oblige him. And then maybe he would leave without further incident.

The stranger lifted his head. "*Queen* Alina?" he asked.

"Yes. That's right."

The man ground his teeth with sickening din, sending the chills that had gone down Dordan's spine back up. He parted his filthy, greasy hair and tucked it behind his ears. He seemed to stare through Dordan, taking angry, deliberate breaths. "Where is King Elijah?"

"He died while trying to save his daughter. Commander Rasi returned his body to Thasula."

"Commander Rasi? And why wasn't that criminal … Rasi … prosecuted and executed for his previous crimes against the kingdom?"

"Executed? Why would he be executed? He was given a full pardon. It was he who helped King Elijah save the queen from the scoundrels who took her."

The stranger squinted like he was trying to figure out the most complicated mathematical problem ever devised. "Helped Elijah? Rasi? That is not possible."

Dordan didn't know how else to answer, so he stood quietly.

"How long since the war ended?"

"Over a month. Where have you been, sir? Do you need some water?"

The stranger's face darkened until the parts of his cheeks not covered in dirt and grime were tomato-red. He planted his feet and his fists quivered at his side. His irises blurred until only the whites of his eyes showed. The scattered groceries on the floor lifted from the ground and floated knee-high as if suspended by invisible strings.

The man's voice deepened, taking on a hateful edge. "Rasi is an enemy of Epertase. You have all been fooled."

Dordan let out an unintentional chuckle. The stranger glared at him with an evil air the likes of which Dordan had never seen before. And he had seen the Teks' black hearts in battle. "I … I have no desire to offend you, sir."

The vagrant turned away and marched through the doorway. The crowd outside parted. Once the stranger exited the store, the groceries crashed back to the floor, sending a jolt through Dordan's soul. Dordan rushed to the door in time to hear the man address the crowd.

"Death or servitude is coming to you all," he said, and continued unimpeded through the streets.

See you all soon for *A Kingdom's Fall*

BIOGRAPHY

Douglas R. Brown is a fantasy and horror writer who lives in Pataskala, Ohio. He began writing as a cathartic way of dealing with the day-to-day stresses of life as a firefighter/paramedic for the Columbus Ohio Division of Fire. Now he focuses his writing on fantasy and horror, where he draws on his lifelong love of the genre. He has been married for twenty-four years and has a son and three dogs. He has had four books published but now publishes under his own imprint of Epertase Publishing.

Douglas's website is Epertase.blogspot.com

Email Douglas at epertase@gmail.com

ALSO FROM EPERTASE

A KINGDOM'S FALL
THE LIGHT OF EPERTASE, BOOK 2

THE RISE OF CRIDON
THE LIGHT OF EPERTASE, BOOK 3

TAMED

DEATH OF THE GRINDERFISH